QUEEN OF MY HEART

"Soft as an angel's wing!" he sighed. His hands caressed her naked skin. Trish tried to knock them away. "I'm not an angel yet!"

He drew a heavy breath, his face less than a foot from hers, his green eyes burning with sexual desire, his hands rising to her throat. Did he want to kiss her or strangle her?

"Why are you doing this? I came here to—give you what you want!" Trish lied.

"Maybe to punish you for leaving me." His voice was a low hiss. "Queen of My Heart, you've made me so sad."

His thumbs squirmed like eels against her windpipe. She found herself whispering, "Don't kill me in front of my child!"

Books by C. K. Cambray

Conditioned To Death
Personal
Programmed For Peril
Where Is Crystal Martin?

Published by POCKET BOOKS

Most Pocket Books are available at special quantity discounts for bulk purchases for sales promotions, premiums or fund raising. Special books or book excerpts can also be created to fit specific needs.

For details write the office of the Vice President of Special Markets, Pocket Books, 1230 Avenue of the Americas, New York, New York 10020.

PROGRAMMED for PERIL

C. K. CAMBRAY

POCKET BOOKS

New York   London   Toronto   Sydney   Tokyo   Singapore

This book is a work of fiction. Names, characters, places, and
incidents are either products of the author's imagination or are used
fictitiously. Any resemblance to actual events or locales or persons,
living or dead, is entirely coincidental.

An *Original* Publication of POCKET BOOKS

POCKET BOOKS, a division of Simon & Schuster Inc.
1230 Avenue of the Americas, New York, NY 10020

ISBN: 0-671-73540-3

First Pocket Books printing August 1993

10 9 8 7 6 5 4 3 2 1

POCKET and colophon are registered trademarks of
Simon & Schuster Inc.

Cover art by Ben Perini

Printed in the U.S.A.

PROGRAMMED for PERIL

1

CHARLOTTE NEVER THOUGHT SHE WOULD GO TO A priest for advice. Normally asking Andrew, Anna, and Michael their opinions gave her all the support she needed. The problem was they all liked and were impressed by her new friend. As she had been at first—and still was in so many ways. Small wonder she was confused and uneasy. If he hadn't churned up the pool of her emotions so completely, she might have been able to move back to that distance from which her normally good judgment could take hold. From that safe place Charlotte Wigman, gynecologist, dispensed sage scientific wisdom affecting southern California's women's reproductive lives. But her new friend had made too much of an impact on her to allow the quick summoning of her professional detachment.

So she had picked Father Juan. In L.A. priests were in shorter supply than ever, but she had chosen as well as circumstances allowed, studying the younger priests who had said Mass in the churches scattered across her sprawling suburb. She chose the one who seemed the most simpatico. Her hesitant phone call resulted in his setting up an appointment. When she arrived he came to the door and invited her into the courtyard of the mission-style parish house. There, a housekeeper brought strong coffee in tiny cups. Charlotte gushed with small talk, despite herself. Who knew how long she might have run on if he hadn't folded his squarish hands low on his chest and asked, "How can I help you, Dr. Wigman?"

She found herself talking first about her new friend's good points—his intelligence first, of course. How much he knew! He was a genius! He had outread and outstudied her in every area and discipline they had talked about during the three months they had dated. Only in medicine was she better informed—and not by all that much. His knowledge of anatomy, for example, was exceptional. And she had called herself educated. She knew who Chaucer was, how the pyramids were built, the significance of carbon chains, the phyla of Earth's creatures, the art of Klimt and Klee, the music of Pergolesi and Parker. . . . Yet when she compared what she knew with the vast resources of her new friend's mind, it was ant to elephant, for sure. As yet she had been too proud to give him the satisfaction of admitting it.

Into this outpouring Father Juan intruded as well. "In that I see no difficulty, doctor. Possibly you could praise the man less. And come to his shortcomings." The priest wore steel-rimmed glasses. He slid them down the bridge of his nose and peered at her over their silvery curves. His smile was encouraging, almost teasing. Charlotte picked up her cup, then put it down. She realized she was fidgeting. "He wants to dominate me—us," she blurted. "I mean my little girl, too. Suzi. She's six."

The priest frowned. "Let's talk about the child first. In what way does he do this?"

Charlotte nodded eagerly. She could easily discuss this part of her problem. "He encourages her musically any way he can. He bought her different instruments. And music. He makes her practice whether she wants to or not. He insists that she play. But . . ." She hesitated. She was in danger of sounding odd.

Father Juan leaned forward. "Yes?"

"It's not going all that well. Suzi starts crying and says she's trying, but . . ."

"You make no effort to rescue your daughter?" the priest said.

"You mean . . . try to *stop* him?"

The priest nodded.

"Father, you don't stop that man. You just wait till he's finished."

That had led her into the heart of the matter. She had contrasted him with her ex for starters. Leonard the Lazy, King of the Couch Crullers, had been quick to spend her money, slow to return to his days as a super salesman. He suffered in comparison to her new friend, who was a driver and achiever. Much impressed with her new man at first, she had lately come to see the compulsion in his behavior, the wobbling of his psyche's flywheel. Similarly his initial generosity—boxes and bundles from Rodeo Drive—gave way to gifts of the tight-fitting outfits that he insisted she wear when they were together. Modeling one for him at his request, she watched him stalk around her like an antebellum buyer at a New Orleans slave market. "Put your palms on your rear," he ordered. When she did he only grunted. She felt she had somehow displeased him. When he said nothing she asked, "Is it all right on me, sweet?"

"You need a haircut. I know a guy."

The guy turned out to be *the* Hairy Krishna of Beverly Hills. He personally cut and combed bangs about down to her brows and stacked the back—her friend's chosen style. Hairy told her she was *charmante, madame*. In fact she thought she looked like a sheep dog after a tough night forming the flock. Her new friend, though, seemed pleased.

Curious how, deep down, she wanted to please him.

She couldn't look Father Juan in the eye when she started with the pleasing, the sex part. She had to talk about it. It was the primary source of her fright. She started with Leonard again; somehow comparisons made it easier. She had once been a good girl. In her life she had been intimate with only two men before Leonard. Leonard had seemed a skillful lover who paid plenty of attention to her needs. Wonderful, she thought. Now she understood that her ex had lacked imagination and, beyond that, insights into the

3

darker side of her eroticism. Did the core of every female heart contain that urge to please? Or was it just hers? To please, though doing so meant physical discomfort, even pain? To agree, to comply, against the grain of intuition?

She fell silent amid her evasive ramblings. Striking in a thunderbolt of vivid memory was a scene only a week into their history. The one that triggered the recent events that had brought her here today. Begin with the music, the numbing African drumming from her new friend's trunk-sized boom box. His explanation: "This is music raised one level above the most primal—our own heartbeat. Love raised one level above common copulation." Her memory clearly presented him naked, burly, strutting around with hairy truncheon outthrust. And herself. Oh, her naked self! She understood only then the function of the wide, high mirror on the wall of the flashy motel room. She saw Dr. Charlotte Wigman—as she was intended to—standing gagged, her hands bound behind her with golden tasseled ropes joined by what he called his Gordian knot. Under the wretched, sweat-matted bangs bloomed blue eyes wide in—oh, Charl-good-buddy, was that *really* surprise? Or desire? Say anticipation!

"You must go on," the priest urged.

In the end she did a botched job of narration. She tried with limited success to communicate her crosstides of desire and fear, and the dread of her next encounter with her friend. And the one after that. What would it lead to? Where would it end? She ran on and on, trying to cover all her hesitancies. Finally, before the priest's accepting gaze, she burst into tears, finding God mixed up in it after all. She fell to her knees before Him.

Father Juan took her hands in his and encouraged her to rise. She expected words then about the evils to be overcome in the contemporary world and the need for strength in the face of temptation. Instead he turned a frank gaze on her and said only, "I recommend you do not see this man again, doctor. . . ."

On the drive to the day care center she found her face in the rearview decorated with its brightest smile. She had banished it since the first concerns about her new friend crept forth. Now it was back. Glad to see you again!

Swinging into the parking lot, she craned her neck in search of Suzi. Where are you, my reason for living? There! On the swings, swooping and gliding, long blond pigtail stirring in her airy wake.

Closer to home her glee faded. Making a decision was one thing. Acting on it was more difficult.

She would have to call her friend and tell him her decision.

She waited until Suzi was in bed and she had fortified herself with three fingers of Finlandia mixed with a splash of grenadine. The phone lay like a mine on her bedside table. She absolutely had to make the call. She picked up the receiver, looked into the mouthpiece grid. She found it as appealing as a wasp nest.

She touched the keys. She hoped his answering machine would kick in. Please, please don't be home!

At that moment she realized how truly frightened of him she was.

He answered. They spoke commonplaces. In a rushed voice she said, "I don't want to see you again. Don't call me. Don't come by. Please. It's all over!"

She hung up.

Sweat emerged beneath the bangs to slide like oil down her forehead.

2

TODAY CHAMP CHOSE TAPE SEVEN OF THE TEN. IT LAY two thirds of the way between her innocence and sweet, total corruption. Each of the ten was a chrome oxide Scheherazade. Each told an irresistible Tale of Sultan Carson Thomas and Queen of My Heart. Sly Carson had winked his approval of the three hidden videocams, but she—she never dreamed. Later Champ's swift hands and natural sense of style and art had made short work of the editing. The rich harvest from the vines of the trio of machines was gathered, culled, compressed, and distilled into ten vintage performances, ten tales for the pleasure of the solitary sultans— Carson and himself. Tell your tales, oh Scheherazade! *Speak!*

Champ viewed one of the tapes every day. It was an element of the new routines begun since his last meeting with Carson. He commanded Champ: new house, new work area, new disciplines. These changes brought sharper, clearer focus to who Champ was and what he wanted from the terrifying tangle of life; his obedience was complete. Always when Carson reentered Champ's life he arrived like a timely messiah, leading him from the wilderness of his tortured, jangled thoughts out onto the purposeful path.

He squirmed on the bed, finding his own nakedness curiously arousing. How his sexual powers had risen lately! Beholding Carson's past triumphs commanded him to strive to regain for himself those sensual heights defended by the armies of time and circumstance. In the attempt he knew he ignored the lesson taught by literature and common lore: One must sail forward, never back. Were he and Carson ordinary men, he might have checked himself. But they were in no way ordinary.

He spoke toward the control unit Carson had conceived. "All lights off . . . drapes closed . . . bed angle sixty degrees . . . on TV One . . ." The wall-wide screen with a resolution video engineers could only dream of—another of Carson's genius patentable toss-away designs—glowed to life. ". . . VCR One on . . . Cue up to sound and stop."

He closed his eyes for a long moment and drew deep breaths, readying himself for this portion of the saga in which Carson, through strength of will, persuasive powers, and masterful eroticism led Queen of My Heart to . . . just exactly what stage of subjugation? He told himself he couldn't recall. His stiffening flesh told him he lied. "Play!" he croaked.

He had added suitable music to the ten tapes. This one began with a lush surge from the Tchaikovsky Sixth. Trite, but what stronger pillar of the Romantic period? What was Carson about, if not the romantic?

The lit screen came to life. There she was! On shackled hands and knees, looking back over the alabaster curve of her shoulder, mink gag a furry parenthesis spreading her lips to a snarl. Above the arch of up-tilted nose the gray eyes sloed in comprehension of her naked, eager anticipation. "Freeze!" he said. Her lovely, contorted face filled the screen, spread motionless like an exotic blossom. Queen of My Heart! Brightest coal on the hearth of Carson Thomas's passion. Queen of his heart, brain, liver, and the hot stones between his legs. Queen of his May and June and July . . . Queen of his hopes and desires, time without end—amen! "Slow motion," he commanded. Speak her initials, QMH; gloat over the squirm of the mouth shaping those letters being so like a loose, arousing kiss. . . . Her long lashes fluttered. Lids descended to bar distraction from focused savoring of Carson's attentions. Her head lolled. Black bangs swung free of the high white brow to stir in the indirect draft of her hot breath.

Behind her crouched red-haired Carson. His green eyes burned. Her perfect buttocks rose before his face, white and flawless as ancient Arctic ice. He pressed his manicured hands to the perfect skin, spread, disclosed the puckered secret. One wide hand was enough to sustain the position. The other raised the shaped plastic rod. . . .

When he was finished, spent, Champ stored the tape, restored all the equipment to its usual locations. He knew he was, in fact, getting it out of harm's way.

When had watching one of the tapes not been followed by Earthquake Anger?

He dragged Siege Restraint, the heavy chair, out into the middle of the nearly stripped living room, slid it clear of the small couch and lamp table. He sat and fastened the Velcro straps to his ankles. His left wrist lay on the wide chair arm. With his other hand he closed the Velcro over it. He slid his right through the tight loop on the other side. He made a fist, trapping that arm, too.

The first distant swell of anger rolled in from the wide sea of his mind, gathered strength and amplitude, crested and broke on the blasted beach of his emotions. He groaned and heaved, his first violent thought always the same: Master Carson deserved better than having Queen of My Heart desert him. The second swell rose more swiftly than the first: Why had she taken their daughter away from him? *Why?* Other swells followed in rhythmic order, thoughts behind their origins growing vaguer, like islands seen through fog. Currents of rage and winds of sorrow for commanding Carson's losses churned his emotions like Africa's western waters spawning hurricanes. His heaves became spasms. Siege Restraint's metal studs beat the floor like a dancer's taps. He babbled. Ripped painfully from his chest, his words coarsened to grunting howls lengthening into one long keening sound: *Awrrrrrooooooowwww!*

Siege Restraint's right arm broke off, three-quarter inch oak splintered like a mast in a storm. He toppled. Howling the while, he thrust and withdrew his unanchored pelvis as though copulating with the air. His free arm with its wooden load flailed the floor.

He quieted. His set jaw's quivering told him Earthquake Anger possessed him fully now. From the depth of that state was flung a dismaying conclusion.

Despite his having followed Carson's instructions absolutely, the man had not been pleased with the results. Neither Dr. Charlotte Wigman nor her daughter had . . . measured up, as his master put it. He, Champ, thought the woman to be of more than adequate—even grand—potential. Not a bit of it, said Carson.

Neither of the other two lady doctors had Carson's right stuff either. Nor had their brats.

Champ differed greatly with those judgments, too.

He howled again, now in despair. Carson had given him another chance to prove Charlotte's worthiness. He now waited for word of Champ's success.

As vile luck would have it, the woman had called to say the affair was over. Champ dreaded going to Carson with word of failure.

He would be so terribly angry.

Angrier even than Champ was at that moment. He howled and thrashed, rolling Siege Restraint over in clunking loops. He swung his right arm. Splintered oak drummed the floor.

After a long while he wept, calmed, and freed himself. He knelt by damaged Siege Restraint. He clasped his hands together below his chin.

He prayed to some nameless, shadowed entity that from . . . somewhere would come salvation.

After a long while he picked up the phone and explained everything to Carson. Then he said, "Tell me what to do next, Master."

Dressed and groomed, he looked sharp, no mistake. He wore his straight black hair and beard long but tidy. A little comb work settled renegade strands. He admired himself in the full-length mirror—bright ascot at the neck, light linen jacket, ruffled shirt, loud print beach trousers, woven straw sandals. Fashions by Whim and Serendipity. Flash that smile—good teeth now. Bonding is beautiful.

He picked up the paper bag and left his house, locking the door behind him. A twenty-minute plunge through deepening dusk in the 'vette was all it took to reach Dr. Charlotte's block. Oh, no, he was not quite ready yet to swing bold and sassy into her drive, even though expected. Not when it had been suspiciously difficult to convince her that their final meeting would be nothing more trying than an easy, good time for the two of them and Suzi. He found a house with no cars in the driveway and pulled up. He got out and walked back across the lot, past the gazebo and pool. He angled over a long patch of dried lawn. Ahead he saw the redwood rail fence enclosing Dr. Charlotte's property. Dusk was closing down to evening. He heard sounds of families at dinner doings but saw no one. And vice versa. How nice!

Nice, too, were the acres of glass in the rear of Dr. Charlotte's house. A little craning and peering allowed him to view the first-level rooms sunk into the side of the sloping lot. Now where would a beefy friend tuck himself away? In the least visible room. The one sunk most deeply into the earth. He edged an inquisitive eye around a foundation slab to peer through the TV room's slit of window.

Voilà! Mr. Shoulders, a refugee from Muscle Beach or Lenny's Lat Laboratory who rented rooms from Charlotte. Hunched close to the flicker of a portable TV.

The presence of hidden first-floor muscle had made Dr. Charlotte careless. The sliding door hadn't been latched. Champ opened it. He stepped into cool AC drafts. He walked toward Mr. Shoulders's room. Handy silent sandals. He paused at the doorway.

"He'll be here any minute!" Charlotte's voice called from upstairs, edged with uneasiness.

Champ slid away from the door frame.

"Be cool! I'm here," Mr. Shoulders shouted.

"Remember, you listen to us, Chuck. If there's any kind of

trouble, I want you up here—fast. In fact, I think I want you at the head of the stairs after he gets here. Right behind the door. Sit on the step and wait—just in case."

"Whatever. If you're so scared, you shouldna asked him over."

"Oh, it'll be all right, I'm sure. I'm just jiggy."

Champ edged his face across the door frame. Mr. Shoulders had returned his attention to the TV. Champ stepped into the room and advanced. Mr. Shoulders was watching a "Gilligan's Island" rerun. Clearly a man of intellect.

From the inside pocket of his linen jacket he drew a stiff piece of wire. Why hesitate? "Audacity!" General Patton said. In French, of course. He held the pointed wire in his right hand. He spread the left to brace the back of Mr. Shoulders's head when he reared back.

With swiftness worthy of a sleight-of-hand magician he reached forward and slid the wire into Mr. Shoulders's right eye socket, through the eyeball—and beyond. How thin the curve of bone behind the eye! Brain meets wire. Wire wins! A weak cry scarcely left Mr. Shoulders's thick throat.

Complicated tools were overrated. . . .

Champ performed his second entrance—front door this time—with equal élan, charming Charlotte despite herself. The caterer had delivered his order of champagne, her favorite raspberry sorbets and Swedish cookies—eighteen dollars a pound! Why no black mask and pistol? The florist had come through with the sheaf of tropical blooms. Champ's tucked-in card offered a brief message of good luck and success. Read between the block-printed lines: no hard feelings, Charlotte (and no handwriting or fingerprints to analyze).

For her part she wore a stylish white suit. Its neatly ironed creases told him, too: no hard feelings, Champ. Oh, she had the potential to be a pleaser! To be another Queen of My Heart and Carson's delight. It *was* there. Carson claimed there wasn't enough of it. She showed too much inclination for the conservative, the correct, the cautious. In short, she had no genius for casting herself down into the dark well of submission.

From the bag he carried he drew a package containing one of Suzi's junk-food favorites: Sno-Balls, concoctions of sweet cream surrounded by chocolate cake covered with a rubbery icing permeated with shredded coconut. The additive list was longer than that of natural ingredients. He opened the package and gave her the pink one. He noticed with great satisfaction that she wolfed it down despite mother's commands for ladylike nibbling.

He asked her to play her penny whistle. That brought a brief twinge of discomfort to her poreless face. Her braid rolled against her back as she shook her head.

"It won't hurt you to try for the last time, Suzi," Dr. Charlotte said. "Mr. Gray won't be coming back again. Please. He did spend so much time with you."

So Suzi put the mouthpiece to her talentless though shapely young lips and tried the tune with which the two of them had struggled so: "This Land Is Your Land." As always, she went flat here and there. Her only true talent was to disappoint. He sent the child off to girlish goings-on, toasted futures with her mother. He nearly persuaded her to take sorbet from his spoon and a cookie from his hand. "Sometimes they put themself in danger to take bread at my hand." Champ remembered Thomas Wyatt's words with a cunning curl of lower lip. Charge her wavering to the Pinot Chardonnay grape from the Zone de la Marne that had loosened stronger resolves than hers and undermined generations of pious virgins.

When the time was right he rose from the small table and moved toward her, smiling, a telling quip on his lips.

Somehow she knew. Instinct. How do mosquitoes know where the skin is thin?

"Chuck! I need you. Now!" She rose, too, chair toppling. She turned expectantly toward the door to the first-level stairs.

He moved swiftly to cut her off from the other room exit. "Chuck! Now!"

She rushed to the door, checking the lock knob, fearing she had forgotten to clear it. Finding it unlocked, she jerked the door open.

It hadn't been easy to prop Mr. Shoulders up against the door. He had needed to use some mop handles and cord. It had been worth it. He toppled out almost into Dr. Charlotte's arms.

It had been a grand touch to leave the wire protruding from his eye.

Oh, see her face! The mouth burst wide, the staring eyes standing every mascared spike to attention. She reeled back—right into his grasp. He cut off what had promised to be a most convincing scream with his spread palm. Keeping the pressure on, he slid his hand up, bending her nostrils closed. Her nose's flesh bulged, then compressed as she tried to suck breath through unyielding tissue.

Complicated tools were overrated. . . .

He turned all his attention to her eyes. How wide they grew! She understood her fatal predicament. All the waving and clawing of her hooked fingers couldn't lessen it one bit. Blue, blue eyes, broad as fields, their illuminating light sprung forth from the sun of terror. Her lids, their fine blue veins behind the picket fence of lashes, descended like dusk over the day of her life. Further blue suffused her face's soft skin as racing blood arrived without its precious oxygen cargo.

She was dying in silence, like the other two. Dying at Carson's orders. There were to be no clues to future recruitments or about his tastes.

From beyond the girl's bedroom door he heard the faint, muted mumble of her TV. Glancing at the motionless Mr. Shoulders, he thought: They sit passive while men of action work their wills.

Dr. Charlotte hung in his arms now, limp as a plucked daisy after a day on dirt. He kept his hand in place for three more minutes. There must not be any miraculous returns from the brink of the grave. He lowered her to the floor, unbuttoned her blouse, and pressed his ear to her chest between the small golden crucifix and the curving satined jut of her left breast. No pulse of life pounded the pressed porches of his ears.

He raised his head a few inches. The bound breasts thrust up beside his cheeks. He felt the tears start up, bitter as acid in his eyes. He had held that nippled flesh in hands hot with love.

But Carson had said she would not do.

Nor would the little girl.

He dared not weep long.

He rose from the still form, dashed tears from cheeks with the backs of his hands. He moved on magically quiet sandals to Suzi's bedroom door. No reason she should see her mother. He looked at his watch. The girl's time was running out, too. Luck provided a button lock on the outside of the door, evidence of some twisted theory of child discipline or a familial quirk of the former owners. He shoved the button home.

From the moment he had pressed his palm to Dr. Charlotte's soft face he had been increasingly conscious of the weight in his right-hand jacket pocket. It was demanding as a blister, as coins in a child's pocket. He could resist the lure no longer. He reached into white linen and removed the pruning shears. . . .

When he finished he looked around for possible sources of later embarrassment, found none. He descended to the basement, left as he had entered. He was getting into his 'vette when his expectant ear caught the faint concussion, no more noticeable than a slammed door.

Carson didn't think that complicated weapons were overrated.

During the drive home he stopped for a Dairy Queen chocolate malted.

An envelope had been taped to his apartment door. From Carson? Oh, yes, of course. Or so it seemed. Sometimes he wondered if . . . Didn't he well know the man's precise hand? He tore it open, trembling. Within, a clipping and a note.

14

He read the clipping. Turning his face skyward, he howled his delight at the stars.

His prayers for salvation had been answered!

He read his instructions, nodding his assent. Yes, yes! He was being sent on an odyssey of which he had only dreamed. What had been lost could be found. Secret dreams could come true!

3

JUNE FIRST. HALLELUJAH! AN ANNIVERSARY OF SORTS, Trish Morley thought. It had been three years to the day since she had set sail on the sea of capitalist commerce in the small-business boat of PC-Pros. ("Personal computer hardware problems? Don't go over*board*. Call PC-Pros!") In those first days she was the only PC pro, and a self-styled one at that. Of course, she was armed with a serious aptitude for electronics and a determination to succeed. Possibly her greatest asset, though, she had at first undervalued. That was how much she had learned during her eight years of informal instruction and collaboration with a true computer wizard. Almost without noticing.

Her commercial boat had grown to a bark now, crewed by a staff of seven. Each month-end, when Lotus 1-2-3 cranked out the financial spread sheets, that vital bottom-line total was larger. Income was up, but so were expenses: PC-Pros had its own attorney, accountant, office cleaners. The idea was to continue to expand the business, going after service contracts with firms that used PCs but weren't organized to handle the blown drive or memory upgrades. PC-Pros bought dead machines and pirated their parts to create used computers sold at tempting prices. There were some software installations and markups that added to revenues.

She turned away from the Bunn-O-Matic, steaming coffee cup in hand, and surveyed her modest empire—two formerly street-level business spaces made one when the common walls came down. The landlord had wanted to rent as was, but Trish said no. She had heard he was hard up to fill the space; the neighborhood wasn't the best. She held her ground. In the end he paid to have the walls removed.

Inside, all the office equipment and furnishings were leased, as were the two service vans. PC-Pros owned only the analytic devices, tools, parts, and components. She had bought them with the money bequeathed her when her father died shortly after her return from California. How sudden that had been! And ironic as well. After decades of daily aerobic exercises and a recent clean bill of health from Dr. Grandman he had clutched his chest as desperately as any three-pack-a-day boozer and toppled. Wife Marylou had stood terrified witness to the massive coronary.

Even without that tragedy those had been brutal emotional times for her. Having him go unexpectedly trashed what little remained of her good judgment. In her grief she had tried to persuade her mother to take the entire estate. Marylou had forcefully declined. "You and Melody are going to need every dollar he left you yourselves—in the worst way," she said. "Your father left me well enough off." Looking back, Trish counted that refusal as one of her mother's more perceptive actions. Insight wasn't normally her strong suit. When dealing with her only child she was usually highly opinionated and officious. Time past, Trish had fled the length of a continent to escape the woman. She had returned at twenty-nine shaken and chagrined, far more willing than previously to listen to Mother. Whether or not that was wise she hadn't yet determined.

Beside leasing what she could, Trish had resolved from the start to have as paper-free an office as possible. She bought software packages to handle business record keeping, leased a computer-operated telephone system that allowed message accumulation and access from distant sites. To further cut costs she hired smart, hungry young people who learned quickly. Their inexperience made them relatively inexpensive. She had imagined her little firm would suffer more turnover than had actually occurred. She suspected that was because she proved to be a better manager than her lack of experience suggested. She, too, was a fast learner. But compared to . . . *him*, she was a cretin. She kicked her attention free of that snare and went to her own PC. Time to see what she had scheduled on her calendar for this first day of the new month.

She walked into the cubicle formed with shoulder-high partitions. She had resolved that in *her* firm there would be no fancy offices. She allocated space solely on the basis of what doing the job required. Flinging herself into her wheeled chair, she slid over to the surge protector lying on the floor. She flipped its switch to on. A few moments of hummings, beeps, and flashes brought her PC system to life.

Hold on.

Her monitor wasn't showing the usual menu. A single line of yellow letters crossed the screen.

RECONSIDER BEFORE SEPTEMBER 1ST

The letters disappeared. Up came the expected menu. Trish grunted. Somebody was fooling around. She studied her menu startup code, looking for renegade lines.

None.

Hmmmm . . . Whichever staff member had been playing games had instructed the machine to erase the code after the message ran. Well, it was no big deal. She had no idea what *Reconsider* . . . meant. So the joke had gone over her head.

She leaned back in her chair, stuck out her legs, and stretched. As always she wore a white jumpsuit, six of which composed her total business wardrobe. She had taken an economic style choice made in her lean days and turned it into the PC-Pros' uniform; all her employees wore white jumpsuits.

She pressed her thighs. Pretty firm. With calves to match. Twice a week hop-till-you-drop aerobics maintained the foundation of her five-nine frame. The rest of her filled the uniform well enough, despite her having given birth to Melody and passed the big three-oh mark. What we have here, Morley, she thought, is a durable model. But not an indestructible one. Last week she had spotted a thin blue vein decorating the back of her leg just above the knee.

She turned to the computer keyboard and pulled up her personal calendar. A day in the life of Ms. Patricia McMullen Morley, suppy—struggling urban professional. 8:00 A.M.—Meet with the two-woman sales force to hammer out strategy for next year; 10:00 A.M.—Visit Marteko Construction, potential client, to provide assurances about service reliability; lunch meeting (subs or McBurgers out of bags) with her three techies to budget for the new fiscal year; and an afternoon devoted to updating the PC-Pros' master workplan. That meant four solo hours trying to balance hope against reality.

The evening she'd spend at her fiancé Foster Palmer's yacht club. He was giving a dinner for his crew members to celebrate their third-place finish in the Marielle Island race. Wives were invited. She didn't find it all that easy to talk to those ladies. They all had pretend jobs or volunteered. None had ever really felt the lash of want, as she had, so they lacked her hunger for personal commercial accomplishment. They devoted their energies to protecting their fiefdoms of marriage and family, climbing to the towers of intuition in search of predatory female infiltrators. They had the luxury to cultivate their insecurities. Trish felt more comfortable with the men, matched their brash kidding with her own, sometimes to Foster's embarrassment. What the hell! A girl had to let go a little in this world, even within the tradition-minded West Manachogue Yacht and Tennis Club.

She was on the road to Marteko in a van when the cellular phone beeped. Whoopee, her mother Marylou. Wanting to talk about—guess what? Her daughter's wedding, scheduled for September fifteenth and counting. Her mother's deceptively slow, Savannah-softened voice purred in her ear, "Patricia, you simply *must* make a decision about the reception site. La Fontanella called. They want a yes or no.

Other brides are interested in the facilities. And you know, I think you should commit."

"They charge like I'm the last Romanov," Trish said.

"So what if they're a bit pricey? Hasn't Foster generously agreed to help out?"

"I'd rather handle it all myself."

"That's quite impossible financially, Patricia. And you know it. The style of wedding you've chosen simply doesn't come at bargain-basement prices."

"Is it the wedding I've chosen, Mother? Or the one you're designing? I'm starting to get the feeling we're talking two different things here."

Ah, Mom's measured silence. I know her every move, Trish thought. But like a second-rate professional athlete playing against a superstar, I can't stop her. Now Marylou would sock her with a big deflator.

"My dear, I shouldn't need to remind you that your marriage to Foster Palmer will be a major turnaround in a life that not long ago could charitably have been described as an unmitigated California disaster," her mother drawled. "I'm trying to help you start that marriage in a style suitable to the social stratum into which—against all odds—you will enter. There has never been any question in my mind that you belong there. And always have. Your father and I raised and educated you to have the opportunity to step up in life. Now that you're on the verge, all I'm asking to get you to the final height is your cooperation. It puzzles me why you won't give it."

The answer, Trish knew, was residual rebellion, a flash of the old fire that had sent her to the coast and into electronic counterculture. Mom had always been the primary mover where Trish was concerned. Dad had been too agreeable, wandering off into his metallurgical books when the domestic going got tough. So it had been Marylou who arranged for the private primary school, then for four high school years at Emma Willard, thrusting up from its Troy, New York hilltop like a castle. There unsure girls often became confident women. Researchers had lately arrived to illuminate its secrets. After Emma she had been graduated from Brown, major in computer science (a snicker now; how little she had known—and not just about computers).

Right about then she "snapped," as she said over the years to come when characterizing her rapid departure. What did it was the ride home from Providence, cap and gown stowed in the trunk atop a debris of dorm room furnishings. Mom had taken the trouble to research computer-related firms, not on the basis of growth or earnings, but on the number of male employees. "The more men, the more *eligible* men, Patricia." When she balked Marylou went on, her Savannah inflection deepening as she entered familiar lecture mode. "You mustn't tell me you subscribe to this liberation chimera. You've studied history in two of America's best schools. Surely you've noticed that men and women related successfully to each other over the last five thousand years by doing what nature decreed. Look between your legs, Patricia, if you need a hint about your role. And don't be a fool. Play it."

The next day Trish got on a plane for Los Angeles.

Marylou was running on about the private club where she thought the reception would go "in a style that the Palmers would appreciate." Trish found the Palmers—Foster particularly—a lot more laid back about "style" than her mother. Maybe that came with being able to buy whatever style suited at the moment, then going on to the next. From burgers to *entrecôte bearnaise*, from tenting to renting Alpine chalets, from sailing Sunfish to sloops, the Palmers had no adjustment problems. They just slid along atop the thin oily film of their dollars.

". . . now, I know the place sounds a bit dear, and the manager *is* a snob, but . . ." Trish pushed the disconnect stud and put the cellular phone back in its cradle. No problem hurting her mother's feelings. She was as sensitive as a tombstone. The wedding to which Trish looked forward so eagerly would before long demand that she deal with its details. Or was it Marylou with whom she had to deal? In either case, not today.

Midway through her afternoon solo planning session she took a brief break and queried the telephone computer for her messages. It played them back. Three were from vendors that could be ignored. The fourth was from Rocco DeVita. Her mouth dried at the sound of his rough voice. Though born in America, he still spoke with the inflections of old Italy. When she had met him at a chamber of commerce get-acquainted party he was startled to discover she was in the same business as he. He called his outfit Computer Service. His dark eyes narrowed as she described PC-Pros. She didn't like the way his glance moved over her, as though she were a pork chop in a display case. He had to look up to do the full job because he was shorter than she. His burly frame rocked heel to toe, and his thick mustache twitched. He could scarcely wait to play the old familiar song, like the organ grinder immigrant he could have been: "Woman looks good as you do should be home with children."

"It's almost two thousand, Rocco. Not eighteen seventy. Women decide what they'll do with their lives. Not men."

He sniffed away her rebuttal. "So I'll buy you out."

"What?"

He nodded. "Everything you got. Maybe I hire your people, too."

Trish scowled. "I can't believe this! PC-Pros isn't for sale."

"Everything's for sale, Gray Eyes. It's just a question of price."

"Please! I've heard that line only about a hundred times." She began to move off.

He held her sleeve and named a figure. "I'll give you, say, three months to think it over."

"Rocco, I don't need three months. I don't even need three seconds. My business isn't for sale." She hurried away, flushed and annoyed. She hadn't spoken to him since then.

Until now. Why was her finger shaking as she keyed the number he'd left? She knew why but wouldn't face it directly at that moment.

Before she could get a word in, he said, "I talked to my

people. They said I should offer you twenty thousand more. So I'll do it. I called to let you know. Come on over my place. We'll sign the papers. Have a wine over a done deal."

"Rocco, your memory isn't very good. I told you PC-Pros isn't for sale. Second, it's worth a lot more than what you're offering."

A moment of icy silence, then he said, "Anything could happen to your business or your people, say next week, next month. . . ."

Her hackles rose. "What do you mean?"

"I mean you take my money, put it in your pocket, you're done. You stay in business, you're always taking a risk."

"Rocco, that sounds like a threat. Are you threatening my business? Threatening me?"

"I don't threaten nobody. I'm making you an offer, that's all."

Trish swallowed. "An offer that expires . . . maybe September first?" She remembered her computer screen's line of yellow letters. *Reconsider* . . .

"You want September first? You got it."

"I don't want"—Trish took a deep breath—"Rocco, did you arrange to have a message show up on my computer this morning, telling me to reconsider?"

Another moment of chill silence during which her mind paraded out of its warehouse all the trite Mafia/godfather/offer-she-can't-refuse nonsense. Finally he said, "Maybe."

Trish clutched the phone like a lifeline. "Well, I'm not going to sell anyway!" She hung up, knowing as she did that she wasn't certain whether or not he . . . Her palms were damp, and she could feel the ooze of sweat atop her brow. She hurried out of the office and into the repair lab. "Guys!"

Fred, Puck, and Tran looked up from circuit boards and scopes. Something in her tone got their complete attention. "I want to know if one of you has been playing joker with my PC. Like making it run a message when I booted this morning."

Seventeen-year-old Fred Purdom, who was quick and impatient, shook his head. "I don't joke," he said. His narrow face that so seldom stretched itself into either a smile or a frown fit his serious-mindedness like a custommade shirt.

Puck's thick glasses turned his inquisitive glance into a small blue-marbled squint. "You mean like 'Have a nice day'?" he said.

"Something like that," she said. "Ran once, and the file self-erased. Know anything about it?"

"*Nada,* Trish."

She looked at the third man, a slightly built Vietnamese. A puckered white scar curved like a scythe from below the white jumpsuit collar up the neck to the back of his cheek. Where shrapnel had torn tracks in his flesh Tran's sense of humor had leaked out forever. His head moved negatively, barely a wriggle. He looked back down at his solder gun. Tran was odd. Everybody who had been in Vietnam back then was odd. He worked like an animal. He had been an inspired hire, even if in no way chatty.

With two sobersides like Fred and Tran, Puck was a necessity. Every business needed at least one wise guy. "You men see anyone fooling with my machine?" she said.

They hadn't. Puck frowned at her. "You look spooked, boss. What was on the screen?"

"'Reconsider before September first.'"

The three looked at her blankly, shrugging.

She went to the reception area, where multitalented Michelle Amritz pounded on a keyboard, entering fresh information into a data base, head cocked to hold the phone to her chin. She spoke into it in rushed, choppy sentences. Michelle was a jane-of-all-softwares. She handled word processing and spread-sheeting; controlled data; ran payroll, accounts payable, and general ledger; and did desktop publishing—when she wasn't playing receptionist and secretary-to-all. After she hung up, Trish said, "You see anybody around here lately who doesn't belong? Somebody who might have messed with my PC?"

Michelle thought a moment, tapping a large white front tooth with a nibbled nail. "Negative." She looked up inquisitively at Trish. Michelle wore her black hair long and straight. Her glasses had gold metal rims that suited her dimpled cheeks. Her only other adornment was cherry-flavored lip balm that she applied in moments of stress. "Anything else?"

Trish shook her head. Samantha Swords and Teresa Stakos, her two-woman sales force, were seldom in the office. There remained only "Leftover" Lewis—Charles Lewis, really, who so often said he handled whatever the other six left over that the name stuck. He was on a van route that afternoon, after which it wasn't always necessary for him to come all the way back to the building. Today, though, he appeared. She asked him about the message. He knew nothing. He cocked his hairy head. "Something funny going on?" he said.

"Maybe. Why do you ask?"

"Funny things maybe out on the road, too."

Trish's heart thumped with a little extra strength. "Like what, Leftover?"

His face was round, ringed with heavy brown beard and hair four months from a barber's attention. With his thick nose he looked like a bear cub—more so when he frowned, as he did then. "Like maybe being out in the van and thinking you're being followed."

Trish cocked her head. "By whom? Driving what?"

"A guy I couldn't see good. Driving a gray four-door Detroit something."

"When?"

"Now and then over the last week."

A lot more of Trish's questions produced very little additional information about Leftover's sometime shadow. What they did produce was an increase in her anxiety level.

How far was Rocco DeVita willing to go to eliminate PC-Pros as a competitor?

Getting into her Acura, she shoved all that off into a corner of her mind. It all might be coincidental and trivial on the close inspection she wasn't willing to conduct right then.

The closer to her rambling Victorian rental she drove, the more her grin turned up.

Melody would be home from school!

Janine was on the porch thumbing through *Seventeen*. A denim headband held her heavy black hair. Her skin was smooth and white. Trish didn't need to know her name was O'Connor to see the Irish in her. Though only thirteen, she had a way with children. Melody liked her. Trish wouldn't let her get away. "How is she, Janine?" Trish said, climbing the stairs.

"Need you ask? Listen."

From Melody's second-floor room came high-pitched, fluid notes.

"Is that her flute?" Trish said.

"When I last looked in it was the Irish whistle. Chieftains look out!" Janine's smile was silvered with expensive orthodontia.

Trish pulled a check out of her purse. New month. Time to settle baby-sitting accounts. Janine tucked the check into the back pocket of her tight denim shorts. "Thanks, Ms. Morley!" She spun on her $150 pump-up sneakers and was gone. She didn't need the money. She was building character.

Trish took the uneven stairs to the second floor two at a time. "Heads up, kiddo," she shouted. "Here comes your loving mother!" The music stopped, sneakered feet thudded. Seven-year-old Melody burst forth at full run, carrot-topped, freckled. Come to me, sweet pea, sweetheart, sweet crumb of my flesh!

She had school papers to show; teacher was cleaning out her desk with only days to go before vacation. Trish lavished motherly praise on bestarred pages of single-number to single-number addition (no carrying yet) and the briefest of essays written laboriously on lines set an inch and a half apart. This fallout from the enrichment program, promising as it was, paled before Melody's musical aptitude. If she heard something once, she could play it on any of her modest battery of instruments: flute, cheap electronic keyboard, plastic clarinet, soprano and alto recorders, or on her latest acquisition, the tin whistle, three dollars at the Irish fair Foster had taken them to last week.

Trish gave her an extra hard hug. "Hey, kiddo . . . pretty soon no more pencils, no more books, no more teacher's dirty looks," she sang.

"You're *flat*, Mommy. Anyhow, after this year I'm never going to school again!"

"In the middle of August you'll be begging to go back."

"No way!"

"We'll see."

"Can I have a Yodel for my snack, Mom?"

"I thought we had you on a health kick: carrots, raisins, and rice cakes."

"Today I want something gooey."

"Let's check your teeth."

"Aaaaaaaah."

Trish peered into perfect pink and white alignment. No decay. No soft spots. Let's hear it for prenatal fluoride! "Come on down to the kitchen."

That room and its adjoining pantry were high-ceilinged and spacious, paneled with dark, waist-high wood—eighty years away from today's trendy free-standing counters and eye-level microwaves. She loved this shadowy old house with its angles and crannies—except in heating season. She opened the package of Yodels, stared down at the twin artificial-chocolate-covered cylinders. Melody's hand was out. "Just one," Trish said. "We'll save the other one for another time—maybe for next year."

"Mom!"

Trish raised a cautioning finger. "You forgetting the rules? No complaining. And no whining." She poured Melody a small Dick Tracy glass of milk. She gulped down the Yodel in less than five seconds.

"Melody! You're making a pig of yourself!"

"I was hungry." She put her dish and glass in the sink.

"That's not an excuse for no manners."

"Okay, Mom." Melody was suitably chagrined.

Trish said, "Do I get to hear your whistle?"

"Sure!"

As always Trish sat, hands on her lap, in her padded chair while her daughter performed with her usual enthusiasm. The girl narrowed her wide gray eyes (oh, you are your mother's daughter!) when playing and wrinkled her button nose, saucy as any Disney cartoon character's beneath its freckle shower. Spooky that she so seldom hit a false note, never mind a child's limited coordination. The names of tunes often escaped her, though their key never did. Somewhere along the way she had learned to read simple music, though no one had taught her. Trish had no reason to doubt that when the childish strings of quarter notes turned to clustered chords Melody would assimilate them easily, as a young bird flutters increasing distances and then one day soars.

The tunes wound their way from the whistle down to her heart. She was reminded again that from the hellish waste heap that her more than eight years in California often seemed this one incredible redheaded blossom had sprouted.

One day, maybe, she would be able to get wholly past the emotional price she had paid for those years. She would heal the inner damage to her personality that snarled and snapped at the heels of her sexuality, even as she attempted to deepen and broaden her relationship with Foster Palmer. How badly she had thus far failed to do so could be proven by what she had avoided telling him. I have been less than candid, she thought. A great deal less than candid. . . .

The rhythm and fluidity of Melody's tune summoned Trish's attention with a sorcerer's power. She had put off beginning her daughter's formal musical instruction. She wanted to see toward which instrument the girl was tugged. What she didn't want to create was a musical freak. Foster had been supportive about that in the face of Marylou's opposite opinions, as he so often was—thank goodness! She felt a surge of warmth for the man.

Melody took the whistle from her lips. Her narrowed eyes widened to normal. "I wonder if Daddy would like to hear me playing this," she said.

"I'm sure he would," Trish said evenly.

Melody frowned. "I miss him. Sometimes I really miss him and want to see him."

"You know how many times I've explained—"

"I know. And I understand."

"Then you shouldn't make it hard for yourself by wondering. Because that's all it'll ever be. Just wondering."

Melody's smooth brow crumbled into a frown. "I can't always do that. I can't always not think of Carson."

Instead of the trial-by-wife Trish had expected, the celebration at Foster's yacht and tennis club was painless. Thank the bubbly. *Père* Champagne anointed even the most conservative lady. No less than Blanche Twerbly burst into song. Though straight-haired and WASPy, she nonetheless passably sang "Empty Bed Blues," to husband Phil's grand astonishment and, as the light dawned, growing embarrassment. Another hidden, adulterous tale from the naked suburbs, Trish thought, glad it was theirs, not hers. She already had too many secrets.

Foster made a speech of thanks to his crew and praised his yacht, the *Emerald Lady*. He stood six-four, hair thinning as he shoved hard at forty. The metal-rimmed glasses that winked as he gestured looked out of place on a face so tanned by sea sun. His long, wiry hands were rough from sailing duties. Trish felt great tenderness for him, marveling that the two of them should have come together and clicked—she the wandering one, so recently settled into respectable business, he a well-off middle sibling who bred English mastiffs for pleasure and played yachtsman. Foster could have done nothing, thanks to his heaps of stocks and bonds, but everyone in his family understood that while work might not be necessary, idleness was unacceptable. His older brother ran a brokerage house in New York. His younger sister imported South American fabrics to her Dallas boutique.

When the party broke up Foster led Trish outside. The moon was out, the June night warm. They strolled toward the marina, where masts swayed to the beat of tides and current. They climbed the gangway to the deck of the *Emerald Lady*. Answering both their unspoken desires, he kissed her. She eagerly welcomed his taste and the grainy scent of his after-shave. His lips' parting sounded dim, melancholy chimes in the cathedral of her mind. The sensuous side of their relationship hadn't gone that well. She was entirely to blame. Having surrendered so totally to Carson, she found she couldn't let herself go at all with Foster. It was as though some vital gear in her erotic clockwork had lost teeth from rough use.

Foster's reaction to her hesitancy was confusing. The couplings that she considered inadequate seemed to satisfy him. So she worried about the breadth of his experience. The problem was that Carson had conditioned her to certain physical expectations—though she wanted with all her heart to dislodge them. Yet she wondered now and then if Foster could satisfy her that way. Did she really want him to? When she tried haltingly to communicate her anxieties he seemed to comprehend too readily, making her think that he was failing completely to understand. She had perhaps naïvely hoped that these matters of intimacy would work themselves out before September fifteenth. Now she wasn't so sure.

The moon rose higher. The *Emerald Lady* stirred against her moorings like a restless cat. She brought him up to date on her mother and wedding plans.

He laughed, a nice deep chuckle that always delighted her. "If she had more to do, she wouldn't be so busy with your life," he said. Trish knew he was fond of Marylou. In gloomier moments she thought the man understood her mother better than she.

Their conversation wound around, then he said, "Lois called again, ears sharp for sounds of divisiveness between us."

"Do you have to talk to her?" Trish said.

"She's a hard person to discourage."

"Sometimes I think you could try harder."

"We kept company formally for four years. Casually for

maybe a dozen before that. We go back. Just the same, she knows it's all over between us."

"Lois Smith-Patton isn't the kind to give up," Trish said. Lois was a predatory divorcée who reminded Trish of a ferret—danger jammed into a small package. She had stalked Foster hard and determinedly. Then, poised to pounce, she found Trish had stolen away her prey. Far from swallowing her disappointment, she prowled about on the periphery of Foster's life. She saw to it that she ran into him "accidentally" now and then, called him on neutral business, then did personal prying. She had on the occasion of her broken engagement come to speak personally to Trish. Trish took a deep breath and wrenched her mind away from the memory. When reviewing *that* scene it was best to be in a strong-minded mood.

This evening Trish felt far from strong-minded. As Foster pressed kisses on her yielding but unresponsive lips a flash of insight illuminated her present life. She had spent the past three years building not a career and a relationship to last the rest of her days, but a house of cards that rising winds were gathering to destroy.

Three days later Michelle Amritz stopped Trish as she entered the PC-Pros' offices. "Got an angry customer for you, chief. Lester O'Day, Pristine Cleaners. I forwarded him into your phone mail. You better put on your asbestos earpiece."

"What's his problem?"

"He lost files. A lot of files. And he's in a real hurry to talk to you."

In her office Trish pulled up the file on Pristine. PC-Pros had set up a network among Pristine's six stores scattered across the city. Last week PC-Pros had installed a loaner at one of the locations and brought a sick machine back, and . . . let's see, she thought . . . Tran had replaced a blown motherboard. Yesterday he had returned the original machine. Trish frowned. How had any of that led to files being lost? Why was Lester O'Day angry?

The moment Trish heard his voice she realized she was

talking to a new Luddite. Overnight he had turned against all computers. Back to pencils and order pads, back to the abacus! Tactful Trish heard him out. Deal with the emotions first, she remembered being told. Then go ahead to handle the real problem. She imagined Lester at the other end of the line, bald and red-faced, wearing one of his incredibly loud neckties. When he seemed to have run down for the moment, she said, "I don't see how your file losses are connected to our work."

"You don't? Well, my nephew knows something about computers. He says the machine you brought back came with a virus. You know what that is, Ms. Morley?"

"Yes, I do." A virus was renegade software that went about its own destructive business damaging "healthy" files. Depending on what type of virus was involved, it could infect and cripple one machine, dozens, or thousands. "But I'm sure PC-Pros had nothing to do with it."

"Like hell, woman! I'm sitting here with six stores that can't take in any work. There was no trouble in the two years we've been running on computers. Then you people get hold of one machine and—*whammo*—we're dead in the water!"

"Mr. O'Day—"

"Forget arguing with me. Just do something to get me going again. Or my next call is to my attorney."

Trish struggled to hold on to her professional voice— forget that fishwife inside begging to be heard. "I suggest instead that you call your software vendor and—"

"They went belly-up six months ago. They shoulda called themselves 'Fly-by-Night-Systems.' You computer types are all alike. You promise everything—and deliver crapola!"

"Maybe if I could speak with whoever on your staff is responsible for the system—"

"It was a college kid we had. He's been gone so long he's as much history as Abe Lincoln."

"What about your nephew?"

Lester O'Day's voice ground deeper into harshness. "No way. No way! You get him tangled up in it, pretty soon it's all his fault!"

"Mr. O'Day, listen to me. Someone is going to have to reinstall backup software onto your central processor."

Silence.

"Mr. O'Day, do you understand what I'm saying?"

"All I understand is I'm going to call my attorney if you people don't get over here and get me out of this. Every minute I'm losing business!"

Trish pressed her free palm to her face, took a deep breath. "Mr. O'Day, we're a hardware maintenance and repair company. Systems aren't our responsibility. It's really up to you to do what's needed to guarantee smooth operation. Things like regularly making backups. If you look at the contract you signed with us, you'll see—"

"You brought in the machine with the virus!"

"You just think we did. There's no proof. And I can't imagine why someone here would want to sneak a virus into your system. If indeed there is one. Which I doubt."

"Let's cut the crap, both of us, Ms. Morley!" Lester O'Day shouted. "The bottom line is you got me into this, you get me out. Or I sue!" Down went the receiver.

Never mind that this was the electronic age, Trish thought. People to the end of time would be ruled by emotions. She, too, felt some specific emotions—dealing with where Lester O'Day and Pristine Cleaners could go and what they could do there. But the professional Trish knew she would have to act for the sake of continued business and PC-Pros' reputation. She explained the situation to Fred Purdom, her poker-faced seventeen-year-old technician. "I want you to go over there and do what you can to straighten them out. Run some virus-killer software. Use his last backup, tell him all the data after that date is gonzo. And don't take any of his BS. Got it?"

"Yeah, I got it." Fred's face as usual betrayed nothing. His voice, though, revealed his concern. "If this is a virus situation, I can't figure how it got on his machine."

"Neither can I."

After Fred had left for Pristine Cleaners Trish lamented the use of her limited resources to placate "Lowlife" Lester, as Fred called him. For a large company a day of a technician's time was no big deal. But PC-Pros' staff was spread thin. The business simply couldn't absorb these kinds of emergencies. She hoped it was an isolated accident of some sort.

She absolutely refused to dwell at that moment on Rocco DeVita.

4

MELODY'S LOOMING VACATION MEANT TRISH HAD TO assemble the mosaic of the child's summer days with all the care of a Byzantine artist. So many days she would spend with Grandma, so many at play groups, half-day summer camps, organized sports and swimming, so many with Mom at PC-Pros, at theme parks, water slides, and varied musical performances. Trish had to write it all out, then go ahead and make arrangements as far ahead as was practical. After the first of June her daughter's appointments and other demands increasingly infiltrated those of the business. She wrote everything down in her Franklin Day Planner, Supermom's secret weapon.

Leave it to her mother to remind her that she was so caught up in Melody's summer that she continued to neglect her own wedding. "You've arranged things backward as usual, Patricia," Marylou said. "The correct order is supposed to be marriage then children, not vice versa."

"Very funny. I don't hear you broadcasting those words of wisdom at your card parties, Mother. In the engagement announcement you had them say "It will be the bride's second marriage".

"Well, of course! We needn't make fools of ourselves, need

we?" Marylou's right brow rose. Over the years a skeptical crease had formed there. Other, thinner creases had etched their way into her upper lip. The rest of her face remained undisturbed, appealingly youthful. Her gray eyes were still sharp and clear, as was her wit—which she turned too often on her daughter. In her mid-sixties she still possessed the southern charm of her youth to which age had added northern assurance. Trish wondered why she hadn't found a more lively companion than Stoneman Gore. Stoneman followed her around like a leashed pug. In fact, he looked a little like one, with his thick chest and rectangular face. She guessed her mother preferred Stoneman's company because he was rich. The only work he did was to clip bond coupons. A well-heeled cipher, maybe he was the perfect match for reflexively social climbing Marylou. This bright June Saturday morning he sat in his favorite chair in the corner facing the object of his affections, whom he devoured with wide, adoring eyes. He spoke seldom and briefly.

"I've taken the liberty of making up a wedding checklist for you, Patricia." Her mother waved sheets as chockablock as those recording Don Giovanni's conquests ("In Spain already one thousand three"). "The very few things you've already done I've checked off." She threw up a free hand. "Heavens, you haven't even found out if your matron of honor has put the weekend aside!"

"We're talking just one person here," Trish said acidly.

"So?"

"There's no need to hurry big time. In fact, there's no real need for a wedding at all. I'd use a J.P., mother, if that didn't mean I'd have to chain you to that couch to restrain your indignation."

"Something else unpleasant you brought back from California: a disrespectful mouth." Her mother's glance carried the hard glint of glower. "You'd have done better to bring back divorce papers."

Marylou just wouldn't let it go, Trish thought. Of course, she wouldn't breathe a *word* in public. There was no way Trish could explain to her mother just what had happened on her way to motherhood. No way she could explain

Carson . . . and other things. In fact, she had explained to no one. That meant she hadn't yet dared present the precise details of Melody's paternity to Foster either—and she regretted it. He labored under some expected misunderstandings that she had meant all along to clear up.

Dimly she understood that her return home in a posture much like that of defeat had been not only a victory for her mother, but a personal crisis in values for herself. She had rushed to California to forge a life based on her own beliefs, ones far removed from those of tradition-minded Marylou. That she had come home broke, toddler in hand, and with no husband in hailing distance her mother saw as justification for her position. Trish's attraction to Foster and his life meant she had, though she resented it, come to share some of her mother's values. Her enthusiastic acceptance of his proposal (made in a rowboat during a stunning sunset, with a secret bottle of champagne dangling submerged on a string to toast "your good judgment and my good fortune," Foster said) was a solid signpost along her life's new road. She had sown her wild oats and eagerly awaited the stability and permanence of the married state. If only she could be more enthusiastic about the wedding!

The maximum time she was able to spend with mother was about three hours. Any longer and the woman provoked her to screams or tears—sometimes both. She fled with Melody and Foster to the first strawberry picking of the year. Down the rows of early berries they duckwalked, he on one side, she on the other. Melody gamboled under the high blue sky—eat six, box one—fingers, lips, and cheeks smeared sweet red.

"Lift the leaves and stems to find the best berries," Foster said. "I learned this during my boyhood growing up on the farm."

"The farm! What farm?" Trish giggled.

"They sent me to camp every summer. The camp had a farm where we did the chores." The sun flashed off his lenses, and he raised his face in laughter. "So they paid a great deal of money to turn us rich kids into poor farm boys."

37

"Berry?" She held one up to his lips. He bit it. The juice oozed onto her fingers. He licked it off. From his box he selected a huge, squarish berry, so deep red that the yellow seed flecks glowed in it like crumbs of gold. He leaned forward across the matted tangle of plants. She opened her mouth hesitantly. He pressed the monster berry against her teeth.

Her memory flashed like an artillery battery blowing away the present, replacing it with a moment years and states away. . . . She lay on her back, blindfolded, her ears plugged with Play Doh, arms out and tied. On the enameled chisels of her teeth Carson split grapes, kiwis, chunks of fresh pineapple, letting juices run where they would. The sticky rivulets teased her chin, dribbled back onto her tongue's rough buds. Then, as always, he went beyond the expected. She had to guess at the taste and texture of ice, raw meat, eggs, still worse things that made her squirm and roll her deaf, blind head in powerless revulsion. What had begun as a daring diversion ended with her howls of repulsion. And still he pressed on, lashing her with the rod of her submission. . . .

She rolled her head away from Foster's offered berry, turned her eyes to the azure sky. Tears of sorrow burned for what she had once allowed to be done to her. How much resisting the past was like shoving a boulder up an incline! She despaired, because she hadn't nearly the strength of Sisyphus. She begged Foster's pardon and hurried away down the row. When she had regrouped she returned to his side with an apologetic grin and too-shiny eyes.

Sunday Foster asked Trish and Melody to go with him, as he often did, to visit his enterprise, Lake Country Kennels. One of the east's highly regarded sources of pedigreed English mastiffs, it provided quarters for fifty of the huge dogs, mostly youngish animals and pups. Among the full-grown specimens were Gog and Magog, Foster's own dogs. Their pointy-eared heads reached well above Trish's waist. While Foster talked business with Doris, the manager, Melody and Trish played with the animals in the fenced field behind the two low buildings. Gentle, patient, and protective, they let Melody try to ride them like horses. They rolled over to expose tan flanks to her enthusiastic if not skillful brushing.

Melody continued her so far unsuccessful pleadings for "a dog of her own," a phrase she had gleaned from a book or TV. "Every girl should have a dog of her own, Mom!" she said. "I'll take good care of him."

"We don't have room for one of these kind-hearted monsters, sweet. Never mind feeding it chow in bulldozer scoop lots."

"Mom!"

"Foster's nice enough to let you play with Gog and Magog. You can have the fun without the responsibility. That doesn't happen often in life, I can assure you."

Melody frowned but knew better than to dare to whine. She went racing across the field, the dogs loping easily beside, as though daring her to put on some real speed.

Trish squinted against the midday brilliance, watching her child gambol with her two protectors. She wanted this moment frozen in plastic like a boardwalk trinket. She would hang it around her neck and never have to worry about her own or her daughter's safety. They would stand forever as they did now, on secure turf fenced by sturdy Cyclone wire, guarded by faithful animals. She wondered at the sources of her impossible longing.

Some of it originated with bellowing Lester O'Day, his business laid low by a virus whose source had to be her loaner PC. Who had been following Leftover Lewis as he made his van rounds? Who had urged her to "reconsider," and what had to be reconsidered? Something business-related, surely. At the bottom of it all lay Rocco DeVita. Somehow she would have to confront him and exert some leverage, if she could find out how to do it.

She succeeded in shaking off shadowy intuitions for the rest of the day, thanks to Foster, who took them both to a dockside lobster restaurant. There they ate from spread newspapers, gobbled steamers and corn, and attacked the red shells with nutcrackers and picks, showing the zeal of berserk brain surgeons.

After Melody was in bed she sat with Foster on the screened porch's old wooden swing. They ate strawberries lathered with sweetened whipped cream. After they put their dishes aside Foster took off his glasses. Without them he looked less bookish, more like the highbred outdoorsman he was. He never kissed her with them on. She wished he'd try it once. She wanted to use her tongue as a windshield wiper, just to see what he'd do. She often behaved outrageously when she fancied him growing too serious-minded.

Amid a long kiss she tried to gauge how much she loved him. To do that she had to know what love meant for her. What she had felt for Carson had begun as love but had over time wandered up a bizarre tributary of that emotion. She had been too swept up in what she allowed to happen to fully explore those waters' tortuous crosscurrents of meaning.

She threw off clinging memories and put her whole self into the kiss. He sensed her soft yielding and rolled his mouth against hers with increased energy. I do love him, she thought. I love him very much! She took hope from her own rising passion, like a wobbly candle flame gathering strength —at last!—despite the chill breezes blowing from her past. Please, please, in the end let it be all right between us!

The phone warbled in the living room. She groaned into Foster's open mouth. He pulled away and breathed, "Let it ring!"

"Melody . . . it'll wake Melody."

She let her arms fall, and he did the same. She stood up on shaky knees and hurried inside, her heart pounding. She snatched up the receiver. "Hello."

Silence.

She could tell the line was open. "Hello? You there?"

No reply. No heavy breathing. Nothing. Just the open line. Well, she wasn't going to nourish the fantasies of some pervert. "Hello? Last chance."

Silence.

She hung up.

Back on the swing she and Foster attempted to resume their kiss and were making satisfactory progress when the phone warbled again. "Do me a favor," Trish whispered. "You answer it this time."

In a short while he returned. "Whoever it was hung up when they heard my voice."

"I doubt there'll be any more calls," she said.

Even so, the mood was dashed.

Monday morning she went to work relaxed and ready for a good week. One message had been left in her phone mail over the weekend, 2:39 P.M. Sunday. She lifted the receiver and dialed in the code for replay. The man's words, like a sudden blast from the air conditioner, made her shiver: *"Reconsider by September first!"*

She sat back in her chair, played the message through twice more. She didn't think she had heard that voice previously, but she wasn't absolutely positive. From then on she was on edge. Not until late Tuesday did she understand her tension grew from wondering what Rocco would do next. She had reached the conclusion that he had somehow been behind the virus afflicting Pristine Cleaners. What would happen when once again she failed to reconsider by not calling him and agreeing to sell out? What new, nasty trick did the swarthy man have on tap? Or was he merely going to torment her from a distance with tactics like yesterday's two phone calls?

The tension caused her to regress as a manager and mother through the rest of the week. She was curt with her staff and impatient with Melody. The last time she had been like this was at the final stages of her stay in California. She had endured Carson's ever-broadening, destructive demands for the sake of her daughter. As more than three years had passed since her return home, she thought herself fully mended from those days and their punishing emotions. Now, to her dismay, she found herself quickly retreating to the mildest of those stressed behaviors: the short fuse, the long, worrying stares into space, the sudden deep night awakenings. A fog of unfocused anxiety rose and clouded her days.

Late Thursday afternoon Leftover phoned her. His voice carried a taut tone she had never before heard. "Somebody stole my van!" he said. "I had it parked and locked while I was making a delivery. Somebody got in somehow and drove off!"

Tremors marched like troops up the backs of her arms. Having fears come true was worse than complete surprise. "What was in it?"

"Tools and two PCs. Two IBM 386s. And an HP laser printer."

"Tell me where you are." When he did she told him to stay put. She ordered Michelle Amritz to call the police, then report the theft to the insurance company. Rates would go up, but what could Trish do?

On Friday the van was found undamaged. The machines were still inside—but badly smashed. It hadn't been sloppily done. The cases had been removed and the innards crumbled with hammer blows. Replacement with equivalents would be necessary. She wasn't going to piece any together from parts, even if her technicians could do it. That meant she would have to put up the cost of replacement and hope for full insurance reimbursement. She'd have Michelle check the policy for her.

So . . . it had been calculated vandalism, the sort of thing she imagined was right up Rocco's alley. She couldn't let him get away with it. She had to let him know she knew what he was doing and stop him.

Among the problems with doing that was that she had no idea how to handle the man, with his hungry eyes and soft-spoken demands to buy her out. She needed advice, maybe that of another small business owner. For a moment she thought of calling Dino Castelli, the baker who had opened up shop a few doors down several months ago. Below his mop of tight curly hair glowed dark brown eyes whose corners were creased from grinning—often at his own bad jokes. The jokes she could skip, but she had become addicted to his bread and sweet cream-filled pastries. He always seemed ready to chat, leaning his six-one frame across the glass cases, his forearms crossed. On one he had a tattoo, a green alligator with a yellow eye and the words "Nam '75." She sensed that beneath his charming chatter he was a tough guy. Maybe he would know how to handle someone who might have mob connections. After brief thought she discarded the idea of enlisting him. She simply didn't know him well enough. She considered asking Foster to help her, but she didn't want to involve him in her business problems. Nor could she imagine him facing down an aroused Rocco. No, not at all. She would have to handle her menacing competitor herself.

She phoned Rocco and made an appointment to talk to him late Friday afternoon about his "business offer." He seemed pleased to hear from her, as though he had expected it. For moral support she took along Samantha Swords, the larger half of her sales department. She was big in the beam, brassy and confident, armed with the large ego a successful salesperson couldn't be without. On the way to Computer Services, for Sam's benefit, Trish hit the highlights of her concerns. "There's only one way to handle a situation like this, Trish," Samantha said. "Bluff!"

Rocco ran his business on three of the middle floors of a rundown suburban office building. The elevator clanked its way up. Rocco himself buzzed them in, smiling around his thick cigar.

When they were in his office with the door closed Trish made the introductions and said, "I know you want to buy my business. But you're taking foolish risks trying to frighten me into selling it."

"Oh?" Rocco wore an open-necked shirt and a thick gold chain. He touched it absently with one hand while the other waved the cigar. "What you think I do?"

She told him about the virus and the smashed equipment. Before he could reply she continued. "Either you stop or I go to the police and file a complaint."

"The police." He chuckled. "Yeah, you go to the police. Maybe they listen. Maybe they get your story. Maybe they come talk to me . . . in six months. I tell them what I tell you now: I don't know nothing about what you're saying. Then the police go away. And don't come back because you got no proof." He jammed the cigar straight into his mustached mouth and raised his hands in a massive shrug.

"You thinking like a woman. You see too much TV. You think about police. You're not important enough for them to help. Forget them and"—his eyes burned into Trish's—"sell out. Save yourself grief."

"You're saying you did try to hurt my business."

"Saying nothing. I'm not a stupid man. You got a witness. I'm asking you to sell out, that's all. Whadaya say?" His inquisitive glance held her eyes and locked in like a missile.

She was dismayed to find she couldn't read him. To begin with, she couldn't tell if he was cunning or dull. Nor could she guess whether or not he was using her assumptions against her. Hearing her tale of trouble, maybe he had, by simply refusing to deny responsibility, characterized himself as a ruthless adversary who threatened to raise the stakes until she consented to sell. She was beginning to feel she had very much gone off half-cocked.

That feeling didn't leave her, even after a postmortem with Samantha during the ride home. Her saleswoman took the positive approach: "Trish, you served notice on him! That's the important thing. He'll think twice before he tries any other cute stuff. He knows if he does, you'll call the cops."

"What if it wasn't him?"

Samantha snorted. "Who else could it be? Who else would sabotage our business?"

"Nobody I can think of," Trish said.

5

OH, GLORIOUS *MARSEILLAISE! ALLONS, ENFANTS* ...
An anthem worthy of the name, whether blasted out by a
Parisian brass choir, sung at *Casablanca*'s Rick's, or whistled as it was now by perfectly pitched Melody, eternal
sweetheart of Carson's rodeo. The sound reached Champ's
ears with the presence and fidelity that only state-of-the-art
Japanese bugs and speakers allowed. How long had it been
obvious who really won World War II? He pressed a plate on
the compact control panel. That minute adjustment further
sharpened Melody's whistle to you-are-there presence. He
conducted, waving broad hands. He was Pierre Boulez on
Bastille Day! His anticipation rose. Would Melody hearken
to the tune's dynamics, this wonder child who had never
beheld the score? Yes, yes, forte, as the anthem soared
to ... *Marchons!* Her whistle grew in amplitude. Champ
the music director kept pace. He grunted with delight, hands
fanning the air like paddles. Too soon she warbled the last
note. "Encore, encore!" he shouted, words echoing from the
walls of the two small rooms he called Resurrection Headquarters. *"Vive la France!"*

Carson would be so pleased to hear that the girl had only
grown in talent. *Vive* Melody!

He cocked his head, his hunger for even one more sweet note strong as an addict's craving. Maybe she would pick up one of her instruments! No, he heard only uninteresting thumpings. She was fooling with clothes, cleaning her room, or carrying on with some other nonsense. Her gift to the world was sound. She needed to be heard—not seen. So he had hidden the two minicams where they would do the most good, one peering into the living room and the other, of course, into Queen of My Heart's bedroom.

It had taken two months to complete the move from the coast. Carson had been so particular about which equipment, components, and tools should be carried and which could safely be purchased in the new city. He issued instructions about where Champ should set up his head-quarters. Charged and gleeful with the unexpected oppor-tunity to recover Queen of My Heart and his child, he had phoned Champ daily to check on progress and issue the next measure of directions, as though his servant's capabilities were unequal to too many tasks at once.

Champ knew his talents were equal to anyone's—save Carson's.

He had slipped in swiftly to Queen of My Heart's home to install the bugs in the rooms and phones on a sunny Sunday afternoon, after which she and the Loathed One returned laden with strawberries. The sleek cameras with their optic wonder lenses and built-in transmitters required more time and care. He had stolen a PC-Pros' van and used it to haul his own tools and equipment. No neighbor would remark on a van parked in the business owner's driveway. He had wheeled in bold as a thieving politician, tool belt around his waist. Wonderful old house, filled with wasted space, nooks, crannies! A thousand and one sites from which to spy on his Scheherazade. Cunning Champ's interior carpentry skills hid the tiny optical eyes as the most adept curbside three-card monte gamester concealed his jack of diamonds among queens.

Business finished, he had driven off and later smashed the computers and printer—Carson's instructions. Hadn't his master kept him busy since his arrival! He had ordered that

PC-Pros' phones be bugged and that a loaner computer be inoculated with a virus. No problem for Champ to enter the building in the wee hours using his Tumbler Tickler, another of Carson's patentable throwaways. He had never found a tumbler lock it wouldn't open. No problem, either, coding in the "Reconsider" message on Queen of My Heart's PC or phoning it in to her computer on Sunday. And phoning her sweet self!—twice on that same Sunday afternoon—and saying nothing. Orders carried out to the letter, General Carson, sir!

Champ sat in a padded chair facing the control panel. The monitors for the two cameras glowed. The bugs in her old house and PC-Pros' offices were all patched into the board, too. Each was identified with glowing LED letters. He could touch a tiny plate to bring up any of them to his earphones, to speaker. He could tape both sound and video. He had to admit the arrangements were seductively elaborate. One of Carson's greatest talents was for too much of a good thing. He was a master of excess. "Nothing succeeds like a *lot* of excess." Rewrite Wilde.

Champ chewed the inside of his cheeks, tasted the brassy drop of blood. He heaved meaty thighs, demonstrating further to himself the extent of his anxiety. Queen of My Heart *would* reconsider, wouldn't she? How could she not, once she realized she was again the object of Carson's particular attentions?

He had spent the better part of ten days here before the board, listening to her voice whenever possible. Previously he had heard it only on the ten Scheherazade tapes, savored its timbre tensed by arousal and pain. Now in more humdrum circumstances he gleaned from its lighter tone a suppler, happier personality. Today's vulnerability and delicacy leavened yesterday's wickedness that had sparked his arousal—and rage. Oh, no, he hadn't forgotten the crimes she had committed against Carson or the ultimate goal of her total resurrection. It *would* come to pass, because Carson willed it. Steps would be taken, each more daring than its predecessor. At what point the escalation would achieve its purpose he couldn't guess. Yet for the first time

Champ realized he would prefer not to have to pierce the flesh or break the bones of Queen of My Heart.

Carson had phoned him a new set of instructions only hours ago. He had outlined the nature of the devices with which Queen of My Heart would be guided a bit further toward her resurrection. Carson the conceptualizer, Champ the actualizer. Oh, grand team! Oh, worthy goal!

He flew toward the workbench and busied himself. He didn't stop until he had to rush out to an electronic supply house. This week's rental car was an ambiguous shade and model. The Blandmobile. Next week's would be the same. Spare no expense. Carson sent a great deal of money. Who would not invest big time to perpetually share his life with Queen of My Heart and sweetest Melody? Champ's frenzy of assembly lasted until midnight, his watch told him. It alone kept time. Resurrection Headquarters had been made windowless with plywood panels. He cared nothing for the sun's daily careening or seasons' sweep. They were incidentals in his life of service to Carson and pursuit of onanistic pleasures.

Tugged by the twin tendrils of sleep and desire, he shucked off his sandals, worn jeans, and underwear. He normally liked sleeping in his Daffy Duck T-shirt, but tonight's pursuit of pleasure meant it would have to go. He slipped into the living area, devoted primarily to bed, TVs, and VCRs. Food? He had a hot plate. Franchisers abounded. Into the VCR connected to the huge projection TV, mainstay of yuppie lounges and sports bars, he slipped the eighth of his ten precious tapes. Earlier he had patched the camera controller through to a hand-held unit. The unblinking eye into Queen of My Heart's bedroom was his to command. He stretched out on his Mattress Warehouse marvel and beheld the owner of Carson's heart.

She slept in nothing more enticing than robin's-egg blue cotton pajamas, head and shoulders out of the covers, skin softened by the weak light of a distant bedlamp. Afraid of the dark, sweet? He panned in till her face, unmoving but for the slow pulsings of her nostrils, filled the screen. He started Tape Eight. On the big screen he saw the same face five years in the past. Its layer of flesh was more meager then, its eyes more wary. Carson's persistent attentions had taught her that threats could be conceived even in the warmest nest of love. The lips and mouth that—Carson had shown her—could be the most adroit tools of love hadn't changed, nor had the dark sheen of hair. Today she wore it cut, fashioned in the style of the businesswoman. On that long-ago day it had been disposed of in a braid that snaked across her shoulder into the tempting valley between her large breasts, flattened as she lay on her back. Their nipples, colored by Melody's conception and suckling, were convoluted like pressed brown prunes.

Carson was speaking to her. The back of his red head faced the camera. His voice was low, set in persuasive mode. On his spread palm lay the six shiny snail-shaped devices he called "whiz-bangs". Another of his inventions, they were placed at key body points where Chinese medicine said sexual energies flowed. All were commanded by a single small transmitter: a hair more current, a whole mane of stimulation! My sexual life as a Lionel train, Champ thought. Aphrodisia for our age. "Batteries not included," Carson snickered into the white shell of Queen of My Heart's ear. See her wanton, responsive smile!

In time, with uneasy grin, she consented. Earlier, persuading her to venture onto new sensual territory took hours, even days sometimes. By the time this tape was made, though, she had learned to obey and allow. Was she not already fastened down with elasticized cords like car-top luggage? Carson placed the whiz-bangs on her skin, calling out in Chinese—he knew a dozen languages—the names of the nerve centers over which they adhered on tiny sucker feet.

Carson stepped out of view to activate the whiz-bangs. Champ tensed expectantly. Having enjoyed the tape previously only sharpened his anticipation of the first flow of current into the white, submissive flesh. His own desire stirred deep within like a worm. He imagined Carson's fingers on the control unit. A flick of his index finger and . . . Queen of My Heart sighed and stirred within her bonds. Her jaw slackened, disclosing the pink treasure of her tongue. Carson reappeared naked, the red pelt high on his back burning like a cape of fire. . . .

Queens of My Heart past and present swam together before Champ, one naked and abandoned, another demure in safe sleep, the lash of wantoness coiled around the unsullied flower. The worm of his desire stirred further, stretched and showed the teeth of lust. He reached over. Atop the crate lay the six silvery snails. He placed them carefully where they ought to be on his own body, his touch gentle as a lover's. He reached languidly toward the control unit. Let the current flow!

See me! A model lover for the Third Millennium. Do not bother me with flesh, blood, or heart and their intricate demands. I am a Don Juan of electric current, transistor, acetate, silver salts, and chrome oxide. A Casanova for long-dead ladies clustered for the lens on the porches of summer cottages fallen now to anty ruin. I press my lips to faces on yellowing high school crush squeegees ("To the next president of GM"). To porn queens and staple-naveled nubile nakeds I offer seminal tribute. Neither their names nor my involvement are real. To images and illusions only do I give my seed. Shall I compare thee to a laser ray? I do not love you, Queen of My Heart! Your real flesh and soul are Carson's. I love only what the tools of illusion and my own imagination have fabricated from the meager materials of your surface and shadow.

Even such a limited adoration did not begin to bar his increasing arousal, flogged as it was by rewinds, repeats, freeze frames, and the rising stimulation of the whiz-bangs. Ultimately, behind closed lids he paraded with Queen of My Heart in acts bearing names spoken only in locker rooms and in spasms of passion. He shared with her positions attainable only by fakirs. He soared up, up, up in the balloon of his expert fantasies. Oh, Queen . . . Queen . . . *Queen of My Heart!*

I will never dare to love you.

After repeating his performance twice more he had hoped to sink back, sweaty and spent, into sleep.

It wasn't to be.

Earthquake Anger again smoldered deep within, linked to his self-abusive passion as inviolably as smoke to black powder detonation. He tried to resist it. He was weary. But it reared up mightily, thrust a grunt through his dry lips. He thrashed on the bed, raised palms trying to drive off the first swells of rage. How could ... *she* dare run away from Carson? Steal his child? He groaned loudly. He hadn't the will to resist the dark wellings of primal emotion. He sat up, tore off the whiz-bangs, now as loathed as leeches. He flung himself to his feet, smeared and panting. His first howl echoed loudly in the small room. He whirled, fists balled. Even the rising waves of rage couldn't submerge his admiration for Carson's foresight.

He had insisted Champ include his mended Siege Restraint in the move.

He howled again. The sound even to his ear carried the timbre of a beast stalking the night forest. He flung himself into the heavy chair and busied himself with thick Velcro straps. Spit flew from his mumbling mouth.

"Awrrrrrooooooowwww!"

6

TRISH DIDN'T HAVE A WEIGHT PROBLEM. IT WAS ALL right to go into Estrella and order two ricotta pies to have with her morning coffee. So they were a *little* heavy. But they were good! Mario was behind the counter, bent and thin, always with a trace of gray stubble on his cheeks. The heat of the place didn't seem to bother him. She had gathered from their brief conversations that he had not long ago been homeless. He was most grateful to fellow-Italian Dino for hiring him. Dino said he had been in a hurry to open up three months ago. He had hired the codger on impulse. Trish had smiled inwardly. Never let it pass brash Dino's lips that he had done Mario a favor.

Mario put the two pies in a small white box and tied them with string. "Next week we're putting in an air conditioner. So it won't be so hot in here, you know?" His grin showed—count 'em!—three missing basic teeth. The survivors had the look of fangs.

She knew Mario slept on a cot back with the mixers and ovens and sometimes helped Dino bake. He played watchman in exchange for a bed. A win-win. Onto her box he stuck something. Oh! A smiley face sticker.

He winked at her. "Special customer that means."

"What's special about me? I only come in here once in a while."

"It ain't what you buy, Trish. It's how you look."

She could still redden. "Mario!"

His fangy grin widened, a bizarre sight, really. "You know what they say: The older the stag, the harder the horn!"

"Stop it! Or I'll think you're a lot less a nice old man than an old goat."

Mario gave her the box. "You get to a certain age, you don't have to behave no more. It's a trade for not being able to . . . never mind." He turned toward the kitchen. He shouted in Italian. Then translated: "Trish is here! The computer cutie!"

Trish said, "Mario, you don't have to—"

"So? Big deal!" Dino's gruff baritone rumbled, muted by plywood and distance.

Mario chuckled. "He *has* to be macho. I used to be that way, too, till I got old, poor, and ugly."

Dino ambled into view wiping his sweaty hands on a black apron. "What's up, lady?" he growled.

"Oh, you know, Dino. Good and bad." Why was she reddening?

"How's your *bambina*—what's her name?"

"Melody's fine."

Several customers came in, occupying Mario's attention.

Dino busied himself with straightening cookies in a display case. He had a solid face and jaw. Good match for the dark eyes and tight curly hair. He was in his mid-forties, she guessed, because he told her he had been in Vietnam. He had worked as a baker in Chicago. When an uncle died and left him some money he decided to return home. An ad announced the sale of a bakery and all its equipment. He bought it all at a good price, then moved it from a poor location across town to this slightly better one. Business so far hadn't been that great, but he was hopeful he would soon make a go of it. Mario's willingness to work long hours in the heat for small pay was an important contribution that Dino greatly appreciated.

She was about to turn and leave when he looked up from a

tray of devil's food cupcakes and said, "So what's 'bad'? In your life, I mean. You said it wasn't all good."

She hesitated. She had cultivated habits of discretion. Being close-mouthed meant less chance of revealing closed California matters. She recalled she had considered talking to Dino about Rocco. Maybe she should have followed her intuition. "You got a couple hours?" she said.

"How about fifteen minutes? I was gonna have a smoke out back."

It took longer than fifteen minutes for Trish to tell her tale of threats and suspicions and her ambiguity about Rocco being guilty.

Dino threw away his butt and folded his arms. His glance was frank. "I see maybe you're not starting at the right end of this. Are you saying you don't want to sell? Or are you saying he isn't offering enough?"

She hadn't expected that question. The problem about what to do with the business after she married had risen to her consciousness from time to time. She surely wouldn't need PC-Pros for financial reasons. "I might consider selling after my wedding in the middle of September."

Dino grinned. Nature, or more likely a good dentist, had given him white, even teeth. "Who's the sucker?"

Trish shook her head in vexation. *"Why* did I decide to tell you my problems? You don't even care—"

"Hey, I just asked a question, okay?"

"His name is Foster Palmer. I don't think I have time to describe him. He's a wonderful guy."

"Every fiancé is wonderful. Then he becomes a husband."

"What do you know about it? You ever married?"

He shook his head. "Single's the way for me to go." He looked up at her, grinning. "Things don't work out in your marriage, you can always look me up."

Just like an Italian, she thought. All macho talk. I'm the greatest lover in the world. And I want to spread it around. Then some woman gets him by the ear, and he rolls over at home like a puppy. She wrinkled her nose. "Thanks just the same. I'm sure Foster and I will be quite happy."

He shrugged. "So what about this DeVita guy?"

She explained how she couldn't read him but feared him just the same. Throwing some caution aside, she told Dino she very much wanted to know her competitor's background. Possibly he was connected with the mob. If that was the case, she would have to take him more seriously. She flashed a tight smile. "Do you think you could . . . maybe find out?" She shrugged. "I mean if you grew up here and all."

"I been away," Dino said.

"I don't know what to do. I can't prove anything to the police—as he reminded me."

"Cops." He shrugged. "Forget cops."

"Easy for you to say. So you don't want to help me—"

"I didn't say I wouldn't." He opened the screen door to the bakery's rear. "I know just what to do. And I'll do it."

"What, Dino?"

"Talk to him. Man to man."

"Will you do that? I'd appreciate it. I really would."

He turned away. "Hang on a second." He disappeared into the hot gloom and came out a moment later with a white bag. He shoved it toward her. "Take." She took it. "A couple apple tarts for your *bambina*," he growled.

"The way to a girl's heart is through her stomach. Anything apple, she goes crazy. Thanks, Dino."

She drove home wondering if the baker would have any success dealing with Rocco. Both were odd men, that was certain.

Melody would have gulped down both tarts at one sitting if Trish had let her. The child's passion for pastry was astonishing by itself. Adding in apple turned her gluttonous. Witness the wicked powers of the apple: Eve, Snow White, and now Melody. "Number two is for *tomorrow*, sweet. Understand your mother on this. We're talking sugar overload here."

On Wednesday afternoon the phone rang. Dino's heavy voice rasped down the line. "We talked man to man. Me and that—" He used an Italian word that sounded derogatory.

Trish pressed the receiver closer to her ear. She was reminded how tense she had become in recent days. "What did you think?"

"He's not your problem. He's not man enough."

Trish frowned. She remembered Rocco and his cigar very well. He hadn't seemed benign to her. "You sure?"

"We talked. I tested him."

Something told her not to ask him just how he had done it. "Then . . . who's causing problems for my business?"

"Dunno. But you can forget Rocco DeVita. I convinced him he oughta be nice to you, Patricia, from here on out."

"How in the world did you do that?"

"We sat down and reasoned together."

She recognized some kind of movie or real-life euphemism in his words. She wondered if his handsome face was split by a grin of satisfaction. It sounded so. She thanked him and said she owed him a favor. Of course he made a ribald suggestion. She hung up laughing.

Her good mood fled quickly. Dino's certainty had convinced her that Rocco had been bluffing. With her only suspect eliminated, she was left in a deepening cloud of menace. That night she woke with a start, a cry on her lips. In her dream she had been bound with velvet ropes, at Carson's mercy once again. She had begged him for both pity and pleasure. She rolled over and sat up. Tears wet her cheeks. She had hoped those nightmares were forever in the past. She looked at the digital clock. Four-ten.

She got up and crept to Melody's bedroom. The child dreamed under her Kermit quilt. She crossed the room, bent, and kissed the smooth cheek. May your dreams always be far sweeter than mine, she thought.

She didn't sleep again. She made a pot of coffee and watched cool dawn break over the high hedge. She left for work even earlier than usual with no appetite, even for one of Estrella's cinnamon buns, still oven warm at this time of day.

She wanted to work energetically to occupy her mind. Instead she found herself repeatedly woolgathering. Her stomach was sour and her nerves on edge.

What was going to happen to PC-Pros?

At nine-thirty her phone warbled. She picked it up. A computer-generated man's voice bubbling with optimism said, "Good morning. Please do not hang up. You have been selected to participate in a survey whose results will be immediately valuable to you. Press one if you are a man, two if you are a woman."

Trish hesitated. These things usually ended up with an offering of Florida condos or something else she didn't need. Well, she wasn't getting work done. She pressed two.

"Thank you, Ms. or Mrs.," intoned the voice. "Now press one if you are between twenty and twenty-five, two if you are between twenty-six and thirty, three if you are between thirty-one and thirty-five."

She pressed three.

"Thank you. Now press one if you're single, two if you're married."

She pressed one. But not for long, she thought.

"Thank you, Ms. Now press one if you're engaged, two if you're not."

Peddling bridal gowns or place settings for twelve, she thought. She pressed one, wondering how the program would swing her around to a particular product.

"Thank you, Ms. Now key in the number, one to twelve, of the month of *your* wedding. Example: If you're a June bride, press the six key."

She keyed in nine.

"You have indicated that you're to be married in September. We strongly insist that you reconsider this intention—"

Trish gasped. Her diversion turned upside down—to torment! "Reconsider . . ." The same word she had seen on the screen and heard on her phone mail!

"—at once. Failing to reconsider will bring to your business and yourself a world of trouble. This warning is absolutely genuine. The determination and resources are in place to force you to change your mind. It would be wise to do so now. One minute will be allowed for you to reflect on your situation and, of course—reconsider! The minute begins now. . . ." Beeps sounded on the second.

She looked at the receiver imprisoned in her clutching hand. Her mind tumbled with thoughts. She snatched at them as they flew by, too shaken to get organized. It wasn't PC-Pros that was her tormentor's target.

It was her upcoming wedding to Foster!

Who knew she was marrying him that wouldn't want it? Who would infect PCs with a virus, smash equipment, and make so many ingenious threats? How vulnerable both she and PC-Pros were in the face of some determined crazy! She whimpered. The programmed voice intoned, "Thirty seconds . . ."

Her eyes darted around her office, found no comfort in the material evidence of her career success. She thought of slamming the receiver down. Some deep curiosity forbade it. Just as she had so often anticipated refusing Carson's increasingly disturbing proposals, then consented out of a similar skewed fascination. Carson belonged now to the past. She had to fling that frame of mind back to him as well. "Fifty seconds . . ." Memories of Carson froze her attention like a rodent before an adder. She thought . . . nothing until the voice spoke again.

"Your period of reflection is over. Press one if you have truly decided to cancel your wedding. Press two to show your stubbornness and poor judgment."

"Two!" she shouted into the receiver. "Two, damn it!" She jabbed at the phone with a rigid index finger. Two, two, two!

"A poor decision. We'll be in touch—much closer touch —soon." The line went dead. She held the receiver in the air for a long moment. Abruptly her thinking focused like a flashlight beam and moved in an entirely new direction.

She hung up gently. To her surprise, she was smiling.

She had guessed who was behind the call and who else had helped make it possible.

Guessing sent her recent panic into retreat. She reached for the phone, then decided against calling. On the way out of the office she told Michelle to reach her via car phone, if necessary. She would be on the road. No matter personal problems, a manager shouldn't be out of touch with her responsibilities.

She drove straight to Danielle's, probably the most exclusive women's clothing store in the city. There amid swish surroundings wealthy customers turned rags to proprietor's riches. Operating the store required sales personnel accustomed to customers whose bankrolls allowed paying four or five figures to cover a woman's back. Though such employees were essential, they needn't be paid a great deal. Large discounts on their own clothing purchases and no grander career ambitions kept them loyal. What better place to work for a stylish woman with social-climbing expectations? What better occupation for Lois Smith-Patton, not long ago—and now very possibly still—Trish's bitter rival?

A hawk-faced woman of forty-five greeted Trish. Her amber eyes moved over the younger woman's white jumpsuit like a laser scanner, trying to weigh her tastes and bank account. "I'd like to see Lois," Trish said.

"Of course, darling. She's with a customer. You can wait in the lounge or go right down to casual wear."

She found Lois attending to a hefty dowager. At five-one she looked like a pilot fish servicing a shark. She was more sharklike in style than the moon-faced woman to whom she said, "The lines are so *good* for you, Philomena."

While Lois concluded the sale Trish looked around at the mouth-watering outfits. If ever her dream of marrying Foster came true, she would start buying here. But not from Lois, of course.

When the small woman returned she saw Trish. Her round face rolled, and her violet eyes flashed. "I can't believe you'd expect *me* to give you fashion advice!" she said. Lois had a high, thin voice that in moments of excitement rose to cut the ear like a metal saw. Trish had been responsible for a great many of those moments over the last year.

"I'd like to talk to you, Lois," she said. "Could you give me ten minutes?"

Lois's eyes hooded with distaste. "I wouldn't give you ten seconds, Patricia Morley."

"It's about you, me, Foster, and the wedding."

She frowned. "I don't understand."

"I think I know what you've been doing. I've come here to warn you. If you don't talk to me, you can talk to the police."

Lois's head bobbed as though in agreement. "This figures. I told Foster all along that you were a disturbed person—"

"Lois—"

"So now, after you've wrecked my life, ruined everything, you finally crack. It figures!"

Trish held her annoyance on a tight rein. Despite Lois's distortions she wasn't too far removed from the truth. She hadn't yet completely gotten over California and Carson. There had been some rocky moments for her and Foster. Through them all Lois had played a host of mental tricks on her former lover, trying to get him to change his mind. She would never accept having lost him.

Lois Smith-Patton had been raised in comfort among the moneyed, went south to college where she majored in social life and reached what at that time was her goal—marriage to a wealthy student. After six years the marriage fell apart for want of commitment and children. Instinctively she knew that for her there could be no other path through life than to marry money. Foster Palmer had been an old friend from her earlier world of cotillions, benefits, and opening nights. She put herself before him. To her great satisfaction and delight he took the initiative. She sailed under favorable winds toward the altar's safe harbor. Then the ship of her secure future ran aground on Morley Shoals. When Trish and Foster's engagement was announced at the end of January Lois had fled the city in shock for three weeks in the Caribbean. There, Trish imagined, she had resolved not to surrender Foster until his wedding day. Thus she conducted her guerrilla campaign of personal intrusions into his life. Because that approach wasn't working, Trish was certain she had adopted stronger, more dangerous tactics.

Her interest obviously piqued, Lois seemed ready to listen. As they walked to the exit of the store Trish confronted her. "I know what you're trying to do, Lois. You're trying to frighten me out of marrying Foster."

"Oh, I am?" Her shaped eyebrow rose. "And how am I doing that?"

Trish told her about the various spoken and displayed messages, the virus, the destroyed equipment. As she talked Trish searched for a revealing flash of guilt. Lois was a fine actress; her expression reflected only bewilderment. "You think *I* could figure out how to do all that computer stuff?"

"You didn't have to. You had Nicholas do it for you."

"What?"

"Your brother is *more* than capable of making everything I told you happen. Isn't he, Lois?"

Trish's glance hardened. Nicholas's skills and personality formed the cornerstone of her suspicions. Foster had told him of the curious relationship between Lois and her gangling, brilliant brother. She had met the man once when keeping a mall luncheon date with Foster. Nicholas had happened by before she arrived. She found her fiancé buttonholed by a tall, completely bald man in his late thirties. His dome gleamed in sunlight leaking down through the atrium glass. He wore an expensive but ill-fitting three-piece suit. From his jacket pocket protruded a folded chessboard. High-tech earphones clasped his neck. Their wire snaked down under a tie that clashed like a cymbal with the charcoal vest. A blind man could have made a better fashion choice.

Odd as he looked, when he turned toward her to be introduced she was nonetheless startled by his eyes. Lying under a high, naked sweep of forehead, their depth and blue brilliance seemed unearthly. She thought of off-world aliens from movies and the pages of the *Enquirer*. Her glimpse was brief because those eyes slid swiftly over her face and didn't return. He looked only at Foster. Mr. Shyboots, she thought.

Later Foster told her that Nicholas Smith-Patton was a genuine hybrid, erratic, eccentric, and emotionally immature. He had attended MIT, where he studied electronics but was never graduated. Study bored him, and he intuitively grasped much of the curriculum. Buoyed by the life preserver of a modest inheritance, he bobbed around on the ocean of life, trying one career after another. He was most successful as an electronic design consultant, solving thorny problems that had choked corporations' best engineers and collecting fancy fees. But he was too much of a gadabout to turn talent into an organization. He operated solo with little more overhead than business cards and letterhead. He had no passion for career. The greater part of his energies were devoted to what for most were mere hobbies: chess and jazz.

Lois served as his gateway into normal society. She advised him about the minimum interactive requirements expected for him to be actively considered a member of the family. Like a comet he soared for long periods geographically and emotionally away from the Smith-Patton clan's solar system. He returned regularly, summoned by the sun of a wiser sister's command. "If anyone controls Nicholas, it's Lois," Foster told Trish.

Knowing all this had armed Trish for this confrontation. She made her detailed accusations: Lois had conspired against PC-Pros and had enlisted Nicholas's considerable skills in her scheme. Her goal was to force Trish to break her engagement or have her business destroyed.

Through Trish's exposition Lois held her purse straps in both hands. She squeezed them with increasing strength. Foster had told Trish about Lois's hot temper, now put to the boil by her charges.

"That is the most absurd mess of nonsense I have ever heard, Patricia Morley! If Foster needs more evidence of your mental instability, you've just given it to him. And he *is* going to hear about this—lunacy. I guarantee you that!"

The heads of other shoppers turned their way. Trish ignored them, concentrating entirely on facing down her adversary. "You can rave all you want, Lois. It's just a smoke screen I see through quite clearly." She rose. "Consider yourself and Nicholas warned. Any more 'incidents' and I'm going to the police with your names."

Lois leaned over and spoke venom to Trish. "I can't

believe how stupid you're being, Patricia. You had Foster in your hands—for life. Now your craziness is bungling him away. And when he's loose I'll get him back again!" She spun and strode away, drawing half the shoppers' eyes. The rest remained on Trish.

She stood still. She felt her previously controlled face reddening. Confronting Lois had seemed precisely the right thing to do. What better way to stamp out her dangerous mischief? Now . . . doubts loomed. In an attempt to end the growing psychological pressure, she had perhaps both over-reacted and jumped to conclusions. Oh, Lord, had she? If so, she had put trump cards in the hand of a moribund rival in a game she had already won, then asked that play be resumed.

Could she have been that stupid?

Later that evening Foster phoned. Would she join him tomorrow on his drive upstate to deliver two mastiffs to new owners? Normally Doris, the kennel manager, handled that, but he was in the mood to get away. When she said she'd like to bring Melody he hesitated a moment before agreeing. That was curious, as he was usually delighted to have the girl join them whenever practical. "I'll pack a picnic lunch," she said. "We'll stop somewhere along the way."

On the way up north Foster focused his attention on Melody, asking her about summer plans and her music. Trish noticed he occasionally nibbled at his left thumb knuckle. She had seen him do that only once earlier, just before he had proposed to her. The man was nervous. She already knew him well enough not to pry. That would raise a storm of denials that would postpone revelation. He would pick his time and moment well enough.

Along the route home there was a state park just off the interstate. As Foster turned down its main road a lake spread out before the van, pale and smooth under the early afternoon sun. They found a grassy stretch. Trish unpacked lunch. She had borrowed her mother's champagne flutes. Into Melody's she poured Cranapple juice, her favorite; into the others Moët. Cold chicken with mustard crumb coating and pasta salad suited soft breeze and fresh air. Carson had cooked, she had learned. . . . She savagely kicked away those memories. Italian cookies from Estrella were the finishers. The three ate sprawled on an old quilt. Alcohol usually made her chatty, but today for some reason it did the opposite. Foster, too, seemed distracted. Their normally flowing conversation was halting and choppy. Trish dreaded what was coming.

Melody had brought along her soprano recorder and penny whistle. She began to tootle on them. Her red hair flamed in the bright sunlight. Foster said, "Why don't you take those down by the lake and play? I'll bet you draw a crowd if you take requests."

"Okay!" Melody was never one to avoid being the center of attention.

When she was out of earshot Foster turned to Trish. He picked up her hand and held it. Did she sense caution in his touch, or was the champagne making her stupid?

"You've hurt my feelings quite a bit," he said softly.

"I did? How?"

"By not telling me about the . . . trouble you've been having."

Trish's heart thumped. She was touched that Foster only seemed concerned about what she had been going through. "I'm sorry you know. It's my problem. I'm trying to solve it myself."

"In my opinion you're not doing very well," he said. "Flying off in all directions, willy-nilly—"

"I flew off in just one direction—well, two, maybe. And I had good reasons for doing so, Foster. The first direction didn't pan out. And I'm sure you know the second was toward Lois and Nicholas—"

"Trish, your suspicions are absurd!"

She drew a deep breath and carefully reviewed her next words. She studied Foster's well-made face, saw the razor nick under his chin, just above the silken rise of his tie. "Do you remember how Lois took word of our engagement? Poorly, right?"

Foster smiled thinly. "To say the least."

"As I recall, she went to you as soon as she heard. And you told me what she said. Do I have to repeat it?"

He shook his head. "I remember quite well. She told me you had mental problems."

Trish fought off the chill those words sent through her chest. "She said other things!" she snapped. "She said if we went ahead, she'd kill me for what I did to her. Do you remember *that,* Foster?"

He frowned with discomfort. "I do."

"If she was willing to kill me, why don't you think she'd be willing to put me out of business to try to get me to cancel the wedding?"

"It was all talk. I know her well enough to know when she's just talking."

Trish drew up her knees and tried to keep the vexation out of her voice as she gave her fiancé a capsule version of Lois Smith-Patton's motivations. Earlier when she had discussed the woman with Foster she had been diplomatic. It hadn't seemed wise to be too critical of a former rival. Now plain speaking seemed in order. She told Foster Lois was obsessed with him. She had fully expected to become his wife. His choosing Trish had turned her emotional world upside down. When it came right again she had resolved to win him back. To accomplish that she would stop at nothing. He couldn't imagine the full extent of her determination. Far from abandoning him as a gracious loser would, she had redoubled her efforts. She would do whatever she thought necessary to destroy Trish and Foster's relationship, including defaming her mental strength and launching a campaign of physical and psychological sabotage. Her ally in it all was her malleable, erratic brother, whose talents were more than adequate to the electronic magic so far shown. Couldn't Foster *see?*

He heard her out, stretched on his back, hands behind head. When she was finished he sat up. "I really don't think she and Nicholas are involved," he said.

Trish's temper flashed. She fought to control it. "How can

you doubt me? Hours after I accused her she was on the phone to you, telling you I was a nut case!"

"She didn't say—"

"Never mind the exact words she used, Foster." She glared at him. "And why do you always defend her?"

He shrugged. "Just my normal fair-mindedness."

"I think, considering that I'm about to become your wife, you ought to bag your fair-mindedness once in a while, and maybe take my side."

He stared at her, his eyes behind their lenses round and cool. "That's difficult to do when you're so far off base."

"How do you know I am?" she shouted. "What makes you so cocksure about what Lois would or wouldn't do?"

His shrug was infuriating, too.

From somewhere behind the shield she raised to hide her emotions flashed a single revealing outburst. "She still means something to you, doesn't she, Foster?"

"I asked you to marry me, didn't I? That should answer your question."

"Well, it doesn't. I think sometimes you still—feel for her."

"Nonsense!" He tried to hug her, but she shoved him away.

"That woman has risen up like a dark shadow over everything we have together."

"Trish—"

"You better be damned sure you love me, not her."

"I do. But when you talk as stupidly as this . . ."

They argued. The volume of their voices had never reached so high during their earlier petty squabbles. Neither the lovely lake nor the perfect sky calmed them. Melody's sweet music in the distance went unheard as, over the next twenty minutes, Trish found her way to tears and Foster to silence.

The ride home was too quiet, broken only by the child's oblivious chattering. Their uneasy parting was lightened little by promises to talk again after they had calmed.

Having no one else in whom to confide, Trish rushed to

her mother. She was having iced tea on the screened porch with loyal Stoneman Gore. Marylou quickly saw her daughter's emotional state. She sent Stoneman and Melody off together for frozen yogurt.

She made Trish sit beside her and lifted the pitcher. Lemon slices floated; condensation dewed the polka-dotted clay. "In Savannah where I grew up, iced tea was considered a steadier," she drawled. "Of course, we often used to add a drop or two of whiskey. Let's try it without right now, shall we?" She gave Trish a brimming glass.

The tale of the quarrel rushed out of her, and with it a few tears. She hated them. Marylou was so expert at making her suffer for her weaknesses.

"Well you might cry, my dear. You're doing a splendid job of trying to undo all the good you've managed for yourself before now."

"Mother, someone's trying to stop me from marrying Foster!"

"And you're helping that someone right along, aren't you?"

"I am?"

"You are, and I can't believe that hasn't somewhat dawned on you. You're a bright girl—at least on paper."

"Mother!"

Marylou waved away Trish's protest. Her brow creased along its sole skeptical line. "I can't believe that at this late date I have to teach you lessons about being a woman."

Trish eased into blubbering and hated herself for it. She sucked in deep, steadying breaths.

"Calm down now, dear. Try to look at the situation from a neutral point of view. What happens to you? Someone starts playing pranks on your business—"

"Pranks! They were so much more than—"

"Hush! Just listen to me. Some pranks. Nothing more. What do you do? You *imagine* that Lois Smith-Patton—who's from a very nice family, you have to agree—is behind it. No proof, of course. What more do you do? You go to her and expose your troubles. She uses what you tell her against you, of course. Then you complete the debacle by quarreling with Foster. In short, you did *everything* wrong. You must see that, child."

"I'm not a child!"

"That very much remains to be seen. Since you wasted those years in California—"

"They weren't wasted!"

Her mother snorted. "Whatever happened to you out there confused your . . . priorities, let's say. Possibly it's up to your mother to remind you that your number-one priority now is Foster—specifically marrying him. This is the very worst time to muddy waters with him. Men in the weeks before a wedding are like deer, easily spooked and anxious for flight. You were wise to try to keep your troubles from him, stupid to take them to Lois, for whatever reason.

"Nothing you do now should disturb Foster. He should see you as tranquil, steady, adoring, and calm. After the wedding . . . well, that's a different story, isn't it? You should do whatever it takes to cement your relationship for the present. That very much includes hiding your own troubles and nourishing your love."

"Mother, that is so . . . bogus."

Marylou's face lost a shade of color. "Don't even begin with that 'modern thinking' drivel! You *must* have Foster as a permanent part of your life, just as he needs you. But your reasons for wanting that are different because you are man and woman. Men trade in money and careers. Women trade in pleasing husbands, raising families, and nourishing emotions. Nothing you or any of your California friends believe will change the way things are in marriage—and life—the way they always have been."

Trish disagreed, but she wasn't sure just how at that moment. Her quarrel with Foster had left her so shaken and unsure! "So what would you do in my place, Mother?"

Marylou's hand came to rest on Trish's forearm. "Mend whatever harm you've managed today. I think you should suggest to Foster that you go away to some romantic spot for a day or two." She nodded deliberately at her. "Give love a chance to heal whatever lacerations you caused. The bed is much better at settling disagreements than the best lawyers. Don't you agree?"

She might have if Foster was more adventurous in his lovemaking, and if she wasn't so experienced. Still, he seemed pleased enough, and generous in his praise of her responsiveness. She wondered how he would feel after she told him as much as she dared about her past with Carson. She had to work up her nerve to do that before the wedding. She had already delayed too long.

Her mother sipped her tea. "So you'll go off with Foster for a short time?"

Trish nodded. It did seem a good idea.

"I suggest you call him about that quite soon."

"Okay." That she was taking the woman's advice told her how much the messages and sabotage of her business—and now the quarrel—had shaken her.

Marylou went on: "As you're here, I thought I might have a talk with you about something that's been on my mind ever since you came back to me more than three years ago." She turned her eyes fully toward Trish's face. "I've bitten my tongue on many occasions."

"Mother . . ."

"I haven't inquired much about what you did out in California or with whom you spent your time. Possibly you're aware of what a different person you became out there."

"I was there more than eight years. I grew up."

The skeptical crease split Marylou's brow. "I suspect a great deal *more* than that happened to you. Whatever did isn't so important as the present—and the immediate future. I want to remind you once again that you've gotten yourself to a point of great potential—marriage into a family of wealth and name."

"You say that ten times every time we talk!" Trish said.

"It bears repeating. The wedding is of the greatest importance to your life. I urge you to do everything you can to get safely to that day."

"Even though somebody is trying to stop it?"

"Those pranks?" Marylou sniffed. "Handle them some

way. Call the police, a private investigator. I'm sure if you do, whoever it is will think better of what he's doing and leave you alone." She waved away that annoyance. "What I have to say to you has to do with what I've come in my little reveries to call your 'California weirdness.' By that I mean all the peculiar habits of thinking and behavior you've shown since your return. I won't catalog them. I think you know what they are." She cocked her head quizzically.

Trish shrugged. "What about them?"

"If you're to succeed in your new, better life"—she squeezed Trish's arm—"you'd best put them forever behind you."

The years with Carson flared up then like wizard's powders thrown into an open fire. California weirdness stranger than her mother had ever dreamed! Memories burst free in her mind. They tumbled and tangled, snagging at her attention with barbed tendrils. They tugged her toward a dark past she had renounced and away from the bright gate of the future. Carson, flame-haired and in full cry! Put aside thoughts of him and those years he ruled like Satan? Yes, she tried, but they came whirling back like boomerangs, threatening to rend to ruin more than her present—possibly her soul itself. Increasingly her relationship with him seemed less a lovers' interlude than a bargain with the devil.

7

"*BAAHBA-DU-ZOT!*" CROAKED "POPS" ARMSTRONG
across the gulfs of races and decades into Nicholas Smith-
Patton's mote-light, $250 earphones. Sing it and play it,
Satchmo! I hear you and Stephane and Django, Eubie, Fats,
Toots, Duke, Count, Cleanhead, Bird, Max, Monk, Milt,
Miles, Mose, Marian McP and Les McC, Cannonball,
Hawk, Bongo Mongo, Little Jazz, Big Mama, Ma, Bessie,
Lady Day and Ella . . . Sing to me from the authentic U.S.
underbelly—forget Mozart!—imported from nowhere, ex-
ported everywhere, even to Japan. Our manufacturers
should be so lucky! The satchel mouth worked its wonders.
The clean cornet riff careened around his brain like laser
light at Epcot closing.

To listen through an entire day, free of all distractions,
was a major personal success. He had succeeded many
times. He had listened on deserted beaches, boom box at his
side. He had stalked through silent woods, Walkman on
waist. He had listened on the bed in his own rarely occupied
room in the family home. There woofers coughed like
cougars and the highs went through his brain clear as
starlight on a transit to Mars.

He listened in the heat of his chess matches. Hearing

jazzmen solve their problems of key and time helped him ponder variations in search of the strongest move. Preparing for a match involved not only review of his best offensive and defensive openings, it meant making fresh, long tapes of the most introspective players, Bill Evans, McCoy Tyner, Tatum. . . . Long because each of the five-game round robins could reach the maximum four-hour time control.

He tapped out the beat on the metal welding table he used as a desk. Technically speaking, he was at work. All that meant was that he happened to be in his office, a water tank remodeled by an eccentric into a place of business. Once a visitor, hopefully in good health, climbed the wrought-iron ladder and pushed up the counterweighted trap, he would find himself in the small reception area of Smith-Patton Systems. There Dolly Hummer, if she bothered to come in, would play receptionist/secretary. He had met her at a jazz concert. Though he had never formally hired her, she started climbing the water tank ladder each morning on a fairly regular basis. From time to time he left a fistful of bills by her computer, though she never used the machine. When there she worked double crostics from a spiral-bound book and talked on the phone. She made efforts to organize him and the office but was largely incompetent herself.

For the most part women didn't appeal to him. Certainly Dolly didn't, with her balloon-sized breasts and tight striped T-shirts. He wondered if she had some personal interest in him. If so, such things had happened before. No matter. All women gave up on him after a while. More than ever now he was indifferent to the charms of the legions of ladies.

He was madly, desperately in love with a beauty as unattainable as world peace.

"When it's sleepy time down south . . ." Nicholas sang along, a gravel-voiced ersatz Satchmo. He got up and moved to one of the six chessboards set up among his electronic equipment. Humming, he let his mind sink into the Pirc Opening. The joke was that the long-gone Pirc alone could play the opening and win. But Nicholas had done well indeed with it. While he touched the pieces he saw the opening tree in his mind, variation branching to variation, without having to move so much as a pawn. If this, that. If that, then this . . . Rudimentary programming. One day before long a computer would be built that no grand master could ever conquer.

He became aware that Dolly had been buzzing him for some time. He shoved the left earphone up and replaced it with the receiver of his portable telephone. "Your sister," she said. "You always take her calls."

Lois's voice beat at his concentration. She was indignant. She sang her song of outrage into one ear while Louis sang of catfish into the other. He began to feel imposed upon, though he would never dream of cutting Sweetest Sister short. Then to his astonishment she spoke *her* name. Armstrong and Pirc fell away. His attention sank into Sweetest Sister's words like needle teeth. He had been insulted, too, she cried. He imagined her standing legs spread by the boutique's pay phone. Sweetest Sister! Five-one by the yardstick, seven-three in her influence on him. Sweet, sweet, Sweetest Sister, glean the rich field of your indignation and share with me tales of *her*, she of the black hair, eyes gray as seas in storm. Oh, behold their past sorrow like flint-colored current in those whirling waters. . . .

He sorted wheat from chaff, surprisingly found hard grain. He questioned Lois intently. She wasn't used to this sort of persistence from him. Oh, no, it wasn't his style. Normally he listened and did her bidding. Life was so much simpler when she led. Not now, though—not when *she* loomed large and troubled on his horizon. He felt blessed, called. It was now written that he who had knelt so long at his worship's private altar should be rewarded for his secret, determined love.

How he did love her! From that enshrined day when he had beheld her for the first—and last—time. To Foster she walked, white and supple as a willow branch in her spotless jumpsuit, long-fingered, capable hand outthrust toward Nicholas. Oh, warm, satin skin against his gritty paw! Oh, cunning curve of lip in restrained smile, its inner moisture glinting like dawn dew under angled sun. So suddenly had the bomb of love detonated over the once-arid plain of his heart that he nearly sank to his knees and wrapped worshipful arms around her white-clad calves. Since then that plain had blossomed lush as Eden, cultivated and watered by his undeclared longings.

How could he dare approach her? Despised as she was by Lois, engaged to Foster, she was declared off limits by two different forces. And by a third, he thought ruefully, his own spidery body with its hairless, gleaming head. A grotesque man could nonetheless long desperately. . . . So many nights he had lain awake, face to the ceiling, and whispered her name to the conspiring night: Patricia, Patricia, *Patricia* . . .

He cut into Lois's monologue again. "You have to answer my questions *specifically,* Lois," he said.

She sputtered. "Nicholas, what has gotten into you?"

"I want to know just what I'm being accused of," he said. "Tell me—slowly—just what happened to Ms. Morley."

His sister wasn't empirically minded. Getting hard data out of her was as difficult as kissing the First Lady. Finally, though, he found out what he wanted. There had been an on-screen warning, code auto-scrubbed. A virus had migrated from PC-Pros' software into a customer's LAN. A telephone warning had been followed by theft and PC bashing. Important point: The machines' cases had been opened to assure destruction. Not the work of some ignorant vandal. Most interesting was the last harassing event: the telephone "wedding survey." Mounting that required a specialized computer and software. Whether or not they were commonly available he didn't know. What was certain: Someone was making a considerable effort to warn Patricia away from marrying Foster. The question that followed from that was how much further was the harasser prepared to go? Or was that the end of it? He didn't think so. Because he didn't, he was prepared to do what so recently was unthinkable.

To approach Patricia and offer not his love, but his assistance. To serve his goddess like the most devout priest.

Off the phone he tried to return to Pirc and Louis, without

success. Before him floated a vision of a frightened love in white, turning, searching in all directions for the help that only someone with his talents could give.

Within an hour he was in the reception area of PC-Pros. He had taken a hand-held chess computer with him, intending to review recent grand master uses of the Pirc. But his powers of concentration had been weakened. Further, his heart pounded, and he drew shallow breaths in the face of possibly meeting Patricia for the second time. He knew the dimpled woman at the desk—Michelle she called herself—was covertly eyeing him. He read her mind. Could anyone really be as gangling and high-browed as he? He was right to spend most of his time alone, away from gawking. He knew he was sweating, despite the air conditioning. Moisture crescents showed on his shirt under his arms. Yet another way in which he was unappealing. He dreaded meeting Patricia again. He dreaded not meeting her. . . . Jazz riffs curled up from memory: Monk at Montreaux, Chet Baker in Paris . . .

"Ms. Morley will see you." Michelle pointed at the inner door. "Cubicle on your left."

Like a pilgrim to the shrine! Muslim to Mecca. Catholic to Lourdes. Hindu to the Ganges. Nicholas to Patricia! He strode carefully, sought to compose himself, dry the sweat. Impossible! He peered around the door frame.

She!

His love sat at her desk, hands folded on its top. "Come in, Nicholas. Have a seat." She pointed at a chair set six feet away from the desk, ten feet from the tip of her outthrust sneaker. "I debated whether or not to talk to you, Nicholas," she said. There was haughtiness in her stare. He wasn't fooled. He had read between the spoken lines of Sweetest Sister's report. This woman was frightened. And he would help her. "I'm well aware of what you and your sister are up to. I assume that she's talked to you, so that you're duly warned, too."

"We did talk, but—"

"Did she give you my warning?"

He blinked. That he didn't recall. He shook his head.

"She must have told you that I understand your role in what's happened to PC-Pros recently."

He opened his mouth to protest. She waved him silent.

"One more incident and I'm calling the police. And giving them your names."

He battled a reluctant mouth. Move! "It's not us," he managed.

"I think it is." Her tones were clipped. "I'm not going to debate it with you. I did that with your sister. It wasn't pleasant."

"L-Lois can be difficult," he said.

She smiled thinly—ah, lips made to match his! Toads lived only to kiss princesses. "I'm well aware of it." She unfolded hands long enough to gesture questioningly. "What brings you here, Nicholas?"

"I—want to help you." He rushed ahead, spewing out a verbal tangle of detail related to what he called the "incidents." There were some key points he absolutely had to make with her. He had assumed her technical knowledge was broad. She would not disappoint him in that way.

She hesitated to interrupt him. He saw in her eyes the gray smoke of partial comprehension. Then the winds of emotion blew it away. "Please stop, Nicholas! I don't doubt you know what you're talking about. What I doubt are your motivations for being here. There's more than a little guilt in your visit, I think. You've come here to try to make the point of your innocence. It's a bit of an overreaction, isn't it?"

"Not guilt." Adoration, but he couldn't say it.

"You say you're here to help. If you really want to help me . . ." Her eyes found his. Spear me with their twin barbs! I am fish made defenseless by the shallow water of my love. "Refuse to help your sister any further," she said.

He flogged his tongue like a mule team master. "Lois and I have nothing to do with your problems. You should believe me, Patricia. If you don't, worse things could happen."

She gasped. "Are you threatening me?"

He groaned inwardly. She was misunderstanding. He babbled out a denial so sincere it sounded like the pontifications of the guilty. Everything was going wrong! What further words passed between them then weren't really clear. His own emotions rose up. Jazz lines and opening moves hopelessly muddied his concentration. I can't get started with you . . . say either, I say I-ther . . . the first six moves of the Cozio Defense . . . let's face the music and dance, dance, dance!

He was at the outer door, his beloved standing by with folded arms. She said, "I don't want to see you again, Nicholas. If I do, it'll be an unfortunate day for you. Good-bye!"

He stood outside the PC-Pros' storefront staring at the bricks. Before he realized it an hour had passed. It was hot. Sweat poured down his expansive forehead. His sides were soaked. Not a glance from anyone within fell upon him. Unworthy of a second look, he might as well be that McDonald's fish fillet container crushed down there in the gutter. He had failed wretchedly to achieve his objective. His love had spurned his help, though she needed it far worse than she knew. In her final sliding gray glance he read that she saw him, rather than as her most devoted lover—oh, far more devoted than Foster Palmer!—as a socially inept, possibly dangerous geek.

What did it matter that she had spurned him?

He would help her anyway.

8

TRISH HAD BEEN SHAKEN BY NICHOLAS'S UNEXPECTED appearance, though she had succeeded in hiding it. She wondered if she could have carried it off in the face of someone not a zero for interactive skills, as Nicholas was. What a strange man, with that huge moon head and long arms! She giggled. He looked a little like a family-sized E.T. Her amusement died quickly. He and his sister were nothing funny together. His behavior had been most revealing. His first mistake was coming to see her at all. The second was protesting his innocence too much. Face-to-face he had rendered his guilt as transparent as plastic wrap. Her instincts had suggested that the Smith-Pattons were behind those nasty stunts. Now she was certain of it. Well, she had personally warned both of them.

She guessed her troubles were over.

She went back to her office. She had to check invoices outstanding. Cash flow was in danger of becoming a problem. She flipped the surge protector switch. Her lit PC screen carried a message. She stiffened, remembering the previous warning. With a rising sense of dread she scanned the lines of yellow text.

ALL YOUR BUSINESS BACKUP FILES HAVE BEEN DE-
STROYED. THE ORIGINALS ON THE HARD DRIVE OF THIS
MACHINE WILL BE ERASED IN EXACTLY 10 MINUTES.
ONLY YOUR INTERVENTION CAN SAVE THEM. TURNING
OFF THE MACHINE OR ATTEMPTING FILE ERASURE WILL
GUARANTEE LOSS OF ALL FILES. AT THE TONE THE 10
MINUTES WILL BEGIN.

She whirled in her chair. Her eyes sought the shelf across
the room where she kept her backup tapes. The boxes were
gone! She groaned. She had meant all along to store them
off-site, maybe in a fireproof safe. Now it was too late! Her
machine was the heart of PC-Pros' local area network.
Without its files her entire business would be brain-dead.

What was going on here?

Beeeeep!

She had the presence of mind to take off her wristwatch
and put it face up beside her keyboard.

Only your intervention can save them. . . . She flung herself at the keyboard, mouth gone dry as sand. She brought
up the hard disk file directory, scanned it eagerly for a
renegade file. There! It was a sizable one. She sent it to the
laser printer. It *whummmmed* to life, spilling out twenty
pages of program code. That was more code than needed.
She guessed that dead ends and mazes without exits
abounded.

Three of her ten minutes were gone.

She snatched the sheets out of the printer tray, scanned
the first. She recognized the language—Delphi. It was one
of those she had learned at Carson's feet. Another of the few
good things she had brought back from the west coast.
Maybe, maybe she could unlock the file, pull its teeth.

She used the intercom. "Anybody in the building know
Delphi? If you do, get in here—fast!"

She dug into the code, looking for the lines that would
trigger the erasure. She didn't see them! Oh, Lord, somehow
Nicholas had buried them. How had that gangling weirdo
sneaked into the building, gotten to the backup files and this

machine? How had he known PC-Pros ran on a local network? She had to force her attention back to her immediate problem.

Tran Lo Dinh came in. He said he knew "some small little" about Delphi. Without looking up she told him what they were up against.

"Only ten minute?" he asked, eyes widening.

"Down to six now, Tran."

"Ah-yi!"

It took her three more minutes—damn all the red herrings!—to grasp how Nicholas had tied the code into the PC's operating system. She understood at once that she had to recode that part of the program so that when the machine was turned off no file erasure would take place. Then she could reboot and kill the renegade lines.

Tran leaned over her shoulder and tried to help. But she knew Delphi better than he. She turned back to the PC and brought up the program. She would have to take out . . . those seven lines there—and put in maybe ten new ones.

They would have to be absolutely correct. She would not enjoy the luxury of being able to test them.

Two and a half minutes left.

She busied herself with the keyboard. Her jaw was clenched. Her heart pounded so hard she felt the pulse rising in her wrists and calves.

"You spell word wrong!" Tran whispered.

She went back and corrected it. "Keep checking, Tran." She told him what she was trying to do. "How does the code look?"

"Don't know. Look good? Maybe so."

Two minutes.

She groaned. She saw she had to include an additional statement! Even as she groped for its correct structure she promised herself that Nicholas and Lois would pay heavily for making her go through this little exercise, whether she was successful or not.

"Do you need bracket there?" Tran's long finger jabbed at the screen.

She stared. "No . . . I don't think so. No time to explain."
She finished typing. "Come on, Tran. Look it over with me.
See anything wrong?"

He made a noise much like a tiny whimper. "Maybe . . .
here." Finger on the screen again. His version of two lines of
code emerged in a rushed whisper. As he spoke her eyes
were drawn to the jagged scar crossing his neck and face.

Oh, Lord, he was right!

She glanced at her watch. Less than a minute. Type very
carefully, she told herself. "Give it to me again." She keyed
in the alphanumerics. "Make sure I got it right, Tran."

"Okay now."

She reached out a shaking hand toward the power switch.
Only when she restarted would she know if they had been
successful. Ten seconds on her watch, and it could be
inaccurate. She flipped the switch. The screen darkened.

She leaned on the desk and pressed her face into spread
palms. "Tran . . . I can't take more of this stuff. If we
screwed up, all our files are history. We can't do business."

"Who do this to us?"

"I know who. And whether or not they wiped us out,
they're going to pay—big time!"

Tran grunted. "Got to reboot, Trish. See soon what
happen."

Trish stared at the surge protector toggle switch for a long
moment. She nodded to Tran. "Go ahead. Do the honors."

Tran flipped the switch, and the PC whirred and clicked
to life. Trish bit her teeth, waiting. She sensed Tran's
tension. She gasped. Another screen message!

CONGRATULATIONS! YOU ESCAPED THIS TIME. BUT THE
FUN IS HEREBY ENDED. IF YOUR WEDDING ISN'T CAN-
CELLED, FAR WORSE THINGS WILL BEGIN TO HAPPEN—
NOT ONLY TO PC-PROS, BUT TO YOU. NO MORE WARN-
INGS WILL BE ISSUED.

Staring at the yellow letters, she felt a wash of fear. The
familiar Delphi code and now the peculiar sensation of

dread made her think momentarily of . . . Carson. But he was far away, had no idea where she was or what she was doing.

Much closer and more hysterical were Lois and her loony brother. Well, she had warned them both. She wasn't a bluffer. She thanked Tran and suggested he say nothing about the threat to PC-Pros to the staff. He said he wouldn't. She could trust him. No one was more close-mouthed than Tran. She dialed Michelle and told her to arrange for off-site file storage both in another company's computer and in a safe somewhere. Tran would make the backup tapes for her. She went to the ladies room and washed her face. She leaned against the sink and took several deep, heaving breaths. Coding under that kind of pressure shouldn't happen to anyone.

She looked up at herself in the mirror. Oh, my, see the thin lines bracketing her mouth! Where had they come from? Or had they been there waiting for stress to deepen their etching? Across her brow familiar shadowed wrinkles were a shade more pronounced. Seeing the unhappy effects of the events of the last two weeks on her appearance only hardened her determination.

She marched back to her office and picked up the phone, intending to call the police. Then she hesitated. Getting the law to act would be a ponderous task. Worse, even her knowing who her tormentors were wouldn't be enough for the men in blue. She would be accusing a prestigious family. Police liked evidence. She knew she had none—not the hard kind that they could measure, count, tag, and store. Nonetheless she was certain!

She put down the phone and paced her office. How to reach Lois, and through her Nicholas? How to make her *listen?*

She found the answer but didn't like it all that much.

She got into her Acura. Driving over to Foster's kennels, she heard her mother's voice: *Nothing you do now should disturb Foster.* . . . Under normal circumstances, maybe she would be right. Even in her state of growing stress Trish felt pronounced guilt at disregarding Marylou's words of wisdom. For as long as she could remember, every act in living her own life was prefaced with battling free of her mother's opinions and advice. Looking back, she saw she had indeed broken loose for her eight California years. Having returned for the good reasons of pure survival, she had not only resumed but intensified the struggle: Marylou vs. Trish in the Classic Mother-Daughter Knockdown. Would it ever come to a head and end in some kind of psychological knockout? Or would it drag on till one of them died? Her face twisted into a grim grin. Ordinarily she would assume that her mother would go first, in the usual way of the world. After today she wasn't at all sure about that. A chill angled into the back of her neck. *Far worse things will begin to happen . . . to you. . . .*

Something like rage at the Smith-Patton pair rose to a boil and stayed with her all the way to Lake Country Kennels. She found Foster in his office going over a computer printout. "We have some things to discuss," she said.

The tone of her voice brushed a brief frown across his brow. He put down the fan-folded sheets. "I assume you mean about Sunday's disagreement?"

She shook her head. "We're both adults. We got carried away. I don't hold any grudge or ill will. Do you?"

He shrugged. "I suppose not."

"Good." She pulled up a stool. "Because we're back to Lois and Nicholas again."

He looked pained. "Must we be?"

"We must. Listen. There've been new developments. First, Nicholas himself came to PC-Pros. He looked guilty as Judas all the while he was babbling about 'helping' me with the problems Lois 'shared' with him."

"Why is that so strange, Trish?" Foster said.

"Why? Because I only met the guy once that day with you. He didn't even look at me. Now he comes over and wants to 'help' me? The real reason he came was he felt guilty about what Lois had made him do. I mean, figure it out!"

Foster sighed. He took off his glasses and polished their lenses on the silk handkerchief stuck in his jacket pocket. "What did you tell him?"

"I told him to take a hike. I didn't need his help." Trish made a sour face. "Anyway, after we had talked a while he just about confessed to having played a major part in all the hateful stunts I told you about."

"Then?"

"I asked him to leave. He did. I peeked out. He stood on the street for an hour staring at our building. He's a nut case, Foster. Small wonder his sister has to take charge of him."

"He's a very high-priced electronics consultant and a more than expert chess player."

"He's a nerd!"

Foster shook his head. "What he's not is one of those harassing you and your business."

"Hang on a minute! You have to hear what just happened." She told him about her and Tran's battle against loss of her computer files. It had been a narrow escape from a fate as owner of a business with no past—and no future. "So you see somehow Nicholas got into PC-Pros during the night to do his mischief."

"It could have been one of your employees."

"None of my employees cares whether or not I get married! Believe me. My problem, though you refuse to believe it, is the Smith-Pattons."

Foster sighed again, annoyingly, she thought. "Why did you drive all the way out here to tell me this? You could have called."

"I like seeing you." She smiled. Despite recent difficulties her affection for Foster was stronger than ever. His answering smile told her he felt the same way. "Well, there *is* another reason," she said.

He sat back. "I thought so."

"I was going to go to the police and give them the Smith-Pattons' names. And make it clear to them who's behind this vendetta against our wedding."

"That's absurd. I tell you Lois is guiltless."

"Lois once said she'd kill me! And her brother does whatever she says. How can you say she's guiltless? I knew you'd stick up for her—"

"Trish!"

"So I thought over what to do. Earlier I tried confronting her and got nowhere. Now . . . I want *you* to face her down."

"Me."

"You. She still loves you. She'll pay attention to whatever you say. I want you to tell her to stop what she's doing. That if she continues, she'll end up talking to the police. And I know enough about the Smith-Patton family to be sure that kind of publicity isn't up their alley."

"Does it do any good for me to say once again I'm sure she's not involved with the incidents?"

"It does not! Foster, she has to be made to understand that what she's trying isn't working. That she must *stop*. And fast! I can't make her do it. The police would take forever. That leaves you as my last resort."

"Trish, Trish." He took her hands in between his, made their favorite hand sandwich, and nibbled her fingers. "Listen to me. You're overdramatizing. 'Last resort.' Come now!"

"Sunday you criticized me for keeping my problems to myself, not sharing them with you," she said. "Well, I'm not only sharing now, I'm asking for your help." She freed her hands and put one on each of his narrow shoulders. "Do you think I *like* asking you to talk to Lois Smith-Patton? Do you think I like sending my love into the enemy camp?"

"There's no danger—"

"I trust you. I know you love me, Foster. Just the same, it's not a super-smart thing for me to do. I have ample proof that she's emotionally very dangerous to our engagement, even without her acts of sabotage. But I'm willing to take the risk of having you two interact. Maybe your understanding that will make you see how desperate I am, and you'll agree to talk to her." She looked deeply into his eyes. "Will you?"

He fussed and fretted then. She let him get it out. She listened to all his reasons why paying Lois a visit wasn't a good idea. As he talked, the issue hanging in the balance, she wondered not for the first time how mentally tough he was. Did he have the right stuff when it came to facing down the assertive, excitable woman whose snares were still set for him? Or had a lifetime spent on the firm foundation of many dollars taken the spunk out of him? Should he do as Trish asked, it might prove a positive sign in terms of their future life together.

At the end of nearly two hours he agreed to pay Lois a visit. His reasons weren't Trish's, though. They were very much his own. "I'm going to come back with proof that neither Lois nor her brother has anything to do with what's happening to you!"

"You do that," she said. She laughed at the outrageousness of his idea. "If she's innocent, then I'll *really* have a problem!"

He wasn't smiling. "Won't you?" he said.

Trish rushed home, motherly guilt weighting her gas-pedal foot. She had arranged for Melody to play with her best friend, Pamela Beestock. She had phoned the girl's mother, Jill, before visiting Foster, asking if she could keep Melody a while longer. "No problem!" Jill said.

Jill Beestock was a "no problem" woman, and at times Trish envied her. If people were cars, Jill would be a Golf—simple, efficient, reliable. She was basic, no neuroses, three kids, an insurance company manager husband. For diversions she talked on the phone, quilted, and was active in her church, one of the newer evangelical ones in which the congregation sang and shouted. Mostly she was a professional mom. When she or others encountered life's problems her philosophy was to "suck it up and keep going." For that reason she was sometimes impatient and a little intolerant of those fallen far into the creepers and quicksand of the human condition.

Jill was a stocky, fast-moving brunette. She wore her hair in a practical ponytail held in place by a thick rubber band that had once clutched a bunch of fresh broccoli. She owned twenty pairs of pants and three dresses. She didn't use makeup. Her only facial decoration was a thick pair of glasses often sliding halfway down her nose. She was short on glamour, long on straight thinking.

On several occasions since their friendship had begun Trish had confided in Jill. When she had complained several years ago of the problem of being both a professional woman and single mother, Jill offered two-word advice: "Get married."

That evening Jill served lemonade and ham sandwiches in the screened gazebo by the pool. Shrieking, Pamela and Melody went in and out of the water faster than seals. Sprawled on a chaise, Trish realized how tired she was. The near loss of her business records, the message threatening worse, and convincing Foster to help her nip Lois's conniving in the bud had about drained her strength. Though it was still light, this being one of the longest days of the year, she nearly fell asleep as soon as she had food in her stomach.

"You have a great girl there, Trish," Jill said. "Rock solid. Polite and good-natured, too. She's a good model for mine. Pam still has a lot of rough edges." She laughed. "One thing you oughta do—make Melody cut down on the junk food. She gulped a package of Yodels and a Sno-Ball about a half hour before dinner."

"Her grandmother's influence," Trish said. "Eat! You can do no wrong." She shook her head. "What do I do with Marylou?"

"That's easy. After you marry Foster, you hire a nanny."

"A nanny?"

"Sure. With all his money that'd be no problem. Then you won't have to ask Grandma to sit."

Trish sipped lemonade, thinking of what else an unlimited budget would mean to her.

"That's assuming you continue not to take my best piece of advice," Jill said.

"Which is?"

"Don't tell me for a minute you've forgotten. The day after the wedding you sell your business. And start living the way a few lucky women still can—at home, with kids."

"You sure you're not playing the shill for my mother? The two of you sound alike." Jill moved off to do some cleanup, insisting Trish sit still, keep an eye on the kids. Trish drifted into a reverie that began with her at the altar—in pastel to go along with Marylou's big lie campaign. How she wanted to be married to Foster! Reaching that goal meant so much:

someone to love always, a secure home for Melody and the chance to begin her musical education with the best teachers, far less dependence on PC-Pros for their livelihood. Basic Jill might well be right.

Past those obvious gains from marriage would come some even more valuable—ones made on the fields of her emotions and personality. Reaching the haven of matrimony meant that California, and all that went with it, would be forever behind her. She was not fooled into thinking that she had escaped her past completely, though some critical distancing had taken place. Too much had happened to be thrown aside, even over a three-year period, to make a complete end of it. Carson's influence and attentions had been too telling to allow an easy exit. Lois's cries of "mental case" hit close to her condition upon returning home. How much inner healing remained to take place she couldn't guess. At moments like this, when her energy reserves were low, she imagined Carson still owned the soul she had obliviously bargained away.

She absolutely had to be married September fifteenth!

She drove a drowsy daughter home. Both of them needed to be between sheets in record time. Breaking discipline, she allowed Melody to get into her pajamas without brushing her teeth or washing her face. Trish hurried into her nightgown, slid into bed, and pulled a pillow over her head.

Despite her fatigue, she slept poorly and awoke feeling more drained than rested. All morning she had trouble focusing her attention. Shortly after noon her impatience got the best of her. She phoned Foster's kennels. He wasn't there. She phoned his home. Houghton the butler said he wasn't there but had gone off in "his motor." She knew she shouldn't hound Foster. He would speak to Lois as soon as was practical. The problem was she was losing her cool. She phoned the yacht club and asked that Foster be paged. In time he said hello.

"Have you talked to Lois yet?" Trish was surprised by the naked haste in her voice.

"Trish . . . I'm doing so now. Over lunch."

Her heart sank. "I was hoping you wouldn't turn something like an inquisition into a social event."

"Those were her terms for talking to me—lunch here. She wouldn't take no for an answer." The line rustled with his familiar short, dry laugh. "Here I am, caught between the demands of two assertive women. If I didn't bring Lois here, she wouldn't talk to me. If I didn't talk to her, you wouldn't talk to me!"

"Foster, this is not funny! If you could have been there when I was sweating over code to save my whole business—"

"Lois insists neither she nor Nicholas has anything to do with your problems."

Trish snorted. "And I'm sure that while denying she managed to take a few shots at me."

Foster's voice cooled. "You asked me to do this. You can't have it both ways."

"She's such a bitch!"

"Trish!"

"Foster, I *know* she's behind it all. Just be sure you tell her that if she doesn't knock it off, the police will show up. And Foster, don't enjoy yourself too much!" She hung up, then stared down at the receiver.

She was making a fool of herself.

As the afternoon passed she became more aware of her mental state. She had so much work to do, but her concentration was worse than before she spoke with Foster. Her nerves were stretched to their limit. Diabolical Lois had discovered Trish's secret: To destroy her business was to destroy her mental stability as well.

To pull out of her tailspin Trish toured her little empire, chatting with employees and reviewing their current projects. She eyed Tran, knowing that he had kept silent about their frightening file save yesterday morning. She had never been able to read his scarred face. This afternoon was no exception. She called saleswoman Samantha Swords on her car phone to ask for her projected month's sales figures. She was sitting in traffic. It was hot. PC-Pros couldn't afford to lease air-conditioned vans. Horns blew in the distance. "Next van we lease, forget the AC," Samantha said. "Just get one with wings!"

An hour later her mother called. She insisted the two of them have a wedding action meeting. So much remained to be done. Trish curbed her normal hostile reaction. The wedding, being threatened, had taken on a greater importance. Detailed preparation would make it seem more of a certainty. She told Marylou she would come over with Melody early that evening. Her mother's intuitions were Cassandra-like in their accuracy. "How are things going with Foster? You're not upsetting him, are you?"

"I've had some more trouble with the business. I had to ask him a favor." Trish couldn't bring herself to tell her mother she had sent him to Lois.

"I think you're being stupid. Are you?"

"Mother!"

"Have you acted on my suggestion that you two go off for a short while together?"

"I have some people here," she lied. "I have to go." She hung up. Her hands were shaking. She took a deep breath, held it, exhaled slowly.

What is happening to me, she wondered.

Michelle had been holding a call. A Mr. Perkins of Zealmont Starr and Perkins. Trish took it, introduced herself. Mr. Fletcher Perkins, though he represented the Smith-Patton family, was calling this first time as a friend. He wondered how familiar Trish was with the laws concerning slander and false accusation. His tone was patient, fatherly even. He had a newscaster's baritone that made one want to believe whatever he said. He summed up the point of his call: Before she went ahead and made the charges she was contemplating against certain members of the Smith-Patton family, she should first check with legal counsel about her liability in the event those charges were proven false. Believing that a word to the wise was sufficient—he actually said it!—he wished her a pleasant day and hung up.

Into the dead mouthpiece she said, "Lois is lying." Then

louder: "Lois is lying!" Against her good sense she shouted, *"Lois is lying!"*

She had to be lying.

If somehow she wasn't, and hadn't been involved in all Trish suspected, then . . . who else cared whether or not she married Foster?

She couldn't imagine.

9

POSSIBLY HE SHOULD ABANDON THE PIRC IN FAVOR OF the old Colle System, recently resurrected with new bells and whistles in interzonal grand master play. Think Colle! Opening sequences—white's first move, black's response, white second move, black response—spun out like spiderwebs. They were swept away, then respun with incremental changes. Pawns inched forward, minor pieces danced into enemy territory or bulwarked advanced forces. Where could he introduce a new move to set back, if not bewilder, his opponent? Possibly he should devise a gambit. Sure, they all were unsound in the end. But across the board, with the clock ticking . . . the strongest response was difficult to find. Maybe he could earn a footnote in the next edition of *Practical Chess Openings*. The Smith-Patton Gambit. Yes!

From his van's homemade CD system Dexter Gordon's sax poured out a bath in which he floated happy as any princess in her milk or demimondaine in champagne. Was he at work or at play? Or busy with something in between? He had no idea, and that was good. Only the happiest man couldn't tell the difference between labor and leisure.

He had never bothered to repaint the van. Its sidelong banner still read "Ed's Sewer Maintenance." And in smaller letters beneath: "Sanitary Engineering for the New Age." Nicholas had bought it at a bankruptcy sale, gutted its interior, and installed the sophisticated array of electronic equipment used in his consulting business. The windowless van was protected from prying hands by a security system of his own design. It delivered whopping electric shocks and tossed off showy showers of sparks to discourage the acquisitive. He had hand-inked the small sticker that adhered by the driver's side door handle: "Protected by Merciless Security." More than once he had driven off leaving a stunned potential thief lying by the curb.

Kings and chords twisted like vines in his mind. He reached his destination and pulled over to the curb. He left the engine running. In the van's minilab he flipped switches, pressed panel studs. Three devices of his own design glowed to life. He threw a toggle activating the antenna motor. From the roof the silvery spike vertically extended itself. He lifted a hand-held scope and a keypad from their cradles and carried them with him to the driver's seat. He put the van into gear and began to follow the route he had worked out on the map in his water-tank tower office. He would drive the blocks bounding PC-Pros.

Lois had been gleeful when she called to report that Trish "was bungling back all that she had stolen." She had cataloged his love's accusations in great detail, thanks to his coaxing for specifics. Foster had gotten into the act; all was a snarl. At the heart of it pulsed his dear one's clear panic. He imagined her high cheeks faintly rouged with anxiety. He saw her hesitant index finger touched to the edge of her mouth, where barely pouted lips joined in dimpled curve. There he, who had never had a woman, began his imaginary fleshy forays. That first stone of reverent attention spread his desire's ripples over the creamy pond of her body. Who couldn't judge from the slender columns of wrists, ankles, and neck the porelessness of intimate flesh masked by jumpsuit cloth? Even he, whose desires ran largely to the wonders deriving from the flow of current and the seductiveness of solitude, could not always elevate his thoughts to that high place worthy of her sanctity.

He clutched the wheel with long fingers. He knew his face carried a smudge of blush, his groin unfamiliar pressure. Foolish biological crankings, because he was merely her most devout worshiper, content and secure though standing only at near distance to her. He would serve her as any loyal sailor had the first Queen Elizabeth, make any sacrifice. But approach her *that* way? Never!

He had pondered Lois's last information, added to it previous bits and pieces concerning his beloved's situation. What he had first considered to be semiprofessional vandalism he judged was something worse. His foray today should serve to clarify both the extent and the determination behind her harassment.

Gordon's sax intruded on his attention. Like a volatile drug the sound rose in his mind to blur all but brain basics and driving habits. He forgot where he was, his duty to Trish. His attention wobbled after elusive chord progressions. In time he returned to this dimension, finding himself parked by a fire hydrant, engine idling. In the pantheon of masters, let Dexter's name be engraved large! More than an hour had passed.

He resumed his foray. He placed the scope in its mount, where he could see it at any time. He made two circuits of PC-Pros. The scope winked busily as his equipment monitored frequencies. At a certain point in each circuit he was cued to pull over and start the tape recorder mounted with the other equipment. Interesting and revealing . . . oh, Trish my wish, I serve you well!

He was certain his adored one would refuse to see him, so he pulled his van up outside PC-Pros and parked close by her Acura. There he waited, not idly, for he never wasted a moment. He busied himself with a consulting project, a hard nut that men who called themselves computer experts had been unable to crack. He had mulled and meditated over the problem for several days. At this moment its solution chose to rush into his brain with the energy of a 747 takeoff. He jotted the key illuminations. The rest of the time required by the project would be less fun: drawing schematics to show the less imaginative his inspired solution. Six figures he charged. His not really needing the money made payment all the more important. They paid with pleasure. . . . Dexter Gordon told him more about man and life than a score of philosophers. Oh, saint, take it to B-flat!

She! There! Her jumpsuit gleamed whiter than detergent-commercial sheets in the late June sunlight. Leggy stride rushed her toward her car. He scrambled out of the van, awkward as usual, like a pale-domed spider. "Trish Morley!" he cried, too moved to lower his scratchy voice. He saw the flash of fright widen her sweet face.

"Nicholas . . ."

"I have to talk to you—now. It's important." He tried to maintain eye contact. But his glance slid away like fingers on smooth marble.

"I don't need to talk to you. I heard from your attorney." She turned toward her car.

He went after her. "Please . . ."

"Nicholas, leave me alone! I'm well aware of what you and your sister are trying to do to me. Your threats against my 'slander' don't frighten me."

He shook his head. He couldn't be drawn into talking. Not this way. In her presence he couldn't achieve mere conversation, never mind the eloquence required to persuade her that he and Lois had nothing to do with her problems. He blurted, "Your business is bugged!"

She blinked. Her gray eyes, hooded against the sun's assault, probed his face. "Bugged . . ."

"I think there are three microphones scattered through the building. They're transmitting on adjacent frequencies."

She frowned. "How do you know?"

He told her about his equipment. On familiar technical ground, he found his analysis pouring out with ease. Yes, the most compact microcircuits were being used, joined to economic jewels of transmitters as miserly with voltage as

Marner with gold. She understood him! Of course she would. Angels understood all the tongues of men. Believing was another matter.

"If there are bugs—"

"There are. I'll prove it if you'll get in the van."

She hesitated. He could nearly read her mind. She was wondering how far he and Lois would go to stop her wedding. Would he try to abduct her, she was wondering. She had to let that idea—and a lot like them—go entirely before she could begin to get to the bottom of her problems. Right then she was far from that point. "You have to hear the tape." He nodded toward the van.

"Leave the door open," she said.

"I'm on your side," he said. Her frown told him she didn't believe.

He cued up the tape and let it run. Her frown deepened. He wanted to make her stop; the lines in her brow did her expression cruel disservice. "Those are the voices of my employees!"

"And yours, I think I heard."

She nodded. "Yes, yes." She spun toward him. "How do I know you didn't install the mikes? Now that I'm putting the heat on you and Lois, maybe you're pretending you found them."

"I'm on your side." He knew he sounded dogged, stupid even. He was incapable of conversing with her, hated his ineptness.

She climbed out of the van. "Why did you tell me about this?"

Anything for you! He stood silent, made mute by adoration. He knew what she saw before her, a gangling, pasty spider-cum-human. With the effort of a weightlifter pressing seven hundred pounds he heaved out a phrase. "I thought you ought to know."

She folded her arms; his time with her had terminated. "It's possible I should thank you, Nicholas. If so, thanks. If you're playing some kind of mind game . . . This afternoon I'll have the bugs pulled out."

"I wouldn't."

"You wouldn't. Why not?"

He blurted: "Knowing they're there puts you one up on whoever put them in."

She smiled thoughtfully. "I see. Just watch what I say. And tip off the staff, too?" He made no reply. She saw the hesitancy on his once again mute lips. "If I'm sure I trust them all. Right?"

He nodded, dome gleaming under sunlight and sweat sheen.

"I have some things to think about," she said, half to herself. She moved toward her car. "Good-bye."

Her Acura sped into the distance. He stood motionless, staring, transfixed. Where did this street lead? Tarsus?

Sweetest Sister's summons came at two-thirty. He was to report at once. She ordered him to her audience chamber, a private room at Napes and Nails, one of the city's premier beauty salons. Annalee was administering a facial with the care and attention of a Roman bath slave. The mask was in place, covering Sweetest Sister's face with its whitish film. Cotton pads blinded her. She was motionless. She heard and felt, and so was not diminished. Oraclelike, she spoke: "You're late."

"Traffic."

"You should have left your car and run—crawled if you had to."

He could not retort sharply to Sweetest Sister. He grunted and looked at the floor where her fallen locks curled like black maggots.

"I want to know what the hell you're doing with Ms. Patricia Morley. What has gotten into you?"

He grunted. He sensed her anger. He reached inward for riffs. Saint Dizzy, defend me with me boss sounds! Hard luck. The cabaret of his mind was soundless as the moon. The group was taking five.

"She called me an hour ago. Do you know why she called me, Nicholas?"

He shook his head.

"She called to apologize to us. For making false accusations."

Trish had believed him! The first, necessary step to solving her problems. He smiled.

"She told me you've gone to her twice—the first time to offer help and the second to tell her she was being spied on. Is that so?"

He could not speak.

"Tell me! Is that so? You saw her twice?"

Annalee, buxom and fortyish, had served Sweetest Sister in this chamber for years. Privy to Smith-Patton family matters of all sorts, she was as close-mouthed as a priest out of the confessional. She busied herself with Sweetest Sister's nails.

Nicholas nodded, hating his limitations, himself.

"You must know that she's my enemy!"

Nod.

"Then why do you help her?"

Silence.

"Answer me, Nicholas. Annnnswer me!" Her voice cooed teasingly. "Why do you want to help that gray-eyed nut case?"

He hoisted heavy words up from his throat as though with a winch. "To show her she was wrong about us."

Oracle Lois sat silent under mask and cotton. In time she spoke. "You've never been a crusader for the family's good name, Nicholas. Have you? That lot seems to have fallen to me. No, I don't think that's the real reason you sought out Trish. I think it's love. Or rather your version of it." She giggled. "Even though I'm your dear sister, I can't imagine just what love would mean to you. And I'm sure you're quite incapable of telling me. Aren't you?"

Describe how he felt beholding the white curve where Trish's neck swept down to become shoulder? Or hearing the purring vibrato of her voice speaking to him of spies and suspicions? He couldn't!

"How has she reacted to your attentions, Nicholas?"

He saw Trish's long hands spread before the tape machine

controls, fingers tapered to sensible nails. He nibbled them, but only in his dreams. He knelt before her, kissed the stitched "Nike" on the side of her Airs. He could not reply to Sweetest Sister.

"I can't believe she'd be interested in you for a single moment, you being what you are. If she were, that would make my life so much easier. I could tell Foster his fiancée has fallen for my brother. That would very likely take care of their engagement. Oh, I'm being so stupid! You haven't said a word to her about how you feel, have you?"

He shook his head.

Sweetest Sister fell silent. Annalee busied herself with cuticle pushers and emery boards. Nicholas dared not move. He knew he hadn't been dismissed. Time passed.

Dreamily Sweetest Sister said, "What does this bitch Trish Morley have? She steals my Foster, a steady, sensible man sitting on top of a fortune. Now my virgin brother wants her, too. He who, up to now, loved only PCs, pocket protectors, and pawns. Bottle it to sell, and I could make a fortune." Another long silence. The acetone scent of Annalee's polish remover filled the air. Nicholas anticipated a change in Sweetest Sister's monologue direction. "Is there really something going on that Trish thought we were behind?"

Nicholas nodded.

"Is she in trouble? Could this—whatever's going on— wreck her?"

A surge of dread broke over Nicholas like a dark wave. He heard snaggle-toothed mermaids' songs shaped to jazz riffs. "Maybe. I have to find out more."

Sweetest Sister's masked head bobbed. "Then you should persist in the stupidity of loving her. Maybe you can win her away from Foster. Yes, yes, you have my permission to love her!" Her laughter was sharp as shards. It cut into him with countless points. "Whatever you find out, Don Quixote, I want to know. *Report everything to me. Do you understand?*"

What Sweetest Sister learned she would use against Trish. How could he serve two mistresses, one whom he worshipped, another he obeyed? It wasn't possible! How the matter would resolve itself he couldn't imagine. He squirmed inwardly, phantoms of fear rushing onstage from the wings of his mind. Already he had moved far from the safe roles of electronics consultant, jazz buff, and chess master. And so quickly, too! Worse, he was being shoved toward the footlights where coming days would demand dangerous improvisation. In the audience sat a sinister man with whom his beloved was tangled in ways he couldn't comprehend. His intuition cried that in her service he would meet him.

And rue that day.

He spun and rushed from Sweetest Sister's presence. Even her most awl-like cry's point driven against the membranes of his ears could not turn him back to her. Never before had he been able to resist her command. Surely she would understand how much between them had already changed.

Back in his water-tower office the computer held a phone message. He listened—and gasped aloud. *Her* voice! He was so smitten that the meaning of her words slipped away from his attention like seaside minnows under a child's greedy hands. His memory thrust forth her face, comely lips to the phone mouthpiece, gray eyes narrowed in concentration, their long lashes beating the air like harem feather fans. "By now you probably know I made my apologies to your sister. I decided to believe you two had nothing to do with what's happening to me. Consider this call my official thanks for your help."

In his van he drove the same route as earlier that day. Late evening had come. Now the streets were shadowed and deserted. Fine for him. He had to stop often and take readings, scampering back and forth from the driver's seat to the equipment racks, where screens glowed into the darkness like monsters' eyes. Art Tatum's sound, a mellow drift at low volume, last stop on the stride piano line, invaded his mind like syncopated fog. "Taking a Chance on Love." He bustled.

He was happy.

He served his goddess.

By nine-thirty he was on the way to her house. How often since that bright day he had met her had he cruised by her Victorian relic! So seldom, though, had he glimpsed her fetching form. He pulled to the curb and got out. His pulse sped. He began to sweat despite the cool June night. Dare even he, the most devoted priest, choose to worship at this latish hour?

He climbed the creaking stair, opened the screened porch door, and rang the bell. Within, scampering young footsteps grew louder. The house door opened. A red-haired girl of seven wearing pajamas stood behind the screen staring up at him. Staring. "Your . . . mother," he said in a voice somehow that of a frog.

The child spun, pigtail swishing, and was gone. Melody. Lois had told him about her. Having issued from his goddess's body, she was as dear to him as his good name. Despite hearing her badly managed cry: "Mom, Mom, there's this tall, *weird* guy at the door! He doesn't have any hair! And he has these big eyes—"

She was cut short by Mother's *shhhh!* Trish could not know the child's unintentional abuse could never begin to compare with that dished out to him by Sweetest Sister from his cradle days.

And here she came again into his life! Jeaned and sweatered against the recent turn in the weather. She hesitated behind the screen door, face smudged by shadow. Yes, I am hard to behold, but not deformed, only strange to the eye. Surely you can welcome your supplicant, however briefly. "I . . . didn't expect a visit, Nicholas," she said.

He played his trump. "I found out more."

"About what's happening? About the bugs?"

He nodded.

White hand behind wire screen, the muted cry of ill-hung hinges. "Come in. Just for a minute. I have to put Melody to bed soon. Should have done it an hour ago." She led him to a small sitting room scattered with coloring books. He so wished he could meet her glance, drink the gray waters of her eyes. If he could, he would be stricken mute. So he snatched glimpses of her face in timing as erratic as his conversation. She didn't invite him to sit. "What did you find out?" she said.

"All three transmissions are beamed in one direction. I measured the signal strength." How easy to talk about the familiar! Hear my eloquence! "The receiver can't be any farther away than a half mile from PC-Pros. The signals are tight. Equipment must be first rate. If you want, I could pull one of the bugs and take it apart."

"Whoever it is would know, though, wouldn't he?"

"If he listens all the time, or runs tape. Yeah. He'd know." He sucked breath like an emerging pearl diver. "Who's doing it?" he said.

"I . . . thought I knew. Now I'm not sure. It's somebody who doesn't want me to get married. But nobody but Lois should care. . . ." Her voice trailed off. She turned sharp eyes on him. "If I tell you anything I do know, Nicholas, does it go right back to Lois?"

He stood silent, blinking, torn by the terriers of cross-loyalties.

"Foster told me your sister is the biggest influence in your life."

He sensed her slipping away, the strand of their connection stretching out to the breaking point. The threat loomed large as Godzilla: defrocked Nicholas driven from the temple by a distrustful goddess. He had to speak! "I'll help you," he blurted. "And keep quiet."

Her eyes narrowed. "Why?"

"I think you need the kind of help I can give. Those bugs are so slick they make me nervous. I want to home in on the receiver. See who's sitting there by it."

She paced. When she turned a cautious smile blessed her face. "Maybe you're the good in the family. I know Lois is the bad." She angled her glance up at him. "I suppose I shouldn't say that, considering your—"

"Lois commands," he said.

She nodded. "Nonetheless . . . I don't want her to be part of any help you might give me," Trish said.

"She . . . won't be."

"And you won't talk to her about me?"

Gray eyes sought his, caught like hooks. The full power of her sorcery flowed into his heart. He knew what lovers who said they melted meant. "I—I'll be discreet."

From the distance daughter demanded attention. "In a minute, Melody!" Trish paced again while Nicholas stood at adoring attention. "Beside trying to get a fix on the receiver, could you do one other thing for me?"

Why did she even ask? Command me!

"Check this house for bugs, too."

His van could have sprouted wings, so high did he soar on the road to his water-tower cot. There he thrashed through the night, beaming into the mildewed dark. Trishes in jeans and jumpsuits jammed his dreams, bid him bound bare through hoops woven of drum-sized resistors, their wires braided like a maiden's hair.

So this was love!

10

WEDNESDAY MORNING TRISH ASKED LEFTOVER LEWIS to move all her furniture to an unused cubicle around the corner from the reception area. The bug in what had been her office would end up overhearing nothing more than an occasional staff conference or the rustling of lunch bags. She was pleased at even this small victory over . . . she didn't know who.

Her phone rang at eight-twenty. The caller identified himself as Lieutenant Stanley. "Bomb squad," he added. He wondered if he could come over and talk to her. This morning. Trish sensed she shouldn't say no. Awaiting his arrival, she found her anxiety rising steadily. What did bombs have to do with PC-Pros?

Stanley was short and heavy. About fifty, he had lost hair. Baldness ill suited his round face. He wore a checkered handkerchief in his suit jacket pocket. He wrapped stubby, dark fingers around his leather badge holder. Trish nodded before the gleaming shield. "I'd love a cup of coffee," he said in a wheezing voice.

While Michelle ran his errand he pulled a folder and notebook out of a slender leather briefcase.

"I'm a little nervous about why you're here," Trish said. "Could you tell me?"

"Sure will." He glanced at folder sheets, then looked up. "Kandinsky Klein and Corman."

"They're one of our customers. A law firm. What about them?"

"Before I answer that, could you tell me just what you've done for them recently?"

Trish turned to her terminal. She brought up the data base. "We maintain all the PCs in their office. Repair, service, some software installations. Says here they had trouble with a Northgate 386. We brought it in for service June sixteenth. My technician Puck O'Brien cleaned and recalibrated the read-write heads. We returned it yesterday, the twenty-first." She looked at Stanley. "We pride ourselves on never keeping a machine longer than a week."

"You should be in charge of our PD machines, then. They're taken care of by the lowest bidder—and the service proves that." Stanley had a moist smile that Trish found unattractive. He made her nervous, too. "This machine you serviced . . . where in the law office did your road man put it?" he asked.

She summoned Leftover Lewis. He said that he had returned the machine to its original location—in the law firm's library. Stanley thanked him, asked him not to leave the building. "While I'm at it, could you ask, umh—Puck O'Brien—to stay handy, too? I'll want to ask him some questions."

"What *about?*" Trish was getting more frustrated. Or was it more nervous?

After Leftover was gone Stanley turned to her. He took a deep breath. He was going to give her bad news! He wasn't enjoying it. She leaned forward, nails sinking into her palms. He said, "Last night at two in the morning the computer PC-Pros serviced exploded."

"What? Computers don't explode! The worst they do is sometimes short and catch fire."

"The explosion blew out all the windows in the law firm's library. The fire destroyed two thirds of the books."

Trish sank back in her chair, dread icing her arms and legs. "That's . . . impossible."

Stanley flashed a humorless grin. "No, it isn't. Not when we're certain the machine held a stick of dynamite and a small incendiary device."

Trish was speechless. She was aware her eyes were widening.

Stanley scanned notes. "Both wired into the computer's clock. Piece of cake: built-in timer. Long way from the old alarm clock, huh?"

"I cannot believe this. . . ."

He had plenty of questions then. All were asked in a polite, well-measured voice. He was most noncommittal. And a careful note taker. He asked about the business relationship between PC-Pros and Kandinsky Klein and Corman. Did any of her employees have a connection with the law firm? Any nasty divorces handled by Kandinsky lawyers? What she couldn't tell him, he promised to find out when he questioned her staff. He hoped she wouldn't mind his taking their time. He sat back and spread his short arms questioningly. "Now, off the record, Ms. Morley, I'd be glad to hear what you think is going on."

She stood up, hesitant, and began to pace. Her old habits of keeping unpleasant information to herself reared up with familiar strength. Yet since she had left the coast, little by little she was modifying that behavior, too. She was learning to have more confidence in others. She asked her intuition whom to trust. This morning it told her this roundish cop was okay.

In the middle of her tale of threatening messages and spying microphones Michelle put through a call. It was Ephraim Kandinsky, Esq. He was going to sue PC-Pros for "negligence," which showed how much he knew about PCs. The suit itself, though, was sure to be no joke. That meant big legal expenses that her business could scarcely support. Unless she could prove that PC-Pros had been a criminal's victim. As Kandinsky droned on, her spirits sank lower. When he finished she was on the verge of tears.

Now badly distracted, she finished her story by explaining

to Lieutenant Stanley that Nicholas Smith-Patton was going to further investigate the bugging. He checked his notes. "Well, well, it looks like there's more to it all than I thought," he said almost cheerily. He gave her a business card and a comforting smile. "Keep me up to date on what your man finds out. We'll be going at it from the bomb end."

Trish shook her head. She felt put-upon, threatened.

"You better warm up your smile a little," Stanley said.

"Why?"

"The press will want to talk to you."

The reporters showed up that afternoon. A woman and two men, one of them with a videocam. Trish thought of not talking to them, refusing to comment. That seemed a bad idea when PC-Pros couldn't really have been responsible for the explosion. She told the trio that someone had wired the dynamite and incendiary into the PC. She had no idea who had done it. She wondered later if she had really expected the reporters to be satisfied with her statement and leave. Instead they began to ask questions reflecting their belief that PC-Pros was indeed responsible for the disaster. Clearly they thought one of her employees was a saboteur.

The woman reporter was the most offensive. She had the strained look of the ill-fitting contact lens wearer and the harsh voice of an auctioneer. She shoved her tape recorder toward Trish's face with a straight arm that would be the envy of an NFL running back. What began as an interview Trish allowed to become a cross-examination. She fought hard for self-control but eventually lost the battle. She found herself shouting, "You people are hyenas!" so she knew it was time to end the session.

She had no idea how to do it.

Sensing her weakness, the reporters gathered strength and bayed ruder questions at her. She begged them to leave, but they ignored her. Tears of frustration gathered, and her sinuses burned. She was going to break down. Desperate, she shouted, "Get out of here!"

The reporters fell silent for an instant, startled.

The door flew open. Through it came Dino Castelli, protective Michelle in his wake. "Whatzis?" he bellowed.

He pointed at the reporters with a breadstick he had been nibbling. "You hassling my girlfriend here?"

The reporters made unkind replies.

He whirled toward Trish. "You finished with these—" He used an uncomplimentary Italian word she didn't know.

"Yes! Yes, I am."

"Out!" He snatched the tape recorder from the woman's hand and tossed it past Michelle into the reception area. The reporter started after it. He raised his foot and gave her rear a shove that sent her stumbling and screaming out of view. Michelle clapped her hands in glee. The heavier of the two men Dino simply lifted off his feet and carried out of the cubicle. His Vietnam alligator tattoo writhed with the exertion. "This interview session is officially over!" he growled in his heavy baritone. He glowered at the remaining reporter, who fled in silence.

While Dino finished escorting the reporters the rest of the way out, Trish smiled ruefully. One didn't find that sort of brash assertiveness in many men. She remembered one of them had been . . . Carson, a dominating force when in full cry, long red hair flying. She kicked her memory free of him yet again. When Dino returned, brown eyes bright with humor, she had nearly composed herself.

"Lucky for both of us I came over to talk to you," he said. "Lucky for you because I got rid of those jerks for you. Lucky for me because I *like* giving jerks the bum's rush." He shouted toward the reception area, "Hey, Ms. Ironeyes, bring in that white bag I put down, okay?"

Dino had brought apple tarts. He gave some to Michelle, left the rest in the bag for Trish. "I put in extra apple because I know you like them better that way."

She dug in her hand. "You're so nice to me," she said.

"Yeah, yeah." He nodded curtly. "You must have hit my soft spot. Maybe it happened when I talked to that *vagabondo* Rocco."

"I want to thank you again for that, Dino. At the time I thought he—"

"Like I said, he didn't do nothing to you." He leaned back and brushed his tight mop of curly hair. "Later I got to thinking. His business and yours are alike, no? And you're gonna be married pretty soon. Right?"

"Yes."

"And you told me you didn't think you'd keep this business. Your guy Foster, you said, has—" He rubbed thumb against curled forefinger. "So I decided Rocco ought to buy you out."

"Dino—"

"I went and talked to him again yesterday. I told him he makes you a better offer, maybe you take it. Then you don't have to worry no more about what goes on here. You get married, stay home, raise more *bambini,* and let your old man bring home the dough. That's why I came over now, to tell you maybe you'll hear from Rocco."

Trish laughed and shook her head. "That . . . wasn't necessary. I mean I appreciate it and all. I did say I was thinking about selling out *sometime. . . .*"

He lit a cigarette and leaned forward. "You still having trouble here? Like you were telling me about before I talked to Rocco?"

She nodded. "I'm afraid it's a little worse than it was." Her intuition had previously okayed Dino, and her faith had been confirmed by his real help. So she told him about the bugs and the bombs.

The phone rang. She picked it up. A man's voice. "Nobody got killed—this time."

"Who is this?"

"Next time it could be different."

"Who—"

"Cancel the wedding!" The line went dead.

Trish's whitening face spoke eloquently to Dino. "That was him, huh?" he said.

She nodded. "The wedding . . . he doesn't want the wedding."

Dino leaned back, blew out smoke. "What you got going on here, Patricia? Who doesn't want your wedding? Why?"

"I don't know!"

He nodded. "Look, I'm a baker now. But you know I was in Nam. I did and saw some hard things. I can still be hard."

She had sensed that. For some reason she found it comforting. "Could you maybe help me—if I need it? I might not. But—"

"You give me a call. That's all."

"I hope I don't have to." She sensed that if incidents continued, each seemingly worse than the one before, she'd need more than odd Nicholas and professionally curious Lieutenant Stanley on her side. She thanked Dino again and led him to the outside door. On Michelle's desk was a small white box. He picked it up and pressed it into her hands. "A couple tarts for your *bambina*. What's her name? Melody, huh?"

She kissed his cheek. "Get out of here, Santa Claus."

Rocco arrived two hours later. The cigar stuck in the middle of his mustached mouth was the same. So was its ascending twist of bitter smoke. What was missing was his earlier inscrutability. Trish remembered she had tried so hard to read the man and had failed. The way he fidgeted today made it clear he was . . . nervous. Afraid might be more like it. Sensing that, she was more easily able to compose herself, put on her business face. He thanked her for seeing him. He said he was more interested than ever in buying her out. He ran an index finger around his neck's gold chains. "I think it over. I talk about it with my uncle. I talk to my shyster and my banker. I want to buy all you got. I keep your people on, 'cause they're better than mine." He named a figure, one far more generous than his previous offer. She was startled.

"Now I have a problem," she said.

"What problem?" Rocco's mouth sagged with disappointment. The tops of his small, tobacco-stained teeth showed. "Not enough dough?"

"No. Not at all. The problem is now I have to take your offer seriously. Not like before, when you underpriced PC-Pros."

"Sure! It's a better offer. You understand that. That's good. Why you got a problem?"

"Because earlier you offered so little I didn't have to really think about selling. Now I have to."

110

Rocco knocked a long ash loose. "My shyster's working on the sale agreement. Get yours to call him. Let them work it all out."

Trish shook her head slowly. "I'm not sure I want to sell just now. I might wait till after my wedding in September."

She read disappointment in the shift of his cigar. Behind it lay other emotions, more elusive, possibly more primal. She leaned forward. "Don't be upset. I'm just telling you what I think at the moment. I'm having more of the . . . problems I thought you caused. Now I know it wasn't you. But I don't know who it is. I might be forced to change my mind and sell before September."

He nodded eagerly. "Sell now!"

She laughed. "You're such a strange man, Rocco! Why the sudden generosity? What happened to your subtle Sicilian ways of doing business?"

His face sagged slightly as though it was a ruddy balloon from which air had leaked. "Your friend," he said.

"Dino? I asked him to talk to you the first time. The second time he went on his own. What about him?"

Rocco's lips twisted toward a snarl. "These Nam vets! They shoulda never let them back in the country. They shoulda put them on an island somewhere and let them kill each other off. Instead they come back here, dopeheads and crazies. And they can kill you in the fifty ways they remember out of the hundred they knew before their brains rotted."

"Dino isn't like that!"

"The hell he isn't! He's as crazy as any of them. Crazier, maybe."

"Did he threaten you?"

"Never mind what he did! He was in Nam, and he'll never be right again. They took all the nice guy out of his head. And put in rules of the jungles he used to crawl around in." He snatched the cigar out of his mouth and crushed it out savagely on her desktop. "Don't send him around to me no more!" He jumped up. "He asks you, tell him I made a fair offer to you. A generous offer. If you don't want to sell, you tell him that. Tell him it's not Rocco's fault!" He rushed out of the cubicle. She heard Michelle's "Good-bye, Mr. DeVita" cut short by the outer door slamming.

She stood up, found herself smiling. No problem figuring out what Rocco feared—who, rather.

Dino Castelli was going to be a more potent ally then even she had hoped.

She called her attorney and explained what lay behind the threatened Kandinsky Klein and Corman suit. The rest of the afternoon she intended to spend running some budget numbers for the third quarter. She stared at the screen spread sheet. Instead of thinking about accounts payable her mind swung as relentlessly as a compass toward the pole of the threatening caller.

Cancel the wedding!

She had at last abandoned her diehard suspicions that either Rocco or Lois was behind the threats. That left her with no suspects. She made a discovery.

She was more afraid now.

Lois and Rocco were knowns—no matter how threatening. Now menace sprang from a dark, alien wellhead. Why did anyone care whether or not she married Foster Palmer? A draft from the air-conditioning duct chilled her. She wrapped her arms around herself and bowed her head. What other shocks were being prepared for her? And who was doing it? *Who?*

She had promised Melody and Pamela Beestock a Pizza Hut dinner that evening. That and a cruise through the Parkland Mall kept them out until nearly nine. They tumbled tiredly back home. She scooted Melody into her pajamas.

"Brush out my hair tonight, Mom?" Melody said.

They conducted their child-devised ritual. Melody lay facedown on the bed with her head over the side of the mattress. Trish knelt beside her with the big hairbrush. First she freed the pigtail, saving the rubber bands. She removed the bow Melody chose afresh daily from the selection in her heaped shoe box. With careful fingers she unraveled the triple strand, marveling once again at the hair's red luster and heavy body. Then she began cautiously with the brush.

Her child, for all her resiliency, was quick to howl at tugged tangles. Once loosened and spread, the hair was ready for long brush sweeps. "Brushyou . . . brushyou . . . brushyou . . ." Trish cooed with every stroke. Better than milk and cookies for getting Melody in that bedtime mood. She was asleep even before Mom could get her under the covers.

She tidied up the room, lifted whistles and flutes to their places, stacked the music. She turned and looked down at her child. She heard the light exhalations of her breathing. Trish's love rushed out like part of her soul. My child, my heart, my delight! Melody! By far the sweetest theme in the symphony of her life. How could she have allowed the girl to slip down in her priorities—even for a week—no matter her personal problems? She felt guilt, the single parent's bosom companion. She shouldn't be too hard on herself. Melody had Grandma and Janine. Not to mention frequent days at the Beestocks' pool under Mother Jill's practiced eye. Plenty of care and attention all through there, for sure. Then there were Trish's additional summer plans for the girl. At the moment unexpected events had put them on hold. But hopefully . . .

She remembered she hadn't read today's mail. She dug it out of the soup tureen where Janine was in the habit of stashing it. "You have already won one million dollars!" "Victims of last year's hurricane are still starving!" Two bills, three flyers, and a 6 x 8 manila envelope. The only piece of *real* mail, she thought.

She sat on the love seat, slipped a letter opener under the sticky flap, and tore it open. She slid the glossy color photograph onto her lap. She leapt up with a shriek, slapping the photo away as though it were a loathsome bug. It looped down to the floor and fell emulsion side up. Three faces looked at her.

Oh, she knew them well!

Only with a strong effort of will did she pick up the photograph. There they were again: she, Carson Thomas, and toddler Melody. All grinned like maniacs on that sunny Sunday four-odd years ago. And in the right-hand corner

Carson's bold hand: *Trish, Carson, and Melody—together forever!*

His brother had taken it on a Malibu beach and brought it back with other prints from the one-hour processor. Carson had scrawled the message as Trish looked on. His green eyes rose to meet her glance, burned in to seize command, as always. "Nothing will ever separate us!" he said.

Trish flung down the photo and groaned, softly at first. Then control slipped slowly away. Her groan rose in frequency till it became a harsh squeal, a nasty sound that tore loose as painfully as flesh from her taut throat. Melody! She musn't wake Melody!

This couldn't be!

She had thought it all over, buried, gone, all her tracks doubly covered by her deceptions and the shifting sands of more than three years. *It could not be!* She gasped for breath. How suddenly sweat poured from her!

With a grunt she snatched up the discarded envelope. "No!"

It was postmarked within the city!

She dug her fingers into her hair, clenched the black mop, and tore at it. *"Ahhhhhhh!"* The world spun free of moorings. A red rush roared in from Regulus and took her along for the ride. . . .

11

SHE REVIVED ON THE FLOOR, TORSO ON THE SCATTER rug. Before she even sat up to check for injuries thoughts of Carson flooded in, threatening to paralyze her. She fought them off. Sitting up, she felt her head. No bumps. She looked at her watch. She had been out for only five minutes. She pressed her face to raised knees. A single question shoved in like the tip of the wedge of all her dread.

How had he found her?

It did not seem possible! She had done so much to hide her tracks, even from one as cunning as he. *How, how, how had he found her?* She couldn't let the thought go, gnawed it like a starved mastiff at a bone.

Sleep? Forget it! Sleep when *he* stood somewhere within the vast spread of city limits planning . . . *things* for her? It took her nearly two hours to make an educated guess as to what had gone so dreadfully wrong. She snatched up the phone and dialed her mother's number. Marylou's voice dwelled half in slumberland. "Mother, listen to me!" Her voice was harsh and dry with fright. "Are you awake yet?"

"Can't this wait until tomorrow, for heaven's sake?"

"Absolutely not!"

"What do you want, Patricia?"

"I want to know where you sent my engagement announcement. The one you *insisted* be made public at the end of January."

Marylou's wits were still befuddled. "News of an approaching important wedding should be widely broadcast."

"How widely, Mother? To what newspapers did you send the announcement?"

"All the important east coast ones: *Globe, Times, Inquirer, Post,* and the *Constitution.*"

"How about the *west* coast?"

"Well, hardly anyone there knew you. So I sent just one announcement. To the paper in that little town you used to live in. La Cornada."

Her mother talked on as Trish lowered the receiver, heavy as heartbreak in her numbed hand. The connection broke, leaving her in silence. So it was indeed Carson . . . again.

Memories of him rushed forward, as impossible to stop now as a supertanker in the mid-Atlantic. She had moved to La Cornada because she could live temporarily with a former college roommate. There she found work as a programmer. In time she set up her new life and a social circle. An acquaintance gave a party. Through such a commonplace chain of events she met uncommon Carson.

From where she stood chatting in the kitchen, his voice caught her attention. Tone and substance both tugged at her. There was a pleasing resonance in his speech. She left her spot by the dishwasher and moved out onto the deck. Carson was making his argument to a half circle of surrounding guests. The topic of discussion was Japanese competition in chip manufacture. The technical and statistical information with which he supported his points was pertinent, brief, and timely.

She never forgot her first sight of him—or her first thought: *energy!* He leaned forward, thrusting index fingers to emphasize the words pouring out in a shower heavy enough to wet down the most resistant counter-opinion. There was energy, too, in the shift of his feet and solid legs in khaki shorts hacked out of a pair of dying slacks. He was a bit over six feet, in his mid to late thirties. Closer, she saw the deep luster of his shoulder-length mane of red hair, the piercing green eyes, and the scattering of acne scars on his cheeks.

One of the gathered turned away and walked past Trish. "The genius has spoken," he said half to himself. "Debate judged yet another win for Carson Thomas."

Not until the next day was she aware of the deep impression Carson had made on her. When she thought of the party, he eclipsed whatever else had happened. She realized she regretted not having been introduced to him.

He remedied that at the post office the next week. His hand fell from behind on her shoulder. She turned. Those eyes! Green *could* be a commanding shade. She shivered inwardly like a schoolgirl confronting her crush. "Carson Thomas," he said. "I saw you at Earthman's party the other night."

"You noticed me? You were busy debating—"

"I notice everything around me. Most particularly women in their early twenties with nifty black bangs and big gray eyes. You're Patricia McMullen Morley."

"How do you know that?"

They were walking together out of the post office. "When I want information, I go after it," he said. "It only took four phone calls. My personal best was twenty-three."

"You made twenty-three phone calls to get a name?"

He shook his head, red hair brushing his shoulders. "Not for the sake of a lady. I was trying to get some information out of the state bureaucracy."

She led him to her Volkswagen, affordable transportation for the recently immigrated. "You'll come over tonight. I'll be doing," he said.

" 'Doing'?"

"I'm always busy. What I do is a pleasure. Sometimes I do for pay, sometimes not. You come over, maybe I can figure a way for you to join in."

"Sounds interesting."

"More than you can dream," he said.

He careened by her on the road out of town. He drove a vehicle like none she had ever seen. Truck or car? Van? Some of each. As it zoomed away on oversized tires she realized he must have assembled it according to his own original design.

The same was true of his dwelling, she saw with some awe that evening. It wasn't just a house, but a flexible living machine. She recognized original modular construction and specialized natural and artificial lighting designs. Wandering forward onto a cantilevered ramp, she found no recognizable door. Carson's voice emerged from an unseen speaker, giving her directions.

Within she found much of the space was turned over to workshops jammed with lighter tools and electronics. She found Carson in a darkened area where blue laser beams angled off mirrors. He studied results through deeply tinted goggles. He sent her to an adjacent cubbyhole to enter readings into a PC. Over the course of the evening he found out that she had majored in computer science. He asked her penetrating technical questions that she felt challenged to try to answer. She was partially successful.

With no change in style or expression he moved from the electronics workshop into what Trish was forced to think of as the food workshop, rather than the kitchen. Time-tested devices like sink and fridge were there in new guises. Other food-related machines of Carson's design and manufacture were distributed with original logistics throughout the area. He maintained the same right-on laser project energy level while producing the asparagus with dill sauce, curry soufflé, crusty rolls, and apple tart. She was astonished at the ease with which he cooked. Had he mastered that art, too? Meal over, they hurried back to work.

Carson didn't live by the clock. "Internal rhythms decree the best schedule," he said somewhere after two in the morning.

"My rhythms are talking sleep," she said.

"I need you for at least another hour."

Trish smothered a yawn. "If it was a weekend. If I didn't have to go to work . . ."

He shoved his goggles higher onto his forehead. "Quit."

"What?"

"Quit whatever it is you're doing. Work for me. I'll pay you."

"That sounds ridiculous!"

Her first lesson then began on the power of Carson's persuasiveness. She fell into a deep sleep on one of the slumber platforms scattered through "Castle Carson," as he called it. But not before she had agreed to become his employee and settled on pay—three times what she made as a programmer. No benefits, though. Except his company. Or so it seemed then.

In the following months she realized her employment carried some rather unusual perks. The first was ongoing, never-flagging education in liberal arts, in their truest meaning. That meant painting the whole rainbow of human knowledge—from art through technology. Carson made a generous living by incessant invention of electromechanical devices that he turned over to some kind of marketing syndicate. Periodically a grossly fat man called Jethro DuMont arrived for an evening of discussion and check passing. Carson's rights and patents provided a steadily increasing money flow. Some he spent. The rest he invested quite profitably according to statistical models and commodity wave theories of his own conception.

Both Trish and Carson enjoyed standing shoulder-to-shoulder at a task while he carried on a steady monologue explaining what they were doing. Often she had trouble following him. When she told him so, he said not to worry. She was doing better than any other woman so far.

When the mood struck he abandoned his projects and, depending on his destination, selected one of his four vehicles. Off he raced with her to city or mountain to frolic. To her amazement his energy level never decreased. In time she came to understand the reason: He was always enjoying himself. To keep up with him she was forced to increase her own energy. She began to prosper on only six hours of sleep a night. She awoke eagerly to greet the day's activities. The colds that had occasionally plagued her vanished.

Accomplishment was contagious. He spun off subprojects to her, telling her to handle them. She did. Her technical knowledge arced up in a grand curve. Her specialty within his inspired cottage industry was mini- and microcomputers. She understood she couldn't imitate his creativity, the inspired soarings of imagination that turned the familiar inside out, but once he explained even the most general task, she could hurry on alone to move specifics toward the objective.

The initial awe in which she held Carson never completely disappeared. She did, however, spice it with respect and, in time, tenderness. She was in love with him months before daring to admit it to herself, and finally to him. Beneath that special emotion lay the sense of security that he brought to her life. The roots of her need for it, she suspected, led back east to Marylou, who had managed her life like the most enthusiastic stage mother. Now Trish needn't ever take her orders again.

She could take Carson's.

She had moved into Castle Carson six weeks after the party. "A holdout record," Carson mumbled. She asked him how many women had lived there with him. He tossed off a red-browed glower instead of an answer.

Carson's energy, of course, extended to lovemaking. He knew as much about women's bodies as he did about circuit theory. She couldn't help but respond to his artful, fleshy intrusions. Yet she sensed he held back physically and emotionally. As though waiting for . . . she didn't know what. No matter. From the silver strands of her own upward-spiraling spasms she wove gaudy ornamentation into the secret fabric of her love.

By the fourth month of their stay together she accepted his expectation that they spend all their waking time together. At first she had resisted. She did have a few friends with whom she sometimes visited. When he refused to go with her to their homes and insisted she not go without him, she surprised herself by consenting. She felt strangely relieved—delighted even—at having pleased him by giving up another small piece of her freedom. She moved all the closer to the center of his life, twined around him like a morning glory on a mailbox post.

Standing before an exposed circuit board one day, she was surprised when he abruptly interrupted his explanation of its function. He put down his nonconducting pointer. He turned to her, green eyes glowing and narrowed with what she had already learned to recognize as desire. "Do not move!" he said.

"What?"

"Do not play stupid, Queen of My Heart!"

"All right. I won't move, Prince of My Pleasure."

"And you won't talk!" He touched her chin. His face loomed, eyes like lanterns in their intensity. "You won't make any noise at all."

He put his hands in her hair, stirring the bangs. Fingertips touched the curling cartilage of her ears. They moved back into her hair. He was in no hurry. Her initial anxiety faded. She could trust Carson.

In slow time his lips found their way to her forehead, brows, temples bared of their scrim of hair. He licked her lashes and the curve between her lower lip and chin. When she raised her head for a kiss he said, "No!" He seized her chin in firm fingers. "You *do not move!*"

She froze.

He gripped the jumpsuit zipper ring in his teeth and pulled it down to her waist. The soft sponge of his tongue washed around her neck, missing not one square inch of so-sensitive skin. Goose bumps erupted down her right side. *There* was one movement she couldn't stop, she thought.

With her hands at her sides he had no trouble sliding the jumpsuit off her shoulders. His fingers and lips took their own maddening time cruising her collarbones, sweeping thoroughly into depressions and across the curve of her shoulders. So slowly he went. So . . . slowly.

He freed her wrists and slid sleeves down her arms. Jumpsuit top fell away to dangle from her waist to the floor, suggesting abandoned marionettes and tattered Raggedy Anns. He turned his patient attentions to her back and chest around the satiny bra. Around and around, but never . . . She wanted to ask him to go *ahead* but knew he wouldn't like it. She understood they were playing a game but didn't mind. It was . . . interesting.

From the workbench he took a pair of pruning shears, waved them before her face. She was startled. He pressed them against her lips. Instinctively she kissed the flats of the cool, gleaming blades. That was allowed!

He snipped away her bra. She recoiled from the chill of the metal on her soft flesh. "No!" She gasped and stiffened.

"Stand still!"

She shuddered but obeyed.

He unzipped and clipped until she was standing naked, weak drafts raising more goose bumps. He stepped back to admire her, clicking the shears as though he had somehow fashioned her with them. His eyes were narrowed—with displeasure. He suddenly jabbed the points against the white swell of her left breast. She cried out at the sudden pain, though the skin wasn't broken.

"You weren't obedient enough," he said.

"I tried."

"You need some assistance." He stepped forward and picked her up, cradling her in his solid arms. He carried her to the closest sleeping bay. There he stretched her, face up. "Raise your arms. Touch your wrists together. Close your eyes."

She obeyed.

She heard a rattle and felt a new metallic chill.

"Open your eyes."

Carson's face was above her, a tiny smile curling the left corner of his mouth. He pointed toward her hands. "Look."

She was handcuffed.

"Gotcha!" he said.

Later she understood that exercise in standing and snipping had been both a test and an initiation. Into just what she was too naïve to understand and, even much later, could not put into exact words. She had no deep understanding of psychology. Had she, possibly she could have attached some comforting euphemisms to his opening the bargaining for her soul.

Still the days were sunny. She and Carson worked happily together. She learned from him that in effective lives, work and play were truly indistinguishable. She added much to her store of technical information, prided herself on becoming more valuable to him. In time he came to fill her life like a vast sun around which the planet of her days turned in slow orbit. Her past diminished; the future seemed beyond reach. Carson, Carson, Carson, her heart sang—even as the handcuffs gave way to silken bonds and the unexpected pain of a jabbed breast to more ingenious but no more physically damaging torture.

She might have continued as his sole satellite until her orbit gradually shrank and she fell too close to the fiery orb of his personality—and perished. She understood later she had neither the strength nor mental toughness to fight free of his domination. She could thank Marylou for prepping her personality for the likes of Carson. Oh, yes, there was a very real danger that Patricia Morley, as previously known, might disappear. Except that . . .

Carson's personality began to disintegrate.

The seeds of disintegration lay in the years he had spent in Vietnam. There he had been an interpreter. He learned languages effortlessly, knew at least a dozen. Through typical military misthinking he ended up carrying out dangerous covert assignments. He talked little of those days. He didn't have to; more than once he woke up screaming. When she questioned him he said he was fine.

Slowly, over months, he began to focus more of his time and attention on her. Already his slave, she felt he was trying to totally eliminate what remained of her independence. So many orders he gave! They fell like sleet on all her waking moments. Just as he could not separate work from play, she could no longer tell over the long sweeps of their violating intimacy when she gave physical pleasure or received it. Commands, bonds, pain smeared into a palette so wild as to make Pollock seem a paint-by-numbers cretin.

The declining Carson's orders became unreasonable, impossible to obey. So the periods of her punishment grew longer, their tools more outrageous. Her humiliation extended like a cancer. She pleaded her case. His pocked face turned stony. "Tell me that you don't enjoy it, and I'll stop." A false promise to counter her somehow false plea. Hadn't her shrieks of delight echoed from high piny ceiling when not transformed into beastly grunts by gags gentle and less so?

Her outward determination, in the face of his opposition, slunk away like a jackal. Inwardly it grew. She had to get away from him! Her sense of time grew inexact. More months passed. She told herself she was going to make a break, escape. In fact, only time was getting away.

On an errand to an electronics supply house several towns down the freeway she stopped for lunch at a plaza where a fountain ran and greenery burst from boxes. A musician entertained the crowd with violin, trumpet, and a devastating wit. He requested volunteers for a skit. Two little boys were quick to fill parts. He needed a woman, too. When no one came forward he selected Trish. He gathered his impromptu troupe and gave them instructions.

He was tall and sandy-haired. His quick smile exposed large, uneven teeth and hinted at an inspired sense of humor. When the performance ended he joined Trish, who was finishing her salad. "I can put you in show business," he said. "I heard you sing. Can you dance? I can make you a star!"

Telling herself she had to leave, she nonetheless stayed and chatted. His name was Ron Verner. He played his instruments wherever he could get booked, from studio sessions to gigs like today's, working for parks and recreation departments. He was open and grinny. She liked him. Though he did most of the talking, when she rose to leave he said, "Why is such a sweet lady so sad?"

Almost against her will she wrote his phone number on the back of a cash register receipt, explaining he couldn't call her. She rushed off like Cinderella to her cruel stepmother. On the way back to Castle Carson she memorized Ron's number and fluttered the receipt out the window because nothing escaped her master's green-eyed gaze. Two weeks passed before he asked her to run another errand. She was delighted; she dared not try to arrange an absence herself. He was so shrewd that he'd fall upon any deviousness like hawk on rabbit.

Her afternoon with Ron sped by in what seemed an instant. When they parted tears smeared her eyes. His gentleness and sympathy fell like a searchlight on the hostile landscape of what her life had become under Carson's rule. She despaired because opportunities to meet her new friend could come only so rarely.

As though to fulfill her hopes Carson committed himself to a lucrative project that required that he travel for a period. He devoted the day before departure to exercising his pleasure at the expense of her submission. By now she greeted these sessions with inner bewilderment. Despite superficial denials of the roles of pain and obedience in her arousal, she climbed to ever higher reaches of ecstasy under his mental and physical lashings. As for him, no mythological satyr could outdo his tireless penetrations of her orifices. When even he was sated he turned to what he called "tricks of the trade," electromechanical devices of his own design. This day he had a new one. He held up one of a set of six silvery snails. "This, Queen of My Heart, is a whizbang. . . ."

He was no sooner on his way to the airport than she rushed to Ron Verner's side. He had a recording studio built onto the side of his small house. There amid speakers and equalizers she pulled him down onto a thinly padded cot, weeping as though from a beating, fingers sunk like claws into his shirt shoulders. "Love me, love me," she cried. "Love me like a normal man!"

She could not dare to have Ron come to stay with her in

Castle Carson, nor could she be long away from there. Carson always called unpredictably. She had to have an excuse for her absences, as though he was still in residence. As to nights, she slept chaste as a nun, hands jammed against her groin. Still she met with Ron seven times during Carson's absence. They made love fifteen times; Carson had led her to the habit of counting. So she would understand that "no one you will ever know could want you more than I." Indeed, how could a mere mortal like Ron reach Carson's astronomical number of performances? Resisting at first, she ultimately told Ron everything about herself and about the man it was all too easy to call "master."

Doodling on his electric keyboards, he pondered and composed "An Exercise for Three Personalities". "Trish's Theme" began as a tranquil melody that leapt into jangly arpeggios. "Carson" was a march with a bass line growling like a demented Wagner leitmotif. His own theme was a lighthearted folk tune. He combined the three, fingers flying over the keys like white sticks in a hurricane. Themes linked, intertwined, spread apart, then joined. He looked at her as he wrapped up the piece.

Carson's theme burst forth, triumphant.

It told her that Ron had a clear understanding of the extent to which he was overmatched. "You'll have to make a sudden, complete disappearance," he said. "It's your only hope with a man like that. I'm not a shrink, but it sounds like his head is getting worse in a hurry."

They talked about how she could make her escape. The answers didn't come easily. Sitting beside him, the bowl of her adoration filling and overflowing, she sank her fingers into his unkempt brown mane. "Who does your hair?" she laughed. "Briggs and Stratton Grasseater?"

"I do—if I think about it."

"Get the scissors," she said.

She did a great job—at least he thought so. Her reward was a copy of the tape of "An Exercise" and frantic lovemaking that continued to nearly Carsonian lengths.

Sentimental slob, she scooped a pinch of hair from the floor and slipped it into a compartment of her change purse.

A month later she realized she was pregnant. Her recent behavior allowed no certainty about which man was responsible. Her initial thought was an abortion. She twisted away from that destructive act. What at first seemed a problem could in fact prove to be an opportunity. A child would weigh favorably on the scale of her struggle against Carson. She badly needed an ally in her battle for the survival of, if not her soul, at least her personality. So what if that champion was unborn? She knew enough of Carson, the egomaniac mystic, to presume he would exult at the chance to pass along his genes. After the child was born she might somehow find a way to use it as a lever to pry herself away from him. She pressed palms to flat belly and spoke a silent prayer for a full-term, healthy baby. Let that be first, she prayed. Then let the infant somehow grow to set her free. For three days she worked at steeling her nerve and perfecting her chosen role: the delighted mother-to-be. Then she went to Carson and told him he was going to be a father.

"You'll bear my child," he ordered. "I'll teach him to be Master of the Universe!"

There followed two weeks of intense work during which she could not leave Carson's side. She wanted to share her news with Ron. Sometimes Carson worked with a TV on, turned always to the news channel. "Talking heads telling us lies," he mumbled, and who dared disagree? The local news sometimes touched on the familiar. One afternoon it touched a great deal more.

A news face announced that the previous night Ron Verner was killed in a one-car accident.

While she dreamed beside Carson, Ron had fallen asleep at the wheel. His Toyota hit a concrete bridge support. Dead at the scene. She could not completely swallow her cry of anguish. It emerged as a harsh cough. Her eyes glued themselves to the screen, where the car in which she had once sat was shown squashed as though with a junkyard pneumatic press. The TV station had found Ron's publicity photograph. His young, handsome face bloomed before her for the last time. She set her teeth, muscles marching across her jaw.

"What's he to you?" Carson asked sharply.

"I saw him playing trumpet for kids in a park one day. The nice guys always buy it." Inwardly she begged to be believed.

"So he'll be playing a harp from now on."

"Guess so." She turned back to her work. She was too frightened to grieve!

Nor could she free herself from Carson the rest of the day. Ironically his desire for her seemed to have been stimulated by news of her condition. He led her to the largest sleeping platform at eight that evening. Fourteen hours later he finally tumbled into sleep. Run away! she thought. *Run away now!* But his demands—and her abhorred but no less enthusiastic response—had left her utterly drained. She had strength only for weeping. Weep she did, until a comalike sleep powerful as death overcame her.

In days to come she understood Carson's unparalleled orgy. He had no intention of touching her again until his child was born. She was now sanctified by pregnancy. Oh, she was still his slave, fetching and obeying, but as her time came closer his demands dwindled, then finally disappeared altogether. Nights he ordered her to bare her abdomen. He rubbed oil into her humped belly with surprisingly gentle fingers.

More than her bondage was on hold during that time. She sensed that his descent into derangement had somehow been checked, too. The tranquillity of the first weeks of their relationship returned like an Indian summer before the bleak winter that she imagined would follow her child's birth.

In her private, brooding moments she prayed that Ron was the child's father. To give birth to a spawn of Carson worsened by tons the weight of the advantage he had already taken of her. In hopes of lightening the psychological burden of motherhood she asked him to marry her. He laughed—deliberately fiendishly, she thought.

In time there came that moment when the child was raised above her torn and bloody loins for her admiration.

Drugged and exhausted, she nonetheless felt her heart sink.

The girl had red hair!

Carson came to pick her and the child up two days later. She buckled herself into the convertible, the unfamiliar creature safely webbed into a car seat. He took an automatic pistol out of his pocket.

"What's that for?" she asked.

"That was to use on you if the kid wasn't perfect," he said matter-of-factly. "I don't hold it being a girl against you."

She stared disbelieving at him. His face carried evil secrets she couldn't read.

In the weeks immediately following she made the decision to stay with Carson for Melody's sake. She was gambling that the reversal in his mental deterioration would continue. He was very well off financially. Castle Carson was clean and spacious, its grounds generous. The child would thrive. She told herself that someday she would change things, but she wasn't sure just when. She remembered her late lover's words: "a sudden, complete disappearance."

Nearly four years passed. In later times she blocked out what might be called Carson's and her intimate moments. Her memories overflowed instead with the unfolding joys of motherhood. Asked earlier, she would have scoffed at her nurturing capacity. Surprise! She took to Melody like lightning to a tall pine.

She was an easy child to love—even-tempered and gentle. In her eighteenth month she surprised Trish by reacting to radio rock. She beat time with her right hand. Shortly afterward she began to sing along—not the words, of course, just the tunes.

She was never off-key.

Carson was quick to be fascinated and to encourage this unusual talent. When Melody was two he gave her a mouth organ. She needed only a week of huffing and puffing to learn how to play the melodies that were already accumulating in her curly red head. At three he bought her a kazoo and slide whistle.

Two hours to learn to get music out of both.

Melody sat for hours tootling recognizable tunes. Trish sang to her—and back came the melodies kazooed or whistled with unfailing accuracy.

On her fourth birthday they gave her a soprano recorder. She sparkled and bubbled. "I can get so many more notes now!" she said with a laugh.

Shortly afterward she discovered she was able to whistle. And whistle she did! She would begin with the tune as she had heard it, then wander off into similar ones that Trish dimly realized were versions in different keys.

Proud mother was delighted with her child's talent. It was a generous bonus to the gift of Melody's existence. Where would Trish be without her?

She thanked her daughter not only for helping her to keep her sanity, but for keeping her alive. Carson never threatened her in the child's presence. Realizing that, she kept Melody with her continually. As the girl's third year passed her father's personality resumed its decline. While formerly continually busy and balanced, now long moments of inactivity appeared in his days like holes in cloth emerging from a loom. He sat staring, silent, mind screwed into some distant, incomprehensible wood.

The unfamiliar woolgathering was interrupted by periods in which he again became the inspired satyr. Without the shield of pregnancy Trish had to endure his relentlessly more imaginative and painful attentions. During the worst of them she would have wanted to die—if she hadn't experienced such exquisite pleasure and wasn't a mother.

Thus it became plain that she was bound to him by two things: his inhuman sexuality and his being Melody's father. The first was destroying her; she was deeply addicted to pleasure-through-submission. The second she hated to accept. She had so hoped that Ron . . .

A phone conversation with a friend while Carson was away turned to a recent court case in which determining paternity played a big role. Attorneys had settled the matter with the help of the testimony of a doctor who had presented irrefutable DNA-related evidence. Trish imagined she didn't need state-of-the-art methods to prove what two heads of red hair in the same house strongly suggested. Nonetheless, on a whim she asked her friend, "Do you remember the doctor's name?"

She phoned Dr. Norrington's office, introduced herself as Carole Sieber, and spoke with his nurse. She explained how the tests were conducted and how much they cost. "Of course, we have to have a tissue sample from the child and the two men involved." Trish groaned. Ron was more than three years in his grave.

Over weeks Carson's broodings extended themselves. As they did his control over her eased. She came and went more freely, using Melody as an excuse for one errand or another. It was during this time that she revisited Dr. Norrington's office. In three envelopes she carried hair: Melody's, Carson's, and, from the deepest recesses of her memory trunk, the lock snipped from Ron's head as a souvenir of love. The nurse looked carefully at the three samples. "I'm betting on the redhead," she said cheerily. When tears leaked down Trish's cheeks the woman apologized, blushing.

Two weeks later Trish personally got the test results—guaranteed accurate. Her dream came true. Ron was Melody's father! The hair? "Recessive genes on both sides, maybe," the nurse said. "Happens sometimes."

She walked out of the office, half liberated. Nothing held her to Carson now but the bonds woven by domination. She would break them cold turkey. First, though, she had to escape her master.

She began to execute a plan for a clean getaway. Her intuition suggested more violent changes would soon occur in Carson's personality. He was already turning his newfound hostility against those with whom he did business. Jethro DuMont, the check-bearer, became a target. During his last visit the two had argued loudly, spurred by Carson's intransigence.

She felt she didn't have much time.

She phoned a distant travel agency and requested all their material on Alaska. When it arrived in the mail she hid it in a niche inside an A/C outlet. She mail-ordered an auburn wig, stashed it beside the brochures. That was the easy part. The rest would be more difficult. With cotton jammed between gums and cheeks, wig in place above sunglasses, she cruised neighboring communities. At last she made a friend at a mall supermarket thirty-five miles from Castle Carson. Eileen, a black-haired part-time checkout girl, was Trish's height. Without her thick glasses she might well . . . do.

Trish worked hard to develop the friendship, found Eileen to be perfect—a free spirit fond of travel but short of money. When they met occasionally Eileen was always happy when her auburn-haired friend Carole picked up the check. At the right moment Trish explained how Eileen could be a big help to her. Understand, Eileen, I'm married to a man whose five stepchildren I'm raising. He beats me. I have a lover who just left the area to make a new start. When he calls I have to be ready to go—right then! This is how you can help me, and this is what's in it for you. . . .

She had to wait, then, for Carson's deteriorating personality to lead to a crisis. The next visit of Jethro DuMont provided it. She huddled in hearing distance as their quarrel climbed to the shouting level. Carson began to howl long and low like an enraged animal. She tensed and clenched her teeth. Doors slammed. DuMont's voice rose still higher. Carson's pistol snapped like a whip. Trish whimpered. Jethro's meaty shout was followed by his heavy running footsteps.

This was her chance. She flew to her hiding niche. She donned the wig and sunglasses, inserted the cotton pads under her cheeks. She pulled out the cache of Alaska materials and hid it in one of her closets, where Carson would eventually find it. On the floor sat the getaway sack purse she had carefully filled in preparation for just this moment. She snatched it up. That left her other arm free to wrap around Melody's waist. She slipped out into the carport, got behind the wheel of the convertible. She saw the flash of Carson's pistol off to the right. She started the engine and flew out of the carport in reverse. She spun the wheel and shot up the drive. The house was between her and the two men. In minutes she was on the road, the only sounds those of the engine and a sleepy daughter's questions. She sped to a pay phone and dialed Eileen's number. "Now. Tonight! Yeah, at the L.A. airport. Meet you where we decided."

At the airport she paid cash for four tickets. One-way on the next flight to Fairbanks for Patricia Morley, who would be Eileen. An open-ended return for Eileen, real name. Enjoy! It was eight-to-one men-to-women up there. Never mind that Alaskan women said, "The odds are good, but the goods are odd." The third ticket was for Carole Sieber, the fourth for daughter "Annie," both one-way to Chicago. There she would book a flight the rest of the way east.

She got a surprise from Eileen. "You can forget about the wig and sunglasses, Trish," she said. "I figured out who you are. You're the one lives with that weirdo inventor out in Spires Canyon in that house from another planet."

Trish's face twisted with alarm. "You musn't say—"

"Hey, I dunno nothing. You want to get away from Carson Thomas, that's cool with me. You oughta tell me sometime why you decided to have his kid."

"I won't be seeing you again. I'm going . . . away."

"Good. Just the same, you need anything, call me," Eileen said. "I won't be in Alaska forever—unless I get lucky. And I never been lucky."

Just before her plane left, Trish went to a pay phone. While Melody hugged her knees she lifted the receiver with a shaking hand. She had to enter the number sequence three times before she got it right. The call went through. The voice she hadn't heard in eight years spoke with the inescapability of history.

Trish's words burst from her throat in the desperate rush she had so hoped to avoid. "Mother . . . Mother, I'm coming home!"

12

TRISH, CARSON, AND MELODY—*TOGETHER FOREVER!*

She let the photograph slide from her fingers. It swooped down to the floor, again falling face up, as though to add to her torment. She had never suspected that Carson was behind all that had happened. *Carson!* Her heart sank at that prospect, at his . . . inevitability.

Over the last three years when, despite herself, her mind swung toward him she had hoped that the increasing mental instability in which she had left him had led to incapacitating madness. Time and distance, though comforting, failed to guarantee her safety as much as would word of his institutionalization or violent death. She was certain that he had been in major decline. Where had that dangerous current ultimately carried him?

She glanced at her watch. It was still a reasonable hour—in California. Through information she found Eileen's number. So she hadn't gotten lucky in Alaska. A man answered. Maybe California was treating her better now. Eileen squealed at hearing Trish's voice. They raced straight into pleasantries, brought each other up to date on their lives. Eileen had spent more than two years in Alaska. "I had a ball! But, hey, you can't really *live* there." When old news had been covered Trish could contain herself no longer.

"Important question, Eileen," she said. "What do you hear about Carson Thomas?"

Instead of replying Eileen shouted at her companion that she needed a few minutes of privacy. Several moments later she resumed talking. Three women physicians and their young daughters had been murdered. The same method had been used to kill the doctors—smothering. "Dead wasn't good enough for him," Eileen said. "He finished up by cutting off toes, fingers, ears, nipples—you name it—and piling them on their bellies. They think he used heavy shears. He killed the little girls by somehow tearing their guts wide open."

Trish shuddered. "Why are you telling me this?"

"They're calling him 'The Doctor and Daughter Destroyer.'"

"What's this have to do with Carson?"

"I'll get to that."

"Were they all the same kind of doctor? Maybe psychiatrists?"

"Huh-uh. First one was a nose and throat surgeon. The second, the paper said, was a tummy and tit tucker. Third one was a gynecologist. He got her maybe six months ago. Three isn't many the way these serial guys go. But he got *doctors*. So the whole California AMA is jumping around. And the papers love writing about it. 'Was the DDD Overcharged?' Stuff like that."

"Carson? What about *Carson?*" Couldn't Eileen hear her urgency?

"You didn't tell me he wasted a guy the day we left."

So he had shot Jethro DuMont down in cold blood. "I didn't hang around to find out, Eileen," Trish said. "Did they catch him?"

"Nope. I called my mom to tell her I was in Alaska, and she got talking about it, 'cause it was in the local paper."

"What's Carson have to do with the Doctor and Daughter Destroyer?"

Eileen lowered her voice. "Look, Trish, the guy I'm living with is a reporter. He's covered some of the case. He said that after the second murder the cops made Carson Thomas one of the suspects."

"Why did they do that?"

"They wouldn't tell him."

"Could he find out?"

"Trish, what do you care? You're three thousand miles away."

She swallowed. "I think he found me. He's starting to destroy my life."

Eileen swore determinedly. "Oh, my God. My God! It makes sense."

"What does?"

"After I got back from Alaska I met an old buddy who talked to Carson after he killed the guy and was dodging the cops. Before the first doctor was murdered. Carson said your running out was worse for him than being mixed up in a murder. He said that you were responsible for whatever he was becoming. Can you imagine that?"

Trish recalled Carson's mad intensity. "Yes, I can."

"He said he'd never forgive you. Never really let you go. I mean, come on, he was nutty."

"That sounds so like him." Trish was aware of the leaden weight of her voice. "Now he's going to ruin my life to get even."

"I can't believe it! Are you sure?"

"Yes. Definitely."

After promising to call Trish if her friend could find out anything more, Eileen hung up. Trish stumbled to bed and thrashed about, arms wrapped around her extra pillow. Sleep? Sometime. Carson's face loomed up in the darkness, realistic as a hologram. So he had killed Jethro DuMont for sure, and possibly three doctors and their little girls. He had been enraged at DuMont over some imagined business-related insult. But why had he killed the doctors? And their children! Seven people!

And he held her responsible.

Had she really thought she could escape her past?

Now all the disorders of the California years were crowding closer. She saw her business, her wedding, her future overturned like carts before onrushing horsemen. Worse, she imagined herself bound again to Carson Thomas, never to escape.

She had attempted to hide the past. Now the time had come to confess something of what had happened. How much to expose of the saga of Carson and Queen of My Heart she couldn't decide that fevered night. Regardless, her next step was obvious.

She had to talk to Foster.

She asked to meet him for dinner at the yacht club. He was always more mellow in familiar surroundings. When she got there she was surprised to find he had reserved one of the private dining rooms, as though he knew their conversation was to be most private.

He wore a white silk jacket that showed off his deepened tan. He had spent the day out on the water. Walking with him through the main dining room, she couldn't help but notice the covetous glances tossed his way by women middle-aged and younger. And why not? He was tall, dark, well-mannered, and very rich. And she was very lucky.

In some ways, at least.

She should have guessed from the table location that Foster brought his own agenda. As soon as their mimosas were served he got to it. He told her Nicholas Smith-Patton had insisted on meeting with him and Lois. He had some important information to share about Trish's problems.

Inwardly Trish writhed. She did not like Foster repeatedly being put into Lois's presence. She sensed live embers still survived in the doused campfire of their attraction. "Why couldn't Nicholas have talked just to you, Foster? Why did Lois have to be there?"

"Nicholas insisted."

"I don't like you hanging around Lois."

"Nicholas told me it was his wish—not his sister's—that we meet."

Trish snorted. "She put him up to it. You know she controls him."

He sipped his mimosa. "I'm telling you the meeting was a surprise to Lois. I sense some . . . shifting in their relationship. Nicholas has become more assertive."

Trish was relieved. Possibly Nicholas was keeping his word not to betray her to Lois. That would depend on what he reported. "So what did Nicholas tell you?" she asked.

Foster told her the stringy man had explained that Trish's recent troubles originated with an unknown person who had done dangerous business, including bugging her business. She wasn't to be blamed for having accused him and Lois. She had been frightened. And with good reason. Whoever it was that wanted the wedding canceled was very clever.

"I arranged for us to be able to talk privately for two reasons," Foster said. "First thing is I want to apologize for being . . . uncooperative when you asked me to talk to Lois. I didn't fully appreciate how upset you were. I'm sorry."

She smiled. He was a good man! "Apology accepted."

"Second, I want to help you figure out who has it in for you enough to do these things, Trish. I won't have our wedding interfered with!"

She covered his hand with hers. She found his determination touching. When viewed in the light of Carson's lunatic genius it seemed . . . quaint. She smiled. "That's the reason I wanted to talk to you, too. I *know* who doesn't want the wedding. I want to tell you about him—and me."

The briefest shadow of a frown passed over Foster's wide brow. "Then it's someone you know."

"Someone I used to know. I left him behind in California—I thought."

Had she meant to make a totally clean breast of the saga of Carson and Queen of My Heart? If so, she failed miserably. What escaped her lips was a bowdlerized version of a relationship whose intimacy burst all normal bounds. How could Foster Palmer of West Thorn Point, Princeton, and Lake Country Kennels grasp the essentials of her domination? To explain that required her to analyze the intricate escapement of her mind's watch movement that had allowed her to play her role with such disgusting enthusiasm. She was dismayed to find she couldn't confess. Instead she hid the open cesspool with verbal lilies.

"So this Carson Thomas was your husband?" Foster asked.

"No, that was another man. Ron. He was killed in an auto accident." Oh, Lord, she was buying into her mother's deceptions! She had never been within twenty feet of an altar.

"Ron, then, was Melody's father."

"Yes." At least that was true.

"I see." She couldn't read his thin smile. "You were rather . . . a busy woman in California, I see."

"I was young and stupid. I didn't have a monopoly on that."

"Let's order dinner, shall we?"

She sensed his shift to coolness. It convinced her that she had done the smart thing in soft-pedaling the twisted nature of her relationship with Carson. Nonetheless, she hadn't begun to touch on his personality. That she absolutely had to do. When the squash soup arrived, she said, "Foster, you have to understand what kind of man Carson is."

"I'm sure he puts his pants on one leg at a time."

"Don't underestimate him!" The sudden raw tone of her voice made him put down his spoon. "He's off the mental scale in two ways. First, he's an authentic genius. Second, he seems to have gone crazy. When he was sane he never followed the rules written for the rest of us. Now that he's slipped over the line, God knows what he's capable of doing. That he's back in my life again terrifies me. Totally! You can't imagine how dangerous a man he is."

Foster went back to his soup. "I sense some exaggeration here."

"None whatever!" Trish's appetite was gone. She had set herself an impossible task: trying to explain Carson without being honest about her relationship with him. She tried further. "Listen, Foster. Carson Thomas was always a devil. On top of it he's now a lunatic." She met his gaze, unblinking. "I talked to a friend on the coast last night. There's a strong possibility he's killed seven people!"

Later Foster insisted that his spoon just happened to slip at that moment. He hadn't even been startled, let alone frightened. Trish thought differently. If she had ever thought her fiancé a match for Carson, that idea was dashed out like the gobbets of orange that flew from Foster's bowl to soil the sweeping sheen of his white silk jacket.

Shortly he said, "It's quite clear what we must do next, Trish. I'll speak to Father. He has some ins with the police department."

Friday morning at ten Foster led her to the police commissioner's office. The commissioner was short and tanned, half cop, half politician. He handled introductions. Standing beside the expansive mahogany desk was a handsome graying man wearing a suit tailored skillfully to his burly form. His heavy lips moved into a weak smile as he was identified as Lieutenant Sarkman. No warmth crept into his pale blue eyes as they shook hands.

With him stood two men. The first was a familiar figure, Lieutenant Stanley of the bomb squad. He announced no real progress on the law firm bombing. Trish much preferred him to Sarkman, even though he chided her gently. "You shoulda told me all this new stuff," he said.

The second man was introduced as Detective Jerry Morris. He was tall, lean-faced, and serious. The commissioner said he would be assisting Detective Sarkman. They would be the principal investigators. Lieutenant Stanley would do all he could from the bomb end.

The commissioner played his role. He expressed his sincere regrets over whatever difficulties the Palmer family was encountering, then bowed out. Sarkman, "very possibly my best detective," would take over from here on out. Morris would assist him. Of course, if there was anything more that he could do . . .

The two detectives led Foster and Trish to a room where a tape recorder was set up. Sarkman took Trish's statement, guiding her with questions familiar to him. They slipped off his tongue so readily that he sounded bored. Worse, she had the distinct feeling he didn't like her or Foster but was too professional to show it. She was still talking when he reached over and turned off the recorder. "I think that'll do it, Ms. Morley."

"I had a little more to say."

He shrugged and looked at the other detective. "We get the picture, don't we, Jerry? We got a classic situation here. We got a jealous former lover who can't stand to have been beaten out by Mr. Palmer here. So he tries threats and malicious mischief. Tries to spy on you, stuff like that." He looked from Trish's face to Foster's. "Nothing very serious, from the police standpoint."

"But Carson is—"

"A weirdo. Okay. There are lots of weirdos around. Jerry and I have met our share. What we usually do is find them and give them a warning. All of a sudden their lost love doesn't seem so important compared to doing short time." He lifted the photo of Trish, Carson, and Melody. "We know what he looks like. It won't take that long to find him. Just leave it to us."

"When can we expect to hear from you, Lieutenant Sarkman?" Foster said. "With a report."

The cop's flinty eyes narrowed. "Hard to say." He got up. "I'll be candid. Malicious mischief isn't my specialty."

"What is?" Trish said.

"Murders."

She said quickly, "I've been told Carson killed one person for sure, and possibly six others."

Sarkman blinked. That at least had brought him up short. "We'll run a check on that through to the coast. Your man hasn't killed anybody here. And I have two dozen local murders on my plate." He waved a manicured hand. "All I can say is Jerry and I will do our best and get back to you sometime soon."

Trish wanted to say so much more about Carson and how anxious she had become since learning he had returned to her life. More, she wanted to explain how formidable an adversary he would be to Lieutenants Sarkman and Morris —or anyone else. There was no time. Sarkman escorted them out briskly, making confident, comforting noises. Morris strode silently in their wake.

On the street she looked at Foster. "They didn't take us too seriously. They didn't like us, either. At least Sarkman didn't. I really couldn't read Detective Morris."

Foster nodded. "I've met many like Sarkman. No, he didn't like us. The reason is simple."

"Oh? What is it?"

"We're haves. He's a have-not."

"And we became his problem because of your family's political pull." Trish glowered. "How can he really care about my problems with Carson? Murder's his specialty. And Carson doesn't want to murder me. He just wants me not to marry you. Sarkman's the wrong man for us. With the wrong attitude." She looked up at Foster. "It wouldn't surprise me if he did absolutely nothing to help us!" She made a note to call Detective Morris. Her instincts told her he didn't share his partner's prejudices.

That evening Nicholas arrived at Trish's home, unannounced as always. In the shadows his wide eyes looked like those of a nocturnal insect, and he spoke about as often as one. Melody sat, soprano recorder on her lap, and stared after his comings and goings. From his van he removed a meter unfamiliar to Trish. He hung it around his neck and slipped on earphones. He wandered her rooms like a silent ghost. Another device in hand, he skirted the rambling house, vanishing into the shrubbery, emerging head down, eyes on a dial.

He summoned Trish away from Melody. In the kitchen he whispered, "Two videocams, sound and picture. One in the living room, the other in your bedroom. No others."

Trish gasped. "How—"

"Doesn't matter."

"I talked to the police today. They should know about this."

Nicholas shrugged. He didn't look at her as he said, "I'll take the cameras out, if you want."

"Yes!"

"He'll know, then."

"Know what?"

"That you know about him. That I know."

Trish tapped her foot nervously. "I can't be spied on like this!"

Nicholas nodded vigorously, his Adam's apple seeming to rise and fall. "Blitzing the cameras will announce you're resisting."

She guessed what that would mean to Carson. The more she struggled, the more he would be provoked, the more extreme his responses.

"Take them out tomorrow," she said in a dry voice. "I'll give you a key." She was joining a battle she could never win.

She asked Nicholas if he had been able to locate the receiver to which the PC-Pros' bugs sent their signals. He shook his head, turning away as though in shame for having failed her. What an odd man! "It's okay," she said. "Just keep trying. If you find it, I'll tell the police. They can go in and arrest Carson."

Somehow she knew it wouldn't be that easy.

Shortly after she put Melody in bed Foster phoned. He wanted to visit. She sensed some urgency in his voice. He walked through the door, arms out. He gave her a tremendous hug. She melted against him. He took off his glasses and kissed her. She couldn't mistake his desire.

He sat and pulled her down on his lap. "This—business that's going on. This man who's making these threats . . ." He turned her face up. "We can't let him interfere with our happiness."

She nodded. "I know."

"I assume you're continuing to make wedding plans."

"My mother's lunging ahead full tilt. I'm doing what she asks. It's . . . backwards. But it's working."

"There will be a wedding!" he said, hugging her harder than ever.

"Yes!"

"I came to tell you that I love you, Trish! The last few weeks have been awkward for us. I know how you feel about my seeing Lois. But your asking Nicholas's help has drawn her into view again. It can't be helped. Don't doubt how I feel about you. Compared to you, Lois is . . . very much less what she once was to me. I want to add that I'm sympathetic to your anxiety about this man Carson Thomas, even though I feel you're exaggerating. I'll stand beside you until he's taken care of one way or the other."

She hugged him, needing the feel of his smooth back.

"Please believe that even though the Palmer/Morley duo has been under some pressure, we're more together than ever," he said.

She recalled her mother's advice. "Foster, let's go away together for a long weekend! I very much want to—and soon. Why don't you pick a place and make the arrangements?"

He nodded and smiled. "I will, my love. Great idea!"

She kissed him. He was here for one further piece of business. . . .

When he tried to lead her to the bedroom she hesitated. The camera . . . Then she reconsidered. Carson was watching. Let him! Let him know that her commitment to Foster Palmer was total. The message would be so direct, so ruthless, that even he might realize the impossibility of his demands. She and Foster would marry and live happily ever after. They had resealed their vows just moments before. Let her nemesis behold their consummation. Then Nicholas would remove the cameras. . . .

Atop her and eager as ever, Foster slowed his pace to prolong the act, practicing his modest sexual techniques. My little vanilla wafer in the vast bake shop of the erotic, she thought wistfully, and she wished for Linzer tortes, Black Forest cakes, *bûches de Noël!* No matter. She loved him. She gripped his shoulders when a ripple of pleasure stirred. As he grunted toward completion her fingers curled. She felt the points of her nails against his skin—and drove them in. Three bent and broke with the pressure. He cried out, startled at the mild, unexpected pain that drove his own pleasure to its crest. He bellowed at release—something new! Sly Trish had spurred his delight. Sweet surprise, my love! I carry so many more to share, if you wish, piled up like Christmas gifts in a loving mother's arms. She cooed and slithered her tongue up his trembling shoulders to suck away the few salty drops of blood.

Carson who?

13

CHAMP STEERED THE RENTAL CAR WITH HIS LEFT HAND. The right was busy on the portable console lying on the passenger seat. Ahead Trish's Acura was caught in heavy traffic. He imagined her irritation this hot day. Did the dew of sweat fall on the soft skin below her hairline, on the pert curve of her upper lip, as it had under the heat of lust's sun? He had made himself master of her earlier face and figure, plundered from the Scheherazade tapes like booty from a pirated vessel. The cameras in her home had allowed him to etch the sensitive plate of his incredible memory with the vision of today's Queen of My Heart. Carson would be glad to hear her shape was intact, seemingly as immune to passing months as a prehistoric insect trapped in the slow drip of amber.

In moments alone in her bedroom she had been careless with post-shower towels, tossing them aside on the way to underwear or pajamas. At those so-rare instants—ah, the trials of a voyeur!—her white skin blossomed for him with the power and brilliance of a Fourth of July star shell.

And last night! Last night had compensated him for the hours staring at her sleeping form or at her fully dressed bustling to and from the bathroom. Carson's rival, the

147

Loathed One, had possessed her beneath the unfailing Nipponese eye. Banzai! Champ looked on in a frenzy of arousal. He could no more keep his hands from his body than not draw breath. Queen . . . Queen . . . Queen of Carson's Heart! He spasmed repeatedly, moaning at his master's once and future good fortune.

His loathing for Carson's rival exploded into Earthquake Anger so quickly that he scarcely had time to strap himself into Siege Restraint. All manner of violence his imagination allowed him to work on the tall man. He thrashed and fought his bonds. His howls reached such levels that dwellers in distant apartments, unheard till now, raised angry shouts for silence. He heaved and howled on, chair legs flogging the floor. . . .

Now, today, memories of last night's torrents of sights and emotions flooded in afresh. Sweat sprang out on his face, and he wrung his hands like a madhouse tenant. He moaned amid the horn blares of the impatient. No matter the condition of his mind, he had his orders—and his equipment.

The override device hooked into the FM frequency. Yes! He turned a dial to kill the station on Queen of My Heart's car radio, so lovingly removed and tampered with last night while her sweet breath perfumed the pillow. He picked the hand mike out of its cradle. He altered his voice's inflection and tone and said, "Trish, Carson, and Melody—together forever! *Trish, Carson, and Melody—together forever!*" He couldn't suppress his chuckle when he pressed the console button that disabled her radio's on-off switch. Now he had a mini PA system with which to broadcast Carson's theme. "Trish, Carson, and Melody—together forever!" he bellowed.

Ahead horns blared afresh. Queen of My Heart had stalled her car. It sat in the middle of the intersection, keystone to gridlock. She was having trouble restarting it. Well, she had silenced her radio—the hard way. Champ chuckled. Carson had such style in his designs! How complete his knowledge of the mental makeup of AWOL Queen of My Heart! Champ's glee was total because she experienced no physical harm. Surely she would soon come to meet Carson's demand to scuttle her wedding plans before it became necessary to . . .

He beat the wheel with both fists and felt the metal bend under its plastic casing. Wheezing, wordless grunts spoke eloquently of the sanctity of Queen of My Heart's white flesh. Other blood he could spill at Carson's command. But hers? His master could never wish it either!

Nor did he, hence the psychological campaign against her peace of mind. Champ had dutifully created the "survey" of Trish's marital plans—a real zinger that! Creating the file erase program and installing it on Queen of My Heart's PC had been a trivial exercise for a man of his talent. Stealing her backup tapes had given *that* challenge for her a sharp, threatening bite. I serve you well, Master!

Her car got underway. With the current flowing again through its electrical system, the radio could speak anew of Master Carson's ruling wish. Champ trailed behind a quarter mile, well within range of the Acura. Every ten seconds he raised the mike to his lips. "Trish, Carson, and Melody—together forever!"

He knew she was headed for PC-Pros. He pulled up in a burger joint's parking lot down the block. The console told him she had turned off her engine. His fingers moved like a pianist's over the console. The office bugs whispered into the earphones he slipped over his wide head. Back at Resurrection Headquarters the tape machines turned, recording every spoken word. The three bugs had, in a way, been a disappointment. He wondered if she had somehow discovered them.

"Carson!" Her voice. Coming in on her office bug. She hadn't used that space in weeks, making him suspect. "I know you can hear me." So she did know!

Ah, her voice! It stirred the stew of his innards like a stick. I am not the master, sweet. I am the servant. Shadowed moon of a Leporello circling the mighty planet of Carson's Don Giovanni. I am not Carson. *I am not Carson!* He closed his eyes, let the honey of her agitated words flow over the tongue of his adoration.

"I know you've bugged my business," she said, a shade of shakiness in her tone. "And my home. I've found the cameras. They're coming out this morning."

How had she found them, Champ wondered. Carson had designed them in ways that exceeded her technical capacity for discovery. Had she found help? Maybe from a PC-Pros' employee, maybe from . . . a dark outsider. He would have to investigate that possibility.

"I want you to know what you're trying to do won't work, Carson. I'm going to marry Foster in September. You might as well just stop right now. I've already gone to the police. That photograph you sent of the three of us came in handy for identifying you. Now they're looking for you." She drew a breath that caught in her throat. "Carson, I know what you did to Jethro DuMont—and to the doctors and their daughters. The police here know that, too. If you think about it, trying to ruin my life is going to get you caught. It's hardly worth it, don't you think?"

How could she so underestimate Carson's determination, not only to return her to the fold, but to punish her for her defection? Did she think the master feared the police? The police! Champ's chuckles burst forth as irresistibly as a tubercular's hacking.

"Do you understand what I'm saying, Carson? You're putting yourself in danger by harassing me." Queen of My Heart paused. "I have a proposition for you. I hope you're still listening. I'm willing to . . . sit down with you and talk it all through. Why it won't work and why you have to stop . . ."

Champ's heart leapt like a stag. Could that really mean she was beginning to reconsider? Would Carson's dreams so readily come true? Oh, he would be delighted to hear this news! Champ himself was swept up on waves of hope because . . . he so much did not want to have to hurt her.

Even as Queen of My Heart amplified her offer he rushed out to the restaurant's pay phone. He called Carson and told him about this new development. Breathless, he awaited his master's response.

He walked back lead-footed to the car. Within she was

rounding out her monologue. She had wasted enough breath. Champ worked the console. In her office stood a table radio to which, weeks before, he had paid technical attention. Now through remote control he turned it on and overrode the FM frequency, spun up its volume. He snatched up the mike and bellowed, *"Trish, Carson, and Melody—together forever! Trish, Carson . . ."* until the earphones told him she had torn the line cord out of its wall socket.

His mind overflowed with the sound of her hysterical weeping.

From the glove compartment he drew out the letter in which Carson had spelled out the next tactical operation in the battle to return Queen of My Heart to his side. On the phone moments ago he had ordered no deviation from that plan. They would be reaching now to a higher level of persuasive energy.

They would try terror.

14

Trish was embarrassed at the volume of her weeping. That damned radio! She glared at its dangling line cord. Michelle Amritz came in with the Kleenex box, quick with sympathy, though she wasn't sure precisely why her boss was blubbering.

Within a half hour Trish had calmed. Knowing she was again involved with Carson should have prepared her for such cunning tricks as doctored car and office radios. She had no idea whether or not he would consent to meet with her. In either case she knew how one-sided the struggle was, even with Nicholas, Foster, and the police on her side.

From a nearby pay phone she called Nicholas's number and left a message with a woman named Dolly Hummer. She asked him to remove the bugs from the building after he finished with the cameras in her home. That positive step improved her frame of mind, but still left her feeling . . . inadequate in the face of Carson's attentions. Dismay hung around her like persistent wisps of fog.

When Dino arrived at her desk with more tarts she decided it was written that he should show up at that moment. As usual he grinned and talked about her *bambina,* though he had never laid eyes on Melody. She invited him into her unbugged area for coffee. His brown eyes studied her over the Styrofoam cup edge. "You been crying," he said.

"An old lover has turned out to be the one trying to upset the apple cart of my life, Dino."

He waved an arm. "The trouble you been having all along? That you thought Rocco caused?"

She nodded. "Rocco came and talked to me the other day. He made a sincere, fair offer to buy me out. I might well sell to him after I'm married. He asked me to tell you that he had made me a fair offer." She leaned forward. "I think you scared him a lot." She thought it diplomatic not to mention that he thought Dino was another half-mad Nam vet.

"Guy like that deserves scaring." Dino took a big sip of coffee.

She groped for words, unsure just how to continue. "You're the only guy I know who could really scare another man."

He grinned, his teeth wide and white as those of a star with a Hollywood dentist. "You don't hang with the right kind of guys."

"Maybe I don't. Not for the trouble I seem to be in." She drank coffee, battling her nervousness. "I need help. I have some, but I need more." She burst into a partial description of her situation and the man who lay behind it. She backed and filled, added, tried to bring it all together. "The whole reason for everything is that Carson doesn't want me to marry Foster. He's been concentrating on hurting my business." She waved her hand to take in all of PC-Pros. "It's the easiest way to reach me. I'll be honest. It's working. I'm getting into an expensive lawsuit over a PC loaded with dynamite that blew up in a law library. Who knows what's next?"

"You want me to meet him instead of you? Want me to scare the hell out of him, too?"

Trish smiled grimly. "I don't know if he'll meet me. But I do know you couldn't scare him. It might be . . . vice versa, you know."

"Oooooh! You're talking a baaad dude."

"I do want your help, Dino. You're right. But I feel very strange mixing you up in my problems."

"You're a good woman, Patricia. You get married, all your problems are over, right?"

She nodded. "Then we're like any married couple. With a different set of problems. The present problem is getting past Carson."

He raised his palms in the Italian shrug. "So what can Dino do for you?"

"For now, if you could, keep an eye on this building. You're only a couple doors down, and you live in those rooms behind the bakery, right?"

"Nah. Just Mario. I live a couple blocks away. I got an apartment. But I'm usually at the bakery. Right now Mario and me are working nights putting in a coffee bar."

"So one of you could maybe walk around this building at night and on weekends? Look in the windows? Make sure nothing's going on?"

Dino put down his cup. He got up and walked toward Trish, arms out. The green-eyed alligator tattoo on his forearm writhed as he gestured. "That don't sound like enough."

"Will you do it?"

"Yeah, Mario and I, we'll do it, but—"

"Right now that's all I feel right asking you to do. Maybe later I'll need your help in other ways. Then I'll let you know."

"How come you're playing your cards so close, Patricia?" His brown gaze was penetrating, demanding even. She felt his inner power. There were men, and there were *men*.

"What do you mean?"

"How much of the truth did you tell me? About you and this guy? This Carson?"

She met his gaze. "As much as you need to know. As much as I can tell a person I just met. Maybe as much as I'm emotionally equipped to tell right now."

He held her forearms lightly in his hands. It was the first time he had touched her. She felt the electricity and saw desire dart across the brown field of his eyes. She pulled slowly away, not breaking eye contact. "So someday you'll tell me everything?" he said.

"I hope it doesn't come to that."

"What happens, happens." He was lighthearted again. "Hey, when do I get to meet your little girl, huh? She want to know who makes the great apple tarts?"

Trish smiled. "I'll see what she says."

After Dino left, Trish sat motionless at her desk, trying to compose herself. Her heart pounded. Why was she so rattled? At first she thought the doctored radio and its repeated message were still tearing at her nerves. Then it dawned on her that what she was trying to get over was Dino's growing impact.

Now that they had met several times she had become increasingly aware that his animal charm, not to mention his subtle intelligence and strength of personality, were affecting her. He wasn't a temptation. She was too serious-minded for that. She loved Foster. Nonetheless . . .

September fifteenth couldn't come fast enough!

Foster phoned. "Clear your desk for the next six days!" His voice was bubbling. "Call on your subordinates, sweetie. Rely on them. Because we are going to be out of here! You wanted to get away. We're going to do it."

"Where are we going?"

"I'll be by your house in the limo. You and Melody. Summer clothes are good."

"Where—"

"Seven o'clock, my love."

She had a frantic afternoon shedding nearly a week's responsibilities. She worked with a smile. She didn't care where Foster took her. Wherever it was would be away from relentless Carson.

She got home to find Melody doing a bad job of hiding her conspiratorial grin. She had combed her hair with Janine's help. She wore her best dress. "What is going on here?" Trish said.

"Surprise." Janine was grinning, too. Trish guessed the baby-sitter had played some kind of role in Foster's plan. The girl hurried off without revealing anything. Questioned teasingly, Melody giggled that she didn't know where they were going.

Not until the Palmer limo pulled up at an airport gate did a beaming Foster lean over and say, "We're going to southern Portugal. The Algarve."

Trish's delight was split by a bolt of anxiety. "Passports! We don't have passports."

Melody giggled and bounced up and down on her seat. "We got 'em. We got 'em!"

"The Palmer Force has been with you," Foster said. "As well as the little conspirator bobbing to your left. We sent some of your photos to a studio. They made passport-sized prints. My attorney's office handled the applications." From his inside coat pocket he pulled two passports. "You need only sign."

How much easier life was when you were rich, Trish thought. She took pen in hand and spread her opened passport on the limo pull-down desk.

They flew first class on Air Portugal. Foster, much the air traveler, suggested no food or drink until morning. The journey was better spent sleeping. This would cut down on jet lag. They caught a flight from Lisbon to the Algarve. Foster explained that the English had been coming to this part of Portugal for many years as vacationers, some to retire. In the markets and shops they heard more English than Portuguese.

He had rented a villa and a sailboat, both nestled into a narrow cove. With it came Josh, a local who served as butler, driver, and interpreter. With the help of his family up the road he also occasionally played the role of baby-sitter.

They sailed by day in the Gulf of Cadiz. Evenings one of Josh's sisters busied herself in the kitchen making kale soup, the national casserole *cataplana,* and doing wonders with fresh sardines. Josh chose and served the Dão region wines.

An unspoken agreement left PC-Pros, Carson, and Lois Smith-Patton on the other side of the Atlantic. They went sailing. They sky was cobalt, the waters calm. Melody in her yellow "boat coat" sat still in the bow playing tunes on her penny whistle that she had heard the fishermen sing while mending their nets. Trish leaned against Foster. One hand on the tiller, he curled his free arm around her. They nibbled and nuzzled while gulls cried and an occasional sardine boat chugged by on the way to port. "Are you happy?" he asked. The only adequate answer was a long kiss.

The villa was ringed with a stone walk angling along stony bluffs high above the sea. They strolled there every night in the breeze. Each day ended with uncomplicated love in a canopied bed wide enough to sleep six.

On their next-to-last night they returned from their walk to find a table set with candles, pastries, and sweet wine. Josh had done Foster's bidding and left for home. Trish went to Melody's room to check on her. She slept the good sleep that follows an outdoor day. Trish came back to find Foster filling crystal goblets with golden liquid. He raised his high. "I drink to my love for you, Trish!" She was speechless, her eyes suddenly brimming. In toast, crystal rims rang in the round room. He reassured her again that recent awkward events had in no way diminished his feelings for her. In fact they had deepened. He held her shoulders lightly and looked into her eyes. "For that reason I think we should get married tomorrow. Here, where . . . no one can bother us. Look!" From his pocket he drew a ring box. He popped it open and removed two ornate wedding rings. "Hand-worked by the best Portuguese goldsmiths." He put them on her palm. The candlelight glinted from the twists of filigree. Dazzled, she gasped.

She was stunned. Doubly so, really. First because he was suggesting a hasty, private wedding. Second, because . . . she hesitated. She heard herself say, "Oh, I . . . can't. Not this way."

The lenses of glasses magnified his widening eyes. "I . . . don't understand. Why not? Now's the time!" Past his surprise lay some other emotions that she couldn't then grasp.

She put the rings on the table and got up. She walked out

onto the darkened stone balcony. Stars blazed above. He followed her, asking increasingly excited questions about her reaction. She tried to gather her thoughts, found them elusive as a journey to one of the distant starry specks. She knew she didn't want to give in to Carson. Not one inch. She wanted to be married on the day she chose, in a style suitable to the Palmer family. At the next instant she wondered if those were her thoughts or her mother's, she for whom the old ways would always be best.

Past that came more, difficult to put into exact focus. In a way Carson's madness was challenging her relationship with Foster. The gauntlet of the days until September fifteenth had yet to be run. When it was, however matters fell out, her love would have been put to a hard test. One she wanted to believe it would survive. Yet as Foster went on pleading, begging even, to have the wedding there the next day, she wondered if what had hovered for a moment in his eyes had been nothing more complicated than . . .

Simple fear.

From her own standpoint, what did her hesitancy mean? Foster said he loved her and wanted to prove it with a quick wedding. She hadn't yet been wholly convinced that his feelings for Lois Smith-Patton belonged entirely to the past. Here, too, more testing, more challenging ought to be done. Or was Trish simply being stupid, playing fairy-tale princess who wanted her suitor to perform impossible tasks before consenting to give her hand? Behind that stance possibly stood something—or someone—else. She needed the time to find out just where a certain man stood in her life. A plain-spoken man with an alligator writhing on his arm.

Dino Castelli.

She never fully figured out, in the end, why she refused Foster's suggestion.

Only Melody enjoyed the return trip. She ran around the nearly empty first-class section and charmed the hostesses and stewards. They found Portuguese sweets and pastries and set a little table just for her. Trish and Foster ate and drank sparingly. In conversation they danced around the wedding that never was. The gold bands lay still potent in

Foster's vest pocket, as laden now with meanings and powers as rings of the Nibelungen.

Once home she rushed to her mother and told her what had happened in the Algarve, or rather what had not happened. To her astonishment this woman who seldom saw her in the right said, "You did the proper thing, Patricia."

"I did?" She wasn't so sure.

She nodded vigorously. Her freshly permed hair scarcely stirred. "Don't you agree, Stoneman?"

Stoneman Gore waved a wrist archly. "I very much agree."

"Indeed. We've been talking over your situation. And what we're certain of is that you're overreacting to these pranks," her mother said.

"Pranks?" She was still calling disasters pranks! Trish thought of dynamite going off in the law firm library. Marylou knew about that, but not about *Trish, Carson, and Melody—together forever!*

"You've talked to the police. They'll handle this annoying fellow, whoever he is," Marylou drawled. "In the meantime, it's your job to go ahead with a wedding that'll be worthy of the Palmer family. I'm working like a mule toward that end, I assure you."

Somehow chastened, Trish spent the rest of the evening cooperating with her mother on wedding details. She spent an hour on the phone with Jill Beestock, her matron of honor. She explained where the bridal boutique was, when she should show up for fittings. More than a month ago she had had her first fitting for the gown she—and Marylou—had chosen. Her mother announced herself pleased with the design, no matter that it cost "a fair portion of your father's generous estate." Trish had studied herself in that inspired cloud of pastel. In the pale color she saw symbolized the tangle of her past. Mother Trish hiding an illegitimacy made wearing white a social impossibility. Father Ron Verner, who would surely have made an honest woman of her, was dead in an accident. Master Carson claimed a throne of paternity not his. . . .

Would she ever escape all that and be allowed to live a new life with Foster? She guessed that wouldn't happen until Carson was in police hands. The police were in touch with her that evening. Detective Morris phoned. She waited expectantly for news of the hunt for her nemesis. Instead he said, "How would you and your daughter like to join my family's Fourth of July picnic?"

"Oh, I . . . don't know." She recalled the cop's silence in contrast to his colleague Lieutenant Sarkman's cool officiousness. See him socially? Foster was sailing on the holiday; they had agreed on a brief cooling-off period. She had planned nothing more than a solo bout with the outdoor grill. One day in the company of a law officer would scarcely compromise her engagement. "Can we talk about what the police have done about my problems, Detective Morris?"

"We can, but I'll tell you up front I don't want to spend the whole day talking business with you. You're too pretty for that. And by the way, you can call me Jerry."

The Morris clan was extensive—dozens of adults of all shapes and ages and hordes of children. Every Fourth of July they rented a pavilion in a park not far from the site of the civic fireworks. No sooner did Trish and Jerry arrive than the softball game started. After that came volleyball. By the time Trish sank down on a bench, beer in hand, she wasn't sure her overworked muscles would allow her to walk to the buffet—even though she was starving. Jerry came to the rescue holding a heaping plate. "You never told me you were a left-handed power hitter," he said.

"My pop-ups over second that fell in? That's not power where I come from, son."

Trish was so relaxed from the exercise and sun that it was almost unwillingly that she wheeled their conversation from easy generalities to what the police had accomplished with her problems. She asked Jerry what kind of a job he and Lieutenant Sarkman were doing on her behalf.

He shuffled sneakered feet. His heavy lashes rose in mild concern. "This is all off the record today, right?"

She shrugged. "Sure."

"Sarkman thinks he's the department superstar. Solving murders can do that to your head. It's our society's most glamorous crime—murder—isn't it?"

"Never thought of it that way. You're saying he'd rather solve murders than help me? Why'd the commissioner give him the case, then?"

"Politics. Sark the Shark has a good rep. So the Palmers think our best man is on their case."

"What's he done for me so far?"

"Not much."

Trish rose and pulled Jerry up. "Let's take a walk along the reservoir." A quarter of the way around she asked him if he could take whatever initiative was needed to find Carson and arrest him.

"Sark told me we weren't really going to give your case priority," he began. When she opened her mouth to protest he hurried on. "But I'll see if there's anything I can do alone." They walked on in silence, the reservoir blue and unblemished to their right. "This guy Carson has you psyched, doesn't he?"

"Do I show it that much?"

"I've been told I have excellent intuition," Jerry said.

"I ask you to accept what I say as is: He's far beyond cunning, and now he's crazy as well. He's a devil. He'll never stop until the wedding is canceled or you arrest him. I guarantee it."

Jerry stopped and leaned against the wall. "He must be very much in love with you."

"Obsession isn't love."

He nodded. "And Foster? Is it love with Foster?"

"Of course! What kind of question is that? We're going to get married if Carson will leave us alone." Was it quite that cut and dried, she wondered. To her surprise she found herself telling Jerry about Foster's wish to marry in Portugal and her surprising refusal. She laughed nervously. "It seems I want there to be more testing of our relationship. It *will* be tested, I know."

He touched her lightly on the shoulder. "If Foster doesn't

pass the test, I want to put in my dibs right now." The late-afternoon light had brought out granite flecks in his brown eyes, hard bits amid gentleness.

She looked away. "I appreciate the compliment. You're a good man. I sense it."

"I'm old-fashioned. I believe in right and wrong."

Trish put her arm lightly around his waist. It was narrow. She sensed a hard belly. "Maybe that's what I need: a dose of simplicity." Even as she spoke she was reminded how elusive that condition was. If she and Foster parted—she couldn't bear to think of it!—Jerry imagined he might step forward as sole successor. It made a certain sense, until she thought of . . . Dino.

"Because I stand behind what I believe in—right and wrong—I won't say anything else personal," Jerry said. "You're engaged. I wouldn't do anything to interfere with that. So when we get together from here on, it'll be only on Carson business."

"You're so sweet, Jerry. I'm not sure I deserve it."

His eyes narrowed. "Spoken like a lady with a past. Is that what you are, Trish?"

She turned away toward the picnic grounds. "Time to get back. To see if Melody's staying out of trouble."

The fireworks filled the night with showers of red, green, and blue fire. Trish wanted the sky to bloom and boom all night. What had eluded her for six days in Portugal she found for a half hour among oooh-ing and aaah-ing adults and screaming children by a reservoir not ten miles from home.

Relief from her problems.

Jerry called her at work the next day. He had double-checked to make sure that Carson's photograph had been distributed to police throughout the city. He had made a formal inquiry for information about the Doctor and Daughter Destroyer. So far as his own investigations went, he lacked both clout and what he called "moral force," meaning that in this city Carson was suspected of no more than committing a minor felony. Unproved suspicions from a continent away added little weight locally. "I have some advice for you, off the record, Trish."

"Tell me."

"You're getting some technical help from private sources, right?"

She thought of odd Nicholas. "In a way."

"You might look to get some more. Private detective, bodyguard. That sort of thing."

"Are you saying the police aren't going to be any help?"

He hesitated. "It's just that not enough trouble has come your way yet."

"Oh, great!"

"Trish, listen. I'll help you. That you can count on. Past that . . . Hey, I'm just being honest."

She remembered her recent chat with Dino Castelli. "You know, I think I've already taken those safety steps." She smiled and spoke in teasing tones. "Well, I've handled *everything* myself, haven't I? What am I getting for my tax dollar?"

"Personal attention that no amount of money can buy. Mine!"

"I'll be more impressed when you actually catch Carson!"

Hanging up, she realized what she had said could have been interpreted as rude. She didn't want to be rude to Jerry.

She simply couldn't deal with yet another man in her life!

15

NICHOLAS MOVED A KNIGHT, PUNCHED THE CHESS clock, and wrote his move down on the score sheet. Move 17. He adjusted his left earphone. Roland Kirk riffed, two reed mouthpieces jammed into his jaw. Blow wild and crazy, Rahsaan! The game's initiative hung in the balance. Playing the black pieces, he edged toward equality. He had trotted out that old vexer, the Petroff Defense, in the face of white's king's pawn opening. White was one of those seventeen-year-old hotshots. Nicholas knew how to handle them: steady, steady play. Seize the initiative and grind, grind, grind. Pimply lads such as the one sitting across from him hadn't enough tournament experience; they always blundered or crumbled.

He had won all three games Saturday. This Sunday morning he liked his game. If there was a secret to winning at chess—besides raw talent, preparation, and experience—it was concentration. Getting the game into your teeth and, like a rat terrier, shaking the life out of the opponent. "I like to watch 'em squirm," Bobby Fischer said. Yes!

Rahsaan was playing two saxes at once. The desperate haste of his play hinted at his instinctive knowledge of oncoming stroke and death. Nicholas gripped Kirk's line and black's best chessboard variation and steadied himself to grind. . . .

Yet, this weekend something was different. Into the impregnable keep of the castle of his concentration glided . . . Trish Morley and her problems. What had she become if not his white queen? White jumpsuits, black hair, white and black like the sixty-four squares. Just as queens ruled the game, she was the most powerful piece on the board of his life. Long live the queen! For so long he had been the subject of a black queen—Lois, Sweetest Sister. Trish had played queen-take-queen and now swept unopposed into the warming chambers of his heart. As she entered there his concentration wavered and wobbled. In the tournament's third game he had made an atypical oversight, then had to call on all his creative chess powers to extricate himself from difficulties.

At that moment he broke a personal rule: Rather than study only the board, he looked at his opponent during a game. The lad's cheeks and forehead were sprinkled with acne, purplish lumps, some ruptured to scabheads. His nose was large, his lips heavy and pressed together. From deep in his chest came a stream of barely audible grunts, *Unh-unh-unh-unh*, as though within worked some steady engine adjacent to the left ventricle. Nicholas thought of him as Gruntman.

What did his smile mean?

He should be analyzing on Gruntman's clock, not letting his mind wander. Fifty moves in two hours, a total of four available to play the game to its end. How precious those last few minutes could be! Now was the time to hoard seconds, yet . . .

The weekend had brought with it an undercurrent of excitement for Nicholas. Friday he had pulled out all stops, arrayed his most sophisticated equipment, and taken it to PC-Pros. He needed the best part of daylight to get a fix on the transmissions from the bugs and clearly identify the angle and degree of the signals. Along that line somewhere lay the receiver. Beside it sat Trish's tormentor. He had identified the likely site just as darkness fell. Fatigue and a weekend totally committed to chess broke off his investigation. To be resumed Monday, he told himself.

Now he was in the thick of the delicately balanced middle game. Thoughts of successfully serving his white queen and turning over the rock that would expose the worm of her adversary intruded on his systematic exploration of the available variations. Bald and spidery he might be, but overwhelming success could transform the ugly like a wizard's wand working wonders on pumpkins and mice. In gratitude Trish might bestow on him a gracious smile or a touch of her long cool hand. . . .

Trish My Wish!

Gruntman's queen arched across the board in a foray Nicholas had to admit he had overlooked. Kingside pressure. He had to take great care. Analyze, analyze! He must sit on his hands till he was absolutely sure his chosen move was the strongest response. He sat, but the teeth of his concentration had loosened in their gums. He studied for twenty minutes, searching for an adequate reply. In the face of possible time pressure he moved a pawn. His opponent made a hasty knight foray—typical of the hothead—and Nicholas sought the crushing refutation that usually lay hidden to all but the deepest analysis. He began his search. Only slowly did he comprehend. . . .

He could not answer the move!

He saw that Gruntman's haste to make it lay in its obvious, irrefutable strength.

Nicholas was going to lose a bishop!

What happened then, he scarcely remembered. He managed to get two pawns for the piece. That meant strong drawing chances. Five moves later he bungled away a pawn, leaving him with a difficult if not impossible endgame. On another, earlier day he would have anchored in his concentration and determination like a barnacle and *willed* himself to a draw.

But not today.

On Move 46 he blundered.

He toppled his king and skipped both congratulating his opponent and officially withdrawing.

He fled, defeated. Not by Gruntman. By love!

Monday morning he resumed his quest for the receiver. His instruments pointed him to a block a quarter mile from PC-Pros. Once there, finer calibrations led to a rundown four-story apartment house squatting amid abandoned storefronts and convenience stores where clerks sat behind bulletproof glass. Nicholas imagined the top floor would be best for receiving nearly unobstructed transmissions.

He pulled his van to the curb in front of the apartment entrance. Idle youths sat about on stoops and fences. He took the necessary hand-held instruments with him, activating the vehicle's potent security system. He saw from the corner of his eye their reactions to his pale, spidery presence. "Hey, man, when the next UFO take you back to Mars?"

The lobby smelled of urine and stale pot. The elevator doors yawned wide into immobile cars spray-painted with graffiti. Three men in filthy clothes lay on the floor, nodding or sleeping off drug doses or binges. He found the stairs, held his nose against the stink there. He met two Hispanic men who glowered at him in passing, imagining he was the representative of some resented authority. He looked over the banister into the stairwell. Climbing up behind him were two of the stoop loungers, one in a black Nike tank top. The other wore jeans and no shirt. Their laughter over some private joke floated up to him. Was he the object of their humor? He decided he ought to be cautious, but thoughts of serving Trish overrode his hesitancy. He was on the verge of discovery! Up he climbed, his wind growing short. Floors six . . . seven . . . and finally eight. He leaned against the scarred doorframe and sucked breath.

It seemed appropriate at that moment to put his earphones in place. Chet Baker, dying from self-neglect and drug abuse, sang about his funny valentine. Nicholas stepped into the corridor. He stared down at the meter in his hand, watched its needles turn, searching for alignment. The doors lining the corridor were reinforced against violent entry. TV and radio babble blasted from most. Could be audio camouflage. His equipment wouldn't be fooled. He made his way slowly ahead. At a turn in the corridor was a silent apartment, 836. This was the one! He raised a hand and knocked. He slipped the phones off his ears. Baker whispered into his neck.

From behind: "Ain't nobody there. Ain't nobody ever there."

He whirled, frightened. The two men from the street stood two feet away. The larger, shirtless man's torso was heaped with bodybuilder's muscles. A horrible starlike scar spread over the center of his chest, as though it had in the past stopped a shotgun blast.

"You with the phone company?" the shorter man said. He wore a black beret to match his tank top.

"No, I'm not." Nicholas's voice was dry.

"What you doin' here?" Beret said.

"Some electronic work. It's too technical to explain."

Beret turned to his friend. "Man be tech-ni-cal. He got tech-ni-cal equipment there, Zak."

"Yeah, technical, Eddie."

With a flash of hand speed Eddie tore the meter from Nicholas's grip. "We want it!"

Zak ripped off the earphones and lifted the tape player from Nicholas's pocket. "We want this, too!"

"Give them back!"

"Give you this!" The scarred man swung a huge fist that caught Nicholas full in his soft belly. The wind went out of him, and he fell to the floor, gasping for breath. His assailants went methodically through his pockets, taking his hand-sized instruments, wallet, and loose change. He tried to resist, but they easily shoved away his hands.

They rose. Eddie put the sole of his boot onto Nicholas's throat. "Who you lookin' for here, man?"

Nicholas sucked air, the paralysis lifting slowly like fog. "I don't know. Maybe whoever's in that room."

"Tole you. Ain't nobody in there." Eddie leaned weight against Nicholas's neck. He coughed, nearly choking. *"What you want here, Mars man?"*

Nicholas tried to speak, but his voice lay broken like a dish.

"Nobody can get in that room," Zak said. "Got some kind of gorilla lock and door on it. We can't get in, we *know* you can't."

At last Eddie took his boot off Nicholas's neck. His relief was short-lived. Eddie kicked him in the head. Darkness closed in like Death's embrace.

He awoke and rose to hands and knees. He vomited, adding his bitter bit to the debris and dried puddles scattered the length of the hallway. He felt his head. Having no hair to protect it, his skull had taken a brutal blow. A nut protruded, too sensitive to touch. In time he rose to shaky legs and glanced at the lock. He knew at once it was electronic; he could find a way to open it.

He tottered down the stairs, holding the banister with both hands like a lifeline. He had to stop halfway down. He sat, waiting for sudden dizziness to pass. His head ached horribly. It had been unwise to come to this building. He now felt the fear that should have kept him away. He had been emboldened by thoughts of Trish. Possibly he had made some small progress on her behalf. Where to go from here he had no idea. As bad as he felt, he was relieved by the thought of his van being protected by its security system.

He left the lobby and found himself in a crowd. It surrounded fire trucks and police cruisers. The smell of burning rubber and paint was overwashed with moisture. Fire hoses arced water onto a dying fire. He groaned and staggered.

His van had been torched.

16

TRISH SPENT AN HOUR OF MONDAY MORNING ON THE phone with Louise O'Day, her attorney. Kandinsky Klein and Corman had indeed filed suit. Louise tried to cheer her up. She told Trish that the criminal actions of someone outside her firm were quite a different thing from negligence. Of course, such actions would have to be proven. Not to worry anyway. By the time the big firm got all its heavy artillery in order Trish would likely have sold out to Rocco or another buyer. A pending suit might lower the PC-Pros' price somewhat, but by then she would be safe within Foster's golden net. A few thousand less wouldn't matter that much.

That theme was repeated when she called the bank. Mr. Beetlebrow, whose real name was Arthur Breed, had reviewed the figures she had recently sent him. Unhappily, it wasn't possible at this time for Commercial Savings to grant another loan. When she became Mrs. Palmer the bank would be willing to reexamine the application, assuming her husband was willing to co-sign.

So it wasn't a great day for a woman who wanted to stand on her own two feet. Nor for one who wished to squirm away from Carson Thomas's attention. She got a call from odd Nicholas Smith-Patton describing his bizarre adventures in a dingy tenement. That he had been injured while working on her behalf struck a tender spot in her heart. He was certain Carson lurked behind the door he had never had time to open. She sensed Nicholas lacked the nerve to return. She thought for a moment. She told him she had a call to make. She'd get back to him. She phoned Dino at the bakery.

"This is Melody's mother," she joked.

"How many apple tarts you want?"

"What I want is some of the help you promised." She outlined what had happened to Nicholas. She continued hesitantly. How much was it fair to ask the man? "Could you . . . go back with him sometime soon? He says he can get the door open. If he can . . . well, this whole awful business might wind down. All you have to do is make sure he doesn't get hurt. The police can do the rest."

"Screw the police! If he finds Carson, I'll handle him."

"Dino! You will *not*. You'll get police help. Carson Thomas is—"

"Who is this Nicholas guy?"

She described him, saying much less about his appearance than his helpfulness and technical competence.

"Sounds like a nerd," Dino said.

"He's just terribly shy and awkward."

"Yeah, a nerd."

"Dino!"

"Have him give me a call," Dino said.

"Oh, thank you!"

"Done nothin' yet."

"Remember, don't try to handle Carson alone. Get help from the police."

"Sure."

"Call Detective Jerry Morris. He's ready to help." Jerry, the one man too many in her disarrayed life.

She felt better after talking to the baker. She could rely on him. Memories of a chastened Rocco DeVita waiting in the wings with a fair offer for PC-Pros spoke to Dino's efficiency. He and Nicholas might well make an effective team.

Michelle brought in Trish's takeout lunch. Foster called. "I'd like to speak with you," he said.

Trish had to talk through a mouthful of takeout tuna on pita. "I'd like you to speak with me. I always do."

She expected his dry laugh at her tuna tones. Instead he said, "In person" in a level voice.

She swallowed heavily to clear her mouth. "I'm really busy here, Foster. I hope you can wait until—"

"I'm not interested in waiting. I don't think you should be either. When the possibility of our future life together is right now in the balance."

"What are you saying?"

"I'll be waiting for you here at home. I'll be in the library. Get here as soon as you can." The line went dead so loudly that she wondered if he had slammed down the receiver—something she had never seen him do.

She tried to take the time needed to tie up the loose ends of her day's projects. No hope! Her attention was as fragmented as a broken light bulb. She made the drive to the Palmer mansion in a wash of worry.

No one greeted her at the door. She hurried toward the building's rear. One of the library's two wide doors was ajar. She edged it wider and stepped through.

Foster sat behind the 1850s heavy black desk. She had expected to find him angry. What she saw was more frightening.

His tear-smeared cheeks.

His eyes were red, though he wasn't weeping at that moment.

"Foster . . ."

"Close the door." She did as he asked.

He nodded toward a chair that faced a TV and VCR on a rolling stand.

"Why did you invite me here? Why the hurry?" She could normally read his lean face like a newspaper. Now it seemed hunched and huddled from her scrutiny. He didn't answer. "Foster . . ."

"Sit. And watch." He picked up a remote control from the

desk. "This morning the mail brought me the videotape you're about to see and will have to explain."

"I don't understand this!" She felt very threatened. Foster had never before come close to being threatening. Anxiety welled up like muddy water. She found herself edging forward in her chair even before he used the remote.

A flash of video snow, then—oh, Lord! It was *she,* naked, bound, blindfolded! How could . . . And there! Carson, *Carson.* He hovered over her, fingers curled, like the devil above a sought soul. She knew the place, the larger sleeping platform at Castle Carson. When? Her heart sank. During one of those endless weeks during which she had lost track of time and he cruised like a man o' war upon the little lake of her life.

Bad enough the color and several cameras at work. Hear the clear sound track! It fell upon her ears as corrosive as acid. She heard afresh Carson's growled obscenities, his vocabulary vivid and imaginative. And her responses! How had she allowed such . . . smut to escape her lips? Her pleas for further degradation betrayed her true nature as the uncontrollable outbursts of a torture victim condemned him to death.

How had this tape been made? Why? Of what use could it ever have been to anyone? Had Carson in his devilish genius found a way to peer into the future? Her stomach heaved, and she felt the color drain from her face. Oh, look at her! Look at what she was doing. . . .

Carson stood over her, thick nine-inch phallus in hand.

"Turn it off!" she screamed.

Foster stared mesmerized at the screen. She wailed inwardly at what must surely be his arousal.

"Foster!" She reached out for the remote. He swung it away, eyes on the screen. Fresh tears gathered in his staring eyes. Even so his face reddened further. She knew what that meant. "Foster, *turn it off!*" He didn't move.

She sprang up and rushed at the wheeled cart. She heaved and bowled it over, howling as it toppled. Though TV and VCR crashed down, they continued to operate. So clever, these Japanese! She dived for the extension cord and jerked it out of the wall with both hands. She lay on the long soft pile of the Kirman carpet, fingers wrapped around the black wire. She pressed forehead to hands and began to sob.

She heard Foster's voice, heavy as ballast. "Explain," he said.

Explain Carson and Queen of My Heart? She had warned him that Carson was no ordinary man. Could an ordinary man have reduced her to what Foster had beheld on that evil tape? She tried to gather herself to rise to the massive task of exposition. When she struggled to stand she shivered as though an icy blast blew on her from the stinking pit of her past.

She first did her best to expand her earlier description of Carson. One of those who achieved success early and often in life, he dared so many more things than those hobbled by mediocrity, she said. With their victories mounting one on another they tossed aside rules and laws meant for common-place people and wrote their own. Those few like Carson, who had fully maximized their potential, exported daring into all phases of their lives. So doing, they didn't hesitate to pursue their tastes, whether for wealth, power, or . . . domination.

As for her, she had been primed for him by her family life. Without ever understanding, she had at that time badly needed a figure to help her organize her days, set her on some meaningful track. Carson had proved to be that person—with a vengeance.

Her fiancé listened without replying. She found his silence terrifying. She was forced to try to read his face while tumbling desperate words from her lips. More! She tried to plumb the depths of his heart to judge the breadth of compassion and forgiveness there.

Even as she explained, tried to some degree to excuse herself, she couldn't help but be awed by diabolical Carson. It was as though he guessed that she hadn't dared to totally explain to Foster the Carson years. He was using her reticence as a sledge to slam down the emotional structure she had built with her fiancé. That he should possess such an incriminating tape! More than ever his destructive powers seemed irresistible. He *was* her devil!

"You have to understand that we started out together normally, Foster." She tried to compose some kind of verbal coda to wrap up the long symphony of her frantic monologue. "Little by little I came to understand he was going crazy. But I was so tangled up with him that I didn't have the will to escape. And I don't think I ever would have gotten free if I hadn't met Ron Verner."

"I remember his name. He's Melody's father."

"Yes! A wonderful man I fell in love with. He gave me hope that I could eventually get away from Carson. If he hadn't had an accident, I might have made the break that much sooner. Just the same, he left me with a little candle of hope that I never let blow out. When the time was right, I got away."

Foster sat unmoving, all too much like an attentive judge on the bench. "I thought you told me you were married to this Verner person."

Everything was coming back to haunt her! When would she learn to be totally honest? *When?* "I had intended to explain that I . . . never married him, Foster. My mother talked me out of spreading that truth. Divorce is more acceptable these days than illegitimacy." She forced herself to meet his gaze. "Don't you think? That's why I won't be wearing white." She felt stupid talking about her gown when the whole idea of the wedding was in jeopardy. Worse, she was even sounding like her mother.

Foster shook his head slowly. "Trish, how could you . . . do those things with Carson?"

Underneath the clear anguish in his voice she heard the weakest whine of sexual jealousy, envy even of the fleshy roads she and Carson had traveled together. "I just tried to explain all that, Foster. He was a dominating personality. I was primed to be receptive." She drew a deep breath. "I'm not that way anymore. I'm using all my strength to try to leave everything in the past. Now Carson's come forward to try to pull me and Melody back there."

"That tape . . . disgusting!"

"Everyone has a past, Foster." Her voice shook as she battled to keep it even. "My past needn't have been shared, particularly when it contained acts like those you just saw. Carson is using it to destroy our relationship." She paused. "Has he done it?"

"I am so bewildered—ahhh!" Foster pulled off his smeared glasses, dropped them to the desk. He stood up quickly and began to walk the book-lined walls. "Who are you, Patricia McMullen Morley? How many other surprises do you have for me? How much more of your past will become my present?"

"It's Carson! And he's crazy. It's not me!"

"Through him I learn about you."

She hurried to his side. "He's my devil. He reveals only my dark side. Not what's good. Think about his motivations!" She held his arms, but he didn't respond.

"Trish, if I didn't love you so much—"

"Don't say it! Because you do love me. You do. You do!" Still his arms stayed woodenly at his side.

Trish straightened her shoulders. She was close to pleading. That didn't become her, nor was it right. Everyone had the privilege of making mistakes and learning from them. She was struggling to free herself from that destructive relationship and chart a new path for herself and her child. If Foster hadn't the insight to put her past into perspective, he was less understanding than she imagined. She took a step backward. She met his eyes. "Do you see that what I have become is so much better than what I was?"

He blinked, as though freed from a hypnotist's spell. "I—I'm not sure what to think."

"Think about loving me. Could one videotape turn that off like a light switch?"

He draped his hands loosely over her shoulders. "You should have told me—"

"No! I gave you enough of an idea about what Carson was like. That was as much as concerned you. I had no reason to want to degrade myself by completely describing him."

He shook his head. "You described him. Not you *with* him."

She groaned inwardly. Oh, yes, there was truth there. She was trembling. She wouldn't break down! She wouldn't give Devil Carson the satisfaction. She went over and plugged in the VCR, put it and the TV back in place. She removed the tape. She looked back at Foster, who stood unmoving, glasses back on his face. "You have a lot to think about, then." She forced herself to go on. "To decide whether or not Carson is going to have his way about the wedding." She would *not* crawl!

Foster nodded. "Yes, the wedding. I have to ponder. . . ."

She left him standing in light streaming through the wide window. His glasses masked his eyes like golden coins as he turned to witness her departure.

On the way home she should have used her cellular phone to check in with Michelle. Something could have come up at PC-Pros. But she didn't. She was paralyzed by the possibility that Foster, in his slow, methodical way, might well be dismantling the foundation of his commitment to her. When he finished, September fifteenth might prove to be no more eventful than the common mill run of her days. In a swift, grim vision she saw the two of them estranged, and Lois Smith-Patton enfolding him at last in the weighted cape of her love. Trish's innards twisted. Her eyes burned with the beginnings of tears. No! She would not cry. She would do something to help herself.

She absolutely had to stop Carson!

She phoned Jerry Morris at police headquarters. She told him about the tape, though not about its contents.

"Oh, great. Maybe that's a break. Bring it over. We'll have the print people go over it."

"Oh! I—I couldn't do that."

"Why not?"

"Have you found out anything at all about where Carson is?"

"Negative."

"Jerry, are you even trying?"

"Very much so. Why don't you want us to see the tape?"

"Personal reasons!" She hung up. Why had she thought the police would be able to help her? Jerry had warned her about Sarkman's preference for murder cases and the limits to what he could manage alone. That left Nicholas and Dino, both of whom wanted to work on her behalf. She phoned Nicholas's office. He answered. She told him who Dino was and that he was expecting his call. She left it up to the two of them as to just how to go ahead. The bald man's soft voice drifted off into a technical current concerning electronic locks where she sensed he was far more comfortable. She cut him off.

"Find him," she said. "Find Carson Thomas!"

17

THIS DINO PERSON DIDN'T LIKE JAZZ. BARBARIAN! Philistine! No sooner had he swung his muscled self into Nicholas's new van than his hoarse voice rose in protest: "Cut the honk and squeak, *paisan!* Put on some country!"

"That's a tape," Nicholas said.

"Kill it like a snake." Dino settled himself in the passenger seat and looked around. "This is quite a piece of tin you got here, worm neck. Smells brand new."

"It is." It had taken tens of thousands of dollars to replace his torched old van and most of its electronic equipment. He had kept Dolly Hummer on the phone in the water tank for a day and a half straight ordering devices from across the country, air expressing everything. She who had rarely been asked to do anything but show up from time to time turned amazed bloodshot eyes on her now-tyrannical boss. He fed her pastrami sandwiches and begrudged every minute she spent in the ladies' room in the gas station down the road.

He labored like an animal to install his purchases and to recreate the machines of his own design that he would need to help his White Queen. The tips of his long white hands carried red twists and lines, nicks and cuts from handling obstinate hardware. When fatigue hung like sash weights from his neck he caught a quick nap and started work again. I labor for my love, he told himself. My white-suited, black-haired, sweet-voiced, honey-thighed, untouchable beauty! Trish My Wish!

"So, are you loaded with bucks, *paisan?*"

Nicholas shrugged.

"You don't say much, do you?"

Nicholas thought his companion more than reached a conversational balance with his incessant chatter, much of it in the form of annoying questions about Nicholas's relationship with his beloved. On the other hand, the small fortune in state-of-the-art electronics that filled the vehicle's rear interested him not at all.

Trish's hasty description of the man failed to do justice to his assertiveness and animal ways. From his wiry black hair down to his heavy flour-dusted shoes he exuded raw force, like a python poised on a branch to crush the next victim passing below.

"What's Patricia to you, really, worm neck?"

Nicholas didn't answer.

"I think you got the hots for her. I think you lie awake at night and think about what she's got under that jumpsuit."

"No!"

"You're a lying sack of scum! Even a zombie like you sees a woman looks like Patricia, you want to jump her bones."

Nicholas sought respite from the verbal pollution of his beloved in riffs, a blast of Cannonball, a swing from the Duke. Their tunes were drowned out by the brutish brass of Dino's persistence. "I wonder if that Foster guy she thinks she's going to marry knows how lucky he is. I wonder if he knows how to handle those coconuts of hers."

Nicholas turned his face from the rainy road and said, "Don't talk about her like that!"

Dino croaked out a laugh.

"They will marry."

Dino's heavy brows rose in frown. "Dunno. Never mind this guy spooking around her life doing her dirt. Hell, we might take him out inside the hour. From what she's said, I don't think she and Foster are a real match. Something not quite right between them. Something tells me it's going to fall apart between them. And when it does, hey, maybe a poor baker will look a lot better to her."

Nicholas's most private heart swooped down. He, too, felt that Trish would never marry Foster. If her unknown adversary didn't succeed in stopping the wedding, then Sweetest Sister somehow would. In the end Lois would march with Foster to the altar like Caesar into Rome. Trish would be cast aside, despondent. Then she might be willing to notice him. How much about the wonder world of computers they had in common! They would sip coffee, and his words would flow eloquently with the caffeine. He would behold a woman's face at long last with more than sidelong glances. Now it seemed even that most secret longing was doomed to be crushed by python Dino's lust. And who would have the power to drive him away?

This outspoken man had changed not only Nicholas's dreams but his wishes as well. When they met at ten o'clock that morning Nicholas wanted to take the police with them to the apartment house where he had experienced his expensive, painful adventure. Dino read his fear as clearly as a billboard and waved it away. "Two reasons why not. First, I'll take care of you, worm neck. Second is, cops have to follow rules. Dino doesn't." He raised a fist and stared at it as though it were a crystal ball. "I figure whoever he is has about forty-five happy minutes left. Then—whamo!"

Nicholas sought relief from his companion's oppressive personality in a chess problem he had committed to memory. Mate in five—a thorny puzzle, even for a man of his abilities. He hooded his eyes in a further effort to shut Dino out.

"Pull over into this parking lot!" Dino said.

"We're not close yet."

"I know. We take a cab, dingbat. You wanta get this thing torched, too?"

While Nicholas gathered up the equipment he needed and

put it in a leather shoulder bag Dino stood outside in the light rain. In his full-length black duster he looked more like a chimney sweep than a baker.

The cab dropped them off at the entrance to the rundown apartment house. Returning to the scene soured Nicholas's mouth. His hands trembled. Glances up and down the street showed him that the usual lounging idlers had been driven indoors by the rain. His relief was short-lived. When he entered the mildewed lobby with Dino he found some of them. Three sipped from bottles hidden by paper bags. "There!" he whispered.

"What?" Dino said.

"Those two men. The one with the beret, the big man beside him. Eddie and Zak. They're the ones who attacked me!"

"They're just punks. Keep walking."

"Look who's back!" Eddie stamped a booted foot in delight. His grin was white and bright. His scar-chested partner, who wore a stained Valvoline sweatshirt against the coolness of the rainy day, chuckled and nodded. "Mars man," he said.

Nicholas hesitated. Dino shoved him in the kidney. "Keep moving. We gotta get this done."

They began to climb the eight flights of stairs. Nicholas felt ill. He reached out for jazz, but the chords chirped weakly in his mind, crushed out by the fall of their soles on the heavy steel stairs.

Below they heard muffled thumps. "They're following us just like—"

"Forget them. They're pussies. They try something, I'll prove it." Dino started taking the stairs two at a time. "Let's get up there and get the door open."

They rushed down the eighth-floor hallway, more stale and sour-smelling than Nicholas remembered. He was short of wind. Exercise played no role in his life. Dino raised a big fist and beat on the door of 836. "Open up, pal! You got trouble now, or trouble soon!"

Silence.

"He's not there," Nicholas panted.

Dino glared at him. "Or he's laying for us. *Paisan*, you got no smarts, do you?" He nodded at the lock. "Can you open it?"

"Of course."

"Do it!"

Nicholas pulled one of his inventions out of his leather bag. He unstrung its earphones and put them on. He knew this type of lock was activated by a generator producing a certain frequency. This device would tell him what it was. All he needed was a little time. He heard footsteps at the end of the littered hall.

"Punk alert," Dino said contemptuously.

Nicholas's fingers shook on the dials. The footsteps drew closer. His concentration fled. He saw Eddie and his big friend a few yards away. Both were grinning. "Can't stay away from that door, Mars man, can you?" Eddie said. "You can't open it nohow."

"Take off, you two," Dino said evenly. "Or you'll get hurt."

Zak snickered. Unlike his comrade's bright-toothed smile, his was marred by a missing tooth and black spots of decay. "Din't you hear we cleaned his clock, man?"

"I heard. Today he brought along the cavalry."

Eddie frowned. "The what?"

"I'll make it easy for the stupid," Dino said. "I'm trouble for anybody who messes with us."

Dino's voice had lowered. Color climbed in cheeks beneath which muscle rose over clenched teeth. Nicholas remembered Trish telling him the man had been in Vietnam. Dino spread his feet slightly, wholly on balance now and menacing. Like a cobra, Nicholas thought. "Now you creeps buzz off before you get hurt," Dino said.

Eddie's kick came incredibly fast. The heavy boot flew up toward Dino's crotch. Faster than Nicholas could think, Dino somehow moved backward. He clutched the exposed ankle at waist height and lunged forward. Eddie went over backward. The back of his head hit the floor with stunning force. His yelling mouth took the full force of Dino's own kick. He screamed as four of his front teeth flew out.

With a curse Zak came in hard and low. Dino jumped aside and lashed at the big man's ears and eyes with curved fingers. When Zak came at him a second time he had a tire iron in his hand. Eddie's whines of pain echoed in the hall.

Dino's smile was horrid, more a rictus exposing his teeth like the fangs of a warring ape or baboon. Was it blood lust or madness? Nicholas felt a bolt of panic. What kind of man was this?

A whirl of black cotton duster and Dino was facing Zak with a sawed-off shotgun in his hands. "My scrawny pal here told me about your chest, *paisan*. You could be the first one on your block with matching blasts." He extended the shotgun, finger on the trigger. "You know about semiautomatics like this? Every time I pull the trigger you get a lead bouquet. At this range it'll tear pieces off you like a bear." He stepped forward and raised the twin metal Os till they were pointed at Zak's skull. "Or take the top of your head off like a can opener."

"Jesus, man, don't—"

Having been frightened badly by the two thugs, Nicholas found himself almost as frightened by Dino.

He sensed Dino wanted to pull the trigger.

Zak broke and ran. Dino swung his weapon down toward sprawled Eddie. He whimpered, scrambled up, and rushed after his companion. On the floor lay a smear of blood and pieces of his smile. "Come back and die!" Dino shouted.

When he turned back to Nicholas his face was florid. His eyes burned like torches. "Scum! Beneath contempt."

Nicholas couldn't bear that hot gaze. He busied himself with the lock, aware of his companion's heaving breath, knowing his blood lust hadn't yet subsided. He concentrated on finding the correct frequency. He found it, then nearly dropped the hand-held unit while reaching for the one to actually open the lock. He steadied himself, feeling half a continent out of place.

When the mechanism clicked Dino said, "Step back!" His voice was a harsh croak. Nicholas pressed himself against the wall. Dino grabbed the knob, turned it. He swung the door wide.

The only sound was Dino's grunting breath.

Nicholas looked over Dino's shoulder. The apartment was dim, shades pulled down. It smelled musty, unused. He followed Dino inside. There was no furniture in the first room. "Nobody lives here!" Dino said angrily. "Goddamnit!"

In the middle of the next room stood a table. On it electronic equipment had been gathered. In an instant Nicholas knew what it was. Before he could speak Dino had lowered his shotgun. "Where are you, you scumbag coward?" he shouted.

The weapon's blast was deafening in the small room. Metal scraps and buckshot careened against the far wall. Some of the pellets ricocheted back. Nicholas winced and cowered.

"Dino, no!"

Too late! Too late. Dino fired twice more, blood lust high as flood tide. When the report echoed down to silence Nicholas rushed to the table. The equipment there had been destroyed as well as with a sledgehammer. His heart sank. Dino rushed ahead into the next room shouting and cursing. "Where are you? Come out so I can blow your friggin' head off!"

By the time he completed his search and returned to the middle room Nicholas knew exactly what had gone on here. "You made a big mistake blowing this equipment apart, Dino."

"Huh?"

"Nobody ever lived here. Carson came in and set up these units to relay the signals from the PC-Pros' bugs to wherever he's *really* holed up. If they hadn't been damaged, I could have used them to lead us to wherever he's hiding. Thanks to you, they're just useless scrap now."

"You sure you know what you're talking about, worm neck?"

"I'm afraid I do. This place was set up as a buffer between us and him—and it worked. The minute you fired he knew we were trying to track him. Now he runs." Nicholas shrugged his thin shoulders. "And maybe we'll never find him." His annoyance had made him nearly eloquent, particularly so because his companion had behaved so stupidly. He was still intimidated by Dino, but now less so.

Dino cursed in lumpish grunts. Spit flew from his lips.

This man is a stupid reptile, Nicholas thought. Worse, quite possibly he is insane.

18

"YES, MASTER. I UNDERSTAND. TERROR. YOU KNOW it's unnecessary to repeat *anything* to me." Champ listened a moment longer. Carson was so meticulous, so unwilling to entertain the possibility of error through oversight. "I hear and I obey!" He chuckled. A common joke of theirs.

Yet . . .

How perceptive Carson was! Could he have guessed that loyal Champ's increasing determination to return Queen of My Heart to his master's life had somehow distracted him from the next step? The nature of the distraction was unclear, even to Champ's exalted intellect and lucid personal insights. While the illness was obscure, its symptoms were not. He had made oversights, little careless errors in carrying out his tasks that astonished him. He was also letting things slide. It had taken him several days to replace the PC-Pros' bugs with more sophisticated ones after Nicholas Smith-Patton had removed them.

That new bugs should be operated without a protective buffer seemed an error to him. The electronic road to Resurrection Headquarters was open, should someone like Nicholas resume his investigations. His unexpected appearance on the scene had distressed Champ. Not so Carson. No matter the spidery one's unmistakable gifts, his master's genius would triumph. Queen of My Heart and Melody *would* be returned to his side.

Yet what of Champ's distracted mental state, he, sole soldier under Colonel Carson's command? What did it mean that when Carson told him to mail Tape Ten to the Loathed One he had momentarily balked? Balked! Then he realized he could easily make a copy. Till then he hadn't recognized how greatly he coveted what the tapes showed: Queen of My Heart's white, twisting limbs, glistening pink disclosures . . . As if to compensate for those few seconds of imagined loss, he was compelled to view all ten tapes sequentially. Dared he count the increasing hours he spent mesmerized by Queen of My Heart's charms? To the sweet cake of her dominated flesh he added the Bavarian frosting of recent footage of her spread and pinned by the Loathed One. Already that tape was a rarity; Nicholas the meddler had torn out the cameras. See her fingernails set in Foster's shoulders like Dracula's teeth! Feel the whiz-bangs charge Champ's blood like an electrolytic! He spasmed on and on and on. . . .

Though stewing and brooding, he was unable to survey fully the shifting plain of his mind. Analysis failed. Never in earlier times had he failed to understand himself. He was the most logical and straightforward of men. His role: obey Carson. His focus had been as sharp as an electron microscope's. Now he sensed . . . dilution of his commitment. Of course, he could never diverge from Carson's goals. Yet he sensed a fault line along shifting inner plates mapped by his growing confusion. No matter that. He still had to carry on!

He shook his bearish shoulders. *Ta-ta-taaah-ta-ta-taaaaah!* blasted the hunting horn in his mind. *Au chasse!* To the hunt! To the chase! To duty!

He carried the necessary equipment to his Blandmobile. Behind the wheel he knew it was a twenty-minute trip through the night to paradise—her home. Her next-door neighbors were on vacation, their drive screened by overgrown pines. In their thick shadows he left the car. Carson's directives had been precise, as always. His destination: Queen of My Heart's garage.

As his steps carried him closer to that structure they faltered. He turned and raised his head. Wolf under the sliver of moon! He looked toward the Victorian sprawl of her home. To his surprise, he began to walk toward it, keeping to the deepest shadows. He left his equipment on the grass. His heart rate rose. Oh! A dew of sweat fell upon his wide brow. His eyes found the windows. Within glowed the dim nightlights of women alone. Lower power bills: sleep with a man. He should be resisting this temptation. Yet his feet set themselves on their own way. Before he knew it he stood before a basement hatchway. Avast! Seaman Champ reporting for duty.

He heaved on the welded handle. Oooh! Open. He descended woody stairs, lowered the hatch above him. His never-die flashlight disclosed an oak door. An impressive lock was set under a knob. How perfect! A tumbler lock. From his pocket he pulled Carson's wonder, the Tumbler Tickler. In eight seconds he was closing the door behind him.

Why was he here? He couldn't or wouldn't answer that question. At the heart of it lay Queen of My Heart. Yet in what connection he sought to bring himself to her presence he couldn't imagine. The flashlight led him through mildew and along whitewashed stone walls to the stairs. Up he went, silent as a bat. Mr. Slyboots! He eased open the door and found himself in a pantry. Wheatsworth crackers and Dinty Moore beef stew, Hi-C juice, Cain's mayo—on these she feasts!

Onward! He entered the kitchen, chose a door. He remembered the house's layout from his earlier visits. Feet close to banister to quiet creaking, he ascended to heights where his angel dwelled. On the second floor he stopped.

He could smell her!

Eau de la Reine. Compounded of shampoo and soap scents, the unseen effusions of her pores, the balm of her breath drawn shallow in sleep. Follow your nose! And hear your heart! It thumped now like a stripper's drummer, as though he had climbed a skyscraper of stairs instead of one modest flight.

His camera had shown him where and how she lay in slumber. But it hadn't blessed him with curtains stirred by a light July breeze, the ratty slippers mating under the over-hang of bedsprings—or his own lumpish form in the closet door's full-length mirror.

He should not be there.

He took four long, silent strides. He stood at her bedside. His bowels shook as though seized with fatal fever. Behold, behold! More that the camera hadn't caught. The tone of her skin, the topography of sheet folds in loose right-hand grip, the glistening track of moisture from the corner of a mouth parted in sleep.

He had feasted first his sense of smell, now sight. What remained but to touch and taste? He leaned forward.

No, no! *She was Carson's.*

He should not be there!

His heart slammed his ribs like John Henry's hammer. A drop of sweat ran down his nose, fell free and struck bedspread, became an ephemeral smudge in the paisley. No, he should not be there.

His arm raised itself, his fingers extended.

Her soft neck seized his attention. It seemed to stretch itself like Alice growing taller in Wonderland.

He spread his hands. Let him wrap that ivory column with the bony ropes of his fingers!

"Mommy, Mommy!" Melody's scream from her room.

He jerked his hand back as though wakened from a dangerous dream. Panic followed. Mothers could raise themselves from the dead on hearing their child's weakest cry.

"Mommy, I'm having a dream!"

Champ rushed from bedside to closet, tore open the door, flung himself among clothes. Queen of My Heart's sweet odor was rent by the rancid edge of his sweat. He stood motionless, dripping amid cloth's caress.

He wondered if Carson's powers extended to the sorcery of an induced nightmare delivered to Melody's brain at that penultimate moment. If somehow his master had known—did Champ even know?—on what acts' edges he had teetered, punishment would be absolute.

Absolute.

"Melody, it's okay! Mother's coming."

And Champ is going!

He heard the give of springs, the faintest rustle of hurried strides. Crack the door. Out with the head. The way was clear! A 210-pound man could move like a wraith on two cat feet. Whoooosh! Down the stairs, to the pantry, the cellar, and out.

In the shadow of the garage he panted, sweat drying too slowly. He shuddered at where he had gotten to, what he might have done. Behind any such forbidden behaviors would lie Carson's wrath, following as surely as thunder after lightning. Next: furious punishment.

More terrifying than Carson in full rage was the vivid lesson he had just learned.

He no longer maintained stony control over his behaviors!

Bewilderment rose like the dew on the grass at his feet.

The Tumbler Tickler got him into the garage and under the hood of her car. At work, with devices of his own assembly in hand, his newfound uncertainties subsided. His mood improved. He hummed as he worked. In time he smiled. He sang in a low voice, "To dream the impossible dream . . ."

19

NICHOLAS HAD REACHED NEW HEIGHTS OF PECULIARITY when making his report, Trish thought, nosing her Acura through traffic. It had taken her a while to translate the evasive eye contact, foot shifting, and dome stroking. Eventually she understood they meant he had been embarrassed and chagrined. Dino's shotgun blasts had sent all his determined technical efforts down the chute.

Trish had hidden her disappointment at the news. Nicholas attempted to hearten himself by sharing with her new ideas about how he would resume the electronic hunt for Carson. She sent him on his way with words of encouragement and cheer that she didn't truly feel. She had put a lot of stock in the odd man's scheme. That it should have failed on Dino's account she found disappointing. It seemed his inner steadiness had been a facade. In his way he was even less reliable than his spidery partner. An odd couple indeed.

Buying bread at Estrella, she found Dino sheepish and apologetic. Sometimes he could be hotheaded, he explained. Trish imagined she heard again frightened Rocco DeVita talking angrily of deranged Vietnam vets.

Dino reached across the counter and touched her hand

where it rested beside the white bag. "Don't give up on me, Patricia," he said. "I can be a help to you. I know it. Besides just me and Mario keeping an eye on your building. I want you to call on me again. I won't screw up. Promise."

Had she more forces in her fight against Carson, she would have politely kissed him off. But a quick tally of troops, especially with Foster's loyalty hanging in the balance, told her she couldn't spare Dino, no matter his taste for the quick and violent.

Thoughts of Foster wheeled her back to memories of their relationship over the last two weeks, shifting like a river delta in floodtime. She groaned, wondering more than ever if they would allow themselves to reach the haven of September fifteenth nuptials. He had ordered a one-week break in their relationship—to Trish's great anxiety—the day after he had confronted her with the lewd videotape. He needed that time to "confer with my heart," as he put it. She feared he would go to Lois Smith-Patton with his dilemma. Trish could well imagine Lois sending a final torpedo into the damaged vessel of his engagement.

To her joy, the hiatus ended with his invitation to go sailing. He set a course for the middle of the bay. She waded patiently through a marsh of his small talk, waiting for his assessment of the status of their relationship. From it would issue the condition of not only their engagement, but his compassion. A man's love was best read when tested.

In time he dropped the anchor, left the wheel, and joined her where she sat sunning in her favorite deck chair. He wore clip-on mirror sunglasses against the glare. They gave him the look of a blind man. She would have preferred to see his eyes.

"Trish, I've been thinking a great deal about us."

"Good thoughts, I hope."

"Good and bad, to be honest."

"I want to hear where you've gotten to," she said evenly.

He sat silent. The gentle swells stroked the hull. "I've had to work hard to deal with your past. It hasn't been easy."

Trish began to speak sympathetically, but he cut her short

with a jabbing gesture. "Before I can say I've been success-ful, I have to ask you a question. I'm sure you can imagine what it is."

She frowned. "I'm not sure I can."

"Oh? I had hoped you would. If you had, you might understand the source of some of my . . . anguish. The question is: Do you have any more surprises for me? Like those I've recently had? The depravity of your relationship with Carson, for example. The minor detail that Melody, sweet as she is, is another man's bastard—"

"Foster! That *word*. It—doesn't *fit* her."

He shrugged. "And that, whatever your sexual adven-tures, you never bothered to marry. Are there more such revelations in store for me? Even one more?"

"No!"

"Are you sure?" The blind man's glasses turned to her in unspoken skepticism.

"Absolutely."

"Your word?"

"Foster!"

"No more weird secrets in Trish Morley's traveling bag?"

"I said no."

He nodded. "Then . . ." He smiled. "Let's go below and make love."

"Yes!"

She remembered Mother Marylou's pronouncement about the bed being the best adjudicator of lovers' quarrels. She scampered down the hatch, giggly and frisky. In the end it was going to be all right!

They stripped on the wide bunk. Midsummer tan lines marked their skin. She reached up. "I'll take your glasses off." Her job in the preludes to their private loving.

"No. I'll leave them on for now."

"You look like a blind man," she said softly.

"I have been."

Trish readied herself for his touch, eager to please. She wove herself enthusiastically into the familiar pattern of his kisses. By now she knew the order of his caresses and anticipated them with delight.

He broke the order.

She opened passion-weighted eyes. He was groping beneath the bunk. She clung to his neck, impatient with the unexpected delay. "Foster . . ." She ran the moist pad of her tongue across his ear.

His hands moved up into view. In them he held short lengths of plastic line. "Give me your hands," he said.

He was going to tie her to the bunk.

She began to tremble, not in fear, but in dismay. Far from getting past Carson and Queen of My Heart, Foster had allowed himself to be infected with the devil's disease. Nothing positive for either him or Trish could come from knotted lines and mock submission. Having Foster conduct himself this way was no more natural than a modern artist beginning to paint like an Old Master. Time and personalities built stronger barriers than her fiancé could ever climb with his timid copycatting.

"Don't," she said.

He ignored her, sliding the previously tied slip knots around her wrists. "It's nothing you don't know well," he said.

Anguish rose in her heart. Couldn't he understand that what he was attempting to do wasn't authentic for him? She had accepted his adequate loving, wishing only distantly for long-gone forbidden pleasures. He, too, should accept the physical side of their relationship as it was. How crucial was self-acceptance to happiness!

No one could be Carson but Carson. No one!

What she ought to do now confronted her with the might of a philosophical question. Should she oppose what he was attempting because in the end it was doomed to fail, or should she go along for now? She faced a woman's dilemma. She had to judge whether or not this was a situation in which it would be wise to defer her own wishes in favor of those of her man. Resisting him might well punch out another board from the already damaged hull of their engagement. On the other hand, submitting carried some messages, too, about how far short her bid to become and remain independent had fallen—when put to a real test.

He reached for her ankles now. She wished he would take off those foolish sunglasses.

This was all wrong.

"I want you to stop!" she cried.

"I don't believe you."

"Foster . . . please."

He ignored her.

"Foster!"

He tried to work a rope around her ankle.

Abruptly she got angry. It was a healthy anger bubbling up from her restored ego. How dare he! Never again would she stand for this treatment. *Never!* "Foster, I'm telling you not to fool with me."

"Is that so?"

"Yes!"

He didn't reply. The glasses masked his eyes. He pressed close to her.

Abruptly she was in a rage. She exploded and drove a foot up into his crotch. "Aaaah!" he howled. He doubled over, white-faced, clutching his middle. Grimacing, he glared wildly at her.

She screamed, "Untie my hands! I let Carson do this sort of thing before. I'll never let him or you or *anyone* do it again!"

Foster grunted and gasped for breath.

"Foster, do as I say! *Now.* If you want a life with me . . ."

He took deep breaths, his pain fading. Still he made no move to free her. She knew his thoughts then, her mortification welling. He was thinking of forcing her.

"Foster Palmer! This instant! *Untie me!*" She saw the beads of sweat blossoming from his recent pain. The creases newly drawn in his face hinted at an aged Foster. He turned toward her, his mouth a narrow channel under the brown disks of the sunglasses.

"Take off the glasses, Foster!" she ordered.

He hesitated.

"Do it!"

He began, "You're—"

"Take them off!"

He did as she ordered. His hands were shaking. "Patricia—"

"Shut up!" She locked glances with him. She sensed he would look away. She sent her gaze like an arrow into his. After a long moment his eyes sought the floor, and relief.

She realized she had won a test of wills. "Loosen the ropes," she ordered.

His long fingers moving over her wrists filled her for the moment with loathing. She could scarcely grasp the extent of her disappointment in him. He had proved himself so much more limited than she had ever dreamed.

He made it worse still by then trying to make a joke of what he had attempted. He babbled on, forcing laughter like corn down the neck of a Gascony goose. She stared at him and gathered fresh insights.

She was stronger than he now. Much stronger. That strength was a searchlight that increasingly illuminated the defects in his personality.

Driving to an appointment the next morning, she took little pleasure from probing her fiancé's character and finding soft spots. She sensed—irrationally, she supposed —that Carson himself had set in motion the cogs of that reevaluation. She felt a chill and shivered despite herself.

She began to feel Carson closing in on her. She imagined him somehow standing unseen beside her. She found herself not wanting to be alone, lest that give him the opportunity to approach, should he wish it. Yet so far as she knew, stopping the wedding, rather than confronting her, was his sole desire.

For now.

Should the wedding be canceled, she sensed he would come forward with some other equally outrageous demand. One that he would force her with glacial strength to meet. She knew Carson. The Master of Excess.

Her fears deepened when she thought about vulnerable Melody, now visiting Washington, D.C., with Grandma. When she came back to walk through the rest of the summer mosaic assembled for her entertainment and education, how could Trish protect her from Carson? Should he kidnap the child and demand the wedding be scrapped, Trish would consent. No question! Blood always told.

She had so hoped Nicholas would lead the police to Carson's hiding place! For the time being he and Dino had failed. How could ordinary men penetrate the secret world of genius?

She groaned with dread.

She pressed a radio preset button to the golden oldies station. *Ba-Ba-Ba-Ba-Barbara Ann . . .*

Coming to the site of a seemingly endless road-bridge construction area, she swung off the highway onto a secondary road, beginning her familiar self-designed detour. Two lefts and a right later she was heading down a narrow street faced with warehouses. Here, too, roads were under construction. But not today.

The Acura's engine sputtered, stalled. Muttering, she spun the ignition key. The engine caught. She drove sixty yards, then it died again. She didn't like this part of the city. The streets were deserted, except for an occasional disheveled wanderer. She tried four times to restart the engine. Grind, grind, but no ignition.

Maybe it was flooded. She sat for five minutes, looking nervously around. If it didn't start now, she was going to use her car phone. No way was she going for a hike in this neighborhood. The warehouses seemed to grow several stories higher and lean out above the narrow street.

She glanced in the rearview mirror. Motion. From an alley on the right emerged a monster road roller, two high, heavy cylinders with a cab in the middle. Great! It was turning in her direction. No way it could get around her. She'd have to get out and explain the situation to the operator as soon as the machine stopped behind her car.

As the roller drew closer its towering front cylinder completely filled the rearview mirror. How slowly it moved! Weight was its thing, not speed. Its size was hypnotic. Having it anywhere behind her car was threatening. She waited for it to stop.

It didn't.

Her radio blasted: *"Trish, Carson, and Melody—together forever!"* That voice! It had already crept as unexpectedly as a snake from previously doctored radios. That didn't make it less terrifying now.

It was worse, because she understood she had been caught in a trap!

The massive roller's metal curve touched her rear bumper.

"No!"

"Trish, Carson, and Melody—together forever!"

The Acura shook. Clatter behind. Her bumper had been broken off! Oh, Lord! The roller operator was going to crush her car!

But not her. No way! She was out of there! She unbelted, touched the electronic door lock button, and flipped the driver's side lever. She flung her shoulder against the door.

It didn't open.

It was still locked!

Baffled, she touched the lock button again. The lock posts stayed down. The electronics had been tampered with! Carson's work!

Grinding from the rear. Two explosions. The rear tires had blown. The Acura's rear sank. The windshield rose before her, pointing the way to the sky, not the road.

She spun in her seat and dug at the driver's side lock post with her thumb.

It wouldn't budge. *It wouldn't budge!*

She was going to be crushed to death!

The noise of thin sheet steel and frame collapsing sounded deafening in the enclosed space.

The window. She could crawl out the window. She pressed the electronic window stud. The glass began to lower! She could get out.

Halfway down it stopped. She shoved the stud harder, but the window didn't budge. She couldn't fit through the opening. Carson had thought of that, too! Her finger slipped, and her nail snapped.

She didn't want to scream. She simply couldn't stop herself.

When she drew breath she heard: *"Trish, Carson, and Melody—together forever!"* She was too panicked to bother silencing the radio.

What did that voice matter when she was going to die?

She flung herself against the door, shrieking when it didn't budge. Behind, the trunk had collapsed. The rear seats tilted forward. Above, the roof began to slant backward. In moments it would press down, crushing her. She would become a smear of blood and bone amid metal and flattened seating.

The side windows' glass followed suit. She felt the heat of friction, smelled torn paint and plastic. Her screams drowned out the sounds of destruction.

Her seat nudged her back. It was folding forward! The roof brushed her hair like a fatal caress. She leaned forward. The wheel! It would crush her chest. She flung herself across the seat. She beat the upholstery in a spasm of terror and panic.

The seat back pressed forward. She squirmed onto the floor. The shift lever dug into her hip. Face up, she saw the roof descend, curved in the arc of the roller.

In seconds she would be dead!

Only after ten rapid heartbeats did she realize the only sound now was her screaming. The roller no longer advanced. She lay motionless for two dozen thrusts of her hurried heart. She had time to understand how uncomfortable she was, how raw her throat from shrieking.

She squirmed up. Her head spun as she peered through webbed windows and windshield. Her eyes were smeared with tears of hysteria. Ahead on the corner thirty yards away stood a figure. Though she couldn't see clearly, she nonetheless recognized who waved and smiled at her.

Carson!

The world roared, darkened, and she was swept away. . . .

When she awoke firemen and police were prying her out of what had been her Acura. They were using a machine with dinosaur-sized jaws. The road roller had been backed off down the street. A paramedic invited Trish into her ambulance for a quick quiz and once-over. When finished she smiled and said, "Not a scratch!"

"At least on the outside," Trish muttered numbly. "How did this army of help find me?"

"You're just a lucky lady. Cruiser on patrol notified us."

The paramedic gave her two capsules and a small cup of water. "Something for your nerves—if you have any left."

Outside the ambulance she found Detective Jerry Morris waiting. He wore a seersucker jacket, dark slacks, and mirrored sunglasses. "Some people stop at nothing to get attention," he said.

"What does one expensive car mean if I could draw a crowd?" Trish was aware her knees shook. She was a long way from being calmed down.

"Want a beer or Coke?"

"A ride would be nice, too."

"Yeah, I guess you won't be driving the Acura again."

In the unmarked sedan Trish said, "Carson did this. I saw him."

"Congratulations. Nobody else has seen him here. Nobody's seen him in California, either, for quite a while. I've been talking to the PDs there about the Doctor and Daughter Destroyer."

"What did you find out?"

"Bunch of things. The most interesting was that when he mutilated the women they're sure he used heavy shears. The garden kind."

Trish gasped. Yes! She remembered Carson working on her clothing with such a tool. Clipping and snipping. Prelude to love and domination. She groaned softly. "Then I'm *absolutely* sure Carson killed them, Jerry."

He slid his sunglasses down his nose and glanced at her. "Funny thing about that. Investigators turned up a witness. Lady said she saw somebody leaving the second murder scene. She didn't get a great make. They showed her the photo I faxed of your buddy Carson."

"And she said it was he," Trish muttered.

"Whoever it was, it wasn't your man," Jerry said.

"What?"

"She didn't get too good a look, okay? They're working with her doing an artist's composite."

"But it wasn't Carson?"

He pushed his glasses back up his nose. "Nope."

"Do the police still suspect him, then?"

"They seem to."

"Why?"

"I haven't found that out yet."

Trish remembered Eileen, who had impersonated her while she made her escape from Carson, telling her she hadn't been told that detail either. She was supposed to be working on it through her reporter boyfriend. Trish ought to give her a call. There had been too much on her mind—and still was.

Jerry insisted on buying her dinner—half a calzone and three Lites, as it turned out. She told him the details of her Acura's adventures with the road roller. Midway through the second beer she brought him up to date on Nicholas and Dino's adventures in search of Carson's hideout. She became aware that the words spilled from her lips in a wild rush. Having been nearly frightened to death had left her nerves in tatters.

Jerry shook his head. "All this to stop you from getting married?"

She nodded.

Jerry leaned forward. "A suggestion? Friend to friend?"

She nodded. "Sure."

"Why don't you marry Foster Palmer right away? Like . . . tomorrow?"

Thoughts of Portugal rushed forward. Abruptly she was leaking tears. "Remember? I told you he . . . asked me to do that!" she wailed. "I said no. I wanted to wait till Sep-tem-ber."

He began to make man noises of sympathy. She shook her head, tears dribbling. "I told you I wanted time to . . . test the relationship. And Foster's not passing the test!" She was bawling like a babe now. Jerry slid his chair over beside hers. He enfolded her in a gentle hug. "Hey, it's okay to cry."

"It's so—public!" she blubbered.

"So we'll go to my place."

He owned a condo with a deck. On the ride there she managed to regain some of her composure. She had surprised herself by confessing her emotional turmoil. Before, she had been very much a private person. Too much so, really. Now, with Jerry, she had no wish to hold her tongue. She didn't understand why. Sitting with him on the darkened deck, she didn't care why. He had made coffee. She clutched her mug as cool breezes stirred.

"You see what's happening, Jerry? Carson is getting his way again. For me he's the devil. Do you understand?"

"Not exactly."

"I thought he was out of my life, that I had escaped him. But he's back again. He knows me so well that he might as well be in my head—like the devil. I've bargained away my soul to him, in a way. Look what he's done. Taken effective steps to destroy my business. He's destroying my relationship with my fiancé, too. He's beginning to reduce me to the dominated person I was. He can only do those things because of his intimate knowledge of me, of my soul. See what I mean?"

"We'll find him. We'll put him away, either behind bars or at Mental Estates."

Trish was glad her face was deeply shadowed. Jerry would think her smile loony. "Somehow I don't think you will. No matter what you try. Even if you had everybody on the force working full-time on the case, never mind your efforts and Lieutenant Sarkman's half-hearted ones. Carson is . . . Carson. Genius unchecked. He's my devil. I'll have to be the one to drive him away. Either I do it, or . . . I'm finished. My daughter and I will be his for the rest of our lives. And . . ." Her voice caught like rag on thorn. "You can't imagine how miserable we would be."

"How do you expect to rid yourself of him?" Jerry said.

"I haven't the faintest notion." She got up and walked to the edge of the deck where flowers grew in long boxes. "He's a contemporary devil. No crucifix and holy water for him. No traditional rites of exorcism would work." She stared off toward other condo clusters. "There's more to it, too, Jerry. I've grown as a human being since I left him. If I'm to grow the rest of the way, to reach whatever potential I have, I have to completely and permanently escape him."

"We have to find him!" Jerry said.

"You've had my photo of him for nearly a month, haven't you? And nobody's seen him except me."

"Oh, he's out there—somewhere. Nicholas is on his track."

"Could you make a cop available if Nicholas comes up with something this time?"

"Maybe. Depends on when. Trish, I just don't have the *authority* with your case."

"Could you talk to Sarkman?"

"The prima donna? Lots of luck."

She spun in the dimness. "Jerry, I need your help!"

"I know one way to help you. A simpleminded way, but at least it'll be something."

"What's that?"

"Get you a pistol and teach you to shoot."

She protested. She knew nothing about handguns. Not to worry, he said. He would teach her. He arranged for her licensed revolver, a smallish, deadly-looking thing. She found its bluish steel and the gleam of copper cartridges fascinating as he made her repeatedly load and unload it. At mutually suitable times he took her to a private range. At first she shot at stationary targets, with sound deadeners clinging to her ears like hi-fi phones. Then, when she felt ready for more adventure, they stalked pop-up figures into which she put bullets with surprising accuracy—and enthusiasm.

"Women are men's equals as marksmen," Jerry said. "It's that they hesitate to kill with their weapons that makes the difference."

"The difference between civilization—and none, if we left it up to the men."

"The only question you have to ask yourself is: Could you shoot at Carson?" Jerry said.

"Just give me a chance."

"I hope the opportunity's all you need."

After their sixth and final three-hour session he drove her toward PC-Pros. "How do you feel after an hour of revolver practice?"

She lowered her lids. "Do you believe—sexy?"

He laughed, Mr. Straight Cop. "It can definitely be a turn-on."

She was tempted to tease him, asking if he was interested. No, that wouldn't do. Jerry was too straight. Think what further confusions another emotional relationship would introduce into her already tumbled life! Foster was her man and would stay so until Carson had done his worst. After that, who knew where—and who—she would be. And what about Dino? For now Jerry could only be a friend.

He had accepted that from the first moment he learned she was engaged. In their conversations during her firearm training he had revealed himself to be a churchgoing man who truly believed in right and wrong. And in God as well. To him it was wrong to become physically involved with an engaged woman. It was also wrong to lie, steal, do drugs, or break the law. In her life, Trish admitted, she had met few such people. When she had, her memory reminded her, she had made fun of them. She arrogantly lived her life according to her own improvised principles. Only recently had she come to lament where that ad hoc ethical system had taken her. How often would she be reminded that she wasn't as smart as she thought? She hoped not too often. It always resulted in embarrassment—or worse.

No matter that Carson closed in on her life in ever-diminishing circles, she was still a mother. She had promised Melody mother-daughter mini-vacations. The girl still had to be driven places when Grandma and Stoneman Gore weren't available. She still had to be readied for picnics and sleepovers and supported during two weeks of day camp.

Foster, too, needed careful care and feeding of quite a different kind. She told him about her nearly fatal run-in with the road roller. He understood her terror, and through it he set a finer gauge on Carson's obsession. He was too much the gentleman to dwell on his dissatisfactions. A sailing race took him away on the *Emerald Lady* for nearly two weeks, reducing tensions and allowing her to gather emotional strength. She was glad she had taught him a lesson about trying to sexually dominate her. It was just so wrong for both of them!

PC-Pros turned as demanding as a sulking lover. Fallout from Carson's sabotage spread. Lester O'Day of Pristine Cleaners closed his account in favor of another vendor. Louise O'Day, her attorney, had politely insisted she be given a substantial retainer. Dynamited Kandinsky Klein and Corman was pressing its suit. Since Mr. Beetlebrow had told her his bank wouldn't give Trish another loan, she was keeping PC-Pros afloat financially by dipping into her own savings. She buried herself in budgeting and long-range planning because she wouldn't accept the possibility that the business might fail.

She worked out a sales strategy with Samantha Swords. The brassy woman did wonders for Trish's own self-confidence. Of course things were going to be all right, Samantha said. How could PC-Pros not fly with both of them on board? Sam stood and waved her beefy arms as though trying to take off. Trish burst into laughter and clapped her hands. A little humor was a rare thing lately.

The phone warbled. She picked it up. Michelle was sending a call through. "Somebody from police headquarters," she said.

"Trish Morley speaking."

"Feeling crushed? Cancel the wedding!"

That voice! The one that had been tormenting her for weeks. Not Carson's voice, though. Whose? "I won't!"

"You should. Do your chubby saleslady a favor." He hung up.

Samantha was staring at her. "Trish! Your face. You look like a compulsive blood donor."

Trish sank back in her chair. "Another threat."

Samantha scowled. "Can't the cops catch that nut?"

"He . . . mentioned you."

"Oh?" Sam was interested.

Trish had spared her staff the details when discussing the

recent troubles. She concentrated on events and avoided providing specifics about Carson's personality and obsession. They knew about the bugging, the virus, the exploding PC, and the road roller. And that someone wanted her to cancel her wedding. Just the same, there was distancing between them and the magnitude of Carson's madness.

Now that would end.

"What did he say about me?" Samantha's hands were on her hips. She looked solid, unflappable.

"Nothing specific. Sam, I—"

"Don't worry, Trish. I won't cut and run."

"There's no reason for you to get tangled up in this. Why don't you take some time off, go away for a couple weeks?"

"What? We just finished working out our sales strategy. I don't remember there being any vacations scheduled."

"Sam, he can be . . . dangerous."

The big woman snorted and made a fist. "I'll take my chances," she said.

"I want you to be careful!" Trish surprised herself with the volume of her warning. Her voice seemed to ring from the ceiling. "Carson isn't a . . . prankster, Sam. He's more like the devil himself!"

Sam turned narrowed eyes toward Trish. "I hear you. I really do."

Trish watched Sam leave, then looked down at shaking hands.

20

I HEAR AND I OBEY! CHAMP CHUCKLED. FOREVER AT
your service, Master Carson. True blue for you! He had just
been given his second assignment as the Masked Marvel.
The first had been a joy. "You can make big bucks as a heavy
equipment operator!" Oh, cunning, cunning Carson! No
ordinary mask this, no domino-on-a-stick, no rubbery rot-
faced repulser to delight delinquents on All Soul's Eve. This
was the king's ransom-priced work of a Pacific Northwest
master. May he rest in peace, his silence assured by Champ's
wire into his left eye socket—and beyond! He carefully
donned mask before mirror. Look, Ma! A new head. Crown
to collarbone. Snug as a condom.

He greeted this latest assignment with his old enthusiasm.
The one he had formerly summoned easily before Queen of
My Heart had increasingly seized his thoughts. His right
role was to admire her image snared by media. The creature
of pumping heart, flesh, and secretions was Carson's. So
spoke his rational mind. Yet . . . he had been moved
by uncontrollable forces to enter her bedroom and hover
over her like Nosferatu. He despaired when reflection
revealed that what he wanted to sink into her was not his
teeth.

He had wailed at comprehending his own frailty. He flew to his Queen of My Heart tapes and whiz-bangs. A dozen spasms followed by seizures of Earthquake Anger restored his self-possession—or so he told himself.

Deep down he doubted.

Today Queen of My Heart wouldn't be the object of his attentions. Another had been selected. He went to his equipment. Like a salmon or Arctic tern her car had been tagged with a pulse source. Busy Champ! Active on so many fronts in the campaign to resurrect Queen of My Heart.

He chose a suitable hat from his collection. Headwear should match the job at hand. Today a blue laborer's cap with a short brim would be just the ticket. He donned it at a jaunty angle.

To the Blandmobile he carried a hand-held monitor. On its screen a reduced map of the city showed her approximate location.

It was time to rendezvous.

A drive across the town, then . . . ah, a visual sighting! In traffic behind her Toyota he waited for the main chance. Yes, coffee break time! Dunkin Donuts. Love their oat bran muffins! Healthy. The careful lady locked her car but left it out of sight of counter and cruller. Error.

Champ nosed the Blandmobile to the curb. Lucky legal parking space. No meters. Tumbler Tickler in hand, he ambled to the driver's side door. A mere flick of the wrist, ladies and gentlemen, and he was inside. Into the backseat, then onto the floor. Happy discovery, a raincoat! It would cover part of his body. He snaked an arm out and pushed down the lock post. Nobody here but us crushed cups and crusts.

One of us with a short, sharp knife.

The door opened. The front seat heaved. This was a solid lady. He smelled distinctive Dunkin Donuts coffee. Made their reputation on it. Clicks and clanks, and then they were underway. When the Toyota was rolling smoothly he wriggled the knife out of his belt. He rose behind Ms. Samantha Swords as silent as Hamlet's first ghost.

Quick-handed Champ palm-muffled her mouth. "Surprise!" he cooed. Their eyes met in the mirror. Frightened she was, but not panicked. A hard case. Well, he would be working on that. Her foot's pressure on the accelerator faltered a moment, then steadied. He shoved the tip of the knife point gently into the side of her neck. "Don't want your dough," he sang. "Don't want your bod. Just settle back and drive this rod!" He wriggled the knife point just a hair. A tiny red drop oozed. No more! "The hand comes off in a second," he said. "No screaming. No careening. Just drive. This knife is sharper than Mark Twain's wit. Got it?"

She nodded. He slid his hand away, the other tensed against treachery.

"Who are you? What do you want?"

He said nothing.

"This has to do with Trish and PC-Pros, doesn't it?"

"Make a left at the next block."

She tried to chat. He gave directions only. In the mirror he studied her face. Start with the stubborn jaw, outthrust and dimpled, the thinnish lips too narrow for the broad face. Nice nose, though, nostrils arched and handsome. The planes of skin were poreless. Brown eyes with curious yellow flecks moved between mirror and road. She was getting a good look at his face. Lot of good it would do her. Above her curious eyes arched bushy brown brows and a high sweep of forehead. Her face was as solid and reliable as her body.

By now they were out of the city. Countryside unfolded. They left the interstate, wound on two-lane blacktop, then off onto dirt road, finally bumping along a grassy track. He ordered her out of the car. She eyed him warily. "Where the hell are we? What are you going to do?" Absence of familiar surroundings: tip of the wedge of breaking her. A surge of inward glee bubbled up in Champ's heart.

This was going to be fun!

"We can go back whenever you're ready," he said. "Just tell me you're going to resign from PC-Pros."

Her eyes narrowed. "So it is. . . . I'm not mixed up in anything that has to do with Trish Morley!"

"You are, Samantha Swords. You work for her. That is, up until you decide you don't want to anymore. That should be in"—Champ shrugged—"two or three hours, maybe much less." He showed her the knife, waved it. "Up the hill, please."

Halfway up she bolted. The arrogance! The thrill of the chase rose up and gave wings to his thick legs. He bounded by branch and bower. She was faster than she looked, prepped no doubt by yuppy health club muscle machines. She screamed. Let her. Only small islands in American Micronesia were more isolated than this carefully chosen spot. She was a super screamer. Lots of diaphragm power in that big chest. Scream on, scream on . . . He accelerated. Tree trunks flew by. Luke Skywalker revisited! Hearing him behind, she tried to dodge and dart. Fit she was, but no NFL running back. He brought her down with a tackle worthy of a Steeler linebacker.

The collision of bone and flesh and the scented sweat of her exertion and fear swung Champ's lash of lust. He felt heaving breasts beneath his chest, each one no doubt two handfuls. He lay on bulky Samantha Swords, the sky above, the grass beneath whirling in a tornado of scarcely checked emotions. Had she been . . . Queen of My Heart. He thought the unthinkable, shoved those ideas brutally away. No! Not even if she were. And she was not.

He fumbled in his pocket for the roll of strapping tape. Zip, zip, rip! Her ankles were trussed together like a holiday bird's drumsticks.

He stood and dragged her to her feet. They faced each other, panting. "Let me go," she said. Her gaze was frank, determined. A woman of character, no question.

"Quit your job," he said.

She hesitated, weighing a lie. Whatever she said now he wouldn't believe. She knew it, too. No dummy here. She had to be convinced. The enjoyable part. He put her over his shoulder and ambled on up the hill.

He found the hole and his shovel and spade. It was hard

work digging a hole six feet deep anytime. Yesterday had been hot. He had spilled much sweat onto the heaped dirt. It would be worth it. It wasn't so much a hole to him as it was . . . the Convincer.

Complicated tools were overrated.

He pointed at the hole. "Get in," he ordered.

She looked sharply at him. He knew she was wondering, Is this it? What now? What would happen to her once in the hole? She didn't move.

Cat-quick he slipped a half-nelson on her, put knife to neck. No more Mr. Nice Guy. *"In the hole!"*

He levered her over the edge. She stood and looked up at him. Her head was about four inches from the top of the hole.

Perfect!

"You are going to leave PC-Pros, Samantha," he said.

"Why, what do you want from us?" she pleaded, lacking the energy of old, he noted without answering her.

He picked up the shovel, adjusted his cap's workmanlike angle. He filled the blade and sprinkled the soil carefully so it fell around her feet. Her eyes widened. "You're going to bury me alive!"

"Only if you're determined to keep your job." He shoveled in more dirt. She jumped to stay on top of the fresh soil. He banged her head with the shovel bottom. "No hopping!" he shouted.

Samantha whimpered and covered the top of her head with hands now smeared with moist soil. "My God!" she cried. *"My God!"*

Champ plied his shovel with the vigor of Fred C. Dobbs in the Sierra Madre. Shortly the dirt was waist-deep and rising. He had been forced to tap Samantha's head twice with the shovel bottom to keep her passive. Time now for a meeting of the minds.

He leaned on the stout hickory handle. The healthy tone of Samantha's face had drained to wedding-cake white. Rivulets of sweat ran down from her temples. Her eyes had widened, giving her a hawklike stare of fright. Nonetheless she fixed a boldish eye on him. "I know who you are. You're the man who's trying to ruin Trish. I saw your picture. You're Carson Thomas."

Oh, no, I am the Masked Marvel, he thought. I am not Carson! To her he said: "Of course. And you're . . ." He chuckled. "In a bit of a hole right now." Silly giggle, uncontrollable at that moment. "You can climb out anytime. Just promise me you'll leave PC-Pros."

She stared, said nothing.

"Ever get a lot of dirt in your mouth and up that shapely nose, Samantha? You'd probably want to get it out right away. Only you wouldn't be able to, because your arms would be weighed down by dirt. You'd heave and strain, but your hands wouldn't be able to help you. . . . But then you're a woman of intelligence and imagination. You see your final reward for stubbornness."

She cocked her head. "Maybe you're making your point."

"And if I am?"

"Then you should let me go. I'll go back to Trish and offer my resignation."

Champ swung his shovel to the ready. "No Academy Award for that acting job, my sweet! The bell-like peal of sincerity was absent." He threw the next shovelful of dirt directly into her face. "Shame! For the attempted practice of deceit."

Samantha squealed and clawed at her eyes. Tears poured forth to sluice the grit and ease the emotions. Yes, she wept in pain and distress.

Good to hear!

He slapped at her raised hands with the shovel edge. "Hands down!" He shoveled on. When her hands, then arms disappeared under reddish heaps her face seemed to drag down, stretching toward panic. He shoveled busily. The dirt embraced her elbows, then her shoulders.

"Please . . . don't cover my head!"

"How can you properly be buried alive unless I do your head, too? You're being stupid. Doubly stupid. A sincere promise from you and you're out of there. You got a taste of soil. Only a plant could love it. What do you say, Sam? Had enough?"

Her face was a smear of tears and thin, gritty mud. A stone had nicked her cheek, drawing a small red ooze. Beneath blood, sweat, and tears ran the hard metal of determination. She had cracked but not broken.

Shovel artist Champ, the True Temper Toulouse-Lautrec, stylishly edged dirt in all around her neck, patted it in place with blade bottom. Her head stood like John the Baptist's on a platter of dirt. He squatted at the edge of the hole and looked down at his living masterpiece. He reached down and flicked crumbs of soil from the pink curve of her left ear. By hand he finished packing in the soil. He left maybe an inch beneath her jaw so she could still speak.

He leaned back on his haunches. "Decision time, my sweet."

She stared at him. "Do you leave me for the varmints, like in the westerns? Or do you have the guts to finish the job?"

Extraordinary! What a woman! Defiance at the edge of the Dark Land. Here he had the potential mother of master industrialists, heavyweight champs, the likes of T. E. Lawrence, Burton of Africa. Nonetheless . . . the faintest demiquaver in her tone told inner secrets. He didn't answer her.

He knew he could break her.

Time for the rubber hose.

Her eyes darted like minnows after his every move. He offered her the length of flexible tubing. Her eyes hooded themselves as she comprehended further adventures in dirt. Her teeth were white and even. They gripped the reddish rubber, lips folding around it. Eros's muted howls rose from his desire's closet, closed now by the will to serve his master. Her eyes shuttered against the lewdness of her situation.

Time's a-wastin'! A dozen energetic shovelfuls covered the crown of Samantha's head. Now her eyes would be closed. Her outer ears would be dampened, but the inner would still function. Surely her mouth gripped the rubber tightly now, sharp enamel edges her only hold on the air of life. Shovel, shovel, shovel! Now only the hose rose from the earth, like a short shoot set out to sprout to sapling.

He leaned over the mounded dirt, put his ear to the hose. Hear the rush of her breath! Like the ocean in a seaside shell.

"Earth to the underworld!" Champ shouted. "Orpheus to Eurydice. Do you read me, Samantha?"

"I want you to dig me out. You madman!"

"I want *you* to resign from PC-Pros, you madwoman. You must be mad, because I ask so little in exchange for your life. Which I believe anyone at this point would agree I hold in my hand." By way of example he pressed the pad of his gloved, spade-wide thumb to the hose hole, closing it. Suction gripped the fabric. He could imagine her diaphragm heaving. And with it a surge of panic rising up like a tsunami. To smother. What a horrid way to exit this life! Who knew better than Champ, the smotherer of three?

Grass-cutting time at last.

After a suitably terrifying string of seconds he slid his thumb away. From the tube rushed first desperate breaths, then a frightened babble. In the rush of words he sieved out the beginnings of sincere pleading. Progress. To the thumb again.

The dirt stirred, heavy as it was. She had the biblical strength of ten. Panic, adrenaline. Further progress. He listened again. She mentioned God, several saints, her mother even. Ah, yes . . . Only at the most desperate moment would any woman call upon the name of her mother.

To the credit of her stubbornness and strong character, it took six more near-smotherings before she cracked. Wild, she promised anything, even things he didn't want. He interrupted her disjointed ravings with a shout. "I need your promise, Samantha. Your most sincere, irrevocable promise. You will resign your job, leave PC-Pros, and never return. Do I have it?"

Still she hesitated. Even now, though he knew she was a broken woman.

He closed the hose, watching the sweep hand of his Rolex Day-Date. Nearly a minute passed. He opened the hose and shouted, "Do I have your promise?"

A long rush of desperate, panting breaths. "Yes! Oh, God, Lord, yes!"

"Your *sincere* promise?"

Affirmative.

He let her breathe undisturbed for a short while. "Your promise must be sincere, Samantha. Because if it isn't, I'll find you wherever you are and kill you. Do you believe me?"

"Yes, oh, yes, Carson. Yes!" She wept, well into the hysteria that, if she wasn't careful, could smother her accidentally.

"You will resign from PC-Pros as soon as you can?"

"Yes!"

He offered gentlemanly encouragement toward calm. An accident now would be a senseless tragedy. He rose and put the spade and shovel over his shoulder. The satisfaction he felt was that of any honest laborer leaving the work site. He hummed. *I dreamed I saw Joe Hill last night . . .*

"Carson!"

"Be patient!" he shouted toward the mounded earth. "Someone will be along sooner or later to dig you out."

"Carson, Carson. *No. Dig me out now!"* Surprising volume of sound she could generate through such a narrow aperture. Fitting that her last words to him should call upon the name of his master. Or was he his own master after all?

He trotted away, her wailing fading finally. Bird songs took its place. Down the hill he strode, step light as a filly's in her paddock. Hi-ho, hi-ho, it's home from work we go!

He drove Samantha's car back to the Blandmobile. At the nearby Dunkin Donuts he ordered a Big One and a half-dozen chocolate croissants. He was nothing if not a man of elegant tastes. He ate three, then phoned the police and told them Samantha's condition and just where she was. He hung up. The last three croissants disappeared in grand gulps. He ate whatever he wanted, in massive amounts. His stomach processed anything. And he greeted each day with grand energy. Hear the Bard! *Now good digestion wait on appetite, and health on both.*

21

TRISH REALIZED SHE WAS SLOWLY PANICKING. LIKE A wall above an earthquake her resolve suddenly was shot through with cracks. While she struggled to feel connected with her small support group of friends, Carson's powers threatened to separate her from them. Then he would fall upon her like a wolf on a flock straggler. . . .

It had been Samantha's phone call that completed the illumination of Trish's desperate mind. Sam's voice! It had been harsh as a crow's cry. She said she was resigning from PC-Pros at once. Trish was shocked to silence. Before she could respond Samantha hung up. Trish phoned her repeatedly through the day. No answer. What was going on? Her evening call was answered by a woman with a stiff telephone voice. She announced herself as Alexis, Samantha's sister. Samantha wasn't taking any calls. She wouldn't tell Trish anything.

Samantha's resignation stole Trish's sleep. She tossed and fretted. Without the assertive woman next year's marketing plan was down the tube. How could she just up and quit now? What had happened to her? Trish ground her teeth with anxiety. Intuition's voice told her that whatever agent of Carson had phoned her had done as he threatened.

It took twenty minutes of persuasion the next morning to convince Alexis to allow her to talk to Samantha for a few minutes. Only after making Trish promise that she wouldn't try to talk her into changing her mind did Sam agree to meet her the next day.

Trish found her former employee sitting in a bedroom chair. She wore a light blue robe and a distant expression. She looked no more capable of making her familiar fist and pumping it than flying. Abruptly Trish was sure Samantha would never work for her again.

Samantha told her what had happened: the living burial, the terror of sightless hours of silence before the first fireman's shout, the shame and disgust she felt after fouling herself in fear. As the dreadful tale unfolded Trish imagined herself in Sam's place. In time she began to weep. Sam's face twisted in distress. "I'll be okay, Trish. Don't cry for me."

Trish's sniffles rose to wails. She cried not for Samantha, but for herself.

She was beginning to unravel.

She battled her growing despair, calmed herself. She used her handkerchief. Deep breaths!

When she had it together she asked Samantha a great favor. Would she visit the police with her?

"I already talked to them, Trish. They asked me bunches of questions. I answered all of them." Sam spoke in a monotone. "Their doctor was the one who checked me over. She gave me some pills."

"I want you to talk to my friend, Detective Morris. Maybe to a man named Sarkman."

Samantha stared at her for a long moment. Something like weariness clouded her gaze. No, it was the towering shadow of Carson's recent attentions. "I'd . . . rather not," she said.

Trish knew that was a final decision.

Trish went to Jerry Morris alone. He suggested coffee in the diner down the street from police headquarters. He had read the officers' report. "What did we find out?" he said. "Carson grabbed Samantha and buried her. He wore gloves, used her car, left nothing in the way of clues."

"There must be *something*."

He shrugged. "We didn't find anything."

Despair stirred Trish's chest. "Carson's winning," she said softly. "Losing Samantha is a big blow to my business. And"—she paused and swallowed the growing lump in her throat—"he's getting to my head big time."

Jerry's long face angled sympathetically. "I wish there was more I could do."

"You gave me the pistol lessons." She didn't want him to think he had disappointed her. Feeling that way told her he meant more to her than she realized. Her emotions were so stirred she knew better than to trust them at that moment. "I'm doing what you told me to: taking the weapon with me everywhere." She touched her big straw summer purse.

"I hope you never have to use it," he said. "If you do, I hope you *can*."

She touched his wrist. "Jerry, what should I do now?"

He looked down into his cup. "Go into conference with yourself. Do some deciding. Like how much more of Carson's meddling can you bear? Do you want to keep your business open anymore? Do you want to marry Foster tomorrow?" He glanced at her face. "How much more can your nerves take? You called Carson your devil."

"He's tangled up in me, inside and out."

"You have to do some figuring. Maybe you should talk to your fiancé."

She felt a swell of despair. How much Carson's activities had undermined her engagement! She imagined neither she nor Foster could precisely describe the nature of their relationship at this moment.

She called Foster and asked to visit. He was at the kennel. She drove out with Melody in tow. Doris the kennel manager could be relied upon to make sure the girl got a chance to play with Gog and Magog. Trish wasn't sure what she would say once she had told Foster the story about Samantha. When she finished she surprised herself by saying, "Darling, I want you to protect me and my business."

He took off his glasses and rubbed his eyes. She noticed

his face had thinned. In fact, his whole body looked lighter. "You've lost weight," she said.

"Like you, I have a great deal on my mind." There was a time when she could read him. A simpler time for both of them. Now his thoughts were riddles.

"What do you mean, protect you?" he asked.

"I—I'm not sure. I have the baker down the street watching my building. Maybe you could hire somebody to look after me. A bodyguard or something."

He looked surprised. "Have you been threatened?"

"Foster! Since that very first message on my PC screen I have been threatened. Wouldn't you say having my car crushed by a steam roller was threatening? Come on, love! My entire business and emotional life are hanging in the balance, in case you haven't noticed."

"There's no need to be difficult, Trish."

"I'm not being difficult." She leaned closer. "How much longer do you think it'll be until *I'm* buried alive instead of Samantha Swords? If not that, then something like it. Don't you see what Carson's doing? He's escalating—that awful word."

"How can you be sure what that . . . madman will do?"

"If it takes my blood flowing for him to have his way, then he'll wound me. Count on it!"

Foster made a face. "I have no idea how to protect you. Isn't that a job for the police?"

"No! It's a job for you. I *need* you." She knew she was being unfair. She couldn't help it. It was her nerves. It was Carson. It was everything! Most of all it was her relationship with Foster slowly unraveling under the picking finger of Carson's devilish genius. When Foster looked at her now he saw not who she had grown to be but who she had been when the loathsome videotape had been made. Her disappointment over his failure of perception was deepened by his single effort to physically degrade her in turn. Her defeat of his attempt to pursue Carson's skewed erotic ghost had staked out her fiancé's limitations like a mining claim.

The discussion of her plea for protection somehow drifted toward an argument. They had disagreed so seldom before!

From her side, the pressure of Carson's determination had tattered her nerves. From Foster's? In time it came to her.

He was afraid.

With his fear came a need he didn't fully grasp—to distance himself from her. That way he might avoid Carson's terrifying attentions. In her present emotional condition she couldn't trust herself not to speak her mind. She broke off their budding dispute, using Melody's schedule as an excuse.

From the kennel driveway she spotted Foster in the rental car's rearview. She watched his figure recede in the distance and wondered if he was receding as well from his central point in her life to some dim, distant promontory.

Grandma and Stoneman Gore were taking Melody shopping that evening. Better they than Trish, who hated stores and always grew impatient. After shopping expeditions Marylou always served milk shakes and demanded a performance on one or more of her granddaughter's instruments. Melody the ham was more than happy to cooperate and then sleep over. She, at least, was going to have a good evening.

Trish had to spend hers at PC-Pros. She was so far behind in her work that she could make no decisions about her company's future until she gathered data and ran some spread sheets. Then she had to look at invoices to figure out whom to pay or stall. She had never enjoyed being in the building at night alone, and with all that had been happening, tonight it was worse. Every click or rap of metal cooling after a late July day's heat made her repeatedly start and jerk her head up from the PC screen.

She used Michelle's work station. The area had no windows. She'd rather no one saw her from the street. She had been working for better than a hour when she heard a muted clatter from the lab. Probably a tool falling to the floor. She tried to convince herself it was nothing, but she needed to check just the same.

She went through the open doorway leading to the cubicles. A touch of the light switch illuminated the deserted area. Through waist-high windows in the far wall she saw the laboratory, heavily shadowed at 10:30 P.M. Its door was open. A sweep of cool air swirled down from the overhead vent. The unit's kicking in had probably started a draft that had rolled a tool to the floor. She moved ahead, paused momentarily at the doorway, then went in, hand groping for the light switch. She flicked it.

The lights didn't go on.

She turned back to the cubicle area.

All the lights winked off.

There was someone there!

Panic lunged up like a grizzly. Her cry was muffled, choked. The lab's emergency door opened directly outdoors. She wouldn't leave the way she had come. No way! She was getting out of there—now! She ran full speed for the door.

She never saw what was thrust out between her pumping legs. She tripped, sprawled, screaming. They were in here, too! Strong hands jammed cloth into her mouth. In seconds her hands were taped behind her. Then her ankles. Two men! She thought of Samantha buried alive. Was it her turn now? She bleated into the gag and heaved wildly. She trembled with fear. For an instant she thought she might lose control of herself, as Samantha had done.

A flashlight winked on, its lens filtered red. One of the men dragged her into a chair. She glimpsed his shadowy face. Not Carson! Oh, not Carson. Thank heavens!

The other's voice was strange, too. "Carson said he wanted you to see what we do to your lab."

She groaned into the gag. The shorter man held a long crowbar. He approached her, bar horizontal, heavy point first. He jabbed it lightly at her chest, then nudged it between her thighs. "Maybe we'll do something to you, too."

Trish felt her strength drain. She sagged in the chair. The shorter man was about to use the bar to smash screens and club instrument cases. With despair she understood that they were going to destroy everything they could. This violence would shove PC-Pros still further toward ruin.

When they finished with the apparatus, would they then turn a different kind of attention to her?

"Hey, look!" The taller man pointed toward the window. Standing square in the window's center was a man with a flashlight turned on his face. In the reddish glow he looked like a Halloween fiend sent forth to torment her soul.

It was Carson!

Her shriek, muffled by rag, left her mouth a hissing wail.

Closer, closer he was coming to her. Now a mere twenty yards. Maybe tomorrow twenty feet. The next day . . . She kicked and heaved in fear. Her assailants' chuckles were dark as a cave.

All before her, present and future, was bleak and hopeless as a bombed-out city.

"Hey, clowns!"

Trish's head spun toward the familiar voice. Dino Castelli!

He stood for an instant in the doorway, then charged into the lab. The short man swung the bar at him. Dino dodged it nimbly and sent a kick into the exposed stomach. The short man *whooooshed* and fell to his knees. Dino turned and found the other man rushing at him. They came together with the *whup* of football linemen. The two went down, rolling and cursing on the floor. Dino broke free but was pulled down.

From beneath his jacket a longish object fell free and clattered to the floor, coming to a stop near a fallen flashlight.

It was a sawed-off shotgun.

The short man recovered his wind and stood shakily. Trish had worked the gag out of her mouth with her tongue. She shouted, "Dino. Watch out! He's up!"

Dino lashed out at the intruder's throat with stiffened fingers. He choked and clawed at his neck. Dino dived free and scrambled toward the shotgun. The other man got up and kicked it away. A knife appeared in his hand, gleaming even in the weak light. "Gonna cut you!" He advanced, right arm ahead, in a shuffling step. Dino retreated. They moved soundlessly. The only sound in the lab was the short man's choking noises.

Though she was staring with all her concentration, Trish

didn't clearly see the knife thrust. The next moment Dino was gripping the knife man's wrist in his right hand. A shift and twist and the knife wielder screamed. His weapon fell to the floor. Dino sent him sprawling and began to grope in the shadows for the shotgun.

Trish's eyes rose to the window. Though his flashlight was off, Carson still stood in the dimness, peering in. "Dino! Carson's outside. Carson!"

"What the hell can I do about it now?" he shouted.

Both men were on their feet. They ran for the exit as Dino rose, shotgun in hands.

They burst out the door as the shotgun blasted, a violent thump that fell on Trish's ears like a fist. One of the men screamed, but both kept running. Dino ran out after them.

"Dino, go after Carson. *Get Carson!*"

He sprinted out of sight. Trish's eyes spun back to the window. Carson was gone. Get him, Dino. Get him!

And if he didn't? What if Carson the cunning somehow overcame him? She would be defenseless. The two men, maybe Carson with them, would return to pay her and the lab their very special attentions!

She squirmed. The tape was tight as wire. Fear just short of panic flared again in her chest. She eased herself off the chair and began to wriggle across the floor. There were phones in the lab, but she didn't know where. In the next area there was one on every desk.

She had to call the police!

She sat up on the floor, drew up her legs, and shoved. Her sneakers found grip on the carpeting. She heaved and scooted her rear along a foot or so. Anxiety gave her strength. She felt the heat of friction through her jumpsuit. Shortly she was through the door and in the next area. The darkness confused her. She tried to slide into a cubicle but couldn't recall just where the entrances were located. Her heart began to pound harder.

She steadied herself. There were plenty of cubicles, plenty of entrances. She needed to find just one. She thought of . . . Carson coming to stand before her as she lay bound and helpless. No! Not him. *Not again!* Breath left her mouth in a groaning sigh. She heaved herself along. The police! She needed the police.

She inched along the bottom of a fabric partition, then sprawled through an opening. Somewhere in there was a desk. She shoved herself till her back came up against solid metal. She squirmed into a kneeling position, rose, and sat on the edge of the desk. Now where was the phone? She forced herself not to think of Carson possibly stalking her. To consider that would freeze her like a rodent before an adder's gaze.

After what seemed minutes her taped wrist brushed against a plastic case. She clawed the receiver out of its cradle. Her arched fingers crept across the buttons in search of the 0 that would link her with an operator and then the police. Her hands shook from restricted circulation and fear. The darkness drew closer and deeper, like an enfolding wrap. She whimpered and despised herself for it.

She saw light. Someone was coming from the lab! She jabbed wildly at the phone buttons. She had no idea if she had pressed the right one. "Operator! Send police to PC-Pros on Linden Avenue!" Her tongue froze.

The shadowed man striding into the cubicle could be Carson's height! Terror vaulted across the fences of her self-control. She screamed loud enough to tear her throat.

"Chill out, Patricia! It's Dino."

"Oh, thank God. Thank God! I thought you were—"

"He beat it. I never even saw him. I chased the two goons away. They won't be back."

She got through to the police, and then the insurance company. Dino told her to come to the bakery "after the cops do their thing."

Two hours later they were sitting at the table in the back of Estrella. Before her Trish had a bowl-sized cappuccino and a shot glass of grappa, the rough Italian brandy. Her second. For the first she had needed two shaking hands to get to her lips. She felt better now. She studied Dino across the table as he explained that his regular night watchman route around PC-Pros had led him to discover the intruders.

"How did you get in the building?" she said.

"Skeleton key. A big boy's toy. I figured I might need one, playing night watchman."

She nodded. "Why no police?" she said.

He sipped espresso, took a huge bite out of a ricotta pie. "Couple reasons. First is they'd wonder why I have a sawed-off shotgun in my possession. Second, maybe I had some trouble in the past. I don't need to have the cops snooping around, asking me questions."

Trish recalled his eagerness to violently confront the two vandals and then to pursue them and Carson no matter the danger. Rocco DeVita had considered him a Vietnam combat casualty, a walking, ticking bomb. How could there be a real question about the man having been in some kind of trouble at an earlier time of his life?

"I don't know how to thank you." She couldn't meet his eyes. "You have no idea how much I fear Carson Thomas. And he was there! Waiting for his stooges to help destroy my business."

He scowled. "Too bad he slipped away."

"He's growing bolder—no, I don't mean that, Dino. He's always been bold. He wants me to know he'll come closer and closer to me until . . ."

Dino cleaned up the espresso machine. "So since we last talked he's been busy?"

Trish recalled her friend's chagrin over his misadventure with Nicholas, when he clubbed away the electronic trail to Carson's den. She dimly perceived his eagerness and energy were partially short-circuited by whatever damage had been done in jungle and mud. Progress undermined: the theme of his life. Her heart went out to him. She found herself saying, "I'll tell you the latest he's done."

Once she began talking she said more than she wanted. She rushed from Samantha's dreadful adventure to the changed atmosphere between herself and Foster. She didn't spare Dino her disappointment with her fiancé's inability to accept the woman she really was. Without knowing it, he was trying to drag her backward toward years treacherous as quicksand.

She stopped counting after her fourth grappa. Well, the

glass *was* tiny. Having been frightened and now feeling safe, she babbled in relief. Just the same, Dino listened with apparently sincere interest. She felt a tiny thrill of vanity when his eyes remained unblinking on her face. She recalled his joking come-ons. She sensed he wasn't like Jerry Morris, the religious, upright cop who wouldn't make a pass at an engaged woman. No, Dino was cut from different cloth altogether. For a brief moment she told herself she, too, had been fashioned from that pattern. She stopped herself. At one time that might have been true. Now she had changed. She had to remind herself at this grappa-and-cappuccino wee hour that she had become a better person.

Dino took his turn at leading the conversation. He wanted to know why she didn't fully face Foster with her complaints about his behavior. Why did she fence and dodge and wave a thin rapier? A sledgehammer was what the job required.

Garrulous as she had become, she couldn't explain the inner conflict between her mother's values and her own. Marylou had taught her women weren't to oppose; they were to accommodate. She waved the topic away with both wobbly wrists.

"You look like an Italian when you do that." He gathered up the cups and plates. With some dismay she realized their social interlude was ending. "So where does the wedding stand?" he asked. "What's Foster think? Is Carson Thomas going to get his way?"

She had avoided those musings. Now, with the question put to her, she pinned down her elusive thoughts. "I—think he's wavering. Maybe he has reason. I don't know."

"Reason not to take you?" Trish found Dino's dark-eyed gaze penetrating. She felt she ought to look away. There was something insightful behind that intensity. No, that wasn't it at all.

It was desire.

"If Foster is stupid enough to break it off, I want you to think about me." Dino's normally husky voice had deepened even further. She had broken eye contact. Now she shook inwardly at the thought of swimming again in those deep brown seas.

They stood close by the door. Grappa and tumbling emotions made her vulnerable as an ice filigree under tropical sun. If he touches me . . .

Each waited for the other to go out. The moment extended itself. They stood within inches of each other. She imagined she felt the heat of his body and the eddying currents of his life energy. As seconds ticked by she wondered . . . why didn't he touch her? She knew he wanted to. She wondered if she wanted that.

When she finally moved, going out ahead of him, she understood what had been happening.

He wanted her to touch him first.

22

"GWINE TO THAT HORSEMEAT MAAAAN!" CHAMP SANG.
"Gwine to that horsemeat maaa-aaayun!" Had the ring of
an old blues tune, no mistake. And only the Blandmobile
interior to hear his eight-bar beauty. He refined the vocal as
he drove beyond the edge of the city. His destination: a meat
processing factory where, in addition to great groaning
machines, dozens of butchers plied their trade. There phone
orders were taken for wholesale lots, even from such offal
fellows as Champ. They had it all! Beefalo and buffalo,
horse and hog, lamb and goat—I kid you not. If man ate it,
and the law allowed, they carried it. By phone he could place
his order for fifty small steaks cut from haunch of horse.
Wrap in packs of ten, please. "Gwine to *eat* that nag cost me
mah pay!" he belted in Janis Joplin imitation. "Gwine to
eat . . ."

He was in the very best of moods at the top of a day
delightful in its promise of action. Carson's orders had been
explicit; Champ's energy as always would assure each was
followed to the letter. For the first time since he had come to
this city he sensed closure in his master's plan. The arc had
been extended, now it curved back around to the starting
point. By and by the circle would be unbroken.

Queen of My Heart *would* be resurrected.

Once-whinnying booty stowed in his trunk, he drove down the road to a rest area. Hands in rubber gloves, he opened the packages and various bottles. He dug out the new paintbrush. He busied himself with his chemical palette, Van Gogh at Arles, Monet at Reims. Tidy rewrapping finished the preparation. And now . . . *au chasse!*

He looked at his Rolex. Right on schedule. He angled along roads north of the city, curved down south. The quarry always took Route 163 to Wednesday's usual destination at an average speed of 47.6 miles an hour, assuming he got half the lights. Chrono and odo told Champ just about when quarry's 4 x 4—oh, he was such a *sport!*—would reach the long, deserted stretch between the junkyard and the motor home park. So he had set the timer installed last night to cut off quarry's engine just about there, give or take a few hundred yards. Champ was nothing if not a reasonably precise man.

He came around a corner. Drat! Construction. Yellow-hatted men swarmed like workers around a queen bee of an asphalt-laying machine. One-lane traffic was controlled by a flag woman. When delay is inevitable, sit back and enjoy it. Study her buttocks beneath the loose Day-Glo safety vest. Imagine peeling off tight bleached jeans, panties, and setting whiz-bangs upon white flesh. He would threaten her with dribbles from that pot of hot asphalt. He imagined the upward-curling steam stinking of methane-chain compounds, heard her screams of fear. But in the end he would press nothing hotter than his kisses against her body's seven portals. In time she waved him ahead, fingers curved fetchingly around the flag rod.

Seven minutes wasted.

He picked up speed a bit, but not so much as to draw the attention of troopers. He would arrive at his quarry's stalled vehicle more than five minutes late. Surely that wouldn't matter.

But it did.

The Good Samaritan drove a Volvo. He had pulled it up behind the 4 x 4. The two men bent over on either side of an open hood. Champ killed the engine and glided the Blandmobile behind the Volvo. Speedy action was required. And little cat feet, too. He kept both in his bag of tricks. From the backseat he pulled a baseball hat. Go, Pirates! He pulled the bill low. Ready, set, *allons!*

Mr. Samaritan was a hirsute man in his late twenties, handlebars and Custer–style locks. Champ angled his approach to partially hide his shadowed face from the 4 x 4 driver. "What's the problem?" he growled.

"Just died as I was going along," the 4 x 4 driver said.

"Oh, that! It's a classic problem with these nineties. I know how to fix that." Sly Champ, the auto authority!

"All right!" Mr. Samaritan said.

"This is all you need to get it going again." Champ brandished his tool.

Mr. Samaritan frowned. "Just that piece of wire?"

"Works wonders. Watch." Wait for that lone car to pass. Now the deserted road stretched out as comforting as written permission.

He lowered his hand into the engine well, stiff wire angled down. Then the moment of truth! Don Champ de los Enfernos in the *corrida,* leaning over the horns of the bull, sword searching for that exact spot on the hide guaranteeing sudden death. Yes! The upward thrust of the wire, the left hand rising behind Mr. Samaritan's head. Reflexive avoidance was a no-no. Bull's-eye! Or was that man's-eye? Whatever, four inches of wire foraged in gray matter.

Champ whipped out the wire, let Mr. Samaritan slump down between the car and the road.

The 4 x 4 driver stood paralyzed, frowning. He wasn't sure what he had seen. He should be running, Champ thought. But he suspected the fellow wasn't that much a man of action. As he hurried around the front of the car the driver took a few backward steps. For the first time he looked Champ in the face.

"You're Carson Thomas!"

Oh, sublime mask! I am not Carson! "And you're Foster Palmer."

"Oh, my God! You know who I am?" Heavy shadows

worked their way across the Loathed One's wide face. "Carson Thomas . . ."

"My fame precedes me," Champ said. "Get in my car. We have important things to do."

"No!"

Champ read his fear as easily as Sunday's Beetle Bailey strip. It had been fermenting for weeks within his WASPy skull. "Get in!"

The Loathed One hesitated. Champ was on him in an instant, bending his fingers until he howled. *"Get in!"* he ordered.

"My hand!"

"Your neck if you resist." Champ's grin was sun bright. He winked. "Or maybe your eye."

"W-what did you do to him?"

"Sent him on a journey to eternity."

"Why?"

The bone of that question fell with a clatter onto the plate of Champ's mind. Why, indeed? He could have found another, gentler way to get the Loathed One into his car, one that would have left no corpse. He . . . hadn't thought. But he always thought. His intellect was premier among his strong suits. He was getting tangled. *Tangled!* First he had crept into Queen of My Heart's bedroom, running mad risks and inviting terrible events that would be followed by Carson's sure, certain punishment. Now he had sent a stranger on the longest journey. Tangle, tangle! He knew who lay at the heart of it—and in his heart. There she swelled like a sublime cancer gently nudging aside the organs of his discipline, loyalty, and cunning.

Queen of My Heart!

Hiding his dismay with iron self-control, he led the Loathed One to the Blandmobile. He dragged Mr. Samaritan into his Volvo and propped him behind the seat. It would be a long time before anyone figured out what killed him. Or was he deluding himself? Never!

When Champ got into the Blandmobile Foster tried to begin a conversation. Champ knew his type. Let us reason together. The mind-set of a man who had never felt the lash of want or come to grips with the violence and uncertainty of human existence. Go to the history books! Nothing like a dose of incessant European wars, religious persecutions, and famine to shake ill-founded self-assurance. How about that Black Death! Probably the man was kind, repressed, tentative in exerting his will. Tranquil years sheltered him ever more deeply behind heaps of dollar bills. He sought the path of no resistance. Had there ever been inner strength in that tallish frame? Behind those wide glasses lurked what? An intellect? Or a spoiled rich boy? The Loathed One!

On this . . . mediocrity Queen of My Heart was going to bestow body and soul.

Oh, wise, disruptive Carson. He raised his exalted master high over the altar of his mind.

Was there any doubt remaining about whether or not the wedding would take place? Today's grand adventures would answer that question without fail.

Negative. Negative!

"Shut up!" he growled at the Loathed One, who was whimpering.

"You can't murder people! You can't hold me hostage, Carson."

"I have pistols and knives. Do what I say."

The other squirmed in his seat. "What are you going to do with me?"

Champ grinned broadly with Carson's face. "Not *with* you. *To* you."

The Loathed One's eyes blinked behind wide frames. "This is crazy," he said softly.

"You ain't seen nothin' yet!"

Lake Country Kennels was better kept than some motels Champ knew. The wonder of money! New paint gleamed. Doggy odors were absent. Give credit to the manager, this Ms. Doris, butchy, banged, and belligerent. He had to show her the long knife, nip some buttons off her no-style blouse, to get her cooperation. He left her roped like a dogie, her ring of keys and their chain now on his belt. Come along, Loathed One. Show time! Always with the questions! A quick back and forth with the side of the pistol opened barber-shaven cheeks and closed his mouth. He whimpered and occupied himself with blood and lightly cologned handkerchief.

Champ put pistol to tanned temple. The man quivered. Why so pale and wan, fond lover? "Just follow along. Don't make trouble. Don't try to get away. Don't talk to me about you and Trish Morley. Got it?"

"What are you going to do?" His voice shook like MTV hips.

"And no questions!" A shove of the pistol left a faint indention of barrel opening on the Loathed One's high forehead. Enough weakening of what seemed to be not that strong a will, Champ thought. To work! The Loathed One wandered before him, attached by a chain of fear. Champ went to the trunk and took out the horse meat. His new bond slave manned the wheelbarrow. Soon they were on the way to the kennel proper, where dozens of residents bayed at the smell of meat. To the Loathed One's favorites first: Gog and Magog. "Feeding time!" Champ sang, raising his face to the cloudless August sky. "Feeding tiiiiime!"

Each mastiff had its own run. Slid into mounted frames were computer-generated summaries of bloodlines. Champ knew the English mastiff breed: huge but gentle, lovers of children and protectors of their owners. Admirable creatures altogether. He ordered the Loathed One to toss Gog her lunch. The bitch fell on the meat with grunting enthusiasm, jaw working like road machinery.

Shortly Gog's forelegs weakened. She sank to her knees. Her haunches bent and folded to the concrete. Gray flanks heaved their last.

"This meat is poisoned!" Loathed One's voice was dull with disbelief.

Down went Magog for the long count. "Onward!" Determined Champ bent upon his rounds. Up and down the runs they went their workmanlike way. Dogs dropped like Aussie troops at Gallipoli. Those without appetite Champ treated to a pistol blast between pointy ears. Along followed the Loathed One, his disbelief long cast aside in favor of shock and horror. "You're just . . . slaughtering these magnificent

235

creatures," he said thrice. Surely the beginning of his true appreciation of Carson's genius. Just wait! Gleeful Champ brayed with laughter. The temporarily surviving dogs howled their response. Beast could recognize beast.

When he came upon puppies he waded in with heavy boots working, popping their heads like small pumpkins in a patch. Thus prompted, the Loathed One asked him what kind of man he was. To which Champ answered true—the very best kind!

Shortly before the last mastiff was dispatched the Loathed One took sick, bending over to puke. He emptied himself of pinkish drip. When he turned moist eyes again to Champ there was something like respect in them. "You're . . . insane!" he croaked, voice raw from retching.

"What I am is loyal and obedient!" Once so, Champ thought. But now?

On the road again, Champ gave chump careful instructions about phase two. A stop at a Burger King rest room, the cleanest in the business, and a change of clothes brought forth yachtsman Champ. See him in a snappy little seaman's cap! How about these nautical twill trousers and Docksiders?

To his companion Champ's motives remained murky. Yes, surprises yet to come, my boy! Champ put chump at the Blandmobile wheel, told him to drive to West Manachogue Yacht and Tennis Club. Do not stop until you reach the gate. There the flunky bid them good afternoon and fair winds, ignoring the Loathed One's Band-Aided cheeks. How phony could you get? Thinking so soon of Christmas tips!

Champ showed chump the pistol again. Not to forget, please, and do just as I say. From the trunk he took the suitcase, stickered for prestige: St. Maarten, Hong Kong, Tunisia. Together they crossed boards and ramps, destination the Loathed One's prized possession: the *Emerald Lady.* "All aboard!" Champ ordered.

My, what a nautical beauty we have here, he thought. Was that teak? Look at its dark sweep! See decks polished and shipshape as those of a British warship in the age of sail. Below, then. Sleeps ten, the Loathed One boasted, pride perking up through his misery and bafflement. And how! Look at the heads, the nifty economy of space. A four-star chef could work in *that* kitchen.

To the bilge! Puzzled chump was reluctant to inform him just where the bulkhead was. But the wave of blued steel before wounded cheeks brought him around.

Shortly they were on their way out of the yacht club parking lot, sans suitcase, of course. A road circled up the high hill behind cove and club. Up Champ drove to the rest area where lovers clinched by night and no one came by day. Except them. He invited his guest out of the car. Below, the yacht club marina spread hard by the score of tennis courts. Floats marked the swimming area where distant children's cries beat the hot air.

The Loathed One was beginning to look dazed. Just wait a minute, Champ thought. Glancing at his watch, he corrected that to: Wait seventy-three seconds. "A lovely vista, no?" Champ chatted.

"What have you done to the *Emerald Lady?*" the other said dully.

"Time will tell."

The Loathed One faced him. "You have no idea of the depth of your insanity, Carson Thomas."

I am not Carson, he said to himself. Or was he? He bared his Rolex. "We have eleven seconds and counting . . ."

"What?" The Loathed One flailed arms against sides in baffled frustration.

"Seven . . . six . . . five . . ."

"Oh, no. *No!*" The light dawned.

"Three . . . two . . . one . . . We have detonation!"

Below, the *Emerald Lady* played airplane for an instant, lifting herself from the water. Then the plastique's gases tore the hull completely apart. A grand explosion rolled like thunder to their vantage point. Red and yellow flashes sent deck and hull planking soaring. Inner debris flew up in a great smoky shower. Check out that splintered section of wet bar, boudoir, armoire—all airborne. Bye, bye, Miss *Emerald* Pie! Fire bit into the settling scrap. Leverage of masts against keelless hulk turned decks toward the vertical.

Once-hidden panels and bulkheads were exposed to sun and sea like chambers of a ruptured insect nest.

Champ turned an eye to the Loathed One.

He wept!

Sentiment was a good thing in a man. Made him more docile. Champ had no trouble taping his wrists behind him and sliding on the blindfold.

On the drive to Resurrection Headquarters Champ pondered the unworthiness of the Loathed One to become Queen of My Heart's husband. As he did he felt wellings of that state of mind so close to being beyond his control: Earthquake Anger. How often had it risen up, its target now this man lying under a blanket in the backseat? He found himself drawing in great drafts of air. His heart thudded like Mongo's bongo. Why was he being gentle with him?

Because Carson had commanded it.

Never before, though, had the Loathed One been within Champ's power. One violent instant and . . . the September fifteenth wedding would be forever impossible. He dared to think that maybe he knew better than Carson. Why couldn't he think for Carson? How much difference was there between them, really? Was there any at all, with his devotion so complete? His breath emerged in shallow grunts. He thought of his hands around the Loathed One's throat, pressing life out of him like toothpaste from a tube. Yes, yes . . . He turned the car from his appointed route toward a hilly suburb. There river and creeks cut through the terrain. The Blandmobile found its own way to an arching bridge over a deep gorge. He pulled up on the shoulder a dozen yards from the span.

In no time blindfolded chump, weepy no more, was on his feet and moving with him to bridge center. Breeze stirred.

"Where are we? What are you doing with me?"

Champ looked over the tubular guards. Rocks and rills, white water aplenty. He shoved chump against the thick tubes, bent him over. Directly below his eyes was nothing but three hundred feet of air.

He snatched off the blindfold.

The Loathed One cried out, "You're going to push me over. *You're going to push me over!*"

Champ's heart thudded, thudded. His brain beat with the pulse. This man. Queen of My Heart. Jumble. Mumble. Tangle. Carson-Champ. Champ-Carson. Carson-Carson. Earthquake Anger . . . The breeze worked up under his pant cuffs, teased his ankles. He needed relief from the soft clasp of the mask. But that could not be. He clutched the seat of the other's pants. He hiked him up a bit, tampering with his balance. The chump screamed. Nerves not what they were? It had been that kind of day.

He goosed the Loathed One up a mite more. With hands bound and feet having no real purchase he was helpless. The idea of going over must have seemed very real because he began to beg for his life.

Music to Champ's burning brain.

"You a praying man?" Champ asked. "If you are, you better start in. You're going over!"

"I'll give you whatever you want!"

"Prayer is more becoming than pleading. Pray!"

Champ's inner self twisted, convulsed like a snake in fire. Earthquake Anger, Carson's commands, Queen of My Heart! He felt at once powerful and weak. He closed his eyes and shuddered. Still gripping the other's pants, he tensed himself to up-and-over the man. A one and a two and—

A car was coming!

He lowered the suspended feet. His left hand rose to hide taped wrists. He leaned forward, too. Look, driver, a matched set of the curious. Aren't we a pair!

The Loathed One howled for help!

He had waited too long. Engine noise was loud. The car never slowed. Champ never turned. So that motorist had been spared. Champ ought to have spared that morning's Samaritan as well. He stared down at the rocks and tumbling water. Maybe they should both go over. . . .

"You shouldn't have shouted," Champ said. "You'll have to be punished!" He seized the other's pants bottom again. Champ the joker.

The Loathed One's voice was a terrified choke. Though he thought he knew the answer, he asked, "How are you going to punish me?"

Champ dropped his feet back to the cement. "Let you live," he said.

Back on went the blindfold. Champ drove uneventfully to Resurrection Headquarters. By now the Loathed One's babbling was somehow soothing, a reminder of how well Champ was succeeding in doing Carson's bidding. And possibly his own as well.

Yet success did not generate the joy it once had.

This late afternoon would see the fruition of all the careful espionage, deceptions, and electronic legerdemain that he and Carson had carried out in preparation. Days and nights they had spent at their computers. He stripped off the blindfold and tape and ordered the Loathed One into a chair by a PC. His face was pale. He rubbed his freed wrists and ankles. His lips trembled. Champ was now tired of his verbal drivel. He told him to shut up. He gave him a shot of brandy to help get him together. He had to be alert to appreciate . . .

The Big Finish!

He activated the communications software. At his command the modem dialed. He entered passwords pirated only after the expenditure of much sweat and energy. The screen shifted as he responded to distant system prompts. "Look," he said. "What's this?"

His guest's dulled eyes narrowed with recognition. *Now* he was alert. "That's one of my accounts!"

"Napoleon Expeditionary Mutual Fund. It had rather a good year, didn't it? Good years, I should say. You're up to nine hundred K there, a healthy piece of change."

"How did you—"

"Great technical skill. Genius level."

His guest's lips tightened. There was still a little fight left in him. The last of it would be hoarded to protect his money, wouldn't it? "So you know what my account is worth. What of it?"

"We do a transfer."

"So? Any funds go into one of my other Napoleon accounts. Checks from liquidations are sent to my address."

"You're dealing with Carson Thomas, chump. Surely by now you must believe a lot of what your love told you about him." Champ read down Carson's software from the connected tape drive into the PC's expanded memory. One of his master's most exquisite programs. He cued it. It spoke with the fund's computer. "A meeting of the minds," Champ tittered.

He responded to menu prompts. "Ahh! The machines are dancing cheek-to-cheek." The screen filled with a list of numbers. "Want to make a choice, chump?" Champ said.

"What choice? What are those?"

"Computer codes for various charities around the world. Go ahead, pick."

His guest sat upright, as though a rod had been shoved up his spine. "What are you doing? Turning over my assets to a charity?"

"Not just to one," Champ said. "That would be too easy to trace. Say to a couple hundred."

"You can't do that. It's impossible!"

"It isn't. Robin Hood lives!"

Champ busied himself at the keyboard. Nine hundred thousand and change flew to legions of the deserving. Champ the one-man Marxist band. "To each according to his need."

"The assets will be recoverable," the Loathed One said.

"Maybe. In time. Maybe not. Take years, likely." Champ angled his masked face to look his guest in the eye. "That was your biggest account, right?"

"Yes."

"Liar, liar." Champ brushed index fingers toward the bespectacled face. "Shame, shame!"

In fact there were thirteen other accounts, three of which held a million or more. Champ sweated over the keyboard. He was interrupted only once, when his guest attempted an unannounced departure. "Bad manners!" Champ chided, tightening his full nelson to pound the point. The Loathed One's scream sang of a full evening's worth of obedience.

Champ returned to his task. The modem kept busy, dialing, transferring, dialing, transferring. "I-O, I-O! To the poorhouse chump will go!" he sang. He queued up jobs. Even at high speed Carson's program would be busy all night.

Champ sat back from a job well done. "I left you your real estate," he said. "Everything else is gone."

"I'll recover it, you madman!"

"Maybe, maybe. Do you know how many charities there are across the world? Ever try to get money back from one? Until you do, you're flat cash broke." Champ chuckled.

His guest covered face with palms, drew in deep breath. It caught in his chest. "You've killed my dogs, destroyed the *Emerald Lady,* and sent my capital to the four winds. Are you quite through?"

"No."

The Loathed One lowered his hands. "What's left?"

Champ rose slowly. He had been a long time at the tube. He took his guest by the shoulders and whispered in his ear, "Do you want to take your pants off, or would you rather I do it?"

23

TRISH HAPPENED TO BE LOOKING OUT THE WINDOW when the Palmer limo pulled up in front of her house. She saw it held Foster. A surge of relief passed through her. She had tried unsuccessfully over the last two days to reach him by phone. His unavailability had made her anxious. Not hard to do. Recently all her emotions floated just beneath the surface.

The chauffeur got out, opened the rear door. Trish smiled. Yes, there was Foster! He unfolded himself slowly and stood. He turned back toward the limo and put out his hand toward the woman still inside. Trish groaned. She clutched her apron and squeezed till her knuckles popped.

Foster's companion was Lois Smith-Patton!

From the street-side door emerged a huge man in a business suit. He led the way up Trish's flagstone walk. Behind came the couple. There was something slow and painful in Foster's walk. Not so with Lois. The petite woman strode like a conqueror.

What was going on here?

She stepped onto the big porch and opened its screen door. "Foster, hello!" she called.

He pointed at the beefy man. "Let Branch go inside first, could you, Trish?"

Branch's moon-wide face split with a thin smile. His nose had been broken more than once. "Pardon, ma'am," he grunted, pushing by her.

"There's nobody home. Melody is at a neighbor's." She felt foolish for saying it.

"I'll have a look anyway," he said.

"For what?"

"Trouble," Foster said, drawing closer.

"Good morning, Patricia." Lois smiled.

As she greeted the woman Trish's apprehension grew. Something was very wrong that Lois should appear on her doorstep in Foster's company. Something *very* wrong.

She held the screen door open. "Come in," she said.

Foster looked beyond her. "All clear, Branch?"

"Looks okay, Mr. Palmer."

Trish frowned. "Of course it is. I told you—"

"Let's get this over with," Lois snapped.

Trish offered lemonade or coffee. Declined. Foster and Lois sat together on the couch. Branch stood with his back to them, looking out door and windows. "He's a bodyguard, isn't he?" Trish said. "What do you need a bodyguard for?"

"I have reasons."

She took her first good look at her fiancé. She could barely suppress her surprise. The man had aged and stiffened. Unfamiliar lines etched his face. A new patch of gray lay in the hair above his left ear. She moved toward him. "Darling, are you all right?"

He flinched at her approach!

She stopped dead. Her eyes turned to Lois. "What did you do to him?"

"Me? I didn't do anything at all, Patricia. It was your 'admirer' Mr. Carson Thomas we have to thank."

"I don't understand."

Foster began to speak, haltingly at first, then more rapidly. Now and then he paused and nibbled left-hand knuckles. She realized he was boiling with unfamiliar emotions. Overlaying all of them was profound shock. Later she would remember with special vividness that late August Saturday morning. The sunlight angled in through the eastern windows. The genuine reproduction grandfather clock's ticks sounded loud as detonations. In the air hung the faint scents of departed Melody's crepe and jelly breakfast.

More than once Foster's voice snagged. Worse was Lois reaching over to touch him on the shoulder like a concerned mother. How dare she! Foster continued to talk, each word falling like a weight on Trish's heart. The poor man! All that had happened to him! His mastiffs! The *Emerald Lady!* His financial resources! The humiliation of reporting all to the police.

She grasped something past the words, something in the angle of his shoulders, the looser set of his jaw. As he talked on, her anguish grew. She was coming to understand what lay now at his core.

Carson had broken him.

"He got into your *accounts?*" she asked.

"I don't know what kind of equipment he used. Or how he could pierce security screens. None of the investment firms know either. They're frightened to death. If Carson could do it . . ."

Could anyone do it, Trish wondered. She doubted it.

Foster continued, "Your friend Carson—"

"He is not my friend!" Trish shouted.

"He's a man for this age, isn't he?" Foster asked. "Way ahead of us? Airborne on the electron while we're like ox carts on paper. My attorneys, my investment advisors, the best professionals can't make me any promises about recovering nearly four million dollars." His voice, already dulled, sank to a monotone. "Luckily the other family members have resources that weren't touched. And of course I still have my real estate." His grin was skewed, disturbed. "One of the many things with which he threatened me was that those other resources *would* be touched unless—"

"Unless you canceled the wedding!" Trish said, her eyes filling.

Foster ignored her. He hadn't finished his story. "Branch, could you go out on the porch for a short time? Thank you."

He waited till the huge man was out of earshot. "I want you to hear everything so you'll understand why—"

"It's more than she deserves!" Lois said angrily. "I was foolish to allow you to do this. A brief phone call would have served the same purpose."

"Would you do me a big favor, Lois?" Trish said. "Shut up! Let him talk. And what's this stuff about you 'allowing' him to do anything?"

"Just listen, Trish. You'll understand." No emotion in Foster's voice. No, he wasn't at all what he had been.

He told her what Carson had done to him on the grimy floor of the squalid room—what had taken hours that, in their loathsomeness, stretched seemingly to weeks. She closed her eyes, turning away to hide welling tears. Lois was yapping about it all being Trish's fault. Her whining words in the teeth of Trish's growing distress sounded as faint as the bird calls in distant trees. The last sentences of Foster's tale emerged in a whisper. Trish pawed at her eyes, used the apron on smeared cheeks.

She went to him, arms out to comfort. Oh, God, he leaned away from her!

"Don't bother!" Lois barked. She seized Foster's short sleeve and shook it. "Now! You have to tell her now."

He raised his face, disclosing an unfamiliar weak, watery gaze. "Trish . . ." He raised a hand toward her, let it fall back. "There won't be a wedding. Our engagement is off—permanently."

After they left Trish flew upstairs and flung herself on the bed. Thank goodness Melody wasn't there to see and hear her frenzy of weeping. What weighed more crushingly than a dead dream?

She drew her knees up, clutched them, and let go. Her choking gasps were at first heavy with hysteria. In time they subsided to steady blubbering. She rubbed her streaming face against a pillow sham. Rising for a tissue seemed as impossible as scaling Everest.

She wept on in bitter disappointment. Not only over the turning of the road of her life away from Foster, but for the man himself. He had rebuffed Trish's tenderness in favor of

Lois Smith-Patton's martial rule. From a potential life of sharing to one of being dominated. Poor Foster!

And yes, poor Trish. Or at least so she thought early in her long siege of tears. In time she came to ask herself about her shattered dream of a safe, moneyed life beside what she only now admitted was a merely adequate man. Whose hopes had she tried to make reality? Hers? Or her mother's? In a moment of painful honesty she recalled the shaky soul she had been when she began the relationship—a storm-tossed ship seeking nothing more than a safe harbor. Oh, how hard it was to admit the commonplace! She had colored and filigreed her motivations to fit the pattern of an outstanding love.

Ended now, it didn't seem so grand.

Looming behind that painful insight stood Carson, tall as a colossus in his total comprehension of how she thought and what she imagined she wanted. He had dismantled her future just as she had learned to dismantle the pistol Jerry had given her. Now her devil had gotten his way. The wedding was off. She guessed he thought that now things between them were as they had been. Not quite.

The distant, submissive Trish Morley was gone. She understood now that the woman who stood in her place was a tougher type altogether. In destroying her hopes for a traditional married life he had annealed her in a fire of emotions and events that forever drove off the impurities that had made her a helpless creature.

Just precisely what kind of person she had become she couldn't yet determine. One thing was certain: She would be a great deal harder for him to deal with than he dreamed. Oh, yes, Carson was wise in that way. But unwise in at least one other: He thought she now belonged to him.

Conceivably he could imagine that he had long ago bargained successfully for her soul. In a sense he, her devil, had possessed it for a while. Well, he didn't own it anymore!

Or so she told herself.

Now what? Carson had finally gotten his way. She wouldn't be marrying Foster. Briefly she hoped that her devil would simply . . . go away. Face pressed to damp sham, her memory spoke: *Trish, Carson, and Melody—together forever!* Oh, no, he wouldn't disappear. Somehow he would edge in closer till he stood by her side, arm outstretched to draw her into his hell of madness. . . .

She dreaded the next days.

She rolled over and sat up. She wouldn't just wait for him! She had to try to defend herself and her child. Yet she couldn't guess from which direction he would approach her. She was so vulnerable!

She would have to tell Dino and Jerry what had happened. And even Nicholas, if she could reach him. Wondering what else she could do, she remembered Eileen in California. There the police suspected Carson of being the Doctor and Daughter Destroyer. The unanswered question was why. Trish picked up the phone.

She caught Eileen at work. She brought her up to date on what Carson was doing to her, the failure of the police to find him. She couldn't hide her rising desperation. "I need all the information I can get, Eileen," Trish said. "What did your boyfriend find out about Carson? Why do the police think he killed the doctors?"

Eileen took several minutes to praise her man. Carl had learned how to work with the police, had been promoted at the newspaper, and was doing work for the local television station, too. His career was on the rise. When Trish thought she would burst from impatience Eileen lowered her voice. "They finally told him—confidential, of course. You know?"

"Sure. Tell me!"

"The reason Carson's name came up was . . . Can you guess, Trish?"

"Eileen! Just tell me! Okay?"

"Both the throat doctor and the cosmetic surgeon had treated him."

"For what?"

"He had nodes on his vocal chords. The first doctor removed them."

"The second?"

"They don't know. Carson stole the medical records out of her office and from the hospital, too."

"He must have had surgery. She was a surgeon, right?"

"Yeah. Don't ask me about the third. She was a gynecologist."

"Why do the police include her, then?"

"Carl told me. All three women were smothered to death the same way. And the same . . . parts were snipped off."

A chill ran like ice water down Trish's body. Her sense of dread lasted through the rest of the phone call and nestled like a rodent in her chest. She walked to the front porch, where the sun angled in to bathe the swing. Her first thought: Carson had changed his face.

But she had seen him! Twice. Once standing on a corner grinning at her in her crushed car, once peering in through a PC-Pros' window. He looked no different. But his voice was different! She had heard it on the phone and through radios doctored to serve his ends. That was a discovery. She sensed she was missing something but couldn't grasp it. Maybe it would come to her.

But what good would it do?

That elusive crumb of knowledge seemed pathetic before the flood of Carson's power. Like a compass needle relentlessly pointing back to north, she was reminded afresh of her inability to defend herself from him.

She spent the rest of the morning and early afternoon in crisscrossing thoughts that left her vexed and anxious. She knew as the day dragged on that her spirits would sink. The end of her relationship with Foster would weigh more heavily as she tired. After Melody was asleep she knew she'd bawl again.

Was this the worst day of her life?

In midafternoon she got a surprise. Jerry Morris and Lieutenant Sarkman arrived on her doorstep. She offered iced tea. Both declined, stony-faced. They were very much there on official business. She wondered what had brought Sarkman, he of the terrier nose and prima donna posture, to her house. With him there she didn't wish to tell Jerry that

Foster had broken their engagement. She would tell him later. It certainly bore on the case. She'd simply have to hang on, no matter the state of her emotions.

"We finally got some kind of break in this deal," Jerry said.

"Even if it cost some poor slob his life." Sarkman's eyes were bright. Trish remembered murder was his favorite subject. Now she recalled they had talked to Foster at great length. "Your boy Carson stuck a wire in a guy's eye all the way back to the middle of his skull. With Foster Palmer looking on."

"Oh, God!" Foster hadn't told her that. Carson, Carson, mad Carson!

"Kind of curious, that way of offing somebody," Sarkman said. "So we got in touch with west coast people to see if maybe he used his wire out there."

"Had he?" Why was her voice shaking?

"Twice. Once the night the last doctor was smothered. There was a dead muscleman beside her in the dining room. Then a couple weeks later up north in Oregon another guy was killed the same way."

Jerry leaned forward. He said softly, "The second dead man made masks for a living. Extraordinary ones. Made of all kinds of modern materials. People with serious facial damage wore his work. Actors, too, when they needed to look convincingly grotesque."

Sarkman said, "He made a mask for Carson. To hide his face. That's why we can't find him."

"That's what I thought at first, Pete." Jerry nodded at Sarkman, his long face angled with intensity. A good cop on the scent. "But I have another idea."

"I think I know what it is!" Trish interrupted. "Not two hours ago I was trying to get a grip on what I bet is the same idea. Carson had surgery that changed his face. The mask he wears looks like his old face! The two times I saw him he wore it so I wouldn't know what his altered face looks like."

Jerry nodded. "Exactly!"

Sarkman scowled. "Hold on, hold on." He got up and walked to the window and looked out. "You people forget we had a witness who saw the killer leaving the second doctor's house. He didn't look like Carson." He dug in his briefcase. "You see this composite, Jerry?"

Jerry nodded. To Trish he said, "They faxed it to us. The witness worked with a coast cop artist. The witness isn't sure she likes it."

Sarkman gave the sheet to Trish. She studied it. Hair! Goodness, flowing beard and mustache, very curly locks. Real? Who knew? Peeping out were the artist's concept's features. Didn't look like anyone she knew. Or did it?

Sarkman gestured at the composite. "That doesn't look like the guy in that photo you gave us, Trish."

"It's a . . . somewhat different face. Yes." She found Sarkman's brusque, know-it-all tone annoying. It sounded as though somehow everything was her fault. She had reason to dislike the man.

"So how many masks does Carson Thomas have?" Sarkman said.

"Maybe it wasn't Carson who killed the doctors," Jerry said.

"Then who did it? And why?" Sarkman pointed at the composite. "Who is this guy—if he's not Carson?"

Trish studied the drawing again. For an instant she thought the face, shrouded though it was, was Carson's. Final recognition squirmed away like an eel. No, she didn't know who it was.

Sarkman put the sheet back in his briefcase. He asked Trish to sit down. He pulled up a straight-backed chair and sat backward in it, facing her. "I think the time's come to ask you some questions. We got too many murders all of a sudden to keep pussyfooting around. We got Jethro DuMont—used to work with Carson. Three doctors, three little girls, one muscleman, one mask maker, one guy who stopped to help out Mr. Palmer. That's ten people! Then this Carson single-handedly about breaks and ruins Mr. Palmer." He tipped the chair, leaning closer to Trish. His thin lips were tight. His eyes narrowed. "What the hell is between you and Carson Thomas?"

Trish stared numbly at him. "I've talked about that. To

you and to Jerry. The man is obsessed with me. It took the shape of his not wanting me to marry Foster." She drew a deep breath. "Now that he's gotten his way with that, we'll have to see where he goes next." Her voice caught, and she closed her eyes.

"Trish!" Jerry's voice. He knew her dream had crumbled.

"It can't be that simple," Sarkman went on. "Some way you're feeding each other. You're both playing some kind of sicko mind game."

"Pete, come on!" Jerry said.

"You come on. You and Ms. Victim here. If all this is so bad for you, Trish, why don't you pick up and leave? Why do you hang around and let people be killed because of you? Why don't you hide somewhere?"

"I already did that once." Trish struggled to keep her voice even. "He found me. Now I have a business, a child in school, and a mother to help me with her. I'm not running again!"

"Something stinks between you two."

"What stinks is you police!" Trish shouted. "You haven't been a bit of good to me. I'm frightened to death, and you haven't done a damn thing to help me. It's taken a murder in your own backyard to get you to really talk to me, Sarkman." She knew she was going to cry. She couldn't help it. And didn't care.

"You've talked to Jerry plenty." Sarkman's terrier face twisted with contempt. "You've got him in your pocket."

"Pete!" Jerry jumped up. "What's with you? This woman is a victim. She's not Carson Thomas's ally."

Sarkman got up and moved his chair back. "She's a type, Jerry. She leads everybody on." He jabbed a finger at her. "How many other guys you got on the string, sweetie? I mean beside our man here. You want to count them up? Maybe I can help you. You got Smith-Patton, that weirdo. He loves your jumpsuited ass. How about that baker been helping you out? I heard about him. Anybody else we don't know about—"

"Stop it!" Trish shrieked. "Stop it this second!" She cried harder. She wondered if, down at the core, there wasn't something to the charge. What kind of woman was she—really? Did Carson in truth own her soul? She lost it about then, edging down toward hysteria.

Sarkman hung on, trying insults and questions in random order. She only howled the louder.

"Shut up, Pete!" Jerry shouted. "That's enough!"

Sarkman cursed and grabbed his briefcase. He rushed out. Jerry tried to stay to offer consolation. She sent him on his way with a wet smile. "I'm better off alone right now."

"Sarkman is a pig."

"Call me . . . later sometime," she blubbered.

She got it together long enough to serve Melody dinner. A video movie and her daughter's fatigue were all the allies needed to assure an early bedtime. She tootled on her instruments for only a few minutes before the silence that meant sleep.

Trish cried herself to uneasy slumber. She woke suddenly to darkness. The bedside clock said 3:10. Great. Well, she wasn't better, but she wasn't weeping. She couldn't fall back asleep.

She refused to let her attention swing to Foster and her flown hopes. Instead she found herself thinking of . . . Carson. Not the controlled, brilliant man she had once known and admired, but a psychopath who strewed corpses coast to coast. For the first time she asked herself exactly what path his madness had taken. The cosmetic surgeon, the masks, the behaviors—taken together, what did they mean? The man who spawned inventions like a milkweed did silky parachutes was no more. Gone was that one who had possessed many women before her and had assumed others would follow. His all-pervasive arrogance and confrontational energy had fled in favor of sneaky warnings, threats made from at least one remove, obsession . . . Could she call it—timidity? Carson timid!

She got up and walked to the window. A weak, warm breeze stirred her nightgown. A concept wriggled up from the moonlit yard. She had assumed her nemesis was the old Carson looming over her physically and intellectually. To be sure, he still flashed his old intelligence and originality.

Yet . . . he was not the same person. She understood what had happened to him. In the years since her departure his personality had disintegrated under the pressure of madness, then reassembled itself following some unknown template. As it did, she wondered if he fully comprehended the metamorphosis.

Did he truly know that he was now a different person?

When Melody came back from an afternoon with neighbor children she told her that she wouldn't be marrying Foster. Her daughter turned up her candid gray gaze. "Why not?"

"Carson frightened him out of it."

Melody frowned. "I guess he could do that."

"Yeah. He could. How do you feel about it?"

Melody thought a moment. "I'll miss the mastiffs," she said.

She didn't know that every one of them was dead.

24

THE REST OF SUNDAY TRISH DEVOTED TO CANCELING the wedding arrangements. She went to her mother's house to do it. Bad enough doing it in her company, worse doing it alone. She sniffled her way through a watered-down version of why it was necessary. She then patiently answered her mother's questions. Yes, this Carson person's "pranks" had been the difference after all. Marylou, a tough cookie, took the bad news nearly in stride. A trembling lower lip was the only sign that her hopes for her daughter's future had been scuttled. She helped Trish make the calls. For the most part she had the presence of mind to hold her critical tongue.

Toward the end of a tough afternoon Trish went to lie down. On her back she studied the stenciled ceiling. She felt miserable, sure enough. In time she came to understand there was a single bright ray angling through the clouds.

Whatever her emotional future, it would be one wholly of her own design.

The weight of years would slow Marylou. Trish's social life would be increasingly private. Any decisions made would be hers alone. Improved insight and personal growth assured her that she would no longer frustrate herself with worries about whether or not her actions originated from her own motivations or her mother's.

All that assuming she could escape from Carson.

Monday morning she woke aching, as though she had spent the whole weekend doing calisthenics. She thought she was coming down with the flu—in the summer yet. Let no one tell her the mind and body weren't yoked together like oxen. She gave Melody her breakfast, then called Jill Beestock. She told her about the canceled wedding and listened to her sympathies. She begged a ride for her daughter to day camp. Considering what had just happened to Trish, Jill offered to bring Melody home, too. Trish felt too sore and sluggish to protest. She called Michelle and told her she wouldn't be in today. She tottered back up to the bedroom with a cup of tea and closed the door. Under the light covers she started to get the chills. She thought she ought to close the windows. She looked out over the coverlet.

The windows were closed.

Curious. She remembered them being open yesterday morning. Melody must have been fooling around. She closed her eyes, still not sure whether she was getting sick or suffering emotional hangover. She felt herself drifting off.

A noise!

Downstairs. She had locked the door. No one could get in. She sat up, her heart pounding. She strained to hear . . . Silence, then a distant creak on the staircase.

Someone was coming up to the second floor.

"Who's there?" she called.

Silence. Then another creak, closer. She slid out of bed and hurried to the door. She turned the knob and jerked. The door didn't open. It was locked. How? She never used the lock! She shoved at the lock lever. It didn't budge.

It had been tampered with!

She whirled, looking for the purse in which she kept her pistol. It was downstairs.

Slow footfalls in the hall came closer!

"Jill? Is that you, Jill?" Her voice cracked.

No reply.

"If you don't answer, I'm calling the police!"

Was that the hiss of heavy breath approaching? She spun and snatched up her bedside phone. She keyed in 911 twice before she realized.

No dial tone.

With a weak cry she threw the useless phone down. She jumped up, stood in the center of the room. She didn't know what to do. She flew to the closed door. "Carson!" she shouted.

The voice through the wood was thick. "No."

"Who are you? What do you want?"

"I have a message from Carson."

Trish gasped and pressed palms to her chill face. "You are Carson. *You are!*"

"No."

That voice! She sensed it was disguised, that she had heard it earlier. Wait. Carson had had vocal chord surgery. His voice had been changed by it. It had been that "new" voice that had threatened her. It had been he all along, not some faceless ally. He had a different voice to match a different face! It *was* Carson beyond the door. "What message do you have . . . from Carson?"

"He knows your wedding won't happen."

"How?"

"He still hears what happens here. Nicholas is clever, but Carson's more so."

There were new bugs in the house! Trish was close to the door now. Carson was on the other side, inches away, though he himself might not realize it through his fog of self-delusion and madness. Long ago, in June, when all this had begun, she suspected it would come to this. Closer and closer Carson had moved, freezing her and closing in. Was this Monday morning the moment when she would again behold his face, masked or naked? She swallowed heavily. "Are you coming in, Carson?"

Beyond the door what had been a slow hiss of breath speeded up. She sensed it catching in a thick throat. After long moments he said, "No. I told you I brought a message."

Trish sagged against the door, tasted relief.

Beyond the wood the hiss slowed under the rein of will. She had heard such sound in her life: the wordless voice of sexual arousal.

She closed her eyes and pressed her fingers against the door. They shook like stalks in the wind. "What's the message?"

"Pack for a long trip. For both you and Melody. Then meet Carson at a place I'll tell you later."

"And after the trip?"

"You'll be together forever."

Just as he had written on the photograph. Trish's despair rose up like fog. "The wedding's no more. That's what you wanted."

"That isn't all he wants. You should know him better than that."

The Master of Excess. Trish closed her eyes and clenched her fists. She had broken the bargain for her soul. She couldn't go back to him. Was she even tempted? If she was, it was only because his devilish powers were so strong. *No!* What could she do to sway him from his purpose? Her mind whirled like a prayer wheel as she sought something to defuse his determination. Something to make him leave her alone. She thought she found it.

"Carson!"

"I am not—"

"I have something to tell you about Melody. Something I always hid from you. Are you listening?"

"Yes."

"You are not Melody's father!"

Silence.

"Do you understand me? It was another man. A man named Ron Verner—"

"That isn't possible. Her hair, her skin—"

"I had tissue testing done." She blurted out the name of the laboratory and the date of the testing. "Check it! Check it and you'll see. I'll fax them written permission!"

There was a long silence. The heavy voice spoke again, rustling like a toad on leaves. "So broken lines from the net of the past are joined. Truth outs. I have a truth for *you* about Ron Verner."

"You knew him?"

"In a way. How the present and past join!" He paused. "Now, again, you must go away with Carson. You and Melody."

"I won't!"

"Carson thought you might take that . . . unwise position. He instructed me to tell you that in such a case you were to know that he will force you to join him."

"I won't! Think about who Melody's father really was. You won't want her—or me either, now."

Delay from the other side of the door. Trish's news, like an animal swallowed by a snake, was proving difficult to digest. Her heart hammered ribs. Her palms were ice. The voice resumed, gaining vigor and confidence. "Until now no one you know has been badly hurt. Should you remain uncooperative, such things will begin to happen. You mustn't doubt Carson's ruthlessness when it comes to the resurrection of Queen of My Heart!"

So that's what he thought it was, her resurrection. Damnation was more like it.

"I brought equipment, some of which I used before."

Trish jumped back. "What kind of equipment? *What are you going to do?*"

"Prove to you that you really are at Carson's mercy. That he can do whatever he wants to you. That you should reconsider at this moment." Pause. "Will you?"

"No!"

"So the past and present themes combine."

She heard a metallic rattle, the sound of an object put to the floor. She backed further away from the door. "What do you mean 'past and present'?"

"I'm going to gas you," he said.

She shrieked. When she quieted he said, "The same gas used on Ron Verner. It entered his car with the help of a timing device right where the high-speed stretch of highway began, before the bridge abutment. It put him to sleep."

"You murdered him! You knew about the two of us! You murdered Melody's father!"

"Had Carson known—if you're telling the truth—Verner would have died in a far uglier way."

Trish heard the hiss of escaping gas. Though she saw nothing, she spun and hurried to a window. She heaved on the sash. Holding her breath, she grunted aloud with the effort. The window wouldn't open!

"Trying the windows?" came the voice from beyond the door. "I sealed them."

Trish whirled from the glass and looked for something with which to smash it.

"This must teach you to feel differently about Carson's proposal. Don't be foolish. Go away with him and be his love. This is proof of his determination. Next, blood will flow."

"No!"

"Blood will flow!"

Trish whimpered and picked up a footstool. She hurried toward the window. A wave of dizziness nearly swept her to her knees. She staggered. She mustn't breathe! A wisp of gas had somehow reached her lungs. She staggered. Dimly she was aware she had dropped the stool.

Somehow she was on the floor.

What would happen to Melody with her dead?

She didn't die. She awoke with a horrible headache. Her mouth tasted of sourish organic compounds. The bedside clock told her she had been unconscious a little more than a hour. She got to her feet, weathered a spell of dizziness, then opened the door—now unlocked. She thought of calling the police. What good would they do? Mad Carson was long gone. He was too clever to leave clues. Sarkman would insult her further. He would ask intrusive questions that tried to link the gassing with the murder on the highway. Nuts to them! She went down to the kitchen and dug out the dusty bottle of Old Granddad. She wasn't a drinking woman, but . . .

She mixed three fingers with hot water in a cup. Towering behind the recent terrifying interlude like summer storm clouds was the next unknown step in the pattern of Carson's excess.

Come away with me and be my love. . . .

If she didn't agree to do so, she had been guaranteed blood.

Her memory flung her back eight years. Ron Verner's face floated like a balloon before her, his amiable smile, curly hair, white fingers flying over keyboards . . . Dead at Carson's hand! *Murdered!*

She sipped the whiskey. Years ago Carson had been a sane, punishing killer. Now he was someone far worse.

Did he himself know just who?

She began to cry. Unlike her recent hysterical howlings, this cry was like warm, calming rain. It allowed her to realize she needed help. She hadn't really found enough of it up to now. As Carson drew closer, his determination looming as irresistibly as the road roller wrecking her Acura, it was time to marshal what forces she had.

One in particular.

Tuesday morning she stopped at the bakery. She wasn't sure just how to begin to raise the subject of her near-desperation with Dino. When he emerged with his usual white bag filled with apple tarts for Melody he said, "Hey, Patricia, I gotta meet your *bambina*. You put me off long enough. Right?"

"Right!" He had made it easy for her. "Come for dinner tonight."

Melody the ham *loved* an audience. She monopolized the first half hour of Dino's visit with soprano recorder and Irish whistle. "Listen to *this* one, Dino!" she cried, rushing from one number to another.

Nearly eight years old now, she had expanded her memorized tunes to include movie and TV themes. One hearing was enough for her to play them. In cases where their keys weren't right for her instruments, she transposed them to fit. Trish tried to see her with Dino's eyes, face showered with summer's freckles, bright-eyed, pigtailed with Mom's patient assistance.

Dino leaned back and beamed. "Whatta kid! Whatta kid!" He chuckled. He looked over at Trish, who was trying not to blush too red with pride. "She take after you, this music?"

She shook her head. "Her father. The talent—"

"Must be something of you in her."

She shrugged. "Blood is blood. She's mine."

Dino listened on. When Trish tried to tell Melody enough was enough he waved his arm. "Let her play a little bit more."

Melody tootled on for another five minutes.

"Hey, even I know that one!" Dino sprang to attention, saluted. *"Allons, enfants . . ."* He sang on in French for several bars, his rough voice and the recorder a bizarre duo. "The Marseillaise! One of the great national anthems," he said.

"You have a good accent, Dino," Trish said.

"Learned the language from my grandma. She was a Canuck." He patted Melody's back. "That's enough, kid. Go have a tart."

"After dinner, Melody," Trish said with a laugh. "Don't forget who gives the orders here."

"You need a man around here," Dino said. Macho man.

"Why? I don't see any heavy lifting needing to be done."

Dino leered. "Men are good for at least one other thing."

"Dinner time!" Trish called.

During the meal Dino grew gradually less patient with Melody, who was hyped and rambunctious after playing for a new person. "Behave!" he said twice. Trish held her tongue. It was their first evening together. She had hoped they would all get along. When Melody was in her pajamas Trish asked her if she wanted a good-night hug from Dino. She said yes, but Dino only waved. "You're a good kid, Melody. Get some sack time."

Later she sat beside Dino with the coffee on a tray. "She's a wonderful girl, Dino. I hope she doesn't seem a trial to you."

He shrugged. "Not used to kids." He met her eyes. "You got something more important on your mind, don't you?"

"Am I that transparent?"

"You been running scared, Trish. You forget how much you've told me?"

"There's more." She filled him in completely on what Carson had done to Foster. He cursed softly from time to time. She finished up with yesterday's threats and her gassing.

"Right outside your door . . . and he didn't come in?"

She did her best to explain her theory that Carson's disintegration had turned him into a different man entirely. She didn't know what to do next in the face of his fresh threats. She wanted both Dino's advice and his help.

He turned his dark eyes to hers. She again felt his inner power. It resonated for her as clearly as a tune heard through earphones. Speaking to me on Station HHFM—How He Floors Me! "I gotta think," he said. He led her out onto the porch, away from Carson's bugs. He turned to her. "Got one idea anyhow."

"Say."

"I turn the bakery over to Mario for a while. I shadow you. You don't see me. Carson doesn't see me. He tries something with you, I waste him."

"I've told you all about him. You've seen him in action. You know what he's done recently. You want to take that much of a chance with your life?"

"He's not God."

"No, he's the devil."

Dino chuckled. "Sure!"

Trish sat on the edge of the swing and closed her eyes. "I'm so desperate and frightened, I'm willing to let you do it. Willing to let you risk your life. Is that selfish, or what?"

He waved away her fears. "Maybe we have a way to make things happen faster. What's the story with your geek friend Nicholas?"

"I—I don't know."

"We know this house is bugged again, right?"

"Yes!"

"So put Nicholas on it. He found that equipment I shot up. I learned my lesson about that. Maybe we can do it again. This time we turn up Carson."

Trish grinned wearily. "Mr. Shoot-First-Ask-Questions-Later." She led him back inside to the living room couch. "Come sit beside me. I could use a little close company."

He sat, and she put her arm lightly over his shoulder. "Let's not talk any more secrets now," she said. She found herself talking about the softer side of her life: Melody, her mother, her and Melody's friends Jill and Pamela Beestock, the happier days of PC-Pros. She found she was dreamily running on. The reason, she realized, was that she was waiting for him to hug and kiss her.

Though his responses were neutral, she thought she felt his desire for her. Woman's intuition, was it? Earlier, after that dreadful night of violence in the PC-Pros' lab, she imagined she had felt the same emotional vibrations in him. She had been so sure! But he had done nothing but . . . was it wait for her to make the first real move?

Jungle battle and Asian horrors could twist a man's heart with a hard brass hand. Who could guess just how Dino Castelli's emotions had been distorted? Just the same, she couldn't take the initiative with him. She had done her womanly stage setting: provided the occasion and the opportunity. The rest was up to him.

So there they sat on the couch like a pair of nervous teenagers. Men, men, she thought, recalling how he had flown like a missile at Carson's two thugs. Those animals had barely escaped with their lives. He had been utterly fearless. Then! Tonight he was timid as a mole.

Time passed. She felt her heart thudding. Was his, too? Maybe, because conversation faltered, then halted altogether. Did he sense the rising emotional pressure as she did? Surely he knew she was attracted to him—even in the face of all her serious difficulties. Maybe because of them. Dino, Dino . . .

The door chimes sounded.

Trish gasped.

"You expecting anybody?" Dino said.

"No."

He got up and moved toward the door. She followed. He stepped into the shadows. "See who it is," he said.

Trish angled toward the door, squinting at the figure standing beyond the oval glass set in the old door. She touched the switch. The porch light disclosed—

"Oh!"

"Who—"

"It's Jerry Morris. I mentioned him. The helpful police detective." She opened the door and introduced the two men. She read the disappointment on Jerry's face.

"I'm sorry, Trish. I didn't know you had company," he said.

"It's okay. I was just leaving." Dino's grin was inscrutable. "We just ran out of things to say. Trish, I'll give you a call. Talk to Nicholas, don't forget."

After Dino's departure Jerry stood uneasily in the entryway. Trish waved him in. "Oh, come on. You can't be any more annoying than the last one!"

"I don't understand," Jerry said.

"Good. That makes two of us."

She made fresh coffee. Jerry confessed his visit was personal. He had been thinking about Foster breaking the engagement. "One reason I came was to tell you how sorry I am. I know you were more than counting on it."

"Carson had his way after all," she said dully.

"There's a bright side. The way I figure, that makes you eligible for me."

As always she found his straight-ahead sense of fair play and honesty refreshing. In turn she responded frankly. She told him about Carson's visit, the threats, and the gas. He said she should have called headquarters right away. He wanted to go upstairs and have her run through the whole thing again. "It's no use," she said. "The man doesn't make mistakes."

"He killed that guy on the side of the road. That was a mistake. He's getting careless."

265

Suddenly Trish was both tired and bored. "It's late, Jerry. And I'm exhausted. Being gassed and frightened nearly to death doesn't agree with me."

Before he left he asked her if she'd be willing to go out with him. She had trouble getting past her vexation with reluctant Dino. "Sometime, sure. Don't ask me when right now, Jerry. Okay? Sometime. After I survive all this. If I do."

25

"TRISH MY WISH!" NICHOLAS REPEATED SOFTLY TO himself while bent over improved van equipment. That her home and business had been re-bugged had astonished him. His monitors' weekly scans had disclosed no signals. He had despaired because he thought he could be of no further service to her. That situation had flung him into an unfamiliar emotional land—depression. Neither Monk nor Miles nor Mose could lift his spirits. Their inspired riffs fell upon his ears with all the impact of elevator music.

Nor did chess seize his mind in its old snapping-turtle jaws. His ego had been wounded by his defeat at anonymous Gruntman's hands. His mind had wandered, so he had blundered. The much more significant truth was that his life was in disarray. Its simplicity had been overturned. B.T.—before Trish—he had his occasional consulting projects, his jazz, and his chess. He took direction from Sweetest Sister. Now the sluice gates of his dammed emotions had swung open. He was inundated, swept away.

The situation had gone even further topsy-turvy. Sweetest Sister had commanded him to appear, tuxed and cummerbunded, last week at a formal dinner. He was astonished to find her again on Foster Palmer's suntanned arm. The purpose of the dinner fell out as the evening wound its way. She was announcing to the world the reclamation of her lost love. Lois Smith-Patton and Foster Palmer were a social item again! Behind the gay phrases falling like petals from the flowers of her upturned lips lay her fangs, sunk again into the man. Sunk far deeper, Nicholas was sure, than when the two had first been an item. He sensed that soon there would be another betrothal for Foster, with a speedy wedding to follow. Sweetest Sister wouldn't make the same mistake twice.

Of course, the matter of the electronic dissolution of Foster's wealth remained very much an open issue. Sweetest Sister had begun to explain Carson's keyboard and network wizardry to Nicholas. His imagination and technical knowledge at once blew away the fog of vagueness clinging to her words. Yes! It could be done—by a man of genius. Recover those losses? Who could say? He said to her, "I never realized you were a gambler."

"I'm not!"

"Foster may end up only well-off, instead of rich."

"Never!" Lois paled slightly under her makeup. "Anyway, I want him, and I'll get him."

Nicholas pointed at thick-chinned Branch, who hovered as close to Foster as his own shadow. Foster and the brute exchanged frequent glances. Nicholas read fear in the thinner man's eyes, reassurance in the other's. "I hope you three have a pleasant honeymoon," he said. He was astonished by his own boldness.

"Three?"

"You, Foster, and Mr. America there."

Sweetest Sister's glare was touched with disbelief at his forwardness. "What are you talking about?"

"You think Foster is the same person he was?"

"Of course he is!"

Nicholas had heard hints of what had happened to Foster while in Carson's hands. "Foster is a diminished man, Sweetest Sister."

"No!" She whirled, white, and stalked off. She failed to punish him for his insolence. Oh, how he and his world were changing!

The moment he grasped that the dinner was the first milestone on the road to the altar for Foster his spirits soared. Trish was available! His will-o'-the-wisp hope had taken form and shape like a released genie. He *had* dared to hope. Could it be that he might one day feel the gentle touch of her hand? See them together! Gangling he towering over lovely she in her white jumpsuit. Emotionally those sizes were reversed. She loomed large, inflated by love and anguish. He was a desolate depth-dwelling dwarf desperate to flourish beneath the sun of her companionship.

Why so timid, Nicholas? He had mind and money—negotiable currency in the mate market. To be sure, he had his . . . ways. "Mars man," the riffraff had called him. That could be changed. There were means. A hairpiece could eclipse the full moon of his dome. He could succumb to Sweetest Sister's long-standing desire "to dress you like a man-about-town instead of a circus sideshow attraction." More: He could enroll in Dale Carnegie courses. There he would speak publicly, learn the rules for basic human interaction. During three hours Wednesday evenings his rough edges would be filed down, then smoothed by bankers and insurance men joined in mutual pursuit of success.

Despite his plans for self-improvement, he knew he could never bring himself to call Trish. He had never made a call in his life without a concrete purpose. Phoning merely to chat, to exchange news, was equivalent to picking up the Hot Line. Then she had called him! She had learned her home and office were once again bugged. Could he help her?

The mere respect he had held for Carson's technical wizardry expanded to admiration. The man had found ways to communicate on uncommon frequencies, those beyond the reach of Nicholas's prior equipment. But now . . . he—no dolt himself—was once again able to get a fix on the signals. The first he found originated from the bugs nestled somewhere in Trish's house. Their electronic voices angled off toward the center of the city. He drove his van to PC-Pros, circled and circled, earphoned and intent on CRTs. He took a reading, carefully noted degree and minute of the second signal's bearing. Somewhere the waves from home and business would cross.

And there Carson would be found!

Or would there be another relay unit? This time he would investigate in advance. He drew out his detailed, expensive city maps, no mere gas station giveaways. He summoned geometry, wielded protractor, and angled straightedges. The lines crossed hard by a structure the map key indicated was a large residential building. He wheeled the van around and headed across town. His spirits rose. He spun the tape volume up. Lockjaw Davis honked loud enough to outdo Gabriel blowing his final set.

Several tours around what proved to be a large apartment building in decent condition convinced him that no signals were being relayed on to another node.

He was homing in on Carson's lair!

He chuckled with glee and triumph. Blow, Lockjaw! Blow me to success! Blow me to hero status! Blow me into the arms of Trish My Wish!

He had learned from previous experience. He drove the van to a parking garage in the next block and left it. What equipment he needed he put into his shoulder bag. This would be an investigative expedition. Finesse and discretion would be his strong suits. He bubbled. He *knew* he had tracked Trish's nemesis down.

From the garage pay phone he called her, pride welling up like water at a mountain spring. He gave her the number and ordered her to call him back from a secure phone. When she did he told her he was sniffing the spoor near Carson's lair.

"Wonderful!"

He heard the delight in her voice, spooned it up like honey. "I'm going to go have a look—very cautiously."

She hesitated. "Are you sure—where are you going?"

"To an apartment house in the north end of the city."

"Nicholas, are you sure you should go ahead?"

"Of course. I'm not seeking confrontation—at all."

She hesitated. "I really appreciate what you've done, Nicholas. But I think you should wait there until the police—"

"Those useless people! You've told me they've done nothing for you. Neither Sarkman nor that Morris man."

"Let me get in touch with Dino. He can go with you and—"

"Play bull in the china shop again? I can handle this. Believe me! We're only talking data-gathering here." Nicholas was doubly delighted with himself. Hear how he confronted his love! Long gone was the tongue-tied twit who trembled and twitched before her. Color him confident. "I'll report back to you shortly."

"Tell me the address."

"I didn't notice the number."

"Tell me what street—"

He hung up. He sensed her lack of confidence in him. Annoying! She must learn otherwise. And surely would when he ran red-haired Carson Thomas to earth. From a safe distance he would watch the police, the National Guard, the army—whatever it took—subdue the man.

Leaving the parking garage, he reminded himself vividly of his initial misadventure at the hands of Eddie and Zak. He wouldn't be making those mistakes again. Not that it was possible. This was a better part of town. No hoodlums loitered by 2260 Manifold Boulevard.

He wore heavy work boots, khaki chinos, an old plumbing services jacket, a cap to mask his dome—and the sullen air of a tradesman lucky enough to be in short supply. When an occupant left the apartment building, he entered before the door closed.

He unsheathed his meter and got on the elevator. He pushed the button for the top floor, ten. He looked at the LED digits as the elevator rose. The reading increased as the car rose, then slid off as it passed the seventh floor.

So floor seven was where Carson was.

On the way down he got off at seven. In his costume with

meter in hand he scarcely drew a glance from a couple he passed in the hall. He was in the best of moods! He drew the earphones up, set the headpiece carefully under his cap. Ben Webster's sax crooned of approaching success, Nicholas triumphant! Chords and key changes sang of a grateful Trish on his arm one sunny, blue-skied day in the near future.

He looked at the numbers and meter in turn. Apartment 712, 714, 718 . . . The meter reading rose. Down the hall he went. It was deserted. His step turned jaunty. All he had to do was find out which of the apartments held Carson's equipment and thus the man himself. This time there would be no need to go in. No, violent confrontations were not his strong suit. Leave such things for Dino Castelli. Those behaviors were the ones expected from men who couldn't tolerate jazz. Couldn't *tolerate* . . . Such ignorance! He hummed along with Webster's familiar soaring improvisation.

Apartment 722 . . . and 724. There! He kept walking right on past. But that was it. Seven twenty-four! At the end of the hall he turned back. No one was there to see him. He took his time returning, eyes again on the meter. Yes, Apartment 724. On his way past he looked more carefully at its door, thinking of the armored one with the electronic lock in the rundown tenement.

This one was slightly ajar!

He paused, lowered his tape player's volume. Ben Webster subsided to background music. From Apartment 724 he heard no sounds. He looked up and down the hall. No one.

He stretched out a hand. He touched the wood, gave a shove. The door swung wide. He angled his head to see inside.

Yes!

He saw electronic equipment, VCRs, a wide-screen TV, signs of habitation. He stepped closer, peered through the doorway. The two small, shadowy rooms could conceal no one. They were deserted. Plywood covered windows. His eyes turned back to the equipment. Some of it clearly carried the signs of one-of-a-kind fabrication, empirical evidence of Carson's talent. In that one area they were brothers.

Another quick look down the hall. Deserted. A further peer into the two rooms. Watch out for that closet! Oh, relax. Why would Carson hide when he had no idea Nicholas was on the way? Not to worry about the closet.

He couldn't resist a quick peek at the equipment—so much of it!—arrayed on rack shelving. It wouldn't be wise to dally long, but . . . He thought of turning off the tape, but Webster's sax nourished as breast does baby.

Several of the handcrafted devices had no cases. Their innards were exposed, revealing, fascinating. Nicholas scanned boards, components, mapping their functions in the more exalted computer of his brain. He tore himself away and stuck his head out into the hall. No one. Back to the circuits! Their secrets unfolded like a wondrous origami flower. A few more minutes only, and he would be away to Trish, triumphant as Hitler in the railroad car.

Instinct told him someone was standing behind him!

He whirled. A man stood smiling in the doorway.

Carson!

Nicholas recognized him from the photo Trish had shown him. *Trish, Carson, and Melody—together forever!* Panic flew through him like a lightning bolt. "Where did you come from?" he asked.

"The apartment across the hall." Carson's voice was such an odd croak that it had to be affected. "I followed you here. Then I sort of . . . slithered in." Chuckling, he turned back and closed the door behind him. "Welcome to Resurrection Headquarters!"

"You must let me leave." Nicholas tried to level his voice. It emerged in leafy tremble.

"Some part of you will leave," Carson said. "Call it your spirit, your soul, that thing which may or may not distinguish you from lower animals."

"I'll go away. I'll leave the city. I won't help Trish anymore!" He astonished himself. Where was Sir Nicholas Smith-Patton, battling valiantly in the lists, Trish's fabric favor fluttering from his lance? He was ashamed, but frightened far worse. *"Please."*

"You're too much a techie gadfly. I can't tolerate talented wild cards in my game. It's much too serious for that."

Nicholas backed away from the equipment toward the bed. Deep in the apartment now, he was aware of the rutty stink of male body. He stumbled over a heavy transformer on the floor and sprawled down among discarded fast-food bags and toppled paper cups. He squirmed to get up. The sole of Carson's shoe crushed down on his ankle, pinning it to the floor. Nicholas tried in vain to pull it free. Carson towered over him.

Carson raised hands to his own neck. He dug into his flesh somehow, pulled at his skin. Like a shedding viper, he had another skin ready beneath! Oh, the first wasn't his skin.

It was a mask! One that covered his whole head. He tore it free and flung it aside.

"You!" Nicholas screamed. "You're not Carson!"

"Maybe I am!"

Savage hands found Nicholas's throat, squeezing off breath. Cartilage and soft tissue stretched and tore. His eyes closed themselves in the face of agony. His assailant was silent save for the hissing breaths of his exertion. Ben Webster's earphoned sax whispered "Moments to Remember" above horrid, constricting fingers. Its key modulated from the major of life to the minor of death. Reflex ordered Nicholas to resist. He gripped thick wrists. His long fingers and spidery arms were feeble as feathers against wire sinews and iron bone. He tried to twist free. Weight crushed him down.

He could burst for want of drawing breath. Terror overwhelmed him. There was no escape! His ears began to ring. Red waves rushed in from all directions. He was being murdered! Doomed, he only wanted it to be over. His mind drifted away to chess, its art and beauty. And jazz! Both were triumphs of imagination over the commonplace. How much they were alike, really. Yes! Everything that rises must converge!

Lost, he marveled distantly at the devilish cunning of his assailant. Past cunning—genius, as Trish had promised.

She was right.

Knowing what he did about the man taking his life, Nicholas understood she was doomed as well.

Poor woman!

26

"READ ALL ABOUT IT!" CHAMP BAWLED AGAINST THE walls of Resurrection Headquarters. "Son of socially prominent family disappears! Massive missing person effort." *Sure* there would be. More like it: "Cops take a break from hounding drug lords and murderers to hunt hothouse flower!"

That flower was bent and broken, chums. Tossed on the temporary compost heap under his bed. His head was as loose and limp as a spring-necked toy's in the back window of a teenager's car. His van Champ had driven halfway across the city, rolled it into a long-term parking garage. Good luck to searchers!

He studied the front page of the local paper. Not a bad likeness of Carson, cropped from a photo he knew well. A lot of good it would do the fuzz. That face wouldn't be seen on the streets for the time being—possibly never again, depending on his master's wishes.

No question matters were coming to a head. Music maestro Carson conducted the players in his personal symphony—him, Trish, Melody, others—into the coda. The themes gathered, assimilated, refined, and were driven to the simplest, most logical melody: *Trish, Carson, and Melody—together forever!*

To work! The note left on the bed by Carson was brief, explicit. Yet there was room for Champ to exercise his fertile imagination. Such a team they made! Carson the Führer, Champ the Desert Fox of execution. Before long now Queen of My Heart's resurrection would be complete. She, Carson, and Melody would sail off into the sunset. And Champ . . . He blinked and shook himself like a dog emerging from water. He would be ever faithful, awaiting new orders. He would . . .

He was startled. Boiling within signaled the shifting of the tectonic plates of his psyche—Earthquake Anger! Earlier it had been sparked by thoughts of Queen of My Heart's intransigence, the Loathed One's unworthiness. Now who or what caused it? He flew to Siege Restraint and its Velcro straps. His shrieks carried tones of bewilderment. His memory thrust forward the Samaritan at the moment the wire entered his brain. *Why?* Why that then? Why this rage now?

Queen of My Heart belonged to Carson! It was their destiny to be together for the rest of their lives. Whence Earthquake Anger? What lay at its core—beside his own increasingly strained service? Charge that to *her!* He knew what bored from within, though he had called forth armies of denial. Oh, yes, he knew. . . .

Carson had raged to hear that he was not Melody's father. He who was always so sure, so very capable of working his will in all things, had been outpaddled by another's sperm. Not even he could escape being twisted on Queen of My Heart's rack! He, too, had burst into tirades of denial, his voice nearly a howl despite the telephone's muting. He slammed down the receiver, no matter Champ's defenseless, loyal ear. Possibly he then rushed off in search of certitude. Who could guess his master's methods?

What was this? He had ripped his arms free! Torn straps fluttered like ribbons from his wrists, then fell away. He lashed the air with free arms. Siege Restraint tottered, fell.

Flailing and twitching, he sent it clattering. He edged sideways across the floor like an angry crab on the ocean bottom. Dimly he grasped that he could free his legs. He dared not, and thus stand free in full rage. He could not let Earthquake Anger reign!

In time the seizure ebbed. It left him whimpering and gibbering, his cheek brushing the floor in a smear of drool. Everything that had been so perfect, so orderly, was slipping away toward chaos. He could not put words to any of it.

He was certain only of his own fear.

After a long while he rose and wiped away oozing fluids with a stained towel. He slumped onto the bed, snatched up the phone, punched in a number. He was panting like a miler. Because soon it would be *her* voice he heard. This time he was Ed Smurd, C.P.A., calling on business. The round-cheeked receptionist put him through. Into Queen of My Heart's ear he howled his song: "Hi, ho, the geek is dead! The geek is dead! The weirdo geek is dead! Nicholas S-P is no more!"

"What have you done to him? *Tell me!*" Her voice was tight and anxious.

"Listen to me! This won't be repeated," he continued. "At noon two days from today be at the Northpark Mall with your luggage and your daughter—"

"I won't listen to this!" Her voice was as choked as if he had his hands around the ivory column of her throat. She would listen.

"The north end of the parking lot is deserted. Park there and wait." Champ drew a deep breath. "Your life with Carson will be resumed."

"No."

"No police. No tricks."

"I won't come, Carson! We won't be there!"

"Listen! I am serious. And I'll prove it. Later today."

"What are you talking about?" Yes, this was the morning for everyone to shriek, Champ thought.

"There will be a single act that will prove Carson's utter sincerity," he said. "One that will convince you to make the rendezvous."

"What are you going to do, Carson?"

"Prove the depth of commitment to you."

"What—"

Phones could be tapped. Calls must be short, no matter the sweet perfume of her panicked voice. Champ laid the receiver to rest. He could not jar her ear as Carson had his. He stared down at the phone. Carson . . . Was there a Carson? Or had his persona seized Champ utterly? Possibly he worked his master's will so totally that he had become him. Was it Champ and Carson, or two Carsons? Or one?

Never had he felt so lost.

He stirred, rose, shook himself. He must rally his wits. Much remained to be done. *Once more unto the breach, dear friends . . .*

The Blandmobile nosed through the rain after the PC-Pros' van. Champ's lengthy observations of the business had taught him that in the face of adversity employees had rallied to Queen of My Heart. Their loyalty translated into longer hours and a redistribution of tasks. Oh, wonder woman, to spark such generosity of spirit!

The slant was chief among the excellent. His kind knew the meaning of hard work. Play? He didn't. Champ understood their ways. Tran Lo Dinh the Loyal. Knight that Galahad now, purest among the Round Table serving Queen of My Heart. He was making a delivery of three PCs he had spent most of the night repairing, working with the owls and moles. Next-day repair service commanded a premium fee. A small fish thrown toward the gaping jaws of impending PC-Pros' bankruptcy. Such a waste of energy, money, and emotion when all she had to do was capitulate to Carson's demands that she go away with him and be his love. How, how had she been so stubborn and foolish over all these months? When in the end Carson's will *would* be done. Amen!

Why then Champ's sense of . . . faltering?

Cautious Tran Lo Dinh locked the van before departing with dolly. Champ's rubber-gloved hands were quick with the Tumbler Tickler. In a mini-moment he was inside, crouching on the rugged floor, waiting for the slant. In his hand, a friend spawned in the armories of Middle Europe, an automatic pistol—Bad Czech. To heighten the mood he hummed the last movement theme from Dvořák's *From the New World* symphony. "Going home, going home," he crooned softly. He hefted Bad Czech, looked again to make sure there was a round in the chamber.

Hark! The rattle of dolly wheels on concrete. Champ positioned himself by the doors. He heard the slant's key. The right door swung open. Champ and Bad Czech filled it. "Get in!"

Tran Lo Dinh hesitated a moment that nearly cost him his life right then. Champ saw the surprise on the badly scarred face. But no fear. This one had started out in Nam. How could you really scare any one of them with just a Bad Czech? Tran began to climb in. Champ seized his thin arm above the elbow and jerked him forward. The top of his head struck the back of the seat. He lay briefly stunned. Champ rolled him face up and shoved Bad Czech's barrel into his loose mouth. "We're going for a one-way ride!" he growled in his best gangster argot. Edward G., R.I.P!

They got underway, Tran at the wheel, Champ riding shotgun, or was it automatic? This was all going smoother than a baby's bottom. He gave directions, the slant followed them. Champ found his eyes returning again and again to the scar that curved out from beneath his captive's white jumpsuit collar and up the side of his face. The man's throat had once been cut. Somehow he had survived. He could talk, but didn't—at least not to Champ. Who knew what was going on behind the bowl-cut black hair and almond eyes? All these Asians were different.

Soon there would be one less.

Their destination: a road construction area. The day of rain had sent the workers off to vacation. He ordered Tran onto an earthy gouge that would one day be new road. He motioned him to pull up behind a trailer. It would screen the van from any passing traffic.

Champ put Bad Czech's barrel to Tran's temple. "You know who I am?" he asked.

Tran nodded.

"No, you don't!"

Carson's orders had been to pull the trigger at that point. But increasingly of late he felt the sprouting seeds of rebellion. He felt like a slave defying an all-powerful plantation owner. No matter the hopelessness of it. "Tell me about Quee—Tell me about Trish Morley."

Tran shook his head.

"Tell me something!" He nudged the yellow temple vigorously with Bad Czech.

Tran said nothing.

"Aren't you afraid of dying?"

Tran touched his scar. "Died once, not afraid now."

Champ wanted words about Queen of My Heart. On them he would drape his desires like strung popcorn around a Christmas tree. "Talk about Trish, or I'll open up your head like a soft-cooked egg!"

Tran turned impassive eyes toward him. "You crazy man," he said.

No! Not crazy! Cunning, sly, odd, a loner—those! But not mad, not by any stretch. He served Carson. He adored Queen of My Heart. Between those poles turned the earth of his sanity. Not even close to mad! "Watch your mouth!" he bellowed. Whence this stirring fit of Earthquake Anger, then? Never had it arisen beyond the walls of his rooms. But here it came, roaring into his brain like an eighteen-wheeler. He felt the rictus grip his face, twisting it. His eyes widened and bulged. He threw down Bad Czech and seized the silent slant's face in both hands. He slid them to the smother position.

Complicated weapons were overrated.

Champ heaved against the slant, half pinning the small, wiry body with his bulk. Earthquake Anger gave him Hulk strength. He stared into the annoyingly untroubled almond-shaped eyes through the red wash of rage.

The little man squirmed. His arms thrashed and twitched ineffectively. Champ felt the small jaw trembling. The slant was trying to open his mouth and bite the smothering hand.

No way! He increased the pressure. The victim struggled all the harder. He didn't want to die, no matter his stolid rhetoric.

Well, he was going to cash in anyway.

What warned Champ he didn't know. The instincts of the beast in the wood or the Cro-Magnon crouched by his fire. He heaved away just as the sharp report of the slant's handgun snapped at his ears.

Pain penetrated Champ's innards and fueled the fire of his rage like gasoline. He had been fooled, deceived, betrayed, conned—*shot!*

He grabbed the slant's pistol arm and broke it like a stick. The light revolver tumbled to the carpet. He re-gripped the face, saw the yellow drain from it. Agony filled the tilted brown eyes like water running into a pitcher. At last!

Champ, in great pain, had no patience now with slow smother. Or with himself for his carelessness. Who was better bred to violence than the historically undefeated Vietnamese? He heaved the little man into a half nelson and broke his neck.

That did not change what the slant had done to him. He was in pain and bleeding. His plan had been to abandon the van and Tran, walk several blocks, and grab a cab or bus. He had to follow an instant Plan B. He dragged the corpse into the van rear. He surprised himself by using time and waning energy to beat the dead head against the carpet. He supposed it had to be done to appease Earthquake Anger. When he at last panted into pause the skull was as soft as a rotted pumpkin.

On the road he adjusted his clothes to see the wound in his lower abdomen. Lucky Champ! His probing finger told him there was an exit wound as well. Shot through, he was. Lots of blood. He found rags under the seat and pressed them against the twin wounds as well as he could.

The injury spurred his audacity. He pulled the van right up behind the Blandmobile. He scooped up and pocketed Bad Czech, then drove the Blandmobile toward Resurrection Headquarters. There he would staunch the bleeding, rest, and ready himself for the final act in the restoration of Queen of My Heart to Carson's life. *Together forever!*

The six-month project was winding down to its final hours.

Why did he feel no elation? Had he been wounded where rags couldn't reach?

27

DETECTIVE JERRY MORRIS AND LIEUTENANT PETE Sarkman sat with Trish and Dino Castelli in her PC-Pros' office. She had closed the business indefinitely after hearing that Tran had been murdered. Last night she had talked with Jerry about her guilt over not having done so earlier. He was patient and caring, urging her not to be too hard on herself.

The two lawmen were finishing up explaining to her the seriousness of the manhunt now launched for wounded Carson. Speedy lab work had matched blood found in the van to the type in his military records. Carson was their man, all right. They had the parking lot of the Northpark Mall staked out. A policewoman Trish lookalike was sitting there now in a vehicle identical to Trish's rental car. Beside her was a midget in a red wig and mask. Trish and Melody's leaving the house late that morning had been as heavily directed as a Cecil B. DeMille movie. The journey included a nifty substitution for both Morleys and their car. Police had manipulated traffic to make the swap nearly unobservable.

Sarkman was in touch by radio with the cops at the mall. So far Carson had not bitten.

Trish sat white-faced, listening to the radioed conversations.

"Hey, you're okay here, Patricia," Dino said. "Don't look so worried."

"If they don't get Carson today . . ."

He frowned. "So? Then what?"

"That's what I wonder. His words on the phone the other day . . . I had the feeling they were an ultimatum. Show up at the mall today with Melody or . . ." She closed her eyes. "It's the 'or' I'm worried about."

"We're a little uneasy about it, too," Jerry said. "If Thomas doesn't go for the decoy, we're going to put a man on you until we find him."

"Good luck!" Dino said. "If you do as good a job finding him as you have on that geek Nicholas Smith-Patton, I'll be a grandfather when it happens."

What had happened to Nicholas, Trish wondered. She had reported that Carson claimed he was dead. She was also the last person known to have spoken to him. He and his van had simply disappeared a week ago. If he had really been killed . . . Oh, it was her fault! In his own odd way he was a dear man. Let him be all right! More guilt she couldn't deal with in her present state.

Sarkman turned his scowl toward the assertive Italian. "We're the murder crew. We don't do missing persons."

"I forget you don't do it all," Dino said sourly.

"Anyway, we got approval to put a man on Trish," Jerry said.

"About time," Dino said. "I been doing your job for you." True, he had been hovering on the edge of her days, almost always out of sight. That nothing had happened to her she attributed gratefully to his presence. That morning, knowing she was joining with police, he allowed her and Melody to drive off alone. At PC-Pros he had picked her up again. "Maybe I can get some sleep now," he said.

She touched his shoulder. "Thank you for all you've done."

"Prego." He leaned toward her ear. "Come over to the bakery if Carson doesn't buy their crap," he whispered.

He was about to step out the door when the phone rang. Trish stared at it for a moment, then giggled nervously at her own paralysis. She looked questioningly at Jerry. He nodded. She picked up the receiver.

"Shame on you, thinking you could fool me with police tricks!" She could not mistake Carson's new, gruff voice that had threatened her so often. She touched a button that activated the speaker phone. "What do you want, Carson?"

"I am not Carson."

Trish frowned in disbelief. "Whoever you are—"

"You leave him no choice."

"What do you mean?"

"If death itself doesn't bring you to him, Queen of My Heart, then he'll find something *worse* that will."

Sarkman cursed softly.

"Carson!" She swallowed. She had no words for him.

"It's only hours now until you'll be together forever!"

"No!"

"Keep him talking," Sarkman whispered. "We have a phone net on this number."

Trish couldn't bear to hear Carson's voice any longer. She slammed the phone down.

"Jesus! Can't you help us?" Sarkman said.

"Can't you help *me*?" She felt tears spring to her eyes. Lord, there was nothing left of her nerves! She sprang to her feet. "Don't you know he *is* going to get me to go away with him? Somehow he's going to do it!"

"My ass he will!" Dino was still standing in the doorway. He dipped a shoulder, summoning her. "Come on over to the bakery when you can. We gotta talk." He left.

She had to meet her bodyguard. Officer Danny D., they called him. Jerry explained that the man would stick close to her day and night. He'd be her shadow until the manhunt turned up Carson. When he got worn down they'd find another man.

"Is he going to tell me what to do, where to go?" she asked Jerry.

"Not unless you try to do something crazy. He just . . .

tags along." Jerry looked at his watch. "He's due here in a few minutes."

Danny D. arrived. He wore a business suit and a perpetual sly smile on his pockmarked face. He chewed toothpicks. His cologne was expensive. "Think of me as Mr. Comfort," he said.

"More than just in name, I hope," she said.

Sarkman left. Danny D. decided to have a look around PC-Pros, just in case. Jerry sat beside Trish. His long face was set with concern. "I want you to know how worried I am about you," he said. "We're doing all we can. Just the same . . ." He put an arm over her shoulder. She allowed him to pull her closer. "Anything happens, you get in touch with me." He gave her both his phone numbers and reminded her that she could also locate him at any time by calling headquarters.

To her surprise he lowered his face and kissed her. His kiss was firm but not intrusive. She returned the pressure, thinking there was something honest in his lips. Matched the rest of him. She was surprised at how comforted she felt. She broke the brief embrace. *Nothing* about her emotions could be trusted these days.

Sweet Jerry left reluctantly. For the moment she was alone in her office. She sat at her desk. She turned on her computer, brought up the calendar. It was September thirteenth.

Two days before what would have been her wedding date.

The breadth of Carson's destructiveness fell afresh upon her. Look at her, an emotional wreck, increasingly isolated and frightened. Her business edged on ruin. Still her demanding devil wasn't content. He struggled on to possess her fully. Instinct told her she would soon have to confront his inescapable evil face to face.

And Foster! Marylou told her his character had drained out of him as though from an open tap. Pale and quiet, he moved largely at Lois Smith-Patton's command now. He, too, had his bodyguard. In his case, though, Branch looked like a permanent addition to the family. Much of Foster's personal fortune had flown to the winds. Hives of attorneys and accountants swarmed after it, their success very much in doubt. Was it wrong to call him ruined?

She recalled Carson's voice on the phone minutes ago and whimpered. Tran's death hadn't changed her mind about going off with him. So what else could he do? Kidnap her? She turned that idea over in the light of his deranged personality. No, his obsession turned a different way.

She had to agree to be his companion.

What had to happen to make her do it?

She spun that smooth stone over and over in her mind. Intruding on her ponderings was her suspicion that Carson's mental deterioration was accelerating. She wondered if he really knew just who he was.

Danny D. returned. His top-dollar cologne floated before him.

"Time to hit the road," Trish said. "You start earning your big money right now."

"Where're we going?"

"You like apple tarts?"

Danny D. checked out the whole bakery, much to Dino's annoyance. Only then did he lounge at one of the tables facing the door and sip espresso and nibble Italian cookies. Dino took Trish back by the ovens. He apologized for having to talk to her there. Mario was taking a few well-deserved days off. "I been thinking about where you are in all this . . ." He waved an arm and mouthed an Italian obscenity. "What it is you gotta do till they catch this Carson guy." He jabbed hands into his apron pockets and paced in a small circle. "Then I figured it out. You gotta get out of town. You and Melody." He snapped his fingers. "Fast! Just like that. You lay low, nobody knows where you are . . . See what I mean?"

She should have thought of it. She was like a rat in a broken trap, too scared to dash off into hiding. "So where do we go?"

"I got a place down at the Jersey shore. A summer place I been renting to people. Nobody there now that the schools have started up."

She hesitated. She wasn't used to running from trouble. Furthermore, she had tried once to escape Carson. She had told Sarkman she wouldn't run again. As she thought about it, though, the idea seemed better. The key element would be to get out of the city without being seen by Carson. She would tell no one where she was going. She looked at Dino. "What about Danny D.?"

"He goes. We need all the help we can get. Once we get there he can tell the rest of the cops where we are—another state. The four of us hole up until crazy Carson gets caught."

She turned the idea over and over. At the heart of her desperate situation was the certainty that she had to do *something* herself to derail Carson's planning. She had tried unsuccessfully to rely on Foster, Nicholas, and the police. All that remained that she still dared count on was Dino, her rough, muscular diamond, and her own limited resourcefulness. She hadn't the mental stamina any longer for detailed planning and the patient weighing of risks against benefits. She had to act!

The longer she thought, the better Dino's idea seemed. Finally she looked up at him. "Okay, let's do it!"

"All right!"

"I won't feel safe till we're on the road." She managed what she hoped was a brave smile.

"Don't even pack. Let's just get up and go."

"Yes!"

This breakthrough to potential safety triggered a flash of revelation. Niggling behind her other worries was anxiety over exactly what means Carson would finally use to crush her resistance. Tran's death hadn't done it. In a burst of insight she guessed what avenue he would take to make her submit.

Melody!

"We have to get Melody out of school right away!" she blurted. "Carson is going to kidnap her!"

Dino was startled. "Why do you think—"

"I just know it! I should have realized it earlier." She was aware her voice was a near-shriek. Her child in *his* hands . . .

"Where's she go to school?"

She told him, halfway across the city.

"Send somebody for her, then. Somebody you can trust."

Marylou. No, Stoneman Gore. He was used to being told what to do. She looked at her watch. Early afternoon. The school day was staggered because of overcrowding. Melody was in the second wave. She would be safe there until Stoneman could get to her. She hurried to the phone. Her first call was to Stoneman: Get Melody and bring her to the bakery. The second was to the school office, telling them what would happen.

With Danny D. following she went back to PC-Pros. She took the time to run a final backup of the computer files onto tape. A lot of information and work was locked up in the machine. PC-Pros had been on the edge of success before Carson started trouble. Maybe one day she could bring it back. That didn't matter now. She took the cassette from the tape drive and locked it in the cabinet safe.

Room by room she turned off the lights. She didn't know when or if she'd reenter the building. Technically she was bankrupt. Even at the edge of total despair she had to bow to Carson's cunning and determination.

Her devil!

She went back to her office to pick up her purse and personal belongings. She glanced at her watch. Stoneman could already be at the bakery with Melody. She locked the door and walked out into the September afternoon. She had to squint against the sun's angled brilliance.

She was in a hurry to see Melody. Danny D. had to stretch his shortish legs to keep pace with her. Once together, the four of them would flee to New Jersey. Let Carson do his worst to find them—before the police found him.

In her haste she nearly walked right past the Cadillac. It was pulled carelessly to the curb, the trunk end edged streetward.

Stoneman's car!

She stooped and looked in. Stoneman was slumped at the wheel. "This is the man who was supposed to bring Melody to me!" She rushed to the driver's door. Danny D. was right behind her. She snatched at the latch, tore the door open. She looked in the backseat. "Where's Melody?" she asked the air.

Danny D. touched Stoneman's thick neck. "He's alive." His hands moved through the older man's closely barbered gray hair. "No bumps. Maybe he had a seizure or something."

"Where's Melody?"

Danny D. dug in the glove compartment, under the front seats. "What the hell's this?" He pulled out a miniature canister. At its top was fastened an electronic controller.

Trish's breath left her throat in a rush. "He was gassed! Carson gassed him, just the way he did me—and Ron Verner. He gassed him and took Melody!" Trish was aware she shrieked but couldn't help herself.

Carson had her daughter!

She couldn't take time to wonder how he had managed it. By now he loomed omnipotent over her life. He had seemingly defied the laws of time and place.

"The paramedics should have a look at this guy." Danny D. said. He moved to stretch Stoneman's wide frame out on the seat. From the breast pocket of his suit coat protruded a yellow sheet. Trish snatched it out. Carson's unmistakable handwriting. She read it.

I knew it, she thought. From the first moment she realized that the man had returned to her life she had expected it would one day come to this.

"What's it say?" Danny D. said.

"Let's go to the bakery. You can call the paramedics from there."

They burst through the bakery door at a lope. Dino looked anxious. "Melody's not here yet," he said.

"Carson has her."

"What?"

She gave him the yellow note. He read it aloud. *"Queen of My Heart—Melody is with me now. When you join us we won't ever be parted again. We're in Apartment 724, 2260*

Manifold Blvd. Come now. No tricks or games. You know me. Be straight. Your daughter won't survive either treachery or your absence. Carson."

"My God!" Danny D. rushed for the phone. "I gotta call Sarkman and Morris!"

"No!" Trish stepped into his path. "I don't want you to."

Danny D. shoved against her. "What are you talking about? This nut has your kid, and you don't want me—"

"You have to take my word for this—you and all the other police can't fool or trick Carson. He's too clever. He'll kill my child."

Danny D. frowned. "So what are you going to do?"

Trish stepped closer to the phone. She folded her arms across her chest. "Can't you guess? I'm going to go away with him."

"What?" Danny D.'s turn to squawk.

Not the truth, Trish thought. What she was going to do was go to Carson, just as he wished. At the first chance she was going to take the pistol out of her purse and shoot him. To do it she'd have to make it look as though she was following his directions absolutely. That meant no police. "Just leave the phone alone," she said.

His response was to push her aside roughly and reach for the instrument. "We're talking kidnapping here."

"We been talking murder for weeks," Dino growled. "What the hell difference has it made? You cops haven't done nothing!" Two strides took him to Danny D.'s side. "This woman may be making the right decision. Why don't you cool off?"

"Why don't you mind your own business, doughboy?" Danny D. began to press the phone buttons.

"No!" Trish shouted. Her eyes found Dino's face. "Don't let him!"

Dino's arm swept down and snatched the phone cord. A sudden jerk tore it from the wall jack.

"What do you want? Trouble?" Danny D. asked. "You're obstructing an officer." He frowned, surprised at Dino's assertiveness.

"Do what the lady wants. It's her kid, to live or die."

"I got responsibilities in a situation like this."

"Bag them!"

"Back off, fella." Danny D. raised a hand as though to reach for a hidden holster. Dino grabbed his wrist, spun him around. Somehow the wrist ended up behind the cop's back. Dino bent the man forward and propelled him headfirst against the side of the heavy oven. He went down with a grunt.

Trish and Dino exchanged a wordless glance of alarm over what he had done. He said, "In that drawer over there is some thick cord. Get it!"

She gave him the ball. "You've got yourself in trouble."

His head spun toward her. "You wanta talk? Or you wanta go and start the rest of your life with Carson? Get going!"

"I am. Now." She snatched up her purse and groped for her car keys.

Dino looked up from his knots. "You know, I could maybe still be some help. Maybe I could sneak over there, too, and try a trick or two that I know. Maybe take Carson out."

"No! I've decided what the best thing is to do." She hesitated. "I—didn't think it would end this way between us. Me gone, and you in trouble with the law."

Dino's smile was a thin glimmer of the real thing. "Story of my life."

"Thank you. God bless!"

Rushing to her car, she thought that should she be successful in saving Melody, one of the first places she would go would be right back to this bakery with its comforting heat and more comforting owner.

She reminded herself it was important that all her actions be completely transparent. It couldn't look as though she was trying anything desperate. Driving with her knees, she pulled the pistol from her purse and checked the action as Jerry had taught her. She cocked it.

As she pulled up in front of 2260 Manifold Boulevard her knees began to tremble. She could think only of Melody. She had rebraided her pigtail that morning, urged her to wear her pretty blue jumper. Off to the bus she had gone with her books and recorder. She couldn't bear not to have some kind of instrument within reach.

She was sure that Carson was somehow watching her get out of the car. Who knew what kind of electronic gadgetry had been mounted to assure him that she was alone? No, there were no concealed SWAT teams, rooftop snipers, rangers, rompers, or rovers to cramp his style. Should even one exist, he would kill Melody.

Because now he knew she wasn't his daughter. Rather than driving him away, that information had only given him a weapon against her.

In the elevator she found her attention flying away from Melody and centering on herself and Carson. Worse than simply being her personal devil, he could peer unimpeded into the worst side of her humanity. He had gathered the fuel for the fire of his four months of increasing torment nowhere else but in the forest of her character. In resisting him she had been forced to change that character for the better. Only now, as she pressed the seventh-floor button, did she understand that the impurities removed from her personality now lodged in his.

She understood she was coming here not only to recover her daughter and her soul. She came to destroy forever the shadowed side of both her heart and her past.

She checked the pistol in her big purse, nudged it butt up, hid it under a swirl of silk scarf. The elevator car rose swiftly. She got out on seven, still feeling that she was somehow being watched. She walked down the carpeted hall. She glanced at the room numbers. Raising her eyes, she counted to 724 in the distance. Along the hallway she went. A cold draft blew through her chest. She found it hard to draw breath. Her knees trembled with each stride.

She stood before Apartment 724. Its unmarred surface was as featureless and unrevealing as the future.

She raised her right hand and knocked. "It's . . . me, Carson." She spoke that too-familiar name in a voice dry as straw.

From inside: "Mom! Mom!" Melody. Trish's heart wrenched. Control yourself! The girl sounded all right.

"It's open." Carson's new voice.

She raised a shaky hand. She turned the knob and opened the door. She stepped forward.

To face Carson again.

Her eyes found him first but slid away toward Melody, who sat in the second small room on the bed's filthy spread. Her schoolbooks and recorder lay beside her. She jumped up. From her lap tumbled an open package of Sno-Balls, one of which she had undoubtedly gulped down. Trish had planned to pull the pistol and fire at Carson. Now Melody was on her in a tangle of hug. "Are you all right, sweet?" she asked the girl.

"I'm scared!" Melody said.

As Trish stooped and hugged she glanced around at the two rooms heaped with electronic equipment. The scanty furniture was cheap, save for a massive oak chair hung with torn Velcro straps. The place stank. The smell of sweat, fouled food, and semen slammed at her nose like a hammer. Rising with them was an unfamiliar sweet, sickening scent.

"Welcome, Queen of My Heart!" Carson stepped toward her. She was wrong; his face hadn't been altered.

Trish untangled Melody. "Go back and sit on the bed, Mel."

"I don't want to be with Daddy. He's not nice like I remembered!"

"I'm a sweetheart, a prince," Carson said.

"No, you're not!" Melody said.

"It doesn't matter now how you feel about me, child."

Carson was very close now, too close for Trish to be able to pull out the pistol and raise it. Her eyes found his face under the familiar thatch of red hair. There was something wrong. . . .

He seemed too tall and broad to be the Carson she remembered. His proportions were Carson's, but . . . Or had her memory failed her? No, it hadn't!

"You're not Carson!" she shouted.

"Of course I am."

"No! Who are you?"

"His servant."

"I don't understand you!" This unknown terror was more frightening than the known devil she had expected. She found herself recoiling, stumbling back across the littered floor.

The man was wearing a mask! She had been right. Carson's features had been altered. The mask was his former face.

Her fright triggered recent thoughts about Carson no longer knowing who he was. The structure of his genius had been undermined when the foundation of his sanity was swept away. Was this Carson or not? Now she wasn't sure!

He flew at her with startling quickness. His big hands found her shoulders. His face loomed like a full moon.

He wanted to kiss her!

"Queen of My Heart!"

"Don't touch me!" She forgot her weapon in her fright. She flailed at his chest with impotent fists. One of her blows found his side.

He wailed and sagged for a moment, then he flung her aside. She flew across the room. Losing her balance, she sprawled to the floor. Her purse flew out of reach. Her cheek burned from the rasp of gritty boards. Her eyes faced the bed legs. Between them she saw . . .

She screamed.

Nicholas Smith-Patton's once-thin frame was bloated with the gases of decomposition. It was their odor that hung in the air like Death's perfume. His bugging eyes stared at her, no more than three feet away. In her wildness of mind they looked accusing.

She rolled over, unable to face that poor, dead thing.

She scrambled up too late to avoid the masked figure. He lunged, and one of his hands found her upper arm in an iron grip. He shoved her against the wall, pinned her with thighs thick as columns.

"Don't hurt my mother!" Melody shouted through her tears. She twisted with anxiety on the filthy bed.

She expected him to try to press another kiss on her. She

turned her face away. She was chilled when, instead, his fingers found her throat.

Trish tried to bat aside the big hands. He caressed her skin. "Soft . . . as an angel's wing . . ."

"I'm not an angel yet!" She punched his side. As before he grunted and sagged. This time his fingers didn't loosen. Instead they tightened. For a long moment she felt the crushing drag of his bulk against her throat's tender tissues. She choked and tugged feebly at his horrid hands.

He righted himself, drew a heavy breath. His fingers relaxed and centered on her throat. His face was less than a foot from hers. He was now so near she saw the line of the cunning mask clinging close even to the edges of green eyes burning with sexual desire.

Did he want to kiss or strangle her?

"Carson, why are you doing this? I came . . . to go away with you and Melody."

"Maybe to punish you for leaving." His voice was a low hiss.

"No, no. I'm here now, Carson!" She was trying to debate with a madman. "You can't kill me. You'll have no one then."

"Queen of My Heart, you've made me so . . . sad." His thumbs squirmed like eels against her windpipe.

That he wanted to kill her made no sense. Just the same . . .

There was absolutely nothing she could do about it.

That she was to die was terrifying enough. But to have Melody witness it worsened the horror. She found herself whispering, "Don't kill me in front of my child!"

"You should have thought of that so many months ago, Queen of My Heart," he hissed. "I did all in my power to keep you from this moment. But you insisted on defying Carson."

She hovered on the edge of the hot crater of hysteria. *"Who are you?* You're not Carson! Why are you doing this to me and my daughter?"

"Far, far too late for questions now, my love. My secret,

true, true love!" He spoke with such tenderness! Even close to total panic she understood his utter sincerity. What was happening here? Was she being murdered by someone who loved her? Was he Carson after all?

His thumbs shoved gently into her throat, hinting at the power in the big hands. She would die by strangling! "Are you sorry for having left me?" he said loudly. "Are you sorry for the anguish you caused me?"

A tear ran from the corner of his eye.

She groaned in despair and bafflement. On the bed Melody wailed wordlessly.

His fingers constricted her throat like a boa. She tried to hit his tender side again. He angled his arm to protect it, lowering his shoulder.

Beyond it she saw movement!

The door to the rear stairs was opening. Dust fell from its top. It hadn't been opened for months. Someone was easing through it.

Dino!

He was carrying a heavy stick longer than a beat policeman's billy club. Oh, Lord, he had followed her! Thank heaven for his stupid brashness! She tried to tear her eyes from him lest she give away his approach. The yellow notepaper carrying Carson's message and this address was stuck in his shirt pocket. She offered a silent prayer that Melody would contain herself.

The constriction on her throat increased. Her assailant's weeping, masked face now filled her field of vision.

She couldn't breathe! She twisted and shoved, glimpsing Dino for a moment.

He puckered his face, demanding her conspiracy. He turned to Melody and put a finger to his lips. His wink was theatrical.

Trish's frustrated urge to draw breath hurtled her toward hysteria.

Dino stood directly behind the curved back of her attacker. She wondered if she had ever been so glad to see another human being.

He raised his club high.

Whack him hard as you can, she thought.

Down came the club on her assailant's head. And burst.

A shower of confetti stars exploded from the crumpled tube. Red, gold, silver bits swirled in the air like snow in an old paperweight. Dino struck again. The tube disintegrated into cardboard tatters. Stars whirled in clouds.

The crushing hands fell from her throat. Dino began to laugh. The man in the Carson mask began to laugh, too. Chuckles gave way to shaky wheezes. Dino waved his arms through the fluttering confetti. Stars clung to his shirt, to the hairs on his forearms where the alligator tattoo writhed above his flailing wrists.

The two men turned and faced her, howling now with laughter. They threw arms over each other's shoulders.

Stars, stars descended on their gleeful faces. Bright bits clung to the tracks of her assailant's tears.

Trish moved away from the wall, touching her bruised throat. Stars found her lashes and clung. She turned toward Melody, whose tearstained face trembled with an uncertain grin. "Is . . . everything all right, Mommy?"

"I don't know." She shook head to toe. "Dino, what's going on?"

The man in the Carson mask spoke. "Now you and Carson live happily ever after."

"What are you talking about?" Trish's voice was a near-shriek. "Who are you?"

"Someone you know," he said.

"Who?"

"But haven't seen in years. Guess who!"

"Stop this!"

He bowed. "Who can't obey the wishes of Queen of My Heart?" He dug under his collar with the tips of both fingers. He wriggled them under the sheer mask tissue. The movements of his left hand were sluggish. Trish remembered even her feeble blows had hurt that side. He was wounded. The police had said Tran's pistol had been fired. The blood in the van matched Carson's type. Yet this wasn't Carson. *Who was he?*

He turned his back to her. The star-spangled mask came off, some of it tearing to tatters in his uncertain grip. Heavy-footed, he moved to face her.

There was no mistaking that meaty face. "Champ!" she shouted. "Champ. Carson's brother!"

28

"'TRISH, CARSON, AND MELODY—TOGETHER FOR-ever.' Didn't you remember I took that photo? You never tumbled?" Champ chuckled giddily.

She stared at him. So many times she had read or recalled Carson's promise of togetherness. And never dwelled on who had taken the photograph!

Now she thought of another hint she hadn't taken: the composite drawing done by the police artist. That hairy face had been close enough to Champ's for her to make the leap of recognition. But she hadn't. She had been wrapped up in trying to match the features to Carson's. How could she have been so dense? "It was *you* who did all those things to hurt me and Foster."

"Most of them." He chuckled.

"You killed Tran!"

He nodded. "The devious slant!"

Trish remembered what lay decomposing under the bed. "And Nicholas!"

He shook his head. "No, I didn't."

Trish frowned. "Who did?"

"Me," Dino said. "I wore a Carson mask and took it off just before I choked him to death."

Trish stared wordlessly at him.

He raised a hand, gripped a handful of curly hair, and pulled. The cunning hairpiece came away to disclose a closely cut red stubble. He spat heavily on his alligator tattoo. A rub of his shirtsleeve smeared away most of it. And a patch of skin tint. His complexion was bogus, too! Fingers to each eye in turn popped out contact lenses. When he looked at her his eyes burned with an all-too-familiar obsessive green fire.

Trish wailed and staggered backward.

"Carson. You're Carson!"

"How delightful that you never saw!"

Melody cried out from the bed. "Daddy! You're my daddy!"

"No, Melody. He isn't," Trish said.

She spun back to the man she had thought was Dino. Now—too late!—she saw what an expert job the murdered cosmetic surgeon had done. The bones of Carson's face remained untouched. But the flesh had been redistributed. Long gone were the familiar acne scars. Even now it wasn't all that easy to see it was he.

Her legs threatened to betray her. She staggered back against the wall. Her mind swarmed with tangled thoughts of his obsession and his struggle with her for her soul. My devil! My dark mirror! Despite her shock and dismay she clung to one thought like a life preserver: She had come here to destroy him!

She was speechless. But her head spun with evidence of her gullibility. Carson had opened his bakery three short blocks away right after PC-Pros got rolling. That he could bake professionally shouldn't have misled her. He had always been a master in his own kitchen. He was a Renaissance man; he could do anything. She knew he spoke handfuls of languages. Why hadn't she counted Italian and the nicely accented French of his Marseillaise?

Also, she had missed all the unintentional hints Rocco had sent her. "Dino" had done all he could to make her selling out to her competitor a real temptation. Without PC-Pros he imagined she would be a big step closer to rejoining him. Hadn't Rocco told her Dino was a crazy Vietnam vet—just as Carson was? She hadn't made the connection!

"Champ set me up when he chased those hoodlums away," she muttered.

Champ giggled again. "I found two homeless men, paid them well enough. I taught them their lines and their pratfalls. Carson did the rest."

She glowered at him. "And you stood outside the window in your Carson mask," she said dully.

Carson smirked. "I just *couldn't* catch him."

"When you blew away the relay equipment, Carson, it was deliberate!"

"Of course. Nicholas was already getting in the way. That slowed him up. Too bad he didn't leave well enough alone."

Champ said, "How nicely we muddied the waters of identity. We arranged some of my calls to be made when Carson was with you."

"Were you impressed when I drove off the nasty reporters?" Carson asked.

She groaned and shook her head. How totally gullible she had been!

Carson reached forward with a star-spangled hand and lightly touched her face. She recoiled in loathing. "You're so much as I remembered you, Queen of My Heart! The talent, the mental quickness. You almost caught us short earlier today when you realized that our snatching Melody would be your last straw. The plan was for Champ to grab her after school today. We had to change that. I phoned him while you were tidying up PC-Pros. He slipped the gas bomb into Stoneman's car when he was inside Melody's school."

Far from herself in physical or emotional balance, Trish sank into a shaky chair. She tore her eyes from Carson. "You . . . had me alone at least twice. Why—"

"Did you feel the currents of desire between us?" The softness was gone from his voice now. Obsession tensed his muscular body. "The currents of desire . . . of destiny! You felt them, too, didn't you? You can't deny it."

"I was drawn to . . . Dino. Not you." She sounded lame and stupid. One couldn't argue with Carson.

"I would have been yours again in a moment, Queen of My Heart. All you had to do was reach out your hand and touch me!"

Her heart twisted over what she had nearly done, over her desire to do so. She despaired, knowing she would always be physically attracted to Carson Thomas, no matter that attraction's lunacy. Was it fascination with evil?

She sat before the two men a more complete and balanced woman than she had been when they first began their campaign to return her to Carson's side. No matter. Carson's madness, skill, and cunning had overmatched even the new, better her. All along her instincts had told her she had no chance. They had ranged, accurate as radar, ahead of her reason.

On how many occasions had Carson appeared as her savior and counselor, the one rock upon which she could rely? Wasn't that a trick of the devil, he of ten thousand faces? "You sat with me and the two cops after they switched Melody and me for doubles. You comforted me, told me not to worry. You made fools of them and me."

"Yes! And what fun it was! I teased you with a little hint when we parted. You missed it."

She stared at him.

"You said we were parting with me in trouble with the law. And I said, 'Story of my life.' I was referring to California more than three years ago!"

Trish shrugged. "Big deal."

"It is a big deal that at long, long last you've bowed to the inevitable. You've decided to join me."

She had been right to come here. He came to take her with him. She came to kill him. Through all the long, one-sided nightmare she had been deceived countless times. By coming here she had managed to deceive him only once. Once would be enough.

Champ played at pretending this was a joyful occasion. He gleefully filled in the details of his obedient service to his brother. It dawned full force on Trish that his insanity outstripped even Carson's. It was he who at his brother's orders had smothered the three physicians and cut off body parts with pruning shears. Then he somehow tore open their daughters. All because they hadn't been suitable replacements for her and Melody. He had shoved wires into the brains of three men. He showed no more remorse than a successful mouser.

Melody slid off the bed and came to her. Trish pulled her onto her lap and pressed a damp face to her chest. "It's okay, princess. No one's going to hurt us."

As she spoke her eyes turned to Carson's for confirmation. What she saw there chilled her. His glance was locked on Melody's face. As though a switch had been thrown, his expression changed from distant amusement to a scowl of loathing.

His face was terrifying to see.

Trish tore her glance away. Her purse had ended up on the floor by the edge of the bed, watched over by dead Nicholas Smith-Patton's bulging eyes. How could she retrieve it? Both men were cunning and suspicious. Possibly she wouldn't have a chance to shoot Carson until they were on the road, rolling toward his imagined future.

Champ moved toward the small closet. As he walked Trish saw his entire left side was stiff. She guessed that the wound from Tran's bullet had turned ugly and gangrenous. But he was so strong it had only slowed him. He opened the door and came back with a white box. He brushed scraps of food and electronic parts off a low table and rested the box on it.

His moon face broke into a grin. "Surprise!" he said. He broke the strings on the box and opened it. Trish saw a round layer cake with black frosting. On it red letters spelled *Trish, Carson, and Melody—together forever!* "Time to celebrate!" He smiled at Trish so intently that she felt herself color.

"I didn't order this to happen!" Carson's face was stony.

"You waited more than three years for this moment, brother. What can it be but joyous? She's yours again!"

"Since when do you act without my instructions?"

In Trish's eyes Carson's altered face seemed to switch between his former features and Dino's. One moment he looked his old obsessed self, the next the character he had designed and acted solely for her deception. She couldn't readily adjust to the kaleidoscopic personas. Could he shift to other faces and shapes for her further torment?

Champ lowered his eyes. "I'm delighted for you both," he muttered.

"That's not your place—delight!" Carson spat. "Your place is *obedience.*"

"I have been obedient, Master."

Carson raised his brother's face with stiffened fingers under his chin. "Not wholly. I saw your recent tears of adoration. Besides, you know I can so nearly read your mind. Can't I?"

Champ nodded.

Trish hugged Melody reassuringly. She whispered into the girl's ear, "It's going to be okay." Her daughter sniffled and looked on with wide gray eyes.

Carson shoved his face toward his brother's. "You've been seduced by Queen of My Heart, haven't you? Just as I was once."

"No!"

"You dare lie to your master?"

"No!"

"You do!" Carson snatched up the cake and smashed it into Champ's chest. Some icing and devil's food crumbs clung with the stars to his soiled shirt. The rest fell onto his size fourteen shoes. He made no effort to clean himself. He whimpered and lowered his eyes.

Trish said, "I'm ready to go with you, Carson."

Carson stepped away from his brother. He turned to Trish, crossed his arms. She had been trying to read him since the moment she understood he was Carson, not Dino. At that moment she succeeded. She saw . . .

Hate.

She tightened her grip on Melody.

"I wanted you with me for life, Queen of My Heart,"

Carson said. "Until you confessed that your unfaithfulness made another man Melody's father." He jabbed a forefinger at her. "No matter what you said, I didn't believe it. I thought you were lying to drive me away. So I checked with the clinic, the way oiled by your instructions." He stepped closer and gripped her throat. Melody shrank away, dragging at Trish's arms. "From the moment I hung up the phone your new destiny was decided."

Champ was puzzled. "What new destiny? Her destiny lies side by side with yours, Master."

"No."

Dread rose like fog in Trish's mind. "What are you saying, Carson?"

"You died the moment I heard the truth about who Melody's father really was."

Trish's heart sank in a flood of dread. She had struggled hard to finally break his domination. Through pain and panic she had succeeded. Carson had been totally in the grip of his obsession until she had broken it, too, with the truth about Melody's paternity. At long, long last! The irony was that . . .

Carson turned to Champ. "She dies for her lies and deceptions."

"No!" Trish sprang up, knocking Melody sprawling. She tried to rush to her purse. Her legs tangled with her daughter's. She tripped and sprawled on cake. The scent of devil's food rose amid the reek of festering Nicholas like a flowered vine around bleached bone.

Carson's foot ground in between her shoulder blades. "Champ, get your wire! I'll hold her head and be the last human face she sees."

A wire into her brain, too! Trish tried to squirm free, but Carson's foot was heavy as a pillar.

"And . . . get the pruning shears, too, I think."

"Master . . ."

"Champ!"

Melody was bawling loudly. Trish twisted her neck to see the girl pressed up against the side of the bed. She was terrified. Small wonder! Even in her desperate peril Trish's heart went out to her child. "Please don't hurt Melody!" she shouted.

"Melody, Shmelody," Carson cooed. "Champ, the wire!"

"You can't kill Queen of My Heart," Champ said softly.

"*You* will kill Queen of My Heart. As a punishment for your infatuation. And you will use the shears."

Champ stood unmoving. Carson's weight crushed Trish to the floor.

"Do as you're told! *Move!*"

"You love her!" Champ's words were a plea.

"I did once. Her betrayal spawned this brat she passed off as mine!"

"Let's leave them both, then," Champ said. "Let's go back to the coast and restart our lives."

Carson shook his head furiously. "She's going to die, and you're going to kill her." He took his foot off Trish's back and turned to his brother. "You've never disobeyed me. This is no time to start. Kill her with your wire."

Champ didn't speak. He shook his head.

With a howl Carson sent a karate kick against Champ's wounded side. His cry of pain was nearly as loud as his brother's shout: "Kill her!"

"No!" Champ was defiant! Trish couldn't believe her senses.

Carson lashed out with a spin kick. Champ's speed afoot startled Trish. He leapt back and caught Carson's ankle, tumbling him down. He didn't pursue his advantage. "Brother, let's leave them. Now."

Carson sprang up, his face mottling as rage flooded unevenly into its disturbed tissues. "Not until they're both dead."

"You loved them both!"

"Not anymore!" Carson thrust a hand toward his brother's chest. "Only *you* love them now, Champ."

Champ's head spun toward Trish and Melody. He nodded. Very softly he said, "Love . . ."

"You are not *permitted* to love Queen of My Heart!" Carson shouted. "She's mine alone to love or hate."

"I know, Master. Just the same, I can't let you hurt her!"

"Hurt her? You're going to kill her!"

"No!" Champ's protest was a howl.

Trish was astonished. This wounded brute had made himself her champion! Defying both blood and a dominated will on her behalf.

"You betray me for her?" Carson's face twisted with anger.

"Don't *make* me betray you!"

"Step aside, Champ!" Carson barked. "I'll do the job." Both his fists were clenched.

Champ, who stood between his brother and Trish, didn't move. He shook his lowered head.

With a grunting howl Carson charged. Brothers came together like two heavy jungle animals in a forest clearing. They rained practiced kicks and open-handed blows at one another, parrying most and cursing violently.

Panicked, Melody ran for the door. She tore at the knob. Cunning Carson had locked it from the inside. No key protruded from the hole.

Champ and Carson locked themselves in struggle. They punished each other with blows from a half-dozen schools of martial arts. When Oriental indirectness failed, shoves and punches served. They howled at each other. Wrapped together, they crashed into a table stacked with electronic equipment. Components tumbled like blocks from the hands of an angry child.

Trish staggered to her feet and rushed for the door through which Carson had entered. It had no inside knob! She slammed her palms against it in frustration.

She snatched up her purse and pressed herself up against the wall. The situation was clear. If Champ battered his brother down, he would set Trish and Melody free. If Carson prevailed . . .

With dismay she saw how badly Champ suffered from the gunshot wound. To his wounded side Carson delivered his most ferocious blows. Blood ran from both their faces, but it was Champ's that showed the pallor of agony and certain defeat.

The struggle went on, destroying the meager lot of furniture. Heavy feet trampled fallen tools, components, and the cloth and paper debris of one who lived alone, oblivious to cleanliness. She smelled the men's musky sweat and in time the saline scent of blood. They raged at each other, their shouted words hard and cutting as their blows. Their naked madness ran like an open sore.

How much time elapsed before the advantage passed wholly to Carson she couldn't guess. Nearly an hour, possibly. Champ was on his knees, pawing the air with his big hands. Carson spun and delivered a horrid kick to the center of his forehead.

Trish had both hands in her purse, gripping the pistol butt. The trigger was slippery under the sweat of her emotions. Melody still clung to her. "Move away a little, sweetie." She gave the child a gentle nudge. In her mind she reviewed her sessions on the practice range, Jerry's tactful corrections. One of the many differences between this moment and those nearly languid days of simple point-and-fire was that she trembled from head to toe. Her emotions boiled from panic to rage to horror.

Carson's killing lust rose like possession. His red stubbly hair was plastered with sweat, stars, and blood from the half dozen gouges on his scalp. His eyes bugged. Cords in his neck stood out like rails. With strength that seemed impossible after such a long struggle he snatched up a heavy computer, connectors snaking from its rear. He brought it crashing down on his brother's head. He raised it again, smashed it down on the defenseless skull. He made a bestial sound in his throat, *"Grnnnk, grnnnk, grnnnk . . ."*

He left the computer covering his still brother's face. When he turned toward Trish he was panting from a gaping mouth. Two of his front teeth had been knocked out. The others protruded like fangs. A red worm of blood crawled amid stars from the edge of his mouth.

"Devil!" Trish shouted. She jerked the pistol from her purse, aimed at his middle, and fired. The report in the small room sounded loud as the crack of doom. He spun around and toppled down on his back. He wasn't dead because his arms were moving.

Trish scarcely heard Melody's screams. She moved cautiously to fallen Carson, pistol gripped before her outstretched arms. She saw she had shot him in the abdomen. His hand was twitching on his chest. Despite all rationality to the contrary, she felt sorry for him—and fear for herself. She knew that pity could destroy as well as hate. His breath came in a ragged rush. The fingers of his right hand were nudging weakly at the yellow note he had written earlier.

What about the note? She had already read it. Never wholly free of fear of the diabolical Carson, she snatched at the yellow sheet, dreading even the familiar. As she did she looked at his face.

Despite the blood and damage there was no mistaking his fanged smile.

She put the pistol atop a smashed monitor and spread the sheet.

Her eyes fell on the familiar message. So? She turned the sheet over. On the its back now was a second message in Carson's hand.

My defense against the possibility of treachery: Champ fed Melody an explosive capsule. A remote timer controls it. It goes bang at five, or if she moves out of range. I'll trade the timer's location for my freedom, or a tune.

Trish's eyes found her watch. Ten minutes to five.

She froze with the paper in her hand. A rush of memory carried her back to the three dead doctors' daughters. Their innards were torn open, the police reported. She had assumed that meant with the help of some sharp edge. Now it dawned on her with certainty that crazy Carson had created deadly devices that blew the children's abdomens open. He ordered Champ to use them. Now he had selected that means to execute the child that he had been outraged to find was not his daughter.

Oh, no! *Oh, no!* She couldn't bear that in the end Carson would win. He *was* the devil!

She had to bring him back to consciousness! She would

put the pistol to his head. She would demand he tell her where the timer was or she would kill him. Not even Carson could want to die. No matter how much he hated her and Melody. She rushed on rubbery legs to the squalid bathroom. She filled a flimsy plastic bucket with water and dashed it onto Carson's face.

He didn't stir.

She felt his chest. He was alive. She had wounded him badly. She shook him. "Wake up! *Wake up!*" He didn't move.

"Mommy, I want to go! I want to leave. Please!"

She turned toward Melody. "Did you eat a Sno-Ball when you first came here?" She held her breath.

"The man that pretended he was Carson gave me one."

"Did you—gulp it down, the way I told you not to do?"

"Mommy, I was hungry!"

Trish said softly, "My dear baby." She hugged the girl for a long moment.

She hurried for another bucket of water, poured it on Carson. Still he didn't move. She knew he was dying. Somewhere in this smelly nest a tiny electronic chip was measuring out the last minutes of her daughter's life. She cursed Carson wordlessly. From between the doorway of life and death he was going to destroy her most precious possession.

She glanced at her watch. Eight minutes to five.

She held Melody's head gently between her palms. "Mel, listen. There was something bad in that Sno-Ball that man gave you." Her daughter's face was pallid. Her lower lip trembled. Fresh tears welled down her already tracked checks. What she had been forced to witness!

And the trouble was far from over.

"I'm going to try to make you vomit."

"I don't want to!"

"Mel, you have to let me! What you swallowed is very bad for you. It's like . . . poison."

She led her daughter to a corner of the bathroom. Together they knelt, as though in prayer. Trish worked her fingers into the girl's mouth, then on back, searching for the gag reflex. At the first spasm she kicked and squirmed. Trish bent her over, whispering softly. "Mel, you *have* to!" She thrust her fingers deeper. Moisture passed her hand, dripped to the floor. Juices only.

She held her hand in place until spasm mounted on spasm. The squirming child's stomach emptied onto stained linoleum. Trish didn't relent until dry heaves told her that purging was complete.

She bent over the disgusting puddle with the intensity of a sorceress who has just cast the bones.

She found no capsule.

She wiped the shaking girl's mouth with her skirt. Either the capsule had passed out of reach further into her digestive tract, or . . . it didn't exist. She put Melody on the bed and stared down at the unconscious Carson. Would he bluff?

It was tempting to think so. She turned over what she knew of his character, sane and mad. Which lay at the bottom of his heart, empathy or the will to punish?

He had killed his brother for his imagined disobedience. What chance was there that he would spare a child?

Trish answered her own question with a soft groan. She looked at her watch. Three minutes to five.

Where was the timer? It wouldn't have to be large. No bigger than a walnut, possibly. It could be hidden anywhere in this wretched, dim apartment. She looked around at the debris littering the floor.

She knelt beside dead Champ. Teeth gritted and lids half lowered, she went through his pockets. Nothing but lint and used toothpicks. About to rise, she knelt again and pressed a kiss to his cooling hand. She was alive because of him. Her "Champ" indeed! He had worn her standard with lunatic love.

She rose and moved toward Carson, then hesitated. He had been far away, playing Dino. He couldn't have carried the timer with him. It had to be in these two rooms somewhere. But *where?*

She began to rush about the apartment, pawing at parts, sweeping shelves clean with anxious hands, searching for a device whose exact appearance was unknown. She was on the verge of panic. She whirled to look at Melody, who lay white-faced and spent on the filthy blanket. Somewhere in her gut lay the seed of pathetic, premature death.

Two minutes to five.

Even in this tiny hole there were too many places to hide a small electronic device. And Carson would have ordered Champ to hide it where she would be least likely to look.

Where would that be?

She thought of one place.

She dropped to her knees by the side of the bed. She grabbed dead Nicholas's bony arm and pulled his puffing corpse out into view. Swallowing her rising gorge, she drove her hands into his pants and shirt pockets.

They were empty.

Beneath protruding eyes his mouth was only barely open. She moved his jaw to widen the space; rigor mortis had passed. The timer could be lodged within. Her face twisted with revulsion as she slid her fingers between his teeth. She scooped within the dead pit between tongue and palate.

Nothing!

Her daughter was going to die.

She sobbed and tore her hand free. She slapped it against the side of her jumpsuit, as though to brush away the dry touch of death.

Amid frantic desperation something niggled. She turned back to the yellow note. What had he written, exactly? She read the sentences again. *I'll trade the timer's location for my freedom, or a tune.*

Forget his freedom! His world had dwindled to the few grimy boards on which he lay. . . . *or a tune.* A tune? What tune?

She understood Carson well enough to know nothing was casual or accidental with him. Further, he had always been fond of testing her imagination and creativity. Blend that with his sense of the diabolical, and she had . . .

A puzzle.

A last straw at which to grasp—in the little over a minute left until five o'clock. Less if her watch and the timer differed.

A tune the two of them had in common meant nothing by itself. It would have to be sung or played to mean anything. To do anything. Do what? Carson's words told her: It would reveal the timer's location.

She began to nibble the ends of her fingers. What tune? She cast her mind back over the years with Carson. Tunes? There had been hundreds! From classics to the latest heavy metal. Carson devoured—and shared—them all with her. She couldn't guess which! She bit hard on finger ends. She felt herself in a vast swamp from which a single unmarked narrow trail led to her daughter's safety.

She had less than a minute left. Not enough time!

Possibly clever Carson had assumed she would think first of the past—and sink there. Within the riddle stood another hurdle that she had to get over. What about the recent past, then?

What about that time Carson as Dino had come to her house? She cast her mind back to that evening. Melody had played! He had sung in French!

France's national anthem. The Marseillaise!

She opened her mouth and began to sing loudly. She didn't know the words, but she belted out the first bars of the tune.

Nothing happened. She closed her mouth, stood bewildered in the close, stinking air. She thought she had caught the straw, against all odds. Instead she had caught only air.

There were only seconds left, by any watch. She froze. She couldn't do any more. Her glance swung toward her child, as though to hold her to this life with the intensity of her love.

Melody's eyes met hers. "You didn't sing that right. It was off."

Trish stifled her gasp. "Maybe . . . you could play it, sweet. On your recorder."

"Are all the bad men dead?"

"Just about. Everything's okay. Could you please play that tune right?"

"You said Carson wasn't my daddy."

"No. It was another, much nicer man."

"Why didn't you ever tell me?"

Trish thought she would burst with desperate impatience. "I—didn't want to confuse you. I've learned my lesson about that."

"Good." Melody nodded as though she thoroughly understood her mother's metamorphosis.

"Will you *play*, sweet?"

"Sure." Melody reached for her recorder with what seemed maddening slowness. She put the instrument to her lips, drew breath. She began to play—and made an error!

Trish was astonished. Melody *never* made errors. Then she realized what the child had seen in the last hours. "Try again, sweet. Please." She held her breath, long past daring to look at her watch. Only a few seconds stood between the child's life and five o'clock.

Melody began again. She played four perfect bars.

A beeping!

Trish whirled, trying to home in at once on the direction. There. On the floor. No, *in* the floor!

She dropped to her knees. The beeping came from beneath a floorboard. Close, she saw one of the shorter boards had a tiny fingernail-shaped slot at one end. She used her index finger to angle up the board. With the other she lifted it out.

There was the timer!

She snatched up the caseless circuit board. She glimpsed whirling LED digits in search of the deactivate switch. Twenty seconds remained. She saw two switches of different sizes. Neither was labeled. She knew one would turn off the unit—and Melody would die. The other would stop the countdown and save her life.

Which one was which?

She couldn't tell from the circuits. Not at a glance. And that was all she had time for.

She had to pick the right one.

Melody continued to play. She was improvising now, caught up in the music. At least for a few moments she was distanced from recent shocks.

How many devices had Trish helped Carson design? Sixty? Seventy? In design he was absolutely consistent.

Despite herself, she found her eyes turning to the decreasing digits on the counter readout. Ten seconds. Don't panic. There was still enough time to think.

She felt fresh anger and resentment that Carson was still able to add one more twist to her long, long torment. The sounding beeper kept the timer vibrating on her palm like a rattlesnake. She shoved her memory years into the past, to the circuit diagrams she had drawn to record the parade of Carson's creative successes. Switch sizes? What were they? She remembered his inserting components into circuit boards, each like a miniature city with high-rises of RAM chips and towers of transistors.

The on-off switch was always the largest.

Up to now.

She couldn't bear to look at Melody, who sped toward certain death even as her swift fingers summoned fetching variations on the French anthem. Trish felt tension so great that it seemed current was being applied to every nerve in her body. What if Carson had reversed the switches as the final, demonic torture? She dared not change her mind. She drew a breath, gritted teeth till the enamel whined.

She shoved her chosen switch to off.

No explosion!

Melody tootled on, oblivious to the flyby of the angel of death. In time she would pass the tiny capsule and never know its peril.

The halted timer showed seven seconds left. Trish staggered and groaned aloud with relief. She knelt and carefully put the device back where she had found it.

Distantly she was aware that Melody had stopped playing. She raised her glance to her daughter. Melody's eyes, focused behind Trish, were wide with shock and fear.

Trish turned her head.

Carson was coming toward her. "Down but not out, Queen of My Heart." He lurched like a fiend—and looked like one. Blood from his head wounds still oozed amid red fuzz and stars. His remade face was swollen from Champ's blows. His left eye was puffed, half closed. A gory stain spread over pants and shirt at his waist. It was clear that his wound's shock had worn off. She shouldn't be surprised. You could not kill evil.

She leapt to her feet. Where had she left the pistol? There! Atop the smashed monitor.

"Clever lady to solve my little puzzle." Carson's gaze cleared further as he drew closer. "Your style and courage have only improved during our separation." A laugh showed his fangs. He winced slightly. His hand waved near his abdomen. "You are forgiven for this, for your disobedience, for your infidelity. For everything."

"I don't want your forgiveness." Trish backed away, angling to get past him.

"We'll go away now together, Queen of My Heart. Reestablish, rebuild, rejoin our minds and bodies."

"No."

"A reflexive 'no.' An uncontemplated 'no.' The true, searched response is 'yes!'"

He reached for her. She ducked under his arm and snatched up the pistol. She whirled back, feet planted, arms out in her shooter's stance. She aimed at the center of his chest. He looked back across the blued-steel barrel. "Open the door and let us out of here," she said.

"We'll leave together. But right now our business isn't quite finished," he said.

"I don't know what you're talking about, Carson. I just know I want that door opened—*now!*"

"I won't open it. And you won't shoot me."

"I already did it!"

"In unnecessary desperation. You made a dreadful mistake." His eyes met hers. "One you can't make again when facing me like this."

She steadied her aim, found the comforting trigger curve. All she had to do was squeeze. . . .

She expected her finger to move. It didn't. She tried to force herself to do what she had done so quickly less than half an hour ago. A surge of dismay rose up behind her disbelief. What was it, then, that she couldn't kill—besides Carson? Surely the dark side of herself that he possessed. She was loath to destroy it after all. She feared that what remained of her would be crippled diminishment. She would inhabit an unmended personality from which old values and behaviors had crumbled. The cold winds of life would sweep pitilessly through the broken shell. Did the devil own her soul after all?

She feared he would come toward her, disarm her with a brutal twist of her gun wrist. He kept his distance. Even wounded and weakened, his insight and cunning remained unimpaired, like rocket guidance components sealed in resins. His fanged smile flashed. He nodded in self-assurance. "You might as well lower the pistol. Your arms will get tired."

She tried again to pull the trigger. Couldn't! Her dismay blossomed from a single dark flower into a black blanket covering the hill of her hopes. The depth of the evil power with which Carson still held her dawned with full force.

Her arms began to tremble with fatigue and impotence. Against her will the pistol's weight brought them down. The barrel pointed at the floor.

"Fine," he said.

"Will you let us out of here?" Her voice was leaden with the weight of her weakness.

"Soon, Queen of My Heart. Soon. A final bit of unfinished business remains. When it's finished, we can live out our lives together."

"No, no, no . . ." Trish's eyes joined the pistol's floorward aim.

"Mommy!"

Trish looked up. Carson was moving toward Melody, who had sat frozen on the bed for the last minutes. "Come here!" Carson said.

"Mommy!"

Trish looked on numbly. What was Carson trying to do?

He made a grab for the girl. She squirmed just out of reach. She tried to run to Trish. Carson lunged between them. His outstretched fingers brushed the fabric of Melody's jumper. He went after her. "Stop, Melody!" he growled, "or you're going to be badly punished."

"Mommy, make him stop!"

"Carson—"

"Don't try to run from me, Melody. I'll catch you. And when I do . . . So come here!"

Melody ducked away but couldn't get past the big man. She dodged backward toward the doorless bathroom. Had he his full strength, he would have caught her in a moment. Trish saw he would do so eventually because he was cornering her. She screamed at him: "Why are you bothering her?"

He didn't turn. "She's the last smudge of chalk on our old slate, Queen of My Heart. She has to be . . . rubbed out, you might say." He chuckled.

"Carson, don't!" He was going to kill her child! And she was letting him do it.

With painful lunges he bluffed Melody further toward the bathroom. She was wailing in fear. Those cries struck Trish like lashes. They jarred at the inertia that possessed her. "Carson!"

Melody was in the tiny bathroom now. Carson loomed before her eyes, a bloody, fanged horror. *"Mom-mmmiiiieee!"*

That cry shattered the spell under which Carson had placed Trish. She rushed forward, her mind empty of all but the most primitive thoughts.

Carson had caught Melody's arm. His other hand found her neck. The child coughed feebly as his thumb slid to her soft throat.

He was going to strangle her.

Trish raised the pistol, hesitated. If she fired, the bullet might go through him and into Melody. *"Let her go!"* she screamed, so loud she thought her throat might tear.

Carson released Melody's arm and put both hands on her throat. "Rub . . . rub," he muttered.

She angled to the side, stepped close to Carson's exposed ribs. Melody's eyes were wide, bugging, her tongue stiffening in her open mouth.

Trish shoved the pistol into Carson's ribs and pulled the trigger. She kept pulling it despite the deafening sound and the spent powder burning her hands. Not until she heard clicks did she drop the weapon beside his inert body. She threw the pistol at his gory head.

She wrapped Melody in her arms and hugged with her little remaining strength. She carried her out of the bathroom. The child clung to her like a limpet.

"That was all so awful horrible!" Melody blubbered.

"It's never easy to get your soul back."

"What's that mean?"

"Never mind."

29

REVEREND GRAYMOKE HAD PUT ASIDE HIS CUSTOMARY
illuminations of the eternal struggle between good and evil
in favor of a homily on peace on earth and goodwill to men.
Christmas Eve service called for that. Trish enjoyed hearing
from this different side of the minister. Earlier in the year
she had come to appreciate being in Jerry's church, and not
just because he was beside her. The assembled worshipers,
the uneven voices raised in song or muted in prayer, and the
sense of community comforted her.

More than a year had passed since the violence and death
in the two-room apartment—twelve months of outer and
inner changes for her. Melody had been her first concern.
She found a counselor who specialized in the sort of
psychological trauma her daughter had suffered. The three
of them met to talk it through in depth. The first sessions
had been brutal, both she and Melody in tears, hers of
recrimination and guilt. After all, hadn't it been her behaviors that led to her child's terrorizing? Never mind the little
detail of not telling her who her father really was. Initially
the trio met twice a week. Now only twice a month.
Counselor Strong, puffing on his pipe, announced last

Monday that he thought Melody would do fine without him from here on out. It was Trish he was wondering about.

To her surprise, Stoneman Gore had stepped to the forefront of her business problems. The gassing in his Cadillac had startled awake the substantial dormant portion of his talent. His energy level rose. His business acumen sharpened itself. Trish hadn't known he had been a successful entrepreneur in the heyday of the plastics boom. The bonds whose coupons he clipped had been bought with the profits from the sale of his own company to a multinational. While Trish spared her shaky nerves by putting only half days into the shell to which PC-Pros had been reduced, Stoneman brought in a retired accountant friend who did the books. Soon she and Stoneman knew just where the firm stood financially. He next begged the services of a management consultant chum. The three of them devised a business plan for a new, better PC-Pros. It included an executive vice-president to run things day-to-day. Trish realized she had tried to do too much herself. Now with a more ambitious plan for growth and expansion in place, such a position was indispensable.

The problem was that a large amount of capital would be needed to resurrect PC-Pros and raise it to the next competitive level. Again, Stoneman to the rescue! He was prepared to offer her a loan on most generous terms. "The Marylou Venture Capital Fund," he chuckled, because her mother had coaxed him into it, though it wasn't that difficult.

Shortly after PC-Pros' official resurrection Marylou had a stroke. It put her in bed with movement and speech problems. She was mending, but it was clear that she wouldn't ever be the same again. The doctor was honest: Subsequent strokes were to be feared. A nurse's services would be required, at least for the short term. So Trish's moving herself and Melody into her mother's house made great sense. The money she had spent to rent the Victorian rambler could now be used for three-day-a-week nurse's visits. At night and on weekends Trish would be there. Melody would brighten her grandmother's life with her music and chatter. Marylou was kind enough to say her affliction was completely unrelated to the collapse of her daughter's marriage plans.

Seemingly indestructible and relentless, her mother at last proved to be neither. While her shaping of Trish the child and adolescent couldn't be reversed, the forcefulness of her personality was now softened. The mantle of domestic power passed to her daughter. With it came some new perspectives for Trish that carried healing and forgiveness with them. Daughters before a mirror never saw themselves alone; Mother stood always at their shoulder. The lucky saw help there; the unlucky, horror. She supposed Marylou wasn't that bad. She hoped Melody would one day have as good to say about her.

Monthly Trish visited three graves, stared down at new stones: Tran, Nicholas, and Champ. She always took flowers, even in winter. The largest bouquet was for Carson's brother, to whom she owed her life. Hadn't he clumsily sought redemption from an indentured life of violence and murder in the hope of love? That it had been misdirected and lunatic love she didn't think mattered at all. Who could unravel that emotion's many mysteries—or its powers?

During darker moments, though, she thought of Champ as Carson in yet another form. He had worn his brother's face often enough and worked his will with equal demonic genius. The love that had saved her had destroyed him. As though through clouds of silk she saw love and evil perpetually at battle.

No matter before which of the three graves she stood, she always wished she had a fourth upon which she could heap ashes or silent abuse. Carson had no grave, because his body had never been found.

How many times had she reviewed the events following her fast exit with Melody from the tiny apartment? Safely away, she had found a pay phone. Her first call was to Lois Smith-Patton. To her she gave the bad news about Nicholas and the location of his body. She owed her poor gangling friend that favor. She then tried to reach either Jerry Morris or Pete Sarkman. Neither was available. She told the officer on the phone what had happened. It was never clear later just why there had been a long delay in the cruiser's arrival at 2260 Manifold Boulevard. It was suggested that Trish's call had at first been thought a prank.

The two-hour delay gave apartment dwellers a chance to investigate the gunshots. The open door and silent rooms invited both entry and curiosity. Later questioning by the police failed to satisfactorily establish who had first entered Apartment 724, or who might have departed with Carson's body.

A rumor was heard later that Lois, in a fit of rage over her brother's death, had at once ordered bodyguard Branch to go to the apartment. His job was to remove Carson's remains and dispose of them without benefit of clergy. Trish didn't doubt that Lois was that vindictive and hateful. It was the logistics involved that baffled her. Branch was questioned while protected by a battery of expensive attorneys. No reason was found to continue that line of investigation. Nonetheless, gossip persisted.

Not surprisingly, Lieutenant Sarkman was particularly officious and bullying when taking Trish's deposition. He was clearly trying to establish that she had played a role in the removal of the body. Jerry had trouble keeping him civil. Trish was glad she invited her attorney Louise O'Day to each of the three separate sessions, as well as to those during which Melody was questioned. Three corpses, one of which was missing, didn't sit at all well with the police.

Unable to make Trish tangle herself with the missing body, Sarkman was determined to prove that she had only wounded Carson. He had then crept off somehow on his own. Time and again she had to show the cop and forensic pathologists how and where she had placed the pistol barrel against Carson's body. She couldn't be exact, of course, because her eyes had been closed. She could be sure, however, that she had fired five times. Ballistics proved that the four recovered slugs had gone right through him largely undeformed. Just what that meant was unclear. Hard luck for law enforcement.

Leftover Lewis had a theory: police conspiracy. In a

whisper he explained that within the department debts accumulated. Dark obligations had to be met. Accommodations took place. Just how did a corpse fit into all that? Some way, so it had been secretly removed.

After all the fuss Carson's disappearance remained an open issue. Alive or dead? No one could say.

In moments when her rationality was at low ebb, late at night or when she was very tired, she imagined that Carson hadn't died because he couldn't be killed. He was a creature made up of her own moral errors and a darker force that for want of a better concept she called the devil.

In sunshine, though, this idea receded. She had never been one to entertain superstition. There was no devil. There was no ongoing battle for souls. Nothing so simple-minded could prevail. Humanity was only an unsupervised morsel amid a vast, incomprehensible cosmic stew of whirling stars and glistening, icy constellations.

She shared her thoughts with Jerry. He suggested she "give God a try." She argued that that simply wouldn't work for her. He urged her to come to his church anyway. It wouldn't hurt her.

She had begun to see him socially six weeks after the terminal violence. From the beginning many of his planned outings were designed to include Melody. Man and girl hit it off at once. It turned out Jerry had perfect pitch, too. They played music games that drove Trish only slightly crazy. What she liked best about him was his solidness and dependability. And his understanding of her commitments to her daughter, mother, and business.

When they first began to keep company she told him she was an emotional mess and couldn't begin to handle a heavy relationship. He said that was okay. They could keep it light. Just the same, she was uneasy. Not about him, but about herself. She found Carson gone from the halls of her mind, but there was a lot of important dusting and tidying to do there. Odd, but day-to-day she didn't find the time. Then one Sunday in church while others prayed she found herself able to concentrate on these deeper dialogues with herself. Jerry, the traditionalist, said she was praying, too. Do-it-yourself therapy was more like it. She explained she was one of those who couldn't make the leap of faith. It wasn't in her to do it.

Earlier that evening he had given her a Christmas gift: an engagement ring and a proposal. She didn't accept either. She asked him not to take the ring back to the jeweler, though. Hold on to it a while, she said. It was still too soon after Carson for her to trust herself to make a major life decision. She explained again her self-doubts. The sweet man agreed to allow her more time.

Sneaky Melody had overheard. In the bathroom she whispered, "Mom, what is *with* you? You're not thinking!"

The choir director announced the number for the next hymn. Trish was still leafing through the hymnal when everyone began to sing. She realized she didn't need the music. She joined in quietly at first, intimidated by the two perfect pitches to either side. Then as the familiar melody rose all around she raised her voice and smiled.

"Hark! The herald angels sing: Glory to the newborn King . . ."

The *New York Times* Bestselling Author of *Boy's Life*

A NEW NOVEL OF RELENTING SUSPENSE FROM
THE MASTER STORYTELLER OF OUR TIME.

ROBERT R. McCAMMON

THE STORY OF A MAN, HUNTED INTO
THE SULTRY SWAMPS OF LOUISIANA,
ON THE RUN FROM A TRAGIC MISTAKE.

GONE SOUTH

"PART CRIME NOVEL, PART QUEST....MCCAMMON
CREATES A TYPE OF STORY ALL HIS OWN."
—*The Wall Street Journal*

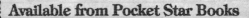

POCKET
STAR
BOOKS

Available from Pocket Star Books

826